The Last Great Edwardian Lady

The Last Great Edwardian Lady

INGRID SEWARD

C

CENTURY

Published by Century in 1999

1 3 5 7 9 10 8 6 4 2

Copyright © Ingrid Seward 1999

Ingrid Seward has asserted her right under the Copyright, Designs and
Patents Act, 1988 to be identified as the author of this work

First published in the United Kingdom in 1999 by Century

Random House UK Limited
20 Vauxhall Bridge Road, London SW1V 2SA

Random House Australia (Pty) Limited
20 Alfred Street, Milsons Point, Sydney
New South Wales 2061, Australia

Random House New Zealand Limited
18 Poland Road, Glenfield, Auckland 10, New Zealand

Random House South Africa (Pty) Limited
Endulini, 5A Jubilee Road, Parktown 2193, South Africa

Random House UK Limited Reg. No. 954009

A CIP catalogue record for this book
is available from the British Library

Papers used by Random House UK Ltd are natural, recyclable
products made from wood grown in sustainable forests. The
manufacturing processes conform to the environmental
regulations of the country of origin

ISBN 0 7126 7561 2

Design/make-up by Roger Walker

Typeset in 11.5/15pt ITC Veljovic Book

Printed and bound in Great Britain by
Butler & Tanner Limited, Frome and London

FRONTISPIECE:
AN EXCLUSIVE PHOTOGRAPH THAT CAPTURES THE GRACE AND
BEAUTY OF THE NEWLY ENGAGED LADY ELIZABETH BOWES LYON

CONTENTS

FOREWORD

This is not a chronological biography of Queen Elizabeth The Queen Mother. There have been any number of those, many of them excellent. Rather, this book is an attempt to see this remarkable lady the way she views herself – through her style.

This is to be seen in her homes and clothes and the way she entertains, in her travels and the way she talks to people. If there is a fairy-tale element to her royal persona, that is deliberate: it is the dressing enveloping and almost completely hiding an inner toughness which has seen her through a century.

The German philosopher Friedrich Nietzsche wrote: 'One thing is needed: to give style to one's character – a great and rare art!' By that criterion, this most genteel of gentlewomen is an artist of exceptional talent.

Age has not dimmed her effervescence nor blunted her performance. She has survived war and social upheaval and royal crises. Throughout everything she has remained resolute in her grandeur and dignity – indomitable, unchanging, yet blessed with a common touch which has made her a national focus in times of both grief and rejoicing.

Born a commoner, she has made herself the most royal of all the Royal Family. To many she *is* the Royal Family. That is her achievement.

As one of her circle, who has known her for forty years, says, 'When the sun's out, she never thinks the sun will go in.'

That is her style.

THE BOWES LYON FAMILY

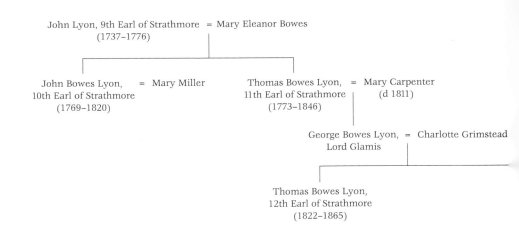

John Lyon, 9th Earl of Strathmore = Mary Eleanor Bowes
(1737–1776)

John Bowes Lyon, = Mary Miller
10th Earl of Strathmore
(1769–1820)

Thomas Bowes Lyon, = Mary Carpenter
11th Earl of Strathmore   (d 1811)
(1773–1846)

George Bowes Lyon, = Charlotte Grimstead
Lord Glamis

Thomas Bowes Lyon,
12th Earl of Strathmore
(1822–1865)

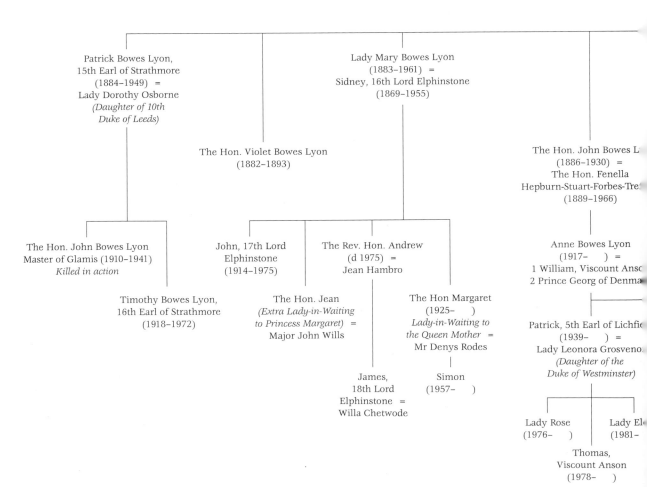

Patrick Bowes Lyon,
15th Earl of Strathmore
(1884–1949) =
Lady Dorothy Osborne
*(Daughter of 10th
Duke of Leeds)*

Lady Mary Bowes Lyon
(1883–1961) =
Sidney, 16th Lord Elphinstone
(1869–1955)

The Hon. John Bowes L
(1886–1930) =
The Hon. Fenella
Hepburn-Stuart-Forbes-Tre
(1889–1966)

The Hon. Violet Bowes Lyon
(1882–1893)

The Hon. John Bowes Lyon
Master of Glamis (1910–1941)
Killed in action

John, 17th Lord
Elphinstone
(1914–1975)

The Rev. Hon. Andrew
(d 1975) =
Jean Hambro

Anne Bowes Lyon
(1917–) =
1 William, Viscount Ans
2 Prince Georg of Denma

Timothy Bowes Lyon,
16th Earl of Strathmore
(1918–1972)

The Hon. Jean
*(Extra Lady-in-Waiting
to Princess Margaret)* =
Major John Wills

The Hon Margaret
(1925–)
*Lady-in-Waiting to
the Queen Mother* =
Mr Denys Rodes

Patrick, 5th Earl of Lichfie
(1939–) =
Lady Leonora Grosveno
*(Daughter of the
Duke of Westminster)*

James,
18th Lord
Elphinstone =
Willa Chetwode

Simon
(1957–)

Lady Rose
(1976–)

Lady El
(1981–

Thomas,
Viscount Anson
(1978–)

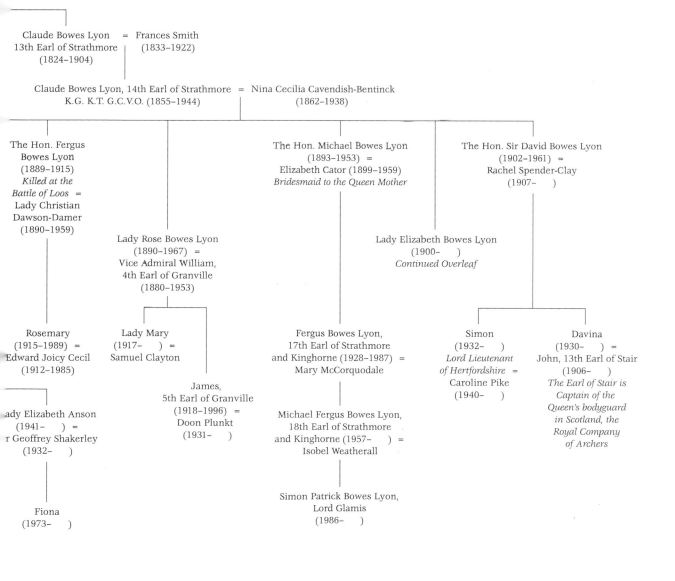

Claude Bowes Lyon   =   Frances Smith
13th Earl of Strathmore | (1833–1922)
(1824–1904)

Claude Bowes Lyon, 14th Earl of Strathmore   =   Nina Cecilia Cavendish-Bentinck
K.G. K.T. G.C.V.O. (1855–1944)   (1862–1938)

The Hon. Fergus
Bowes Lyon
(1889–1915)
*Killed at the
Battle of Loos* =
Lady Christian
Dawson-Damer
(1890–1959)

The Hon. Michael Bowes Lyon
(1893–1953) =
Elizabeth Cator (1899–1959)
Bridesmaid to the Queen Mother

The Hon. Sir David Bowes Lyon
(1902–1961) =
Rachel Spender-Clay
(1907–   )

Lady Rose Bowes Lyon
(1890–1967) =
Vice Admiral William,
4th Earl of Granville
(1880–1953)

Lady Elizabeth Bowes Lyon
(1900–   )
Continued Overleaf

Rosemary
(1915–1989) =
Edward Joicy Cecil
(1912–1985)

Lady Mary
(1917–   ) =
Samuel Clayton

Fergus Bowes Lyon,
17th Earl of Strathmore
and Kinghorne (1928–1987) =
Mary McCorquodale

Simon
(1932–   )
*Lord Lieutenant
of Hertfordshire* =
Caroline Pike
(1940–   )

Davina
(1930–   ) =
John, 13th Earl of Stair
(1906–   )
*The Earl of Stair is
Captain of the
Queen's bodyguard
in Scotland, the
Royal Company
of Archers*

ady Elizabeth Anson
(1941–   ) =
r Geoffrey Shakerley
(1932–   )

James,
5th Earl of Granville
(1918–1996) =
Doon Plunkt
(1931–   )

Michael Fergus Bowes Lyon,
18th Earl of Strathmore
and Kinghorne (1957–   ) =
Isobel Weatherall

Fiona
(1973–   )

Simon Patrick Bowes Lyon,
Lord Glamis
(1986–   )

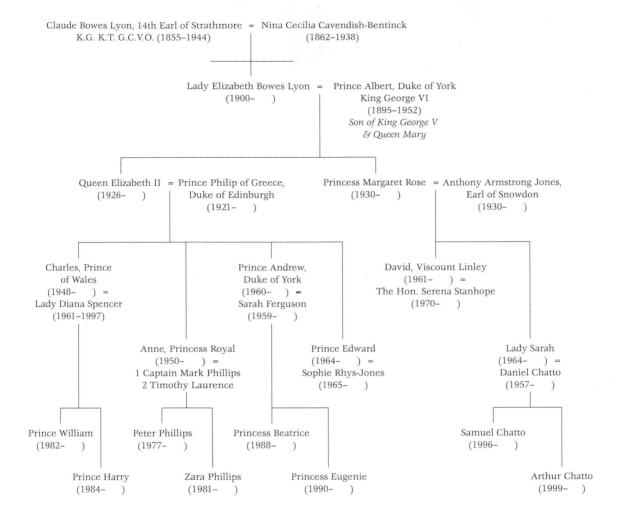

Claude Bowes Lyon, 14th Earl of Strathmore = Nina Cecilia Cavendish-Bentinck
K.G. K.T. G.C.V.O. (1855–1944)   (1862–1938)

Lady Elizabeth Bowes Lyon = Prince Albert, Duke of York
(1900–   )   King George VI
                                                     (1895–1952)
                                                Son of King George V
                                                     & Queen Mary

Queen Elizabeth II = Prince Philip of Greece,   Princess Margaret Rose = Anthony Armstrong Jones,
(1926–   )   Duke of Edinburgh   (1930–   )   Earl of Snowdon
                                (1921–   )   (1930–   )

Charles, Prince   Prince Andrew,   David, Viscount Linley
of Wales   Duke of York   (1961–   ) =
(1948–   ) =   (1960–   ) =   The Hon. Serena Stanhope
Lady Diana Spencer   Sarah Ferguson   (1970–   )
(1961–1997)   (1959–   )

                    Anne, Princess Royal   Prince Edward   Lady Sarah
                    (1950–   ) =   (1964–   ) =   (1964–   ) =
                    1 Captain Mark Phillips   Sophie Rhys-Jones   Daniel Chatto
                    2 Timothy Laurence   (1965–   )   (1957–   )

Prince William   Peter Phillips   Princess Beatrice   Samuel Chatto
(1982–   )   (1977–   )   (1988–   )   (1996–   )

        Prince Harry   Zara Phillips   Princess Eugenie   Arthur Chatto
        (1984–   )   (1981–   )   (1990–   )   (1999–   )

CHAPTER 1

INTRODUCTION

At the time of writing Queen Elizabeth The Queen Mother receives a fixed annual payment of £643,000 a year from the Civil List. That, however, is nowhere near what it costs to keep this grand old lady in the manner befitting her station. No-one, and certainly not the Queen Mother herself, knows the exact sum involved. One shrewd calculation puts the figure the Queen has to find to support her mother at an extra £2 million – and that is probably an underestimate.

The Queen, caught up in a chronic budget crisis which has seen the Household expenses of the Royal Family subjected to public scrutiny, will raise an occasional protest at the lavishness of her mother's lifestyle. With taxes to pay and the shift in public and political opinion against the perceived extravagance of the monarchy to contend with, she is having to keep a watchful eye on the royal exchequer.

Yet no-one has ever seriously suggested that the Queen Mother should be brought to financial account. After a lifetime devoted to duty this remarkable woman has put herself above such strictures. The accountants have taken over – in the City, in industry, in the media. But Her Majesty Queen Elizabeth the Queen Mother, continues to live as she always has: in the style of a great Edwardian lady. It is impossible to describe her otherwise.

As a young girl, travelling by train from her family home in Hertfordshire to the Strathmore Castle in Scotland, she learnt how to make a banana last the whole journey by nibbling a tiny piece and then folding the skin back again. In much the same way she has managed to make her resources stretch well beyond reasonable expectations.

The Queen Mother's own money ran out years ago because no-one, herself included, ever thought she would live as long as she has. But her longevity has made not the slightest difference to her way of life which remains rooted in the expectations of a bygone age. Her year is organized around the sporting calendar. She travels the country with an entourage of twenty servants. She maintains one country house, one castle and two homes, Royal Lodge and Clarence House, which are palaces in all but name. She owns a string of racehorses. Her couture dresses all look the same – she never throws any away, but still feels compelled to order dozens of new clothes and hats every season.

Were she anyone else, the mob would be baying outside the gates of Clarence House. Prince Charles, who has been greatly influenced by his grandmother and shares many of her opinions, is constantly under attack for being out of touch and old-fashioned. Such criticisms are never directed at the Queen Mother.

But then the Queen Mother is not like anyone else and when, on her arrival, the crowds gather, it is to cheer her. Recession and downsizing do not affect her. When Britain's inner heart was hidden behind a mask of manly constraint she was the face of feminine compassion: soft, huggable, tender, comforting. If she hadn't existed it would have been necessary to invent her – had she not already invented herself. It is a role which established her as the 'nation's favourite grandmother' and if people consider the cost of the performance, they reckon she is worth every penny.

The woman the royal household still call Queen Elizabeth has always had that effect. She has an ability bordering on genius to put people at their ease, to make them feel important, to sprinkle them with a pinch of the magical dust of her majesty, to secure their affection.

Underlying her performance is what might be described as sleight of hand. Lady Celestria Noel, who wrote Jennifer's Diary in *Harper's & Queen* magazine, recalled walking behind her at a flower show in the Scilly Isles. After the Queen Mother had moved on, the people she had spoken to all remarked how interested and knowledgeable she had been. Yet, as Lady Celestria noted, all she had actually said was: 'How lovely.' But she had said it in such a way that everyone was left with the decisive impression that she was as fascinated by their flowers as they were. The key to her accomplishment, Lady Celestria concluded, is that she is 'such a good listener'.

The Queen Mother put it slightly differently. 'I love life, that's my secret,' she once said. 'It is the exhilaration of others that keeps me going. Quite simply, it is the people who keep me up. I love talking. Meeting people', she added, 'is good for me'. Being kind to people, she says, gives her the greatest pleasure. And it shows.

It is a gift any politician would envy. But then that is only to be expected, because the Queen Mother is one of the most consummate politicians of her time. She has held the monarchy together during the crises of abdication and war, and provided the backbone lacked by an unpromising king during the nation's darkest hour. Her life is the story of Britain in the twentieth century, and she has accomplished it with a dignity and grace that neither the country nor its leaders have always managed.

She has also got her own way most of the time, not by shouting commands, but by hint and subtlety. She speaks in an old-fashioned way, bobbing her head, clutching at her pearls and saying, in a breathless whisper, 'Oh, do you really think so?' when faced with possible opposition. What she means is that she doesn't think so at all and it is her view which normally prevails.

To the Queen Mother, talking is a vital skill, and from an early age she was taught that socially silence must never fall. Many of her age-group used to drop their 'R's' as an affectation, but she puts them in. The word 'lost' for instance, she pronounces 'lorst'. Emphasis and repetition also play their part, and the Queen Mother has a cache of favourite phrases including 'great joy', 'delightful', 'rather charming', 'rather lovely', 'made to doctor's orders' and 'this is a treasure' with which she peppers her conversations.

She listens keenly to other people, entering a conversation on the correct beat like the consummate verbal musician she is. Irritated by the tongue-tied, she expects her guests to sing for their supper – sometimes literally – and likes to include amongst her weekend guests at Royal Lodge at least one amateur musician.

She exerts considerable influence over her daughter the Queen who, even after forty years on the throne, still bows to her mother's authority in many things, most particularly when it comes to the question of how the monarchy should be run.

The Queen would have liked, over the years, to have introduced a number of reforms to the way the Royal Family conducts itself and its business. She saw the need to build a post-Imperial monarchy shorn of much of its old pomp and ceremony. She also wanted to restructure the way Balmoral and Sandringham are administered. The Queen Mother, however, was against any swingeing reforms. Her opinions frozen in time and background; she was determined that everything should stay very much as it was when her husband, George VI – the King, never the late King, as she insists he is called – was alive. Prince Philip would fume. The Queen would exclaim in exasperation: 'Oh, Mummy!' But that was usually as far as their protests went. Taking on the Queen Mother, as her family have learnt, is not a wise thing to do.

The Duchess of Windsor discovered that. So did Peter Townsend whose romance with Princess Margaret foundered in part on the rock of the Queen Mother's opposition.

And so did Diana, Princess of Wales.

Princess Anne, whose attitude towards both the late Diana and the Queen Mother might best be described as ambivalent, once compared her grandmother to her sister-in-law. What she meant by that was that they were both surprisingly tough and manipulative.

Like the Queen Mother, Diana was the daughter of an earl of prestige and property. Each woman, in her way, found marrying into the Royal Family a trial. But Lady Elizabeth Bowes Lyon, as she was, was prepared to play by the rules and submerge herself in the institution she was wedded to; Lady Diana Spencer was not.

The Queen Mother, both as Duchess of York and as Queen, could be stern and uncompromising. When her husband lingered for too long after dinner over the port with the men, she would do a little drawing of a teapot, hand it to a footman and tell him to take it to the King. After dinner she preferred tea to coffee and this was her signal that she wanted him to join the ladies – immediately. The ever-compliant Bertie was always to submit to her gentle but firm command. In public, however, she would push him forward, always careful not to steal his limelight.

Diana the modern woman was not prepared to play that hierarchical game. She wanted a role for herself outside her husband's orbit. The Queen Mother believes in keeping up appearances, in playing by the book, in doing one's duty no matter how prosaic and difficult that might be. Diana, more spontaneous, more emotional, wanted very different things. It was a fundamental difference in approach, and one which made a clash between the grand matriarch and the wilful but unhappy *ingénue* all but inevitable. The Queen Mother has devoted her life to shoring up the Royal Family – the Royal Family she is substantially responsible for creating – and she became convinced that Diana was doing it irreparable damage.

THE QUEEN, PRINCE CHARLES, THE QUEEN MOTHER, PRINCESS DIANA AND LADY GABRIELLA WINDSOR WATCHING THE TROOPING OF THE COLOUR, JUNE 1992.

It is commonly supposed that the Queen Mother, through her friendship with Diana's grandmother Ruth, Lady Fermoy, played the matchmaker in Diana's marriage to Charles. Shortly before her tragic death Diana denied that story to me and conveyed some of the anger she clearly felt towards her ex-husband's family and the Queen Mother in particular.

Over morning coffee at Kensington Palace she said to me: 'The Queen Mother was not instrumental in arranging the marriage with Lady Fermoy. Charles and I arranged it. It is a myth it was the Queen Mother. She didn't do anything.'

Diana spent the night of her engagement and the night before her marriage as a guest of the Queen Mother at Clarence House. Diana said: 'When I went to stay at Clarence House I thought she was meant to help me, to teach me, but she did not do anything at all. I hardly saw her.'

The Princess concluded: 'She is not as she appears to be at all. She is tough and interfering and she has few feelings.'

By then the feeling was mutual. The week after Diana was killed and the nation was in the throes of an unprecedented outpouring of grief fuelled by rising anger against the Royal Family, the Queen Mother telephoned an old friend and said: 'Who would believe that she could be even more tedious in death than she was in life?'

It was one occasion when the Queen Mother's uncanny ability to capture and encapsulate the popular mood of the country deserted her. It was an uncommon lapse in a woman who, more than anyone else, has managed to weather the changes that have overwhelmed Britain this century. She might play ostrich (and in times of trouble she usually did) but when her head came up again (and it always does) she provided an emotional focus for the country she spent her life serving. When she stood on the balcony of Buckingham Palace, for instance, watching the flypast commemorating the 50th anniversary of VE Day, and wiped a tear from her eye, an occasion of profound poignancy was put into human context.

She may not be, as Diana pointed out, quite as nice as she appears. But then she herself is the first to admit that. It would be wondrous if she were, given the upheavals she has survived.

The Queen Mother has an interest in spiritualism and the 'other side', including speaking to the dead via mediums and seances, which many people would find distinctly odd. Her opinions are old-fashioned; she is annoyingly unpunctual. In private conversation she is politically incorrect (though not a racist): when a piano player of mixed Scottish and Indian stock was employed to serenade her at luncheon one day she put a hand to her pearls and said, 'What a cocktail!' She does not enjoy sharing the spotlight with anyone, including her daughter the Queen. To call her a snob would be stretching a point, given the obvious and genuine enjoyment she gets out of talking to and making friends with people from all backgrounds, but she is not above saying, in one of her breathless whispers, that so–and–so 'isn't quite one of...' The 'us' is left unsaid.

Not even the most diehard of republicans is immune to her charm, however. There is something endearing in the way she dresses, in the way she pores over her racing tips and sniffs the bottle of Dubonnet to make sure it hasn't gone off before tucking into a leg-buckling cocktail.

All important is the Queen Mother's style. She is forever saying things like 'What goes up must come down' and 'All good things must come to an end'. She is not talking about herself. She is still up there, and for her the good times never came to an end. At one point the ill-health of old age appeared to have reduced her spirits, but after she had undergone her first hip replacement she was quickly back on her feet, exuding energy and dancing Scottish reels late into the night. Her ambition is to see out the century and live to be a hundred; this would make her the longest-living crowned Queen, beating Queen Victoria's record, as she mischievously observes, by twenty days. In an era consumed by rush and stress, in a country unsure of itself and its position in the world, fearful of its future, there is reassurance in contemplating a woman who moves with the stately confidence of an older, more secure Britain. She is nostalgia personified.

Even the inevitable does not appear to disconcert her. She has taken a personal interest in planning her funeral, going over the details with the former Lord Chamberlain, the Earl of Airlie, choosing the hymns and inspecting the route at least twice. Because everyone else who has ever played a part in organizing such royal occasions is long gone to what the Queen Mother calls 'greener pastures', the format was borrowed for the funeral of Princess Diana. One can only speculate on the feelings of the Queen Mother given the differences between the two women and their lives, however, the Queen Mother's funeral – code-named 'Operation Lyon' – will be a far grander event, conducted by herself from beyond the grave. She has overseen every detail personally and inspected the route every inch of the way.

In the meantime Elizabeth is determined to carry on living on a scale worthy of her position, and that has cost the Queen a fortune out of her own purse. But then she is Britain's last Queen-Empress. She is the last in the line. And of one thing we can be absolutely certain – we will never see her like again.

CHAPTER 2

EDWARDIAN CHILDHOOD

Elizabeth Bowes Lyon was born in the high summer of Imperial Britain, into a family both ancient and grand. Hers was a society secure in its certainties, assured of its pre-eminence, set in its castes, and the little girl who would one day become Queen started life in the cocoon of extravagant privilege which typified such a background.

It is a world she would never leave.

The Empire she reigned over is no more. The aristocracy to which she belonged has all but vanished off the political landscape, dispersed by the winds of democratic advance and economic progress. The Royal Family she married into and which she came to represent is looking ever more old-fashioned and isolated. The old certitudes – of class and status and prerogative – have gone. Yet Elizabeth survived, untouched and all but unscathed by the sweep of change – the glorious, singular relic of a bygone era.

The thunderous march of history in this most cacophonous of centuries was reduced to the faintest of murmurs by the rampart of privilege which surrounded her, as thick and protective as the

8

walls of Glamis Castle where she spent much of her childhood. While others of her background were trundled away in the tumbrils of egalitarianism, she remained sublimely where she was, safe in rank and comfort.

Everything she had grown up with and had learnt from girlhood to take for granted was still there, right to the end, unaltered.

There was, for example, the choice of magnificent homes; the crested prams and the liveried footmen; the clothes and the jewels and the dressing for dinner. These were accompanied by biases and preconceptions, and the indulgent disregard for the vulgarities of money and its common kinswoman, frugality. Even the servants stayed *in situ*, as attentive and deferential as ever.

Had the child that she was strayed into her own old age, she would have found herself comfortably at home. She had been, by turns, a lady, a duchess and a queen. In terms of lifestyle, however, nothing changed and she remains the same – the eternal Edwardian lady.

ELIZABETH AND DAVID HAD AN IDYLLIC CHILDHOOD. SURROUNDED BY ALL THE TRAPPINGS OF WEALTH, THEY WERE FREE TO ENJOY ENDLESS SUMMERS PLAYING IN THE WELL-TENDED GROUNDS OF THE FAMILY'S PALATIAL HOMES.

The daughter of an earl-to-be, Claude George Bowes Lyon, Elizabeth was born on 4 August 1900, five months before Edward, the King who gave his name to the age that was already in full spate, ascended the throne. Where she actually made her début remains a mystery. Officially, the ninth of Lord and Lady Glamis's children came into this world at St Paul's Walden Bury, the family's Hertfordshire home. There is a Wedgwood plaque in the twelfth-century parish church proclaiming that this is so. In fact she was born somewhere in London, possibly at her parents' apartment in Grosvenor Gardens, possibly in a horse-drawn ambulance, perhaps even in a taxi. The query over the exact location of her birth gave rise to speculation that she was not the daughter of the Countess but the consequence of the Earl's clandestine liaison with a Welsh servant girl in his employ.

The suggestion was malicious gossip. While some aristocrats did on occasion forge close relationships with their more comely

A VERY EARLY
PHOTOGRAPH OF
ELIZABETH ANGELA
MARGUERITE
BOWES LYON,
BORN 4 AUGUST 1900,
THE NINTH CHILD OF
LADY GLAMIS.

employees, it would have gone against everything their lineage stood for to have pretended that the resulting children were their legitimate offspring. And even if the Earl had contemplated such an action the grand Countess would never have countenanced the subterfuge.

Elizabeth herself never gave the matter a thought (there was no reason for her to do so) and she remained sublimely unconcerned by the odd gap in her records. Asked if she was really born in the back of a taxi, she, by now the Queen Mother, replied, in her best Lady Bracknell voice: 'In the back of a taxi? How quaint.'

Such insouciance towards life's mundanities was to become one of Elizabeth's notable characteristics, as indeed it was of her father. Marion Crawford, governess of his granddaughter, the future Queen, called him 'a countryman through and through. He timed all his movements by country things – the coming of the migrants, the wild geese on the river, the rising of the sap'. Nothing was allowed to disturb his routine and while his wife was in London giving birth, Lord Glamis was in Scotland where, on 23 August, he made nine runs out of his side's total of 303 for 9 declared in the annual Glamis v. Strathmore cricket match. He did not get down to England until the third week in September – and was fined 7/6 (37p) for the delay in registering his daughter's birth.

That was a due which an aristocrat of his status could well afford to pay. Upon the death of his father in 1904 he became the 14th Earl of Strathmore and Kinghorne, Viscount Lyon and Baron Glamis, Tannadyce, Sidlaw and Strathdichtie, Baron Bowes, of Streatlam Castle County Durham, and Lunedale County York.

To help him live according to his multi-titled station, the Earl also inherited 50,000 acres of land, ironworks, coalmines and an estimated income of £100,000 (or some £5 million in today's money). By the immoderate standards of the day, he was not exceptionally well-off – the collapse of farm prices in the 1870s had made inroads into the family's reserves, and the determination of the Lord Strathmore's father, the 13th Earl, to build Episcopalian churches all across Scotland had encroached further – but he was rich enough.

Much has been made of Elizabeth's 'idyllic' and 'normal' childhood. And so it was, but only in comparison to those of similar background, and there were precious few of them. To the great mass of Britain's population at the time, she was living at a rarefied level which they could only approach with their heads respectfully bowed.

The Lyons, as they doggedly called themselves, can trace their descent from Scotland's kings. (The other half of their surname, along with the greater part of their fortune, came into the family when the 9th Earl married Elizabeth's great-great-grandmother, Mary Eleanor Bowes, the daughter of a Durham colliery owner who made over his money and his estates to his son-in-law on condition that he took his name.) Their lineage goes back into the mists of the Middle Ages and the violent history of the north is written in their blood (one forebear was burnt at the stake for witchcraft, one was killed in a duel, two were killed in the interminable feuds with neighbouring families, three fell at the Battle of Flodden in 1513). Elizabeth's mother, Cecilia, a cousin of the immensely rich Duke of Portland, also possessed a fine pedigree – and the aristocratic assumptions to go with it.

LADY ELIZABETH AT GLAMIS CASTLE WITH A TOY HORSE. HORSES WERE TO BECOME HER LIFELONG PASSION.

They were not, as the 14th Earl insisted, part of the Court circle. Indeed, the father of the future Queen went so far as to declare: 'If there is one thing I have determined for my children, it is that they shall never have any post about the Court.'

This was an attitude born in equal measure out of a devout churchgoer's disapproval of the louche behaviour of Edward VII and his friends, and the innate reservations many of the older aristocratic houses harboured about the Hanoverians and their descendants (the Strathmores' earldom had been bestowed on them by the Stuarts). That did not imply disloyalty of any kind. These were atavistic feelings, drawn from the collective but unacknowledged subconscious which Elizabeth's grandson, Prince Charles, lays such store by. As part of the established order, the Strathmores acknowledged the primacy of their sovereign who at the beginning of the century existed on an almost mystical plane. It would have been inconceivable for Elizabeth to have been brought up to think otherwise. Her family motto was clear and precise: 'In thou, my God, I place my trust without change to the end.' As for God, so for the monarchy.

What her parents did have was a healthy provincial suspicion of the frippery and fawning that was such a feature of court life under Edward. Though her family were of Society, they were not at its hub. They had their estates and sumptuous town house where they based themselves during the Court-ruled London Season. But, as is often the way of those who stand on the edge of the circle, they were mildly contemptuous of Edward VII's dandified, obsequious coterie. As Lady Strathmore observed from the commanding heights of her own genealogy: 'Some people have to be fed royalty like sea lions with fish.'

Lyons they were. Sea lions they most definitely were not. Theirs was a family that saw itself as a clan, complete in its own company, content to stay within its own parameters, certain of its place in the order of things.

In London, in the fine (and very large) Adam house in St James's Square the Earl had taken when he had succeeded his father, they were treated with the respect due to their lordly rank.

At Glamis in Angus, the seat of the Strathmores' authority, their position afforded them almost feudal devotion. There they grew their own food, had their own bread baked for them and made their own dairy products in the still-room. There was a laundry, a carpentry shop, a stonemason and a private railway station. The Industrial Revolution which had shaken the United Kingdom and made the Bowes Lyons rich had hardly touched upon their remote fastness. The tyranny of the motor car had not yet taken hold and new ideas travelled slowly over the rough-hewn roads leading to their timeless keep, redolent of legends and ghosts. According to

Lord Gorrell, briefly Secretary for Air in Lloyd George's Coalition Government, the Strathmores were gracious and easy-going. 'No stuffiness, no aloofness anywhere, no formality except the beautiful old custom of having the two pipers marching round the table at the close of dinner, followed by a momentary silence as the sound of their bagpipes died away gradually in the distance of the castle. It was all so friendly and so kind.'

The Strathmores, nevertheless, were of their time. Caps were doffed as the lord drove by in his carriage. Housemaids curtsied as her ladyship went about her inspections. And their youngest daughter, who had acquired the first of her many titles at the age of three when her father inherited the earldom, was always referred to as 'Lady Elizabeth' by the army of servants whose duty in life it was to make the lives of their lord and his family as comfortable and carefree as possible.

Their Edwardian days revolved around a succession of meals. Breakfast offered a dozen choices from eggs, bacon, kidneys, haddock and cold partridge, scones, toast, jam and honey served

St Paul's Walden Bury in Hertfordshire. The country home of the Strathmores where Lady Elizabeth spent part of her childhood.

on tables heaped with exotic fruits and flowers from the estate hothouses.

In autumn the Lyons took to the hills for the shooting. When she was old enough Elizabeth went with them, sometimes on an old donkey, more usually on foot.

'She loved walking and could out-walk the guns, the keepers and the beaters,' Sir Alec Douglas-Home, a former Prime Minister and Elizabeth's lifelong friend recalled. 'She could walk all day and then dance right into the night.'

But Elizabeth never walked on an empty stomach. The shooting lunches usually took place in tents erected in the middle of ploughed fields. There the rustic atmosphere ended. Inside the tent would be carefully laid tables covered in white linen cloths, the food served on silver dishes by footmen in full livery. The six-course lunch would finish just in time for the guests to rush back to the house to change for a full-scale tea of sandwiches and cakes. It was a wonder that they could face dinner, which consisted of twelve courses. Tiaras, orders and decorations glinted in the light from candles and the gas mantles on the wall (electricity was not installed until 1929). And at the meal's conclusion, the pipers would appear.

It is a tribute to the boundless energy of the period that anyone had the strength to rise from the table, never mind dance. But dance they did – and Elizabeth carried on doing so into her nineties.

The routine was less hectic at St Paul's Walden Bury in Hertfordshire where Elizabeth spent most of her infancy. She remembered it as an enchanted place of secret walks and mysterious hiding-places. An adult would have described it as an imposing Queen Anne mansion. It was run in a rather easy-going way (when water started pouring down the drawing-room wall, Lady Strathmore was heard to request: 'Would someone be very kind and move the sofa'). But, like Glamis in those labour-intensive days, the house nevertheless required platoons of servants to keep it running smoothly.

Every year the Strathmores would travel from one end of the country to the other, north to south, and back again, according to the sporting calendar, accompanied by a retinue of personal servants. It was a stately journey Lady Elizabeth undertook, involving railways, horses, carriages, carts, ponies and trunks groaning with toys and books, clothes and crockery. But for the addition of the special trains it resembled nothing so much as a medieval progress. This, of course, is precisely what it was – and one which she would re-enact as Queen and, later, as Queen Mother.

En route Lady Elizabeth would stop over at Streatlam Castle in County Durham which, like St Paul's Walden Bury, had come into the family upon the 9th Earl's fortuitous and far-sighted marriage and which, like all their other properties, came with its own complement of staff.

Lady Alice Montagu-Douglas-Scott, daughter of the Duke of Buccleuch and Lady Elizabeth's future sister-in-law (she married Henry, Duke of Gloucester), recorded that during the Season there were sixty-eight staff in permanent residence at her family's London home alone. As an earl, Strathmore did not feel compelled to run his establishments on quite such a lavish scale, but it was still extremely grand.

Including butlers and footmen, factors, cooks and skivvies, valets and ladies' maids, bootblacks and chambermaids, coachmen, grooms and stablemen, parlourmaids, nurses, gamekeepers, stalkers, ghillies, gardeners, gatekeepers, farm labourers, carpenters, stonemasons, nannies, governesses, nursery-maids and the host of other posts vital to the family's well-being, Lord Strathmore employed several hundred people in different parts of the realm.

In old age Elizabeth would recall entering the vast kitchen at Glamis and finding a kitchen-maid asleep on a camp-bed set up under the table for the staff to take their naps between meals. She also remembered Barson, a valet-cum-butler whose incorrigible drunkenness led him to spill food and drink over his master's guests. (He was frequently dismissed but invariably reprieved, which perhaps explains the amused affection with which Elizabeth later treated those members of her household who so frequently over-served themselves.)

Edwardian society was strictly segregated according to class. Friendships that transgressed the social boundaries were firmly discouraged. As the Earl's youngest daughter – and a notably engaging child by all accounts – Elizabeth was petted and fêted by the staff. 'The little imp! I was forever chasing her out of the

ELIZABETH WITH HER
BROTHER, DAVID,
PHOTOGRAPHED AT
GLAMIS CASTLE IN
1909, DRESSED
RESPECTIVELY AS A
LADY FROM THE REIGN
OF JAMES I AND A
COURT JESTER.

kitchen,' one of the family's cooks recalled. She was not allowed to make friends with the servants' children, however. That, to use a colloquialism of the day, simply wasn't done. Like all her contemporaries, she was brought up to know her place in the pecking order – and to keep it.

Her position most certainly did not give her any right to be rude or haughty. The old rural aristocracy to which Elizabeth belonged made a great point of treating their staff with politeness and consideration, and she was taught to be thoughtful and courteous. Her father said: 'Lady Elizabeth is most popular with all the tenants and villagers. She was always more interested in her dolls' houses and her dolls than in how to tease the workmen on the estate and her tutors.' She could be imperious and would tell the kitchen staff: 'If you could make the pats of butter a little smaller, it would be much better. Persons leave some of the big pats on their plates and that is very wasteful.' She got away with that. But if she stuck her tongue out at someone her nanny, Allah, would slap her soundly across the back of her legs. 'Miss Manners', as her nannies and nursery-maids called polite behaviour, was always in attendance.

Noblesse oblige makes a poor playmate, however. The Edwardians invented the house party, but little children did not accompany their parents on their leisurely round of visits. They were left in the care of nannies and governesses. It was an isolated and often friendless environment for a young child.

Princess Alice recalled about her own very similar childhood, 'looking back, I was somewhat starved in my affections. I prayed every night for my teddy bear to come to life.'

Princess Alice's cousin, Anne, Viscountess Cowdray, agreed. Like Lady Elizabeth, she was the daughter of the country-based Earl of Bradford. 'We were not allowed to play with the local children,' she remembered. 'Life could be very lonely at times – especially when the weather was bad and we could not play outside.'

There was no place for complaint in the tedious emptiness of rainy days. 'You must learn to amuse yourself,' was a refrain familiar to every Edwardian child. And Elizabeth's mother would not allow boredom in the house.

Elizabeth's father was a grandfatherly forty-five when she was born and remained a forever distant figure who refused to eat eggs (he considered them poisonous) and daily devoted hours to crossword puzzles. He was more concerned with his cricket and shooting and the running of his estates than the obligations of parenthood (as witnessed by the lax manner he had greeted her arrival). Much of his time was spent lopping off the branches of trees and tying them into bundles. He liked nothing better than venturing out in the dead of night to collect firewood which he would bring back and chop up in his bedroom. 'Good for the trees – and good for me,' he said.

Elizabeth was fortunate in her mother, who took an unfashionable pleasure in her maternal duties and devoted what for the period was a considerable amount of time to her youngest daughter's welfare and development. It was her younger brother, however, who provided Elizabeth with the companionship that children so crave. Her seven surviving siblings were between seven and seventeen years her senior – an unbridgeable gulf in the lifetime of a child. It was to her good fortune, then, that when Elizabeth was fourteen months old Lady Strathmore gave birth to her tenth child, 'a darling bruvver' as her youngest daughter called him. He was named David and the two became inseparable, 'almost like twins', as Lady Strathmore observed.

They were nicknamed 'the two Benjamins' by their mother (Benjamin being the youngest son of Jacob and Rachel) and they were complete unto themselves. No-one else was on hand (because no-one else was allowed) to intrude into the genial little world they created for themselves at St Paul's Walden Bury, where they spent much of their year. There they had their rocking-horses and their well-worn stuffed animals and their pets. This was where Elizabeth and David played their games of Red Indians and where she learnt to ride, on a Shetland pony called Bobs who would sometimes follow her into the house.

Elizabeth herself recalled, through the sepia-tinted gauze of memory (and in the regal third person): 'At the bottom of the garden, where the sun always seemed to be shining, is THE WOOD – the haunt of fairies, with its anemones and ponds, and moss-grown statues, and the BIG OAK under which she reads and where the two ring-doves, Caroline-Curly-Love and Rhoda-Wrigley-Worm, contentedly coo in their wicker-work "Ideal Home."'

David, too, wallowed in the recollection of those far-off, cloudless days. He and his sister had their secret hideouts, as he told Lady Cynthia Asquith who wrote the first authorized biography of Elizabeth which was published shortly after her marriage to the future George VI. There was the Harness Room and the Flea House which 'could only be reached by a very rotten ladder, the rungs of which would certainly have broken if an adult had attempted the ascent. Consequently our nurse was unable to come up and retrieve us.'

ELIZABETH PLAYING
CARDS WITH DAVID.

BELOW:
ELIZABETH AND DAVID
AT GLAMIS.

There they kept their supply of 'forbidden delicacies, acquired by devious devices...apples, oranges, sugar, slabs of chocolate Meunier, matches and packets of Woodbines... To this blissful retreat we used to have recourse whenever it seemed an agreeable plan to escape our morning lessons.'

It is a picture shining with untarnished nostalgia, and it provided Elizabeth with the philosophical framework which was to sustain her for the whole of her life. To that, her mother added the practical guideline: 'Life is for living and working at. If you find anything or anybody a bore, the fault is yours.'

It was a providential principle to instil in a girl who would spend her adulthood speaking to people she had never met before and was unlikely ever to meet again. Effort and and training were needed for that, just as they were when she had laboured as a child to keep boredom at bay.

Without the ready fix of television or the mobile social life afforded by the motor car, Edwardian children had to make their own amusements. The only theme parks existed in their imaginations. Elizabeth played with dolls (she liked the ones with eyes that opened and closed), learnt to ride, learnt how to make daisychains, organized games of hide-and-seek.

With her brother in hand, she would toddle off unescorted to the village shop at Glamis – the world was a safer place then for young children – to buy sweets. They were the Lyon children. They 'couldn't bear' the name Bowes, Elizabeth confided to the artist E.Gertrude Thomson. 'We never use it.' (Their parents would have happily followed suit, but old Mr Bowes had made legally certain that they would have to use his name when he handed them his fortune).

When it rained she would lie reading on the floor until her knees and elbows were chafed raw (*Black Beauty* was her favourite book). She was keen on charades. She had her own dancing master, Mr Neal, whose white beard was rubbed away on one side by fifty years of playing his fiddle. He would skip around the room with Elizabeth and David as he played.

Just as she would when an adult, Elizabeth enjoyed dressing up and took great delight in raiding the family dressing-up box.

Mr Stirton, the local minister, recalled being treated to an impromptu performance by David and Elizabeth dressed respectively as a court jester and a lady from the unifying reign of James (the Ist of England, the VI of Scotland) who awarded the Lyons their earldom. With unctuous hyperbole worthy of Jane Austen's worthy cleric Mr Collins, Mr Stirton declared: 'As the dance proceeded the glamour and illusion seemed to increase. Was it reality, or had the psychic influence of historic Glamis clouded the mind and conjured up a scene to delude the senses? No "crystal ball" experience could have been more effective.'

At the end of the performance Mr Stirton, whose ability to say the right thing about the right person would be rewarded with the post of Chaplain to King George V at Balmoral, asked the young lady who she was.

'I call myself the Princess Elizabeth,' came the prescient reply.

Such impromptu performances were a well-known aspect of Elizabeth's family life at Glamis. Lord Ernest Hamilton, brother of Scotland's premier duke, the Duke of Hamilton, noted: 'It was at part singing that, as a family, the Lyons chiefly excelled. At any moment they would suddenly start, just as the spirit moved them, on some madrigal or sextet – during dinner, out walking in the park, sitting round the fire in the billiard-room, or driving to the station in the family omnibus – it didn't matter where; one note was given – with a tuning-fork or otherwise – and off they started. Their voices, being all made according to one pattern as it were, blended most delightfully, and the effect was fascinating beyond belief.' It is a family trait that Elizabeth continued all her life – to the pleasure of those who witnessed her suddenly burst into song. Veronica, the wife of the adventurer and diplomat Sir Fitzroy Maclean, was one treated to such an outpouring. She said: 'It dawned on me that Queen Elizabeth is a born performer and that it is easy and natural (and fun) for her to project herself before one, two, three or ten thousand people.'

PORTRAIT OF THE
COUNTESS OF
STRATHMORE, 1923.
PAINTED BY MABEL
HANKEY.

The darker side was determinedly excluded from this idyll. Danger and unpleasantness were locked away, like the fearsome Monster of Glamis, the misshapen son of the 11th Earl, who was born in 1821 and incarcerated for the duration of his wretched life in a sealed cell in the castle walls. 'We were never allowed to talk about it,' Elizabeth's sister, Lady Rose, admitted. 'Our parents forbade us ever to mention the matter or ask any questions.'

Nor was the monster the only unfortunate member of the family to be locked away, out of sight if never entirely out of mind. In 1987 two of Elizabeth's nieces, daughters of her brother John, were discovered in a mental hospital where they had been confined for almost the whole of their lives.

They too had been expunged from all conversation. They were never referred to, never discussed. They were treated as though they did not exist. Officially they didn't. *Burke's Peerage and Baronetage*, the authoritative stud-book of the aristocracy, had them listed as dead – on information supplied by the Bowes Lyons themselves. But they were in fact very much alive and, along with the Monster, they cast a malevolent shadow over this otherwise open, breezy family.

It was shame, not malice, that induced the Bowes Lyons to treat their ill-fated relations so heartlessly, and in that they were by no means unique. The Strathmores were of an age and a society which set great store by keeping up appearances. There was no place in this milieu for what the locals described as a monstrous, hairy freak with spindly limbs dangling from an egg-shaped body or two pathetic, vacant-eyed ladies. One did not discuss such 'failures', just as no-one drew attention to the uncomfortable fact that Lady Strathmore suffered what was most probably a series of nervous breakdowns beginning in 1911 when her third son, Alex, died after being hit on the head by a cricket ball, and culminating with her collapse in 1915 on the death at the Battle of Loos of her fourth son, Fergus.

Other families, too, had their skeletons and, as at Glamis, they were kept quietly under lock and key. It was an approach to a problem that made an indelible impression upon Elizabeth, for whom family secrets were matters never, ever to be discussed.

Not all tribulations could be so avoided, however. The Strathmores' nurses were fleet enough in their pursuit to ensure that the two Benjamins attended some of their lessons and got at least the grounding of an education. Their mother played her part in ensuring that this was so. 'My mother taught us to read and write,' David recalled. Both the Strathmores were conscientious and committed Anglicans. Family prayers were read every morning and religious instruction was an important part of their children's curriculum. 'At the age of six and seven we could each have written a fairly detailed account of all the Bible stories,' David said. 'This knowledge was entirely due to our mother's teaching.'

Lady Strathmore was an expert horticulturist who planted the two-acre Italian Garden at Glamis and gave her daughters the names of flowers (Violet, Hyacinth, Rose, and, for Elizabeth, Marguerite). It was from her that Elizabeth inherited her love of gardening. 'She also taught us the rudiments of music, dancing and drawing, at all of which my sister became fairly proficient,' David recollected.

Elizabeth's mother also made it her business to introduce her children to the rudiments of good taste. On carriage drives into

Hitchen, Hertfordshire, she would point out to her daughter a perfectly proportioned Georgian house and compare it to its ugly Victorian neighbour.

Cecilia Strathmore, who was less forbidding than her formidable demeanour suggested (she looked, she said, more like a grandmother than a mother to her youngest daughter), had inherited her artistic tastes from her own mother.

Having remarried after Cecilia's father died, and been twice widowed, Mrs Caroline Scott, as she now was, moved to Italy in 1882. With Lady Strathmore's unmarried sister, Violet, in tow, she took an apartment in Rome and a villa in Bordighera on the Italian side of the border with France. Her principal residence was the Villa Capponi outside Florence where, in typical English fashion, she set about creating a garden. Mrs Scott's niece by marriage, the *outré* Bloomsbury hostess Lady Ottoline Morrell, described the villa thus: 'The old house was filled with Italian furniture and pictures, and the perfume of tiger-lilies, and it was to me a haven of joy.'

Lady Ottoline's cousin, Lady Elizabeth, was equally enchanted. Lady Strathmore made several trips to Italy and Elizabeth always went too. It was an exciting experience for a child and in old age Elizabeth fondly recalled the thrill of the cross-Channel boat and the night-train ride through the still French countryside, the restaurant-car meals, the colour and beauty of her grandmother's Italian home, 'the glamour of being "abroad", the gabble and gesticulations of foreigners'.

The house stood on a hill. Inside, so Elizabeth recounted, 'everything was in perfect harmony with the surroundings, and one can imagine how impressive to a child must have been the great room with an organ at one end, a fireplace in the centre and dark panelled walls – a stately solemn room, yet full of comfort and brightness. Lovely furniture, flowers, books, beauty everywhere. And the little chapel with its few exquisite pictures, and walls covered with red damask.'

Her grandmother and, more particularly, her aunt Violet took familial pleasure in introducing Elizabeth to the splendour of Florentine art. The tan had yet to be invented, the sun was to be scrupulously avoided and there were no swimming-pools for the little girl to play in. Instead her days were spent exploring the city the British declared the most beautiful in the world. Wearing a long white dress and a large straw sun-bonnet, she was taken on tours through the cool of the churches and galleries.

Elizabeth enjoyed her outings with her aunt to look at paintings in the Uffizi Gallery and the Pitti Palace. She also liked going afterwards for refreshments at Doneys where she would be given a small glass of vermouth – the drink to which she developed a life-long attachment.

Her interest in ornate Italian art also dates from this time. There are a number of paintings in the style of the Florentine Renaissance Revival in her bedroom at Clarence House. And on the headposts of the painted headboard of her bed stand two winged angels dressed in real robes. Elizabeth bought them in Bordighera when she was eight years old. She bargained the price down to three lira, a trifling sum even then. The stallholder said he had been honoured to serve her. This would be a familiar refrain.

Holidays, even for a child as favoured as Lady Elizabeth, do not last for ever. And there was a limit to how much time even someone as accommodating as Lady Strathmore could spend with her children. Elizabeth's eye was being trained; her mind had to be, too. With no great enthusiasm, but nonetheless inevitably, the formalities of education had to be tackled and completed.

School was the obvious option – but only for the Strathmore sons who followed each other to Eton with clockwork regularity. Girls were a different matter altogether. It was no wonder that Elizabeth burst into floods of heart-rending tears when David, aged ten years old, was sent away to begin his formal education. 'I miss him horribly,' she said. The little girl who had once written that her favourite pastime was 'making friends' had lost the only real one she had. Now she was being denied the opportunity to meet new companions. The Countess's friend, Lady Cynthia Asquith, observed: 'Lady Strathmore never submitted to the growing fashion of banishing daughters to boarding school.'

Making friends, however, was not an urgent priority for large families like the Strathmores; in the Royal Family it was positively discouraged. Queen Victoria had ruled against it. 'You are right to be civil & friendly to the young girls you may occasionally meet & to see them sometimes – but never *make friendship*,' she wrote to her seventeen-year-old granddaughter and namesake, Princess

Victoria. 'You are so many of yourselves that you *want no one else.*'

Elizabeth did attend Dorothy and Irene Birtwhistle's 'select classes for girls' in central London when she was nine, but only as a day-girl – and only for two terms.

Elizabeth loved London. It was a dirty, unhealthy place compared to the bucolic opulence of Hertfordshire or the dour majesty of the Highlands. Thick, choking yellow fogs called 'pea soupers' descended in winter, cloaking the city in a grimy darkness so dense that Elizabeth could not see the street from her nursery window in St James's Square. No matter how tightly her windows were closed, the fog penetrated into her bedroom, leaving speckles of soot on the curtains and coating the cornices with a black film, filling her young lungs with 'foul vapours'.

Yet, in this Dickensian filth, life acquired a verve and excitement which no amount of country make-believe could equal. Here she had what the countryside could not provide: the companionship of children of her own age. During the Season the great families flocked to 'town', as they called the heaving capital of the Empire. They brought their progeny with them and Elizabeth was allowed out to mix with children whose background met with her parents' approval.

There were outings to the public parks where the hordes of uniformed nannies installed themselves with great pomp on the benches which they regarded as their private preserve, reserved according to the status of their employers. (This unwritten but strictly enforced hierarchical demarcation continued into the 1950s. Prime Minister Harold Macmillan's grandson, the Earl of Stockton, recalled being taken to Regent's Park as a young boy. When his nanny found a nursery-maid sitting on 'her' park bench she asked the unfortunate girl who employed her. 'Mrs So-and-so', came the answer. 'This bench is reserved for the families of earls and prime ministers,' the Macmillan nanny witheringly informed her. Duly chastened, the interloper slunk away, pushing her uncrested pram before her.)

Hyde Park when Elizabeth was small was a clamorous place, bustling with heavy prams with high tussore canopies, babies, pushchairs and parasols, children, horses, carriages and activity. Back then it even had its own flock of sheep 'which stood in the middle distance weighed down by sooty fleeces'.

Elizabeth also enjoyed occasional afternoon teas taken with the children of the grand houses of Mayfair, Belgravia and St James's.

There was the excitement of being a bridesmaid, a function Elizabeth first fulfilled in 1908 when her eldest brother, Patrick, married the Duke of Leeds' daughter, Lady Dorothy Osborne, at the Guards' Chapel.

ELIZABETH – WHO HAD RECENTLY BEEN CHOSEN AS ONE OF PRINCESS MARY'S BRIDESMAIDS – WITH HER FATHER, THE EARL OF STRATHMORE, AT GLAMIS CASTLE.

Best of all, there were the parties. The gregarious Elizabeth adored, and still adores, parties.

She would arrive by horse and carriage and later by chauffeur-driven limousine, accompanied by nannies and maids and footmen. Untroubled by shyness, she bloomed with gaiety amongst the jellies and chocolate cakes. The Marquis of Salisbury's son, Lord David Cecil, met her when she was seven and he was six at the home of the Marchioness of Lansdowne. With the eye of the historian he was to become set firmly on the future, he would later recall being besotted by her 'small, charming, rosy face around which twined and strayed rings and tendrils of silken hair, and a pair of dewy grey eyes. Her flower-like mouth parted in a grave, enchanting smile, and between the pearly teeth flowed out tones of drowsy melting sweetness that seemed to caress the words they uttered...Forgotten were all the pretenders to my heart. Here was the true heroine. She had come. I had seen and she had conquered.' Mr Stirton could not have put it better.

Cecil was not the only one to be captivated by the vivacious little girl. Two years earlier she had attended the Countess of Leicester's children's party. She wore a long blue-and-white party frock; the long hair she was never to discard was tied in bows. The

Countess introduced her to George V's son, Bertie, the future George VI. Elizabeth was five and confident. Bertie was ten and gauche. To put him at his ease she gave him the glacé cherry out of her piece of cake.

To add polish to this natural poise Elizabeth was enrolled at Madame D'Egville's dancing classes (her report called her 'graceful and intelligent') and given musical instruction.

Lady Strathmore would write when Elizabeth was ten: 'The children's class at the Mathilde Verne School of pianoforte playing is wonderful in many ways. My children have attended two terms and have made extraordinary progress.'

So impressed was the Countess with Madame Verne's abilities as a teacher that in 1918 she employed her herself – for the most poignant of reasons. 'I have cataracts in both my eyes, and am thinking that, later on, music would be a great joy to me again,' she explained to the music teacher.

Elizabeth, who later in life would also suffer from cataracts, did not share her mother's enthusiasm at first. She rejoiced in dancing. The repetitious monotony of learning to play the piano was less to her taste. Madame Verne recalled her young charge struggling with one particularly laborious exercise. 'I looked at the child. Though fervent of face, there was a warning gleam in her eyes as she said to the teacher, "Thank you very much. That was wonderful," and promptly slid off the music-stool, holding out her tiny hand in polite farewell. She always had perfect manners.'

Like it or not – and for all her manners, she most certainly did not – Elizabeth was made to continue with her lessons. Along with a passable ability to sing, paint, dance and speak French, playing the piano was one of the 'accomplishments' expected of a well-brought-up Edwardian lady of good family. Mathematics and science were not required; even subjects like history and geography only just made it on to the educational curriculum.

'Serene to the point of casualness', Lady Strathmore attached no great importance to academic achievement. Nor, when her maternal turn came, did Elizabeth. Childhood was there to provide a storehouse for carefully selected memories. To Lady Strathmore's way of thinking, school, with its demands and disciplines and pressures, did not provide what she wanted for her daughter. The Birtwhistle experiment was not deemed a success. Elizabeth was taken out of school and back to Glamis, and her education was again entrusted to the family governesses whose qualifications for the task were measured by the soundness of their characters.

These ladies were usually French, only occasionally British, and the first one, a Mademoiselle Lang, arrived when Elizabeth was just a toddler of four. Many more were to follow. Some were pleasant enough. Others were more demanding. 'Her hands are too small!' one declared. When she was twelve, a sturdy German named Kathie Kubler was taken on. David, on his visits home from prep school in Broadstairs, detested her. When he shot his first hare she ate it all herself, leaving not a morsel for him. 'This crowning offence caused a rupture,' Lady Cynthia Asquith recorded. Elizabeth had quite liked the sturdy German Fräulein but David was adamant in his hostility. 'Diplomatic relations...were finally broken off and she departed from Glamis.'

David Lyon was delighted. The whole castle, he said, had been shaken to its foundations by her Teutonic tread. (Elizabeth never shared her brother's opinion of Fräulein Kuebler and the two exchanged letters throughout the Great War.) Elizabeth watched her tutors trip and tread their way into her life and back out again. She noted: 'Some governesses are nice and some *are not*.'

Such a turnover was unusual. Governesses, often gentle-women whose families had fallen on hard times, were expected to stay to see their charges through to the end of what passed for their education. Most wished to do this; a position with a family as eminent as the Strathmores was much sought-after and consequently difficult to achieve. For some reason Elizabeth was denied continuity in her tutors and at an early age was forced to develop and practise dealing with the comings and goings of strangers.

Sir Alec Doulgas-Home observed: 'She moved around the tenant farmers on the estates talking to them about their animals, the crops, their dogs and the farm life. I think if you lived in that part of Scotland you couldn't avoid being to a certain extent a philosopher, competing with the elements, understanding the ani-mals and the rhythms of life. I think this laid the foundation of her ease of manner with a whole lot of different people.'

Without a readily available pool of children of her own age to draw upon, it was inevitable that Elizabeth should spend a lot of her time in the company of grown-ups. She did so with a charm and an ease of manner that impressed itself on everyone she met.

Aged three, she greeted her father's forty-five-year-old factor by saying: 'How do you do, Mr Raltson? I haven't seen you look so well, not for years and years, but I am sure you will be sorry to know that Lord Strathmore has got the toothache.' At that same tender age she would invite visitors to come and sit beside her – and then talk happily away to them for three-quarters of an hour.

By the time she was seven the family were putting her gift to practical use. If a guest proved particularly taciturn or difficult Elizabeth would be sent into action because, as they said, 'She can talk to *anyone.*' Such was her social composure that from her early teens onwards her father would occasionally allow her out of the nursery to join him for dinner – including the unique occasion when he had four former Viceroys of India seated at his table.

Being almost the youngest of a large family also helped smooth away any self-consciousness Elizabeth might have experienced. The Lyons were a rowdy troupe, as Lady Cynthia Asquith noted.

'Brothers and sisters, though devoted to each other, used at times to quarrel furiously, using hands and teeth on each other with all their youthful vigour.' To which Lord Home added: 'She had to take the rough and tumble with all those countless brothers and sisters. But she gave as good as she got.'

It was Nanny's responsibility to restore order and provide the bedrock of attention and unwavering affection.

When Elizabeth was one month old Lady Strathmore engaged a new nursery-maid. Clara Cooper Knight was seventeen years old, the daughter of a Hertfordshire farmer who tilled a parcel of land near St Paul's Walden Bury. Her new position began an

A REFLECTIVE STUDY OF THE YOUNG DUCHESS BY MICHAEL HOPPÉ.

association that would last for the rest of her life. Elizabeth and David called her Allah which was as close as they could get to pronouncing Clara.

It was a cosy, neat, regulated nursery that Allah presided over. While the children frolicked, she sat in her rocking-chair in front of a coal fire, sewing, chiding, comforting, ever-watchful, dispensing simple homilies.

'All good things come to an end,' was one. Others included, 'Say your prayers properly and don't mumble. You're talking to God'; 'Say please *and* thank you'; 'If you can't say something nice, don't say anything at all'. For generations to come these would sound like so many platitudes, but they encapsulated the Edwardian approach to life and Elizabeth took them to heart.

The role of Allah was an unusual one, as it was for all Edwardian nannies. She was suspended half-way between the mother and the rest of the staff, half parent, half servant, and her nursery was an establishment in itself. It consisted of a day nursery room, a night nursery, a pantry and even a room for Nanny's own servants. (These would consist of an under-nurse and sometimes a nursery-maid for each child.) It was separated from the rest of the house by a green baize door, cut off even from the other servants.

They were usually happy places (the cliché of the cruel nanny belongs more to fiction than fact, though the treatment meted out to Elizabeth's future husband and his brothers and sister by the nanny proved a sorry exception. She particularly disliked Bertie and would snatch his food away from him almost as soon as he'd starting eating. This treatment resulted in the chronic stomach complaint which was to plague him for the remainder of his life). At St Paul's Walden Bury the nursery occupied the entire top floor of the house and all her life Elizabeth carried a picture in her mind of the day-room. 'Its high fender recalls comfortable dryings by the fire and the delicious smell of toasting bread,' she recounted to Lady Cynthia who wrote: 'This pleasant room had not been subjected to the fickleness of fashion, its walls being still adorned by the favourite story-pictures that were framed and hung up by the gardener twenty years before'.

Parents hardly ever intruded. When they were very young Lady Strathmore had indeed spent a considerable amount of time in her children's company. Once they were out of their infancy, however, it was Nanny who was expected to implement the routine and provide them with their comforts. Mother might look in for half an hour at around ten o'clock in the morning; Father almost never did. At teatime the children, scrubbed and shining, would go down to the drawing-room for an hour. Lady Strathmore, engagements permitting, made a point of reading her youngest their bedtime stories. And their father sometimes allowed them to play with his flowing moustache (he would part it before kissing them). But that, apart from high days, holidays and Sundays when the family went together to church, was usually all that parents saw of their offspring through their childhood years.

To a later way of thinking, this approach would seem cold to the point of indifference. That was certainly not the way Edwardians such as the Strathmores saw it. To them childhood was not a state complete unto itself, with rights and entitlements. Those were the prerogatives of adulthood, to which childhood was merely a stepping-stone. They saw nothing out of the ordinary in the way they treated their children. Quite the contrary: by their own standards and in comparison to many of their peers, they were a warm, loving and closely-knit unit.

Elizabeth certainly thought so. As she said, the sun always shone when she was a little girl, just as it had for those other gilded youngsters fortunate enough to be born into families blessed with wealth and social prestige. They had everything to look forward to. They were too young and innocent, too self-absorbed and self-assured to suspect that the world to which they belonged was about to come to its cataclysmic end.

On 4 August 1914 Lady Elizabeth celebrated her fourteenth birthday. She had just passed her Oxford Local examination, the precursor of GCSEs. She awoke that morning in her nursery bedroom at 20 St James's Square to a pile of telegrams and presents.

That evening her birthday treat was to be taken by her mother to the London Coliseum. From their private box they watched Lipiinsky's Dog Comedians, the jugglers Moran and Wise and the Russian ballerina Fedorovna.

At eleven o'clock that night King George V declared war on Germany and the British Empire marched off to its grave.

The Edwardian way of life went with it, never to return. By the century's end Elizabeth Bowes Lyon was its only survivor.

CHAPTER 3

THE ROARING TWENTIES

Elizabeth Bowes Lyon adored men. She responded to them in a open and alluring manner and even in old age the presence of a handsome male would visibly lighten her spirits. It was this flirtatiousness, much more than her looks which were never outstanding, which made her so popular in her youth and gained her the attention of would-be suitors.

She grew to love her husband, Bertie, the future King George VI. But she did not love him at first, not by any means. She felt protective towards him and was fond of him, but she preferred her men debonair and good-looking. He was neither of these things.

Indeed, had it not been for the pressures brought to bear by an ambitious mother (urged on by a fearsome Queen making the best of a ruling introduced by an opportunistic Prime Minister seeking political gain from the post-war anti-German feeling), it is doubtful that Elizabeth would have married Bertie. She turned him down at least once. Left to her own devices, she would probably have turned him down again, for the good reason that she was not in love with him.

Neither her qualms nor the ruthless tactics employed behind the scenes were allowed to intrude into the glowing picture of romantic perfection which was presented to the public on their eventual engagement. Elizabeth, her official biographers wrote, was a 'born homemaker' who, when Prince Albert made his proposal of marriage, allowed 'feelings, not reason' to take command because 'she just found she couldn't do without him.'

The uncomfortable fact that Elizabeth had first rejected Bertie's offers of marriage was glossed over by Mabell, Countess of Airlie, and Lady Cynthia Asquith in their authorized accounts of the courtship. Elizabeth, so Lady Airlie wrote, was 'afraid of the public life which would lie ahead of her as the King's daughter-in-law'. Lady Cynthia agreed. Elizabeth was worried, she said, that marriage to a prince of the blood 'would entail too great a sacrifice of that independence and privacy which is the birthright of every subject'. Helen, the wife of Bertie's future private secretary, Lord Hardinge, weighed in with the observation that 'Lady Elizabeth had nothing against the Duke himself but...having been so happy in her own family, it was hard for her to have to face a situation in which privacy would have to take second place to her husband's work for the nation.'

That Elizabeth was actually in love with someone else was tactfully never mentioned.

In that tightly-knit aristocratic clique to which she belonged, however, affairs of the heart were not something to be left to the vagaries of youthful emotion. The Great War had swept away many of the old mores, but not in her circle. There the old Edwardian customs still held firm, and marriage for the daughter of one of the grand patrician houses was still about position and security. Love, if it entered the equation at all, only did so as a bonus.

THE BODY LANGUAGE SAYS IT ALL; ELIZABETH WAS RELUCTANT TO ACCEPT BERTIE'S PROPOSALS BECAUSE SHE KNEW SHE DID NOT LOVE HIM; HE BELIEVED THAT HIS LOVE FOR HER WOULD HELP HIM OVERCOME HIS GAUCHENESS.

It took persuasion to bring Elizabeth round to that way of thinking. She was vivacious, full of the passionate optimism that went with a brimming social life, intent on having fun without too much concern for the future.

In the summer of 1920 she was presented to King George V and Queen Mary at their court at Holyrood House in Edinburgh.

It was the occasion of her 'coming out', the moment when girls of background and breeding made their formal début into Society, which was the polite way of saying that they entered womanhood. The débutantes dressed demurely in white to signify their virginal purity – a vital consideration in the marriage mart they were about to enter. A headdress of tulle and ostrich feathers was compulsory. So was a train, which before the war was required to be exactly three yards long. After the war that was reduced to no more than eighteen inches, 'in the interests of economy'.

SPECIALLY POSED FOR THE *DAILY MAIL*, ELIZABETH AT 17 BRUTON STREET JUST AFTER HER ENGAGEMENT TO BERTIE WAS ANNOUNCED.

'It was over in a flash,' Elizabeth's near-contemporary Loelia Ponsonby recorded. A future Duchess of Westminster and the daughter of Lord Syonsby, assistant private secretary and equerry to Queen Victoria, Edward VII and George V, Loelia wrote: 'One reached the head of the queue, handed one's invitation card to a splendid official. He shouted aloud one's name and tossed the card into a rather common-looking little waste-paper basket, one advanced along the red carpet and made two curtsies to the King and Queen, who were sitting on a low dais surrounded by numerous relations, and then walked on.'

This presentation was the formal prelude to a Season of dances and luncheons, charity balls, weekend house parties, race meetings, picnics and regattas, and Elizabeth entered into the social flurry with alacrity. She came to London and from her base in St James's and then at 17 Bruton Street where her father had taken a house when his lease on St James's Square expired, set about the none too arduous task of enjoying herself to the full. She was popular and her days were a breathless round of gaiety, punctuated by recuperative visits to St Paul's Walden Bury, where she

retreated for occasional Sundays, before whirling off on the next social round.

It was frivolity with a serious purpose – to find a suitable mate. She was not short of suitors. 'Lady Elizabeth was very unlike the cocktail-drinking, chain-smoking girls who came to be regarded as typical of the nineteen-twenties,' Mabel, Countess of Airlie wrote. Rather, so the Lady Airlie insisted, it was the demure virtues of 'radiant vitality and a blending of gaiety, kindness and sincerity' which made her so attractive. That prim opinion was expressed many years later, after Elizabeth's reputation had been carefully airbrushed by royal marriage. She was not, it was true, one of Evelyn Waugh's Bright Young Things, that hedonistic, fatalistic, sensation-seeking generation who came to epitomize the spiritual

PRINCE ALBERT AND ELIZABETH BOWES LYON WITH HER PARENTS, THE EARL AND COUNTESS OF STRATHMORE AT GLAMIS.

ennui of the post-war era – they came a few years later – but in her time she was regarded as being up there with the best of them when it came to enjoying herself.

Elizabeth was also very funny – 'a wag' as one of her former admirers described her – which in those days was rare for a woman in her circle, and she was certainly not averse to cocktails, the drinking of which became an essential and much cherished part of her diet. She never actually called them cocktails ('too American,' she said, and instead referred to them as 'drinkie-poos') but well into her nineties she was still drinking two large measures of gin and Dubonnet before luncheon and a brace of serious dry martinis before dinner.

That is not to imply that Elizabeth was guilty of anything that might possibly have been construed as unseemly or untoward. The young men of her class were allowed their sexual freedom. Most of the gallants who escorted Elizabeth would have had some experience in such matters: in his bachelor days even that pillar of moral rectitude, George V, had kept one girl in Southsea and another in St John's Wood whom he shared with his soon-to-be deceased elder brother, Prince Eddy. ('She's a ripper,' George wrote unabashedly in his diary.)

What was sauce for the gander was most definitely off the menu for the female of this rarefied social species, however. The men were only permitted to take their pleasure with 'actresses' and women of what were called 'the lower orders', never with girls from their own caste who were required to save themselves for the marital bed.

There was a large measure of hypocrisy involved in this, for once a woman had married and produced an heir (and preferably a spare) it was tacitly conceded that she was at liberty to follow her own romantic desires, provided, of course, that discretion was maintained. This inverted morality was exemplified not only by the behaviour of Edward VII and, later by his grandson, the future Duke of Windsor, and their respective mistresses, but also by the cut and colour of the clothes of the Edwardian era. Mothers ventured forth at night in provocative reds and blacks with décolletages which plunged in open invitation. Their unmarried daughters, meanwhile, were dressed in gowns of pale pastel, cut in a manner designed to show the minimum of flesh. The war had wrought a change in women's fashion. Hemlines had risen, ribcrushing stays and bustles had been relegated to the dressing-up box in the attic. But the sartorial symbolism remained the same, its message unmistakable: sensuality, in that era before the Pill and the permissive culture of youth, was still the prerogative of adulthood.

'It was made very clear to me by my aunts, the first time I was let loose in London by myself, that I was not to go anywhere alone with a man,' Lady Rachel Cavendish, the Duke of Devonshire's daughter and Elizabeth's close friend, recalled. And to ensure that they did not stray, a close watch was kept on the Season's crop of débutantes. As Elizabeth's niece, Lady Mary Clayton, confirmed:

'In those days you were heavily chaperoned wherever you went.'

There were nonetheless plenty of opportunities for everyone to get to know each other. That, after all, was the whole object of this formulated fan dance of courtship. And dancing was the obvious way of bringing couples closer together. Arm in arm, cheek to cheek, they waltzed and foxtrotted at teatime, after dinner and sometimes until dawn. In an age when a kiss was a dangerous thrill and half a dozen tantamount to an engagement, such activity provided an energetic substitute for what they really had in mind. Elizabeth was an excellent dancer.

She also had the gift of looking as though she were truly interested in what people, and especially men were saying to her, and that won her more suitors than many of her more beautiful contemporaries. As Elizabeth's next-door neighbour Mrs Alice Winn, niece of Britain's first woman MP Nancy Astor, enviously observed: 'She had the ability to listen and make everyone feel special. The men returning from the horrors of the First World War found her irresistible.'

Quite how irresistible Elizabeth was is a matter of conjecture. Lord Gorell proclaimed: 'I was madly in love with her. Everything at Glamis was beautiful, perfect. Being there was like living in a Van Dyke picture...I fell *madly* in love. They all did.' The diarist Chips Channon swooned: 'She makes every man feel chivalrous and gallant towards her.' Lord David Cecil eulogized about her 'sweetness and sense of fun'. According to George VI's official biographer, Sir John Wheeler-Bennett, 'she took London by storm.' Prince Paul of Serbia called her the prettiest girl in Britain.

Those testimonies were glowing enough. There is, however, a shading of flattery to the silken phrases which is hard to reconcile with the appealing but by no means ravishing young woman peering demurely out across the decades from the photographs taken at the time. But then flattery went with the territory she had moved into when she was married into the Royal Family. Elizabeth was certainly not going to be the one to deny the perfection which a worshipful company of admirers decide with hindsight she possessed. 'I'm not as nice as you think I am,' she once remarked, but she was undoubtedly charming and vivacious enough and in the carefree days of those post-war Seasons that was quite sufficient to ensure that her dance card was always full.

Elizabeth's charm also brought her to the romantic attention of a number of appropriate men. There was talk at one stage that she would marry Viscount Gage, owner of Firle Place, a magnificent Tudor house set in a fold of the Sussex Downs. Gage's flatmate, the Oxford-educated Prince Paul of Serbia, was also said to be in the running for her hand, as was barrister-turned-stock-broker Sir Arthur Penn, fifteen years her senior and a close friend of her brothers. All were invited to stay at Glamis, sometimes together (the Great War during which one in every five officers had died had significantly reduced the numbers of available young men), but in the end these various suitors went their separate ways.

There was one man, however, who did make serious amorous progress with the young lady of Glamis, daughter of the 14th Earl of Strathmore. His name was James Stuart, son of the 17th Earl of Moray.

Elizabeth first met him at a London music-hall during the war where they were introduced by her brother, Michael, a fellow officer in the 'Royal Scots' who, like Stuart, was back on leave. (Michael returned to the Western Front to be captured, Stuart to win the Military Cross and Bar.) In September 1919, Stuart was a house-guest at Glamis where he stayed for ten days. He became a regular visitor and by the following year he and Elizabeth were on the most familiar of terms. At the Forfar County Ball held at the castle on 8 September, she twice allowed him to partner her on the dance floor. Stuart happened to be engaged to the daughter of a wealthy Glaswegian industrialist. That was no barrier to a man destined to be remembered as one of the most notorious philanderers of his generation, and Elizabeth the captivator was quickly captivated.

And why not? Jamie Stuart looked as if he had come striding out of one of Sir Walter Scott's romantic novels. He was a dashing war hero with an insolent sense of humour. He also possessed the bonny looks which made David Niven his fortune, and had that actor's same brand of easy charm which women, despite their better judgement, often find so compelling. His daughter, Davina, described him thus: 'He never had to make the slightest effort;

JAMIE STUART, IN
DRESS UNIFORM,
COLLECTING HIS
MILITARY CROSS AT
BUCKINGHAM PALACE.

26 APRIL 1923. LADY ELIZABETH BOWES LYON, DAUGHTER OF THE 14TH EARL OF STRATHMORE, LEAVES THEIR LONDON HOME, 17 BRUTON STREET, MAYFAIR, FOR HER WEDDING TO THE DUKE OF YORK AT WESTMINSTER ABBEY.

women just fell at his feet. He had a take it or leave it attitude and they couldn't resist it.' Elizabeth's dresser, no doubt echoing her mistress's thoughts, called him a 'heart throb'.

There was talent and determination behind Stuart's insouciant manner. He became an MP at 26, was Winston Churchill's Chief Whip in the Second World War, served as Secretary of State for Scotland and was created Viscount Stuart of Findhorn in 1959. Apart from a disappointing lack of ready funds, the youngest son of one of Scotland's noblest earls was an ideal match for the youngest daughter of another.

40

That was unquestionably Elizabeth's wish. If looks and panache and pedigree were the measure of a suitable husband, then she was not going to do any better than James Stuart. Once he had broken off his engagement to the unfortunate Elfie Finlayson, which he duly did two months after the Forfar Ball, many thought that his betrothal to Elizabeth would shortly follow. There are some who are convinced that Stuart actually took the step of privately asking her to marry him – and that she accepted.

This was one love affair that was not going to have a happy ending, however. Forces beyond their control were already at work, grinding relentlessly forward. And, by sad irony, it was Stuart himself who had unwittingly set the royal wheels in motion.

After he was demobilized, Stuart went to Edinburgh to read law, at which he proved less than successful, and to play golf, at

THE WEDDING DRESS OF SILK CHIFFON MOIRÉ, DESIGNED BY MADAME HANDLEY SEYMOUR, THE FRONT DECORATED WITH BANDS OF SILVER LAMÉ EMBROIDERED WITH SEED PEARLS, IRIDESCENT WHITE BEADS AND SILVER THREAD. THE LOOSE FITTING BODICE HAS A LOW, SQUARE NECKLINE AND SHORT SLEEVES. A SHORT TRAIN IS PLEATED INTO THE BACK WAISTBAND.

which he excelled. He also took up competitive motoring with his brother John, the future 19th Earl, and it was through him that Stuart was introduced to Louis Greig, former Scottish rugby captain and, more pertinently, the naval surgeon who had been delegated to nurse the sickly Prince Albert through the war. After being introduced to Bertie by Greig, Stuart recalled: 'He was young and did not want to stay in the Palace all the time. Thus a

OFFICIAL PHOTOGRAPH TAKEN AT BUCKINGHAM PALACE. THE DUKE OF YORK AND HIS BRIDE SURROUNDED BY THE EIGHT BRIDESMAIDS.

few of us used to organize small parties and dances for the entertainment of the young prince. What I did not know was that this meeting with Louis Greig, and hence with Prince Albert, was to prove the turning point in my life.'

In the spring of 1920 Stuart was offered the post of equerry to the Prince at a modest salary of £450 a year, plus a room at Buckingham Palace and all the food he could eat. His career as a lawyer obviously going nowhere, he accepted the royal appointment

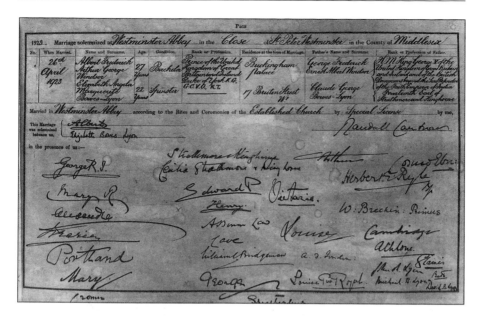

PHOTOGRAPH OF THE MARRIAGE CERTIFICATE IN THE WESTMINSTER ABBEY REGISTER SHOWING THE SIGNATURES.

with its attendant duties, the most important of which was to organize the Prince's social life.

On 20 May that year he accompanied the Prince to a ball at 7 Grosvenor Square given by Lord and Lady Farquhar. Lady Elizabeth Bowes Lyon was there and enjoyed several dances with Stuart under the watchful eyes of Lord and Lady Annaly who were chaperoning her.

Unbeknownst to Elizabeth, the Annalys were not the only ones looking at her that night. So was Prince Albert. He could not take his eyes off her and cornered Stuart with the words: 'That's a lovely girl you've been dancing with. Who is she?' The Duke of York, as he became in June, later confided to Mabell Airlie that he had 'fallen in love that evening', and acknowledged 20 May 1920 as a momentous day in his life.

Bertie was far too shy to make any advances at that early stage. He was stricken enough, though, to ensure that his equerry took him along when he next went to visit the Strathmores at St Paul's Walden Bury. And when the Court moved to Balmoral, Bertie accompanied Stuart on a visit to Elizabeth at Glamis.

Elizabeth, honoured though she was to have the Prince as a visitor cannot have been over-impressed by him. Stuart was suave and handsome; Bertie was neither. He stuttered and suffered from an irritating facial tic, was prone to temper tantrums and drank so much whisky that his father's courtiers feared he was turning into a drunkard. Even Stuart was forced to admit, in violation of the code of uncritical discretion expected of an equerry, that the Prince was 'not an easy man to know or handle'.

He suffered in the comparison to his older brother. The Prince of Wales was the most famous man in the world, with an aura of glamour that rivalled anything the fledgling Hollywood film industry had so far produced. (*The Sheik,* starring Rudolph Valentino, had been released two years earlier.) David, as the Prince's family always called him, was regarded by upper-class society as the most eligible man currently available. Bertie was quite the reverse, and there is a lingering suspicion that it was the Prince of Wales that Elizabeth was really interested in.

'To put it politely, she wanted to marry me,' the Duke of Windsor, as he became, claimed shortly before his death. It is the bitter remark of an old and disappointed man, and the suggestion is hotly denied by Elizabeth's friends who argue that she had quickly seen through his glamorous veneer to the selfishness and moral weakness that lay behind.

But, whatever David's failings, they hardly worked to Bertie's advantage, not at this stage. He was, it was true, a first-rate tennis player – with Louis Greig as his partner he had won the RAF Doubles championship at Wimbledon – and a nimble dancer, but to an impressionable twenty year old in the throes of her first love affair, that counted for little when compared to the jaunty Jamie. Sex was not something that Elizabeth had any practical experience of (or theoretical either: the subject was never mentioned in polite society), but intuition would have told her that Stuart had a lot more to offer in that department than the Duke of York.

Fighting off the advances of a prince of the blood was no easy matter, however, especially when he had the backing of such a formidable ally as his inquisitive and domineering mother. It had not taken Queen Mary long to learn of her son's infatuation. Up until then she had been appraising Lady Rachel Cavendish on Bertie's behalf. She now turned her attention to Lady Elizabeth.

By the rules then in force, any union between the Prince and a woman who for all her noble pedigree was still by definition a commoner, would be a new and innovative departure. In medieval times royalty could marry whom they wished. With the advent of the Hanoverians that freedom of choice was removed,

THE DUCHESS OF YORK WEARING HER GOING-AWAY OUTFIT AT A GARDEN PARTY HELD AT GLAMIS CASTLE, 1924. SEEN HERE THE MATCHING COAT IN HEAVIER SILK CRÊPE, WITH APPLIQUÉD CIRCLES OF RUCHED FABRIC, ENLIVENING A VERY SIMPLE CUT.

for amongst the many arcane Teutonic dictates introduced by George I was the one which forbade a royal prince to marry anyone other than a woman of royal rank. If a prince defied that rule and married one of his own subjects, the marriage was deemed not to exist officially – the excuse used by the Prince Regent to get out of his union with Mrs Fitzherbert.

The tide of anti-German feeling which swept the country after the Great War resulted in a change in regulations. The Royal Family had already been forced to change their name from Saxe-Coburg-Gotha to Windsor. Then, in 1920, the Prime Minister David Lloyd George, playing to the mood of the electorate, 'advised' George V that the Government would not tolerate any more marital alliances with foreigners. That meant that for the foreseeable future the Royal Family was prohibited from raiding the royal blood banks of Germany in search of brides for their sons. Henceforth they would have to draw their spouses from the British aristocracy (but only from the first three ranks of dukes, marquesses and earls – it would be another three generations down the genealogical line before a Duke of York would be allowed to make a 'Miss' Sarah Ferguson his Duchess).

The King disliked Lloyd George's slippery and sometimes blatantly dishonest way of doing business, and was forever launching into vitriolic tirades against a Prime Minister he suspected of the cardinal sin of socialism. Regarding himself as the Fountain of all Honours, he also took furious umbrage at Lloyd George's cynical sale of noble titles, flogged off to the socially aspirant to help fill the Liberal Party's coffers. In this instance, however, the King went along with Lloyd George's directive banning foreign marriages.

'I don't think Bertie will be sorry to hear that,' Queen Mary observed shrewdly. As she confided to her Lady of the Bedchamber, Mabell Airlie: 'I have discovered that he is very much attracted to Lady Elizabeth Bowes Lyon. He's always talking about her.'

What the law allowed and what Elizabeth wanted were two very different things, however, and when, in the spring of 1921, the Duke made his proposal she turned him down flat. He had not even had the courage to declare his own love and his offer of marriage appears to have been made by an intermediary. Who that person was remains shrouded in mystery. Was it the Prince of Wales whom Elizabeth would come to detest so heartily? Or might it perhaps have been Bertie's own equerry, the soon-to-be exiled Jamie Stuart? If it was, it must have been a painful and humiliating moment for them both.

Lady Strathmore was not best pleased, either. Those early reservations she had harboured about life at Court had evaporated when she had scented the opportunity of securing a position at the centre of British life for her youngest daughter. A modern view, holding romantic love as an important factor when deciding on marriage, would regard the Countess's change as calculated commercialism tempered with unconscionable snobbery. To women of Lady Strathmore's background, however, such dynastic manoeuvrings would seem perfectly normal. Like Queen Mary and Lady Airlie, the other two compelling forces manipulating her daughter's future, she too had been eased into a marriage with scant regard for her own feelings.

The aristocratic marriage market was tough and competitive. It was possible to buy one's way in, as witnessed by the success of Elizabeth's three times great grandfather, the Durham colliery owner, but beauty

THE DUKE AND DUCHESS OF YORK ON THEIR HONEYMOON AT POLESDEN LACEY AND ENJOYING A ROUND OF GOLF.

could also play a part. Showgirl Rosie Boote, whose negotiable morality was the subject of much scandalous gossip, demonstrated this by marrying the Marquis of Headfort in 1901 and provided Mrs Kate Meyrick with her cue. Mrs Meyrick owned the notorious 43 Club in Soho whose members included not only the Crown of Sweden but also 'Brilliant' Chang, London's most successful drug-smuggler. She was sent to prison in 1924 and again in 1928, yet despite such apparent handicaps she succeeded in marrying her three daughters to peers – Dorothy to the 26th Lord de Clifford in 1926; Mary to the racing driver Lord Kinnoull in 1928; and her youngest, Irene, to the Earl of Craven in 1939. These marriages were very much the exception, though. Most young men of position preferred to breed within their own caste, with pedigree rather than beauty the real alternative to fortune.

The upper classes of the period took great care in the breeding of their dogs and their racehorses and devoted equal attention to the bloodlines of their prospective spouses. The genealogical riddles of collaterals and distant cousins so many times removed, which were all but incomprehensible to an outsider, provided a constant subject of interest to those whose names appeared in *Burke's Peerage*, first published in 1826. The law of diminishing returns applied just as rigorously in this market-place as it did in any other, however, and the further away from a title and its attendant wealth and prestige she stood, the harder it was for a young woman to secure herself a husband of consequence.

As the great-granddaughter of the 3rd Duke of Portland and a first cousin of the 6th Duke, Lady Strathmore's stock was sound enough. There was no money there, however. Her father, as the son of a younger son, had been forced to enter the Church and was considered fortunate indeed to have secured such a propitious match for his eldest of his three dowerless daughters. It was his only success. One of Cecilia's twin sisters died unmarried at the age of 68; the other had to wait until she was thirty-seven before eventually finding a husband in distant Philadelphia.

Queen Mary was all too aware of such difficulties. Her grandfather, Alexander, Duke of Württemberg's morganatic marriage to a non-royal Hungarian countess had lost his son (Mary's father, Francis of Teck) the throne of Württemburg. This flawed pedigree would have made her ineligible to marry the future George V, had it not been for the personal intercession of Queen Victoria, who had taken a liking to her impoverished first cousin once removed and was grand enough to make her own dynastic rules.

On the whole the system worked well. Like families intermarried, thereby creating a vast network of interrelated dynasties intended to secure long-term prosperity, property and position. What was not guaranteed was happiness. Queen Mary, a woman blessed with an enquiring mind and natural good taste, was forced into an intellectually barren straitjacket by her uncultured husband. Mabell Airlie, whose marriage had been 'settled', as she put it, between her father, the Earl of Arran, and her husband's intimidating mother, was so 'very unhappy' at first that she considered leaving her husband and was only prevented from doing so by the 'terrible disgrace' which would have resulted.

Lady Strathmore appears, more fortunately, to have enjoyed her

THE DUKE AND
DUCHESS OF YORK
TAKE TIME OUT TO
RELAX, SHORTLY AFTER
THEIR MARRIAGE IN
1923.

marriage to the Earl right from its beginning. He was, it had to be admitted, a trifle eccentric. He ate plum pudding for lunch every day of his life and was wont to throw bread rolls at his wife at dinner. But she bore him a total of ten children and he was seen to embrace her in public, a remarkable show of affection for the period. For all that, she remained what she had been brought up to be: a lady of the old school who was far less concerned with something as ethereal as her daughter's romantic satisfaction than with her material well-being. She saw it as her maternal duty to secure the best match possible for Elizabeth and by her careful reckoning the Duke of York, for all his faults, was a much better prospect than the impecunious Jamie Stuart. She was most put out, therefore, when Elizabeth refused him.

Lady Airlie recorded: 'Lady Strathmore too was sorry: she was the soul of kindness and the Duke looked so disconsolate. "I do hope he will find a nice wife who will make him happy", she wrote to me. "I like him so much and he is a man who will be made or marred by his wife."' And the woman who should be doing the making, Lady Strathmore firmly believed, was her daughter, Lady Elizabeth.

Queen Mary shared this belief and she was not one to be thwarted in such matters, as Elizabeth should very well have known. On one of her regal perambulations around the great houses of Scotland, the Queen had stayed at Glamis with her only daughter, Princess Mary. In the house party was the 7th Duke of Buccleuch's son and heir, the Earl of Dalkeith, with whom the Princess was conducting a clandestine albeit chaste romance. Taking if not their lives then certainly their good names in their hands, the pair arranged to meet secretly after afternoon tea in Lady Strathmore's private sitting-room which had been given over to the Princess. The Queen, alert as ever, got wind of what was going on. Imperiously sweeping past the the servants who had been posted as look-outs before they had the chance to raise the alarm, she burst in on the couple.

'The Queen was beside herself with fury and the shouting could be heard all over the castle,' one old retainer has recalled.

It was not Lord Dalkeith's ineligibility which had so infuriated the Queen – as the son of one of Scotland's grandest dukes and a direct descendant of King Charles II, he fitted very neatly into Lloyd George's new guidelines – but the fact that she had already determined that her daughter was to marry Viscount Lascelles, the son of the immeasurably richer Earl of Harewood. And what Queen Mary wanted, she almost invariably got.

Princess Mary was in her twenties and presumably old enough to know her own mind, but that mattered not a jot. She was told where her familial duty lay and that was the end of the matter. As for Lord Dalkeith, he was immediately ordered out of Glamis, without being allowed the time to gather his belongings, which, in final humiliation, were sent on afterwards.

So forewarned, Elizabeth must have faced the Queen with considerable trepidation when she next descended on Glamis, on 9 September 1921. This was no spur-of-the-moment courtesy call. She was there for one purpose and one purpose only – to inspect at firsthand the young woman who had had the effrontery to reject her son.

Lady Strathmore, whose maladies were now chronic, was indisposed when the Queen swept in from Cortachy Castle where she was staying with Mabell Airlie, accompanied by a regal entourage of a gentleman-in-waiting, his servants, two dressers, a detective, a footman, a chauffeur and an under-chauffeur. Lady Strathmore's illness is a measure of just how keen the Queen was on bringing this project to a successful conclusion. Like the King her husband, she had a morbid fear of ill-health (her old maternity nurse would recount how the Queen as a young mother had refused to visit her own children in their nursery when they were sick). For the sake of her son, however, she was prepared to break the habit of a royal lifetime and put herself at risk of infection by entering Glamis. She was pleased with what she found.

Chips Channon observed that talking to Queen Mary 'was like talking to St Paul's Cathedral'. Elizabeth, however, acquitted herself well, serving the tea and impressing the Queen who placed great store by such things, with her knowledge of the Lyons' family history. By the time she swept out again she had formed the firm opinion that Elizabeth would do very nicely.

Lady Airlie recalled: 'In the setting of the grim old castle, where the traces of past bloodshed and terror can never be completely banished by any cosiness of the present, Lady Elizabeth filled her mother's place as hostess so charmingly that the Queen was more than ever convinced that this was "the one girl who could make Bertie happy", as she told me afterwards.'

But how was Elizabeth to be brought into line? With breathtaking disingenuousness, the Queen declared that she would not say anything to either of them because 'Mothers should never meddle in their children's love affairs.'

That restriction did not apply to Lady Airlie who, with the Queen's connivance, promptly assumed the role of matchmaker. When Elizabeth was in London, she would invite her to tea where she 'continued to plead his cause from time to time'.

Barely a fortnight after his mother had descended on to Glamis, Bertie was back there for some partridge-shooting and stayed for a week. On 29th September he went on his first-ever rough shoot with his future brothers-in-law, Michael and David. Between them they bagged nine partridges, a hare, four rabbits, a snipe, two ducks and four pigeons. The Duke thoroughly enjoyed himself and this form of shooting, in which the gun walks up his quarry rather than waiting for it to be driven over his head, henceforth became a regular part of his sporting calendar.

His affection for the Bowes Lyons (or Lyons as he steadfastly called them), and not just for the youngest daughter of the house, was growing. He felt comfortable and at ease with them in a way he never did with his own family. When Lady Strathmore underwent an operation shortly afterwards, he kept in sympathetic touch and when Elizabeth returned to Glamis to help nurse her mother through her convalescence, he sent her copies of the latest dance tunes. It was considerate. It was also inexorable, as slowly but surely Elizabeth found herself drawn into the royal net.

In a singular mark of royal favour, Elizabeth was invited in February 1922, to be a bridesmaid at the wedding ordained by the Queen, of Viscount Lascelles to her daughter, Princess Mary whom Elizabeth knew but vaguely. It was not a happy occasion. The dour groom was fifteen years older than his bride aged twenty-four, and the Princess spent the night before her wedding in tears. The King, jealously possessive of his only daughter, had 'quite broken down' when he collected her to escort her to Westminster Abbey. Only the intractable Queen managed to maintain her composure, and only because she 'so much feared' that Mary would start weeping at the altar. The sombre mood afflicted Elizabeth, who looked so glum that she was painted out of the official portrait.

It was not just the funereal atmosphere that made its gloomy impression on Lady Elizabeth that day, for by then it was quite clear that she was being forced in a similar matrimonial direction to the Princess. The Queen's mind was made up. Lady Airlie was bringing pressure to bear. Bertie was snuffling around like the sad, neglected bloodhound he so resembled. And, just in case she missed the point, James Stuart, the man she really loved, had been summarily removed from contention.

The Queen had let her feelings be known, Lady Strathmore had consulted with Jamie's mother, and together the three women came to the decision, as his son the second Lord Stuart put it, 'that it would be best if my father went away for a while.' A few days into the New Year of 1922, James Stuart had been dispatched to Oklahoma to work the oilfields as a rigger.

HER MAJESTY THE
QUEEN WITH H.R.H.
THE DUCHESS OF YORK
AT BALMORAL CASTLE
IN 1923.

For a young Scottish aristocrat with Stuart's interests, it was the social equivalent of exile in Siberia. For Elizabeth, life carried on very much as before. There were no scenes, no tantrums, at least none that anyone can recall. If she wept, it was in private. The only time her composure slipped was when the *Daily News* predicted that she was about to announce her engagement to the Prince of Wales.

That happened on Friday 5th January 1923, almost exactly a year after Stuart had been shipped out to America. Elizabeth was spending the weekend in Sussex at a house party hosted by Lord Gage, and it was with some consternation that she read the headline proclaiming 'Scottish bride for Prince of Wales. Heir to Throne to Wed Peer's Daughter. An official announcement imminent.'

Elizabeth certainly knew the Prince but their relationship had never been a close one. He was frivolous and irresponsible: very different from the conventional British ideal man of the time. That may have heightened his appeal, especially to the inexperienced, but, given the strong streak of conformity that ran deep in Elizabeth's character, it would seem unlikely in this instance; like tends to attract like.

Besides, Elizabeth was already spoken for. Queen Mary had her marked out for Prince Albert and that would have been quite enough to deter the Prince of Wales, assuming, that is, that he needed any deterrent, which is doubtful in the extreme.

To have her name so publicly linked with his nonetheless made for a most embarrassing weekend for Elizabeth. Her fellow house guests at Firle tried to make a joke of the newspaper story, bowing and bobbing and addressing her as 'Ma'am', but for once Elizabeth's gaiety deserted her. The ubiquitous Chips Channon, who was there, noted in his diary how 'unhappy and distraite' she looked. It was an indication, and an unwelcome one at that, of just how quickly she was being reeled in to the Royal Family.

Getting Bertie to play a leading part in the melodrama which was being orchestrated for his benefit was not proving easy, however. After this first proposal had been rejected, he had retreated even further into his shell of self-doubt. Eventually the royal advisers felt compelled to try and put some backbone into their royal charge. In July 1922 the Duke had gone to Dunkirk to lay the foundation-stone for a war memorial. At the instigation of Louis Greig, he was accompanied by Sir John Davidson, the MP for Hemel Hempstead. Six years older than the Duke, who was twenty-six, and much more worldly, the future Viscount Davidson spent three hours alone with Bertie in his cabin on the voyage back to Harwich. The Duke, casting discretion to the North Sea wind, unburdened himself. He had, Davidson recalled, 'reached a crisis in his life... He declared that he was desperately in love, but that he was in despair for it seemed quite certain that he had lost the only woman he would ever marry.'

Bertie went on to explain, so Davidson recorded, how it was that 'the King's son cannot propose to the girl he loves, since custom requires that he must not place himself in the position of being refused, and to that ancient custom the King, his father, firmly adhered. Worse still, I gather that an emissary had already been sent to ascertain whether the girl was prepared to marry him, and that it had failed.' As it was bound to, if Stuart had indeed been the emissary.

To avoid any repeat embarrassment, Davidson advised the Duke 'that in the Year of Grace 1922 no high-spirited girl of character was likely to accept a proposal made at second-hand; if she was as fond of him as he thought she was, he must propose to her himself.'

QUEEN MARY WITH THE DUKE AND DUCHESS OF YORK AT BALMORAL CASTLE, SEPTEMBER 1924.

Elizabeth *was* fond of him. It was marrying him which was the problem. A few days after the Firle house party she again went to see Lady Airlie and asked for her advice.

'I meant to make a final effort,' Lady Airlie said, to persuade the unhappy young woman where her best interests lay. Instead she spent the time talking about her own marriage – about the problems she had faced, the adjustments and compromises she had had to make, how it had taken her time to settle down but how, in the end, it had all proved worthwhile.

'After she had gone,' Lady Airlie recalled, 'I feared I might have bored her by bringing up a chapter of my past which had closed before she had been born, and wished I had talked more of the Duke.'

As it transpired, talking about herself did the trick. It would have required more resolve than Elizabeth possessed to reject the Duke again. The pressures brought to bear on her by her mother, her mother's friends and by the Queen herself, had proved irresistible. Faced therefore with what amounted to the inevitable, she needed reassurance – about her future and what it might hold in store. Without consciously meaning to, Lady Airlie had succeeded in pointing the way forward.

At the end of that decisive week the Duke of York went to St Paul's Walden Bury to press his suit. After first asking the Earl of Strathmore's permission, he took Elizabeth for a walk in the fairy-haunted wood which had featured so prominently in her childhood and, in person this time, asked her to be his wife. Elizabeth is said to have replied: 'If you are going to keep it up for ever I might as well say "Yes" now.' And just in case that sounded a little off hand, the press added that she had laughed merrily as she said it.

This chapter of aristocratic courtships was now drawing to its close as one by one Elizabeth's friends selected their partners (or had them selected for them) and retired from the market-place, having secured another generation of alliances.

In 1921 Lord Dalkeith had married Verda Lascelles, third cousin, as Elizabeth worked out by poring over her *Burke's*, of the Viscount Lascelles who had married her friend Princess Mary.

In 1923 Prince Paul married Princess Olga of Greece whose sister Marina married Bertie's brother, the Duke of Kent. Appointed Prince Regent of Serbia, he led his country in 1941 into an alliance with Nazi Germany, was ousted in a British-backed coup and spent the rest of the conflict in disgraced exile in Kenya.

Lord Gage waited until 1931 before marrying Lord Desborough's daughter, Imogen. He is best remembered for his droll remark during the debate in the House of Lords about D.H.Lawrence's *Lady Chatterley's Lover*. Asked whether he would allow Imogen to see the book, he quipped: 'I would certainly show it to my wife – not to my gamekeeper.'

More poignantly, James Stuart married Lady Rachel Cavendish on 4 August 1923 – Elizabeth's twenty-third birthday.

By then Elizabeth was herself married. On the morning of 26 April 1923 she left her father's home at 17 Bruton Street, Mayfair to become the first commoner in 300 years to marry into the Royal Family. She wore a dress of ivory chiffon moiré embroidered with silver thread and pearls, sleeves of lace specially woven in Nottingham and a train of Flanders lace lent to her by Queen Mary. More than a million people crowded into London to see her being driven by state coach from Westminster Abbey to Buckingham Palace. They saw a young woman who looked diffident and slightly bemused. The smile that would become her trademark was there, but only just, playing on the side of her mouth, never quite bursting forth.

It would not be long coming, though. The circumstances leading up to her wedding had been trying, but the vivacity which was an essential part of her style was undimmed. She very quickly learnt to use it to the best advantage, both for the institution she had married into, and for herself.

CHAPTER 4

BRIDE OF EMPIRE

All her life the Queen Mother has been a traveller. No other member of the Royal Family covered so many hundreds of thousands of miles or visited so many countries with quite so much enthusiasm.

Her journeying started in childhood when, as a member of a grand aristocratic family, she was forever on the move from one home to another, accompanied by suitcases and trunks, animals, maids and footmen. It continued when she became Duchess of York, accompanying her husband on tours around what was the British Empire. It carried on after she became Queen. It was confirmed as the pattern of her life after she became Queen Mother.

She travelled for reasons of politics, state, Empire, Commonwealth, pleasure, sport and habit. She travelled to cement old alliances and win new allies. And she always travelled in the most sumptuous style.

It was a prodigious performance which only came to an end when age and infirmity made any more trips a physical impossibility. At times there was more than a hint of obsession about the way she took herself off around the world and not all her tours were quite the resounding success she would have liked. Controversy tinged a number of her visits while others, in retrospect, seemed utterly pointless. The unkind might even go so far as to say that, by the end, she was just another blue-rinse matron filling in her old age by taking the royal equivalent of a world cruise.

Yet if at times it looked like travel for travel's sake, there is no doubt that, by her willingness and energy, the Queen Mother did as much as anyone and more than most to promote a spirit of unity in the Commonwealth that had once been an Empire. With a smile and wave she wove an emotional web. And if it were an intangible web, so was the institution she served. She herself would come to regard such international bonding as one of her life's achievements, although there was no hint of what was to come when, in 1924, twenty months after her wedding, she set off on her first overseas visit.

The Duke and his popular Duchess joined the P&O liner *Mulbera* on 1 December 1924, in Marseilles bound for Kenya.

Earlier that year the Yorks had visited Northern Ireland. Bertie, in thrall to his wife's easy charm, had noted when writing to his father, 'Elizabeth has been marvellous as usual & all the people simply love her already. I am so lucky to have her help as she knows exactly what to do and say to all the people we meet.'

That had been a business trip. This time the couple, for all the talk of official duty, were going on a glorified holiday, as the Duke acknowledged in a letter to his father: 'I don't think I really thanked you properly for allowing Elizabeth & me to go.'

They were accompanied by two aides, one lady-in-waiting and filthy weather, which did not clear until they reached Port Said at the head of the Suez Canal.

After that it was plain sailing. To the coaling station of Aden where they went ashore to see the sights of the Arab bazaar; across the Equator where the Duke was subjected to the traditional ritual of being doused in a bath of sea water and shaved with a wooden razor by a ship's officer dressed as King Neptune; on to Mombasa, entrepôt for British East Africa, where they arrived on 22 December.

The royal couple had come well-prepared for their journey into the heart of what they and most Europeans still called the

Dark Continent. Their cabin trunks were laden with all the paraphernalia regarded as vital for any African outing – quinine and salt tablets and safari suits and those sartorial essentials of Empire, the solar topees and red flannel spine-pads designed to protect the wearer from the sun.

And then there were the guns. The couple were going on safari and in 1925 that meant big-game hunting. The success of a safari was judged not by what was seen but by the number of animals killed, and the Duke was very much looking forward to shooting the wild life that existed then so abundantly on the great plains of Africa. Elizabeth, similarly enthusiastic at the prospect of hunting, had kitted herself out with a fine .275 hunting rifle from Rigby, gunsmith to the aristocracy and makers of the world's finest and most effective elephant guns.

There were other distractions. Over the next four months the royal couple would make their way from the coast of Kenya up 7,600 feet to Uganda, then down the Nile and on into the Sudan. In Mombasa they were entertained by 5,000 'uncouthly bedizened natives (who) danced wildly for their delectation' as one contemporary description had it. In Kampala they had been treated to a dance performed for them by the warriors of the Kabaka of Buganda. In the Nuba mountains to the east of the Nile town of Tonga they watched a march past of 12,000 Nubian warriors.

The dances performed by near-naked natives were not to the Duke's taste. They were too hot-blooded, too primitive, too suggestive. They were, he noted with euphemistic understatement in his diary, 'very weird'. It was the hunting which provided the focal point of the tour. This was something he understood, something which posed no threat to his sense of moral propriety and he recorded his successes in enthusiastic detail.

He wrote: 'We found one Oryx alone shortly afterwards & we got up to him within 200 yds by keeping a tree between us & him. I took a rest off the tree & fired & hit him. He was facing me. He went off & we followed & hit him 3 more times when he lay down. I was going to finish him off when we saw a Rhino on the edge of a thick patch of bush. We forgot about the Oryx & went after the Rhino. We followed him into the bush & suddenly came upon not one but two Rhinos lying down in the thickest part of the bush 8 yds away. One came towards us & Anderson fired & killed it. I did not fire as I could not see him properly. It was exciting. The other ran away. After this we went back & finished off the Oryx. It was very hot by now at 11.30 & we were glad of the mules to ride home on. Elizabeth came out with us in the afternoon after tea to look at the Rhino.'

Everything was done to ensure a respectable bag for the Duke, just as it had been for his father when he had visited India and set a record by shooting five tigers in one day. Ever the 'sportsman', however, George V had insisted on the release of a goat that was about to be fed to a pride of the subcontinent's almost extinct Indian lions which were being held in captivity. The goat was given a silver collar; the lions presumably went hungry.

By safari's end the Duke's trophies included two elephant, one with tusks that weighed ninety pounds. He also managed to shoot a rhino of his own which he brought down at a range of thirty yards as it charged towards him.

The Duchess was no mere spectator to the slaughter. She was petite and armed with a winning smile. But she was also deadly with a gun, practised hard and took pride in her ability. Guided by a Portuguese white hunter nicknamed the Hoot, she bagged a waterbuck, an oryx, an antelope, a Grant's gazelle, a steinbuck, a hartebeest, a wart-hog, a jackal, a buffalo and a rhinoceros.

It was an impressive tally – and one that attracted criticism even at the time. There were complaints in the press that the Duke was shooting on Sunday (to which he waggishly replied that he doubted very much if the rhinos knew which day Sunday was). Concern was also voiced in Britain for the safety of the Duchess. Some questioned the seemliness of a woman indulging in what many considered a man's sport.

Some brave souls even questioned whether it was right at all to shoot animals for pleasure, but they commanded little attention. Hunting and shooting were generally still regarded as perfectly respectable pastimes. It would be another thirty-five years before preservation replaced the excitement of the hunt as the prime environmental consideration.

The Yorks paid little heed to these doubting whispers. There was no reason for them to do so (although the Duchess, taking the hint, refrained from shooting the rhino she was licensed to kill). The Duke was a nervous man who wondered sorrowfully if he was up to his duties. His Duchess, a woman of more forceful a character than her fragile appearance might have suggested, shared his concerns. But neither questioned their world or their place in it. It was the Indian summer of Empire and the Royal Family stood at its pinnacle, bathed in the warmth of adoration, secure in their majesty. Wherever they travelled they remained within British-controlled-territory, and they were treated with all the deference due to the second son and daughter-in-law of the King-Emperor.

But they were still young enough to enjoy a natural empire as great (if as equally vulnerable) as their own, and they revelled in the wild majesty of the African bush.

On the train ride up from Mombasa to the frontier railhead at Nairobi, the couple occupied a seat on the front of the engine the better to enjoy the animals – giraffes, zebras, wildebeest, ostriches, baboons, hyenas and antelope of all sorts – flashing past them. The line had been completed twenty-five years earlier at the cost of £5 million of British taxpayers' money, and more than a hundred lives of the indentured Indian labourers who had been devoured by the man-eating lions of Tsavo.

On the safari itself they struggled through swollen rivers, got mud-bound, pitched their tents facing Mount Kenya eighty miles in the distance, and heard the roar of lion prowling through their camp at night. In the rain forest on the way to Meru one of the cars in their convoy got waterlogged and seven of the party had to squeeze into one small Buick (the American cars, with their bigger engines, were considered most suitable for the African bush). On more than one occasion the Duchess found herself knee-deep in mud and one night her tent blew down twice.

Camp life was free and easy. They were called at 5.15 a.m. and after breakfasting on tea and biscuits were out on the hunt by ten to six. Lunch was eaten shortly before twelve. Then, like their quarry, Elizabeth would rest up out of the noon heat before setting off again at 3.30 for the afternoon hunt. They returned to camp at 6.30, and after bathing in the portable canvas tub, ate what they had shot before retiring at 9.30, to be lullabied to sleep – and on more than one occasion kept wide awake – by the sounds of the African night.

For Bertie it was an exhilarating taste of independence, free of the strictures imposed by court protocol and a severe and demanding father. For Elizabeth, who until then had never been further afield than France and Italy, it was the first sample of the elixir of travel which would become a lifetime's addiction.

Africa's lack of inhibitions had another result. The royal couple returned from Africa on 19 April 1925. They had been married for two years yet Elizabeth was still without child. In an age when royal brides were expected to reproduce as soon as decently possible, this had given rise to inevitable Court rumour – that

something was wrong with Elizabeth, or worse, that there was something very wrong with the highly-strung Duke.

For all their apparent gentility, the British upper classes can be cutting to the point of cruelty in their observations and, when a child failed to materialize, the blame was put on the Duke who was said to be impotent. The birth of their daughter Elizabeth one year and two days after their return from Africa did nothing to quash that calumny, and within a few years people were saying that both Elizabeth and her sister Margaret Rose, born four years later, were the product of artificial insemination.

Barney Wyld of the Human Fertilisation and Embryology Authority, discounted the story, pointing out that 'artificial insemination was not available in Britain until the late 1930s.'

THE DUKE AND DUCHESS OF YORK ON SAFARI IN KENYA IN 1925.

Sir John Peel, the present Queen's Surgeon-Gynaecologist from 1961 until 1973, was equally dismissive. He said: 'It is a bit of a fantastic story which is incapable of being proved so anyone can say anything. In those days just getting a specimen and injecting it would have been very unlikely to have worked.' The techniques and technology were simply not good enough. As Wyld explained: 'Even when artificial insemination was generally introduced in 1945 it was highly controversial.'

It is fortunate, therefore, that Nature appears to have done what medical science was not yet capable of. Sex, in the modern sense of unbridled lust, was not something that was ever allowed to feature prominently in the married life of the Yorks – they had too many inhibitions for that to have been possible – but the languid atmosphere of the tropics does seem to have put their relationship on a more intimate basis. As Princess Alice, Countess of Athlone, wrote to her sister-in-law, Queen Mary upon the birth of Princess Elizabeth: 'Kenya is famous for having that effect on people, I hear!'

But if on one level the Empire was a playground of romance and opportunity for those with the social and financial credentials to enjoy it, it was also a business that had to be tended and administered. George V took his friend the poet Rudyard Kipling's notion of the White Man's Burden very seriously. Like Kipling he believed in the Empire as a force for good, with a heart-felt commitment to the eradication of such human woes as slavery, disease and barbarism. And in his own family he saw the emotional glue that held together this diverse, far-flung, loosely structured edifice which covered a quarter of the earth's land mass. As a young man he had visited its outer reaches. He had dispatched his son and heir, the charismatic Prince of Wales, on a series of world tours. Now his second son was called upon to shoulder his share of the Imperial load.

This was a task to which Bertie was singularly ill-suited. The Duke was a man of unsound health who had had his naval service cut short by a series of stomach complaints which may well have been psychosomatic in origin. He was also afflicted by a severe stammer. He found it especially hard to say his Ks and Gs, Qs and Ns which, most revealingly, made it all but impossible for him to pronounce the words King and Queen.

The Duke, who referred to his mother and father as Their Majesties, called it 'the curse that God has put upon me'. God's anointed subject, George V, was the more likely culprit. Sir Louis Greig, the former Comptroller of the Duke's Household, and the surgeon who had nursed Bertie through the war, believed the impediment had been induced by the King's angry impatience with his son's left-handedness, a diagnosis shared by Eileen Macleod, founder member of the Society of Speech Therapists, to whom the Duke turned for help. But whatever its cause, the stammer rendered him a poor candidate for the round of official duties his father forced upon him. Time and again, when called upon to deliver a speech, he would freeze into excruciating silence in mid-sentence, to the intense discomfort of everyone, including himself.

Had it not been for the pert and confidence-boosting support of his young wife, it is debatable whether Bertie would have been allowed to undertake any official duties of a significant nature. Even with Elizabeth beside him, there were still doubts, and they were certainly harboured by Stanley Bruce, Prime Minister of Australia.

To leaven the long-standing and often bitter rivalry between the states of Victoria and New South Wales, it had been decided to create a purpose-built federal capital, just as the Americans had done at Washington. The great project at Canberra was now complete and Bruce requested that one of the King's sons should come to Australia to open the new Parliament House.

He was banking on getting the ever-popular Prince of Wales. When he learned that the British government had decided to send the dowdy Duke of York Bruce was most displeased, and expressed his disappointment vociferously. The King, too, was concerned, while the Duke himself was consumed with self-doubt.

This was one kind of crisis, however, that Elizabeth, was trained to handle. She had learnt how to deal with injured and shell-shocked men during the Great War, while nursing at Glamis, and she took her stricken husband under her wing. She coaxed and coached him, held his hand when fear took its icy grip, ignored his rages of childish frustration and treated him with the love and patience he might more usually have expected of a mother.

On the recommendation of Eileen Macleod the Duke put himself under the care of Lionel Logue, an Australian ex-engineer turned faith-healer with a successful practice in London's Harley Street. Logue prescribed a ten-week remedial course involving breathing exercises and an hour of voice projection every day. The improvement was noticeable, and when in January 1927 the royal couple boarded the blue-and-white painted battlecruiser HMS *Renown* there was at least the hope that Bertie would be able to perform his duty without reducing the Antipodeans to cringing embarrassment.

The tour was a grand Imperial progress. This was an age when the royal yacht was still a wind-propelled plaything designed for nothing more than pleasure cruises in home waters. When on tour, the Royal Family went by battleship, not gin palace. But the Duke and his Duchess did not lack for comfort aboard the mighty warship. A promenade deck had been established above their quarters and Elizabeth had her own sitting-room, decorated in blue and white chintz that matched the ship's paintwork. She served afternoon tea, played deck quoits and enjoyed dancing in the evening.

Again the couple were subjected to the indignity of the Line Ceremony and this time Elizabeth had her forehead anointed by Neptune and was presented with the Order of the Golden Mermaid although, as a lady of the first rank, she was spared the ceremonial dunking. That night they were entertained at dinner with cabaret in the wardroom on the quarterdeck which had been converted into a restaurant. The Duke and Duchess arrived in a 'taxi' made out of two wheelchairs.

They were fêted at every landfall. They went ashore on the Canary Islands and toured Jamaica by car. In Balboa on the Panama Canal Elizabeth stayed out until past midnight at the smoked-filled Union nightclub, listening to jazz. She went shopping in Panama City and was mobbed.

It was jollity which exacted a terrible personal cost. Her baby was eight months old when the Duke and Duchess sailed out of the English winter on 7 January 1927. Elizabeth would not see her daughter for another six months. She missed the child's first steps and her first words which were 'Let's pretend'. Her daughter did not recognize her when she returned in June.

The Duchess had cried when she kissed Princess Elizabeth a last goodbye at her parents' home in Bruton Street, Mayfair. She was, she said, 'quite broken up' and had insisted that the car taking her to Victoria Station drive several times around Grosvenor Gardens so that she could compose her face.

There had been a finality about the parting almost unimaginable today. It was a time before satellite communications, a time before proper telephones. The first international manual telephone exchanges to Australia would not open for another year. In 1927 the only means of voice transmission was beam wireless and, even when one was connected, the static usually made it impossible to understand what the person at the other end was saying. The only reliable means of keeping in touch was by letter, which took up to six weeks to make the 12,000-mile journey to Down Under. Elizabeth had not just said goodbye to her daughter; she had effectively cut her out of her life for the period of her visit.

But she had gone nonetheless. It never occurred to her not to do so. Whatever her inclinations, she kept them to herself. It would have been an inconceivable act of wilfulness for her to have behaved otherwise.

There was nothing in the least unusual in this. The aristocracy had always been distanced from their children, but they were by no means the only ones for whom parenting was a long-range activity. The British Empire was a vast organization which spanned the world and was run by an army of civil servants, administrators, and soldiers, the majority of whom were drawn from the middle classes. Because of the dangers of disease and the belief that if they were brought up where their parents were stationed they ran the peril of 'going native', children were routinely shipped home to Britain and into the care of boarding schools or relations at the age of six or seven. It might be several years before they were reunited with their parents. The experience was heartbreaking for all concerned, but one that was accepted with the stoicism born of necessity.

During the Second World War, moreover, tens of thousands of children were evacuated from the poorer urban areas and removed from their generally uncomplaining parents to the safety of the countryside. Over the centuries, including schooling and wartime evacuations, several million people were subjected

HMS "RENOWN" - AUST

LAS PALMAS
KINGSTOWN
COLON
PANAMA
MARQUESAS ISLES
FIJI
AUCKLAND
RUSSELL
WELLINGTON
PICTON
STEWART
ISLES

Whereas by Our Kingly Condescension We have this day
Our Royal Domain on board His Britannic Majesty's
the necessary initiation, We by these presents do giv
that the aforesaid has become one of Our Loyal Subj
We further require all Sharks, Dolphins, Sea Snakes,
to treat the aforesaid with the respect to which all Our duly

Given at Our Court on the Equa

W. L. Wyllie

Elizabeth

LASIAN CRUISE 1927

SYDNEY
HOBART
MELBOURNE
FREMANTLE
MAURITIUS
& HANISH
ISLANDS
SUEZ
PORT SAID
MALTA
GIBRALTAR
PORTSMOUTH

A

PROCLAMATION

To all whom it may concern

ted _____ Mᵣ U Osborn _____ to enter

Cruiser **"Renown"**, and whereas he has undergone

is Royal Warrant under Our Sign Manual in token

such as have not yet entered Our Royal Domain

ied and Loyal Subjects are entitled.

is 31ˢᵗ day of January, 1927.

N R

C. Hazzledine

Albert

A SIGNED CERTIFICATE PRESENTED TO EVERY MEMBER OF THE ROYAL PARTY ON BOARD HMS *RENOWN* AFTER THE CEREMONY OF CROSSING THE EQUATOR.

to these enforced shipments and separations. It was the British way and, judged by Britain's success in the international arena, it appeared to work. It was not until the 1950s, when the Empire and the values which sustained it were in rapid retreat that people started to question the system.

Diana, Princess of Wales, adopted a very different approach. Imbued with American ideas about parenthood's responsibilities, she insisted on taking her sons with her whenever she could. Her grandmother-in-law did not approve and this provided yet another area for dispute in their continual differences of opinion. To the Queen Mother, as she by then was, Diana's way of doing things smacked of sloppy, sentimental self-indulgence.

Like everyone else of her generation, Elizabeth had been brought up to put duty to King and country ahead of self, and certainly ahead of children who were expected to be seen and not heard – and, in the case of this Antipodean tour, not seen for several long months. The fact that the King happened also to be her father-in-law only emphasized the point: she was a member of the King's family and it was beholden to her to set a good example.

Not all Elizabeth's royal relations were quite so dutiful. The King was already harbouring doubts about the character of his eldest son, the charming but superficial Prince of Wales. His youngest son, George, Duke of Kent, whose tastes ran to amoral débutantes, men and drugs, also gave grave cause for concern, although it is doubtful if the King was ever appraised in detail of the extent of George's deviations. But these were not Elizabeth's concerns. She was much tougher and a great deal more selfish than popular image would have her – a fact that her granddaughter Princess Anne would later acknowledge – but she always operated within the parameters of propriety.

And, for all the tears she shed when she bade farewell to her baby in Nanny's arms, there is no doubt that she enjoyed her six-month Antipodean sojourn.

She had every reason to relish the tour. It was the dawn of the age of international celebrity, of movie stars and popular singers. And royalty, especially British royalty, was up there in the firmament with them. The Prince of Wales was probably the most famous and revered man in the world, and the Duchess of York found herself at the centre of the same hysteria. Coming, as she did, from a grand aristocratic background, she had adjusted easily to the deference that was royalty's natural due. Now she was experiencing the different and altogether more heady delight of mass adoration, and she was intoxicated.

The tour proper started in New Zealand, and she was mobbed wherever she went. Officially it was the Duke who was there on duty but it was his Duchess they turned out to see. The crowds broke through the police cordons at the quayside in Auckland. When they tried to go for a walk in Ellerslie Gardens they were surrounded by well-wishers and the police could do no more than watch helplessly as the Duchess, in her dark blue cloche hat, vanished in a sea of people. Later, what was supposed to be a disciplined drill display by 15,000 schoolchildren became a near-riot when they broke ranks and besieged the royal car.

The Duchess played her part with grace and flair. She smiled and waved, always said the right thing even if it were not very much, and, in an exercise of memory that was to become her

THE DUKE AND DUCHESS OF YORK ARRIVING AT WHAKAREWAREWA ACCOMPANIED BY MITA TANOPOKI, THE VETERAN CHIEF OF THE ARAWA TRIBE AND THE WELL-KNOWN GUIDE, BELLA, TO VIEW THE WONDERS OF THE DISTRICT.

hallmark, had an uncanny knack of remembering the faces and names of the servicemen who had passed through Glamis a decade before.

The Duke caught the popular mood and at one wayside station jumped off the royal train and ran alongside, unrecognized, with the crowd cheering his wife. When she fell ill with tonsillitis, so convinced was he that the success of the tour depended on Elizabeth that he considered cancelling the rest of his engagements and returning to Wellington to be at her side. Only the gentle but forceful reminders by his staff persuaded him to carry on.

SUVA, FIJI. RATU POPI E. SENILOLI, THE GRANDSON OF THE LATE KING CAKOBAU, PRESENTING A 'TABUA' (TOOTH OF THE SPERM WHALE), A SYMBOL OF HOMAGE AND AFFECTION, TO THE DUKE OF YORK.

It was the same story in Australia. There had been fears that this country on the other side of the world, where national pride often had an anti-British slant, would not take kindly to the representatives of a system many had chosen to renounce by emigration. In the event crowds even larger than those in New Zealand turned out to greet the Duke and the woman Sir Tom Bridges, the Governor of South Australia, dubbed 'the smiling Duchess'. The reception in Canberra was 'tumultuous' and everything went according to plan. The Duke succeeded in delivering his speech at the opening of the new Parliament without a hitch while the Duchess, for her part, had the immense satisfaction of starting a fashion.

In Africa, apart from the occasional official function when she had been required to put on a formal hat and frock, she had dressed in a khaki safari suit and a wide-brimmed bush hat. They were clothes the sporting Duchess, who had spent so much of her youth on the moors of Scotland, felt comfortable in; in New Zealand, too, she welcomed the chance of pulling on her old mackintosh and striding out to the river bank. The fishing there was as spectacular as the shooting had been in Kenya. The trout

THE DUCHESS OF YORK OUT ON AN EARLY MORNING FISHING EXPEDITION AT TOKAANU. SEEN HERE CROSSING A STREAM IN WADERS AND MACKINTOSH.

were the size of the Scottish salmon, and such is the change in water temperature caused by volcanic activity that it is 'possible to catch a trout in one pool and cook it in the next' as she wrote.

Such excursions, however, like the one to Lake Taupo on New Zealand's North Island, were the exception. For the most part this tour was a formal round; of official receptions and march pasts, and remembrance services and dances. There was also that new and strange event called the 'Public Reception' where the Duke and Duchess were required to stand on a dais like two waxwork figures in Madame Tussaud's while the public filed past, four abreast.

The Duchess needed suitable clothes for her appearances, and that meant fur and feathers, satin and silk and velvet. It was her cloche hats, however, with their upturned brims and feather and flower decorations, that caught the eye of the fashion-conscious Australian women. The millinery shops in Melbourne and Sydney and, later, Adelaide and Brisbane and Perth, were soon full of cloche copies, and in colours that even the Duchess, whose taste in such matters could never be called understated, found a trifle dazzling.

When the couple eventually boarded the *Renown* for the long voyage home, accompanied by three tons of toys and twenty live parrots, gifts for the daughter they had not seen for six months, they left to a cacophony of cheers and praise. Prime Minister Bruce telegraphed the Duke: 'The personalities of yourself and the Duchess have brought vividly before us how human is the tie that binds us to our kinsmen overseas. As an Ambassador of Empire you have brought the Mother Country closer to Australia.'

Sir Charles Fergusson, Governor-General of New Zealand, telegraphed the King: 'It is quite unnecessary to say that they have both made themselves adored by everyone.'

Sir Tom Bridges wrote to the King: 'This visit has done untold good and has certainly put back the clock of disunion and disloyalty twenty-five years as far as this State is concerned.'

Sir Tom added: 'The Duchess leaves us with the responsibility of having a continent in love with her.'

This was sycophantic hyperbole, certainly, but hyperbole that nevertheless reflected popular opinion.

Yet, for all the praise and plaudits, despite the glowing newspaper headlines and the sheaves of congratulatory telegrams that arrived at Buckingham Palace, the tour was not the uncritical success the Duke and his Duchess had hoped.

Britain was in the throes of industrial unrest and there were complaints about the cost of the trip. Two Labour MPs, Ammon and Kirkwood, had asked of the House of Commons why the Yorks had been allowed to undertake 'a pleasure trip of this kind'; why, 'in spite of the country's distress it can afford to vote £7,000

THE DUKE AND
DUCHESS OF YORK
LANDING AT
PORTSMOUTH. ALSO
SEEN ARE THE PRINCE
OF WALES, PRINCE
HENRY AND PRINCE
GEORGE.

to send out their Royal Highnesses to the uttermost parts of the earth.' To underscore their point they added: 'It would not matter one iota to the welfare of the country supposing they never returned.'

The King was infuriated by what he regarded as a 'flippant, discourteous' attack on his family. The MPs, the King raged, had no comprehension of the 'almost terrifying schedule of dinner, receptions, garden parties, balls and other official duties relieved by brief fishing excursions.'

Intriguingly, however, the King himself was not entirely satisfied with the Yorks' performance.

George V adored his daughter-in-law. 'The better I know and the more I see of your dear little wife,' he informed his son, 'the more charming I think she is and everyone falls in love with her.' Normally a stickler for punctuality, he was even prepared to forgive her chronic lateness. 'If she weren't late she would be perfect and how horrible that would be,' he said. Once, when she arrived for dinner after everyone else, he told her, 'You are not late, my dear. I think we must have sat down two minutes early.'

Being late for dinner was one thing: missing the whole ten-day tour of New Zealand's South Island was quite another matter. To the King-Emperor who nine years later would try and struggle off his deathbed in order to fulfil his engagements, the Duchess's decision to cancel hers due to tonsillitis smacked of dereliction of duty.

It was for his son, however, that George reserved the full force of his displeasure. He arranged private screenings of the newsreel footage of the tour and then fired off finicky missives to the set-upon Duke. One read: 'I send you a picture of you inspecting the Gd of Honour (I don't think much of their dressing) with yr Equerry walking on yr right side next to the Gd & you ignoring the Officer entirely. Yr Equerry should be outside & behind, it certainly doesn't look well.'

As a mark of honour, the King deigned to meet the returning couple at Victoria Station. But again he insisted on treating the Duke, now a married father of thirty-one, like a not particularly bright schoolboy. 'Frock-coat & epaulettes, without medals & riband, only stars,' were to be worn he instructed. 'We will not embrace at the station before so many people. When you kiss Mama take yr hat off.'

Bertie, ever the dutiful son, did as he was told without complaint. It was somewhat galling for his wife, however, to find herself relegated to the role of appendage after all the adulation she had so recently enjoyed. Even her reunion with her one-year-old daughter Elizabeth, who did not know who she was, was taken out of her hands.

FACING PAGE:
THE DUKE AND
DUCHESS RETURNED
HOME TO GREAT
ACCLAIM AND TO A
JOYFUL REUNION WITH
PRINCESS ELIZABETH.
ON 28 JUNE, 1927,
THEY GREETED THE
CROWDS FROM THE
BALCONY OF THEIR
HOME AT 145
PICCADILLY.

Elizabeth had hoped that it would take place in the privacy of her own home at 145 Piccadilly. Queen Mary decided otherwise and ordered child and mother to Buckingham Palace. The Duchess obeyed and when she did eventually get her daughter home, she did as her father-in-law, the King-Emperor, had bidden her, appearing on the balcony and holding Princess Elizabeth aloft 'like a football cup' for the crowd below to cheer.

It was compliance that brought no practical reward. When George V, as Duke of Cornwall and York, returned from his own

successful tour of Australia and New Zealand in 1901, his father, Edward VII, had proclaimed him Prince of Wales. There could be no such elevation for Bertie, of course; that job was already taken. But he was anxious to build on the confidence he had gained in Australia and told his father that he was keen to undertake more royal duties. It was an ambition his wife was happy to support.

This was not to be. George V was not like his father. (It is something of a wonder that a man as easy-going and generous of spirit as Edward produced a prig such as George.) Royal duties there were, but they were of the parochial kind. The Duchess performed them with grace. 'She lays a foundation-stone as though she had just discovered a new and delightful way of spending an afternoon,' *The Times* noted admiringly. But never again did the crotchety King entrust an overseas tour of significance to his second son and his wife.

It would be another decade before Elizabeth was able to resume her travels. By then her husband had ascended the throne. And she was his Queen-Empress.

CHAPTER 5

$\mathcal{L}$ONDON LIFE

Becoming a member of the Royal Family was one thing. But what to do now that she was there? What was her role, her function? How was she expected to behave? When it came down to it, who was she?

They were questions that would defeat the next Duchess of York and cause the future Princess of Wales such anguish. They also threatened to confound Elizabeth.

The vitality that had been such an essential facet of her character seemed transformed as the veil of royalty was drawn across her life. There were no more references to Elizabeth 'the irresistible' whose vivacity had 'taken London by storm'. From now on it was Elizabeth the dutiful fiancée and then wife, Elizabeth the homely, an icon perched on the pedestal of her new-found royal status.

She was even denied a voice. A few days after her engagement had been announced, she had given an interview to a newspaper. Seated in the drawing-room of her parents' home in Bruton Street, Mayfair, she said how happy she was, that she was embarrassed by the fuss and was finding it difficult coming to terms with the public attention, and that her engagement ring would be made of sapphires.

'Do people really want to know about my ring?' she enquired of the reporter. 'Do they want to photograph me?'

It was bland, innocuous, endearing in a naïve way. It was also unprecedented. The *Daily Sketch* noted: 'Never before has the bride-to-be of a prince of the blood-royal established such a link between the teeming millions and the private affairs of the exalted few.' The writer went on to add: 'But I shouldn't be surprised to find a complete cessation of these interviews in the very near future.' He was right. King George V, Elizabeth's soon-to-be father-in-law, was furious. Members of the Royal Family, he sternly informed her, did not give interviews.

When their time came, Diana and Fergie would fight tooth and nail against being swallowed whole in this way, and the royal interview became a powerful and destructive weapon in what degenerated into open warfare with the family they had married into. Elizabeth, on the other hand, accepted her situation. A few weeks before her wedding she wrote to a friend: 'The cat is now completely out of the bag and there is no possibility of stuffing him back again.' Ever the team player, she took her captain's advice to heart and throughout her long life never gave another interview until well into her eighties, when she made the occasional appearance on television to talk about her gardens or her horses.

Henceforth a smile and a wave, highlighted by the occasional 'Charming' and 'Oh, really' became her only means of communicating with those teeming millions around the world over which her father-in-law, and in their turn her husband and daughter, reigned. Her silence did not entail complete acquiescence, however. Compliant she undoubtedly was but at the same time she had a sturdy determination to fashion a life for herself, in her own way and on her own terms and according to her own taste.

She choose her battleground well. Forced into the role of home-maker, she set about making those which suited her and gave expression to the personality which still bubbled beneath the royally varnished surface.

Her husband once said: 'Elizabeth could make a home anywhere.' She did so many times in the various homes she created, whether it was a palace or log cabin by the river. In her advancing years her eye for detail was not as attuned as it once was: the flowers lingered in their vases longer than they should have and the carpets became a little threadbare in places. Her ability to establish her own unique ambiance never deserted her, however, and as with so much else in her life, it was from her childhood that she drew reference and inspiration.

White Lodge – now the Royal Ballet School – was the first house to bear her imprint. There could not have been a tougher beginning, for the Georgian villa sited on a hill overlooking Richmond Park had once been the childhood home of no less a personage than Queen Mary. It was from here she had left to get married and it was where she had returned to give birth to her first son, the Prince of Wales. It was here too that both her parents had died, and the Queen took a close and proprietorial interest in everything that happened there.

When George V gave it to the Yorks in 1923 the Queen declared how pleased she was that they were going to 'keep it in the family'. What she really meant was that she was going to keep it firmly under her own control.

The house where Horatio Nelson had outlined his plan of attack for the Battle of Trafalgar over luncheon, on a little round study table with his finger dipped in wine, was in a ruinous state when the Yorks moved in. There was no heating and it wasn't until they had lived there for some time that they managed to get the hot water to work properly. At one point Bertie was moved to write to his mother saying, 'the boiler is actually finished, and marvel of marvels it worked on Sunday.'

Queen Mary interpreted that as her cue to do what needed to be done and while the Yorks were off on their extended honeymoon, first at Polesden Lacey in Surrey and then Glamis, with the last fortnight at Frogmore in Windsor, she moved in and set about re-creating the house in her own sombre image. Elizabeth returned in mid June 1922 to find it cluttered with dark, lugubrious furniture. Tactfully, the young Duchess described the look as 'airy'. It was far from airy, and nothing like anything Elizabeth had in mind. Her idea of what a home should be had been shaped by St Paul's Walden Bury.

'Few houses have been so thoroughly lived in,' Lady Cynthia Asquith recalled of Elizabeth's childhood home. 'Here, one feels, were no very strict regulations as to the shutting of doors and wiping of shoes, no statements that dogs should be kept in their place, nor that children should be seen and not heard. In all of these rooms children certainly were heard.'

Dogs and children would feature prominently in all Elizabeth's future homes. So would the nurtured family atmosphere of St Paul's, which Lady Cynthia Asquith described as being 'bound together by a contented and unspoiled affection that embraced also every friend who enjoyed the hospitality of the house'.

With that memory in mind, Elizabeth set to work on White Lodge, removing the furniture her mother-in-law had put in and replacing it with pieces chosen from amongst the tons of wedding presents she had received, despite the scathing remark of the former Liberal Prime Minister Herbert Asquith, who said, 'not a thing did I see that I would have cared to have or give.'

Driven by necessity, Elizabeth took a closer look. There were gifts such as an English oak chest stacked with twenty-four pairs of wellington boots and galoshes from the Patentmakers. ('I look forward to an opportunity of putting to a practical test the contents of this beautiful chest which you have so generously given me,' the Duchess wrote.) There was also a Sheraton bow-fronted chest of drawers, an ornate ormolu bureau and some Chippendale mirrors which helped transform White Lodge into a home more suited to a young couple than an old Queen.

THE DUKE AND DUCHESS OF YORK ON THEIR EXTENDED HONEYMOON. PICTURED HERE IN THE GARDENS OF POLESDEN LACEY, NEAR DORKING, SURREY.

Quite what her mother-in-law would make of it was another matter, and it was with some trepidation that the Yorks invited the King and Queen to lunch on the Thursday of Ascot week. 'I had better warn you,' the Duke wrote to his mother, 'that our cook is not very good, but she can do the plain dishes well and I know you like that sort.'

The King at least was suitably disposed. The Yorks took him on a conducted tour of the house and afterwards he recorded in his diary: 'May and I paid a visit to Bertie and Elizabeth at White Lodge and had luncheon with them. They have made the house so nice with all their presents.' If Queen Mary had any misgivings she chose not to voice them. Tactfully she described the house as 'very nice'. Elizabeth had won the round. It was hardly a knock-out blow but it did confirm her right to a measure of the independence which marriage had so seriously curtailed.

WHITE LODGE IN RICHMOND PARK – THE FIRST HOME OF THE NEWLY MARRIED COUPLE.

The glory of living in Richmond Park with its stunning views and herds of deer could not justify the expense of running such a large house, however. That came to £11,000 per year – a very large sum indeed in those days.

Privacy was another consideration, even then. In summer the Park was a popular place for Londoners to spend the day. White

Lodge was besieged by trippers who arrived in cars and chara-bancs and stood at the gates and gawped.

Its distance from London also counted against it. The Duchess's 'smiling presence' was in such demand that she was being asked to attend eight to ten functions a day and in the Twenties when motor transport was slow and unreliable, getting to and from London was both fraught and tiring. The journey was especially difficult in winter when White Lodge was often fogbound and on more than one occasion the Yorks' chauffeur lost his way on the unmarked roads.

Within a year the Yorks had had enough. London was still full of great town mansions occupied by the families who had built them, and run by a staff of thirty or forty servants, and for a couple so committed to the royal round of official duties Mayfair was the place to live.

At the beginning of the 1924 Season, the Yorks accepted the offer of the loan of Chesterfield House, the London home of Princess Mary and her husband Viscount Lascelles, for their base of operations. On returning from their annual holiday in Scotland in the autumn of 1925, the Duchess discovered she was pregnant and the search for a suitable London home intensified.

Neither Queen Mary nor King George could understand what she had against White Lodge, but, in her quiet, unmoving way, the Duchess was insistent she should find the type of home she wanted for herself and her family.

The Yorks stayed for several weeks at Curzon House in Curzon Street, which is now the Saudi Arabian Embassy. They considered Norfolk House in Norfolk Street, Mayfair, but when that proved to be not quite right the Duke arranged to rent a house in Grosvenor Square from a Mrs Hoffman. The King could have offered them one of the many grace and favour residences at his disposal but he did not. It was left to Elizabeth's mother to solve the problem by giving them the use of the Strathmore home at 17 Bruton Street.

It was at this time that the Duchess heard about 145 Piccadilly, an empty property belonging to the Crown Estates which stood on the edge of Hyde Park Corner, across the road from the house that once belonged to the Duke of Wellington, victor of the battle of Waterloo. Behind it was an enclosed space known as Hamilton Gardens, from which a gate led into Hyde Park. From the top

THE DUKE AND
DUCHESS LEAVING 17
BRUTON STREET, THE
HOME OF THE
STRATHMORES,
LOANED TO THEM BY
ELIZABETH'S MOTHER.

windows of the house was a view of what is now the Lanes-
borough Hotel, formerly St George's Hospital.

The Duchess took to it at first sight. The Duke was less enamoured. Although the house was considered a grace and favour
residence, the Duke paid a substantial rent. He also agreed to pay
for the renovation, adding a fire escape to the nursery floor and
carrying out various necessary and overdue repairs. He had the

house redecorated according to his wife's taste in fashionable beiges and pale greens, colours which the Queen Mother continued to use throughout her life. The total costs were almost equal to those needed to maintain White Lodge.

But it could not have been more central – Wellington's adjacent house is colloquially known as Number One London. Most importantly it was a home of their own choosing, a major consideration

THE ANXIOUS YORKS LEAVE THEIR LONDON HOME, 145 PICCADILLY, FOR A CRISIS MEETING AT WINDSOR. WITH WALLIS'S DIVORCE, ABDICATION HAD BECOME INEVITABLE.

with the Yorks. The arrival of a daughter, Princess Elizabeth, in the spring of 1926 had whetted the public attitude for all things royal and a large crowd gathered outside to cheer when they finally moved in on their return from their tour of the Antipodes in June 1927. It was said to be the first time in history that members of the Royal Family had lived in a house without a name, and during the ten years of their tenancy it was always referred to as 'One Four Five', as if it were a semi in suburbia.

According to Marion Crawford, the governess of the Yorks' daughters, the house was 'neither large nor splendid and might have been the home of any moderately well-to-do young couple starting married life'. The estate agents' particulars told a slightly different story, suggesting that in royal circles size and splendour are in the eye of the beholder. The agents described it as an 'important mansion... which is approached by a carriage drive used jointly with No. 144 Piccadilly, contains spacious and well-lighted accommodation, including entrance hall, principal staircase hall, a secondary staircase with electric passenger lift, drawing room, dining room, ballroom, study, library, about 25 bedrooms, conservatory etc...' The imposing double-fronted door with its stone porch was guarded by a policeman who vetted the visitors as they walked up the stone-flagged doorsteps and rang one of the two porcelain doorbells marked 'Visitors' and 'House'.

THE PRINCESSES ELIZABETH AND MARGARET WITH SOME OF THEIR TOYS AND THE COT FORMERLY USED BY THEM BOTH, AT THE EXHIBITION OF HISTORIC AND ROYAL TREASURES ASSEMBLED IN PRINCESS ELIZABTH'S ROOM AT 145 PICCADILLY IN 1939.

To keep the house running smoothly the Yorks enlisted the help of Captain Basil Brooke their Comptroller, Mr Ainslie the butler, Mrs Macdonald the cook, and Mrs Evans the housekeeper. In addition were an under-butler, two footmen, an odd-job man, a steward's-room boy, three housemaids, three kitchen-maids, a nursery-maid, a dresser, a valet, an RAF orderly, a night watchman and a chauffeur, to say nothing of the equerries and ladies-in-waiting who came in on a daily basis.

'Bertie and I sent our butlers to the Portlands [The Duke and Duchess] to be trained, as our own household wasn't large enough,' the Queen Mother remarked many years later. This was a clear indication that despite what seems such a large number of staff by today's standards, she viewed their lifestyle as comparatively simple.

Once inside the hallway, shut away from the noise of Piccadilly – which was clamorous with the new covered-top buses, cars, motorbikes and horse drawn vehicles – tranquillity and the smell of fresh flowers prevailed. The decoration was contemporary, with the new café au lait brown carpets and pale green walls, while the large morning-room on the ground floor had peach curtains which opened on to the sooty gardens behind. Over the mantelpiece was a painting of the young Princess Elizabeth by the artist Edmund Brock, and a Persian carpet covered most of the floor.

Favourite books including those by famous Scottish authors were piled in corners on the floor, a habit the Queen Mother still enjoys. Her heritage was also evident in the china figures of Scottish soldiers on the mantelpiece. Framed photographs of family and dogs vied for position with some fine bronzes which the Queen Mother would later move to the Castle of Mey.

Children, of course, had their place in the decorative scheme of things. There was a menagerie of toys piled behind the largest table in the room, and behind a black lacquer screen were two scarlet dustpans and brushes which Princess Elizabeth and her sister, Princess Margaret Rose, who was born at Glamis Castle in August, 1930, used for playing at housekeeping. Off the morning-room was a small boudoir where the children did their lessons, although the nurseries themselves were situated upstairs on a landing beneath the glass dome, which formed part of the roof.

The house boasted two telephones with Mayfair telephone numbers which were operated in the daytime by a Boy Scout. To make a call, one lifted the handset on the side of a large box on a shelf on the wall and asked the operator for the number required. The telephone system was still in its infancy, however, with only half a million subscribers, and most of the Duchess's business was done by letter. Waking at seven but never appearing before eleven, the Duchess would devote her mornings to going through her correspondence with the help of one of her ladies-in-waiting.

Only a small number of the invitations she received could be accepted, but a glance at the engagement books of the time reveals the surprisingly large number of functions she did attend. Foreign holidays and nightclubbing were not for her. She was only ever seen to be doing good and, what is more, enjoying herself in the process.

The Duchess's performance on these occasions was enhanced by her genuine interest in the work she was doing. Various people from the charities she was connected with were invited to One Four Five so that she could gather more information. Here, according to Lady Cynthia Asquith, they were 'encouraged to talk shop and if any of them felt shy she would be very skilful at setting them at their ease.'

She also enjoyed hosting small dinner parties for friends (everyone was required to dress formally, the ladies in full-length gowns, the men in black and often white tie). Dinner was always served at 8.15, except when she made one of her visits to the theatre or the cinema, when a light snack was served beforehand followed by a late supper afterwards.

The royal couple both liked musicals and in 1928 they went to see *Showboat* with the legendary Paul Robeson who would later enjoy a scandalous relationship with Edwina Mountbatten, the wife of the Duke's cousin Dickie. And just before Christmas 1929 the Duchess accompanied Queen Mary to Edgar Wallace's *The Calendar* and was described by the Bloomsbury author Virginia Woolf as 'a simple, chattering, sweet-hearted, round-faced young woman in pink; her wrists twinkling with diamonds, her dress held on her shoulder with diamonds'.

Just occasionally even these paragons of familial virtue could hit the wrong note, as the Duchess did in 1931 when, with three million unemployed, she was criticized for 'fishing for champagne bottles' at a charity fête while the workers were starving. For the most part, however, the Yorks were seen by the public as a family united in domesticity. That was certainly the way they saw themselves, particularly the Duke who liked nothing better than to stay home with his wife, to play with his daughters and then listen to the wireless (later in his life he would insist on listening to his favourite programmes during dinner and the family would sit at the table eating and laughing at Tommy Handley's *ITMA (It's That Man Again)* or the comedy programme *Much Binding in the Marsh*). This was how the Duke would have liked to have lived for the whole of his life. But events beyond his control were conspiring against him.

On a December afternoon in 1936 the Duchess, who had taken to her bed with a severe bout of influenza which always afflicted

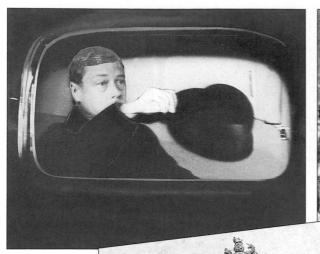

ABOVE:
THE NIGHT AFTER
HIS ABDICATION,
THE REALIZATION OF
WHAT HE HAS DONE
SEEMS TO HIT THE
FORMER KING AS HE
LEAVES
MARLBOROUGH HOUSE
AFTER A FAREWELL
DINNER WITH BERTIE
AND QUEEN MARY.

RIGHT:
THE INSTRUMENT OF
ABDICATION, SIGNED
BY THE KING AND
WITNESSED BY HIS
BROTHER AND
SUCCESSOR, ALBERT,
DUKE OF YORK.

INSTRUMENT OF ABDICATION

I, Edward the Eighth, of Great
Britain, Ireland, and the British Dominions
beyond the Seas, King, Emperor of India, do
hereby declare My irrevocable determination
to renounce the Throne for Myself and for
My descendants, and My desire that effect
should be given to this Instrument of
Abdication immediately.

In token whereof I have hereunto set
My hand this tenth day of December, nineteen
hundred and thirty six, in the presence of
the witnesses whose signatures are subscribed.

Edward R.I.

SIGNED AT
FORT BELVEDERE
IN THE PRESENCE
OF

Albert

Henry.

ABDICATION

Daily Mail

THE KING HAS CHOSEN

WE have passed through the most anxious and astounding day in the history of our Empire. At its close no longer did King Edward the Eighth hold the most glorious heritage that ever fell to the lot of a ruler. His "final and irrevocable" abdication fills every heart with an overwhelming sense of tragedy. Indeed, the event far transcends man's capacity to realise it and all that it implies.

The King's decision was stated in an historic message, such as no English Sovereign has ever before penned. It was read by the Speaker of the House of Commons. "The burden which constantly rests upon the shoulders of a Sovereign is so heavy that it can only be borne in circumstances different from those in which I now find myself," declared the King.

The voice of contention is stilled as the Empire sadly reflects on its great loss. The King's subjects had hoped against hope that the Throne would for many years be filled by a Sovereign so well equipped to lead a great Empire through the difficult days that lie ahead. Yet the whole Empire is now aware that King Edward has reached his decision only after heartsearching reflection. As far back as November 16 he informed Mr. Baldwin of his intention to marry Mrs. Simpson and that he was "prepared to go."

"This Heavy Task"

Then later his proposal for a morganatic marriage was rejected by the British Government after consultation with the Dominions, the King's determination became unshakable. To no great figure in history has an issue so momentous presented itself in a form so stark and uncompromising. King Edward was faced by alternatives each awe-inspiring in its implications. He could renounce the Throne

"I Ha
To
T

AT 3.3

CROWDS GATHER IN
THE STREETS OUTSIDE
PARLIAMENT ON 10
DECEMBER 1936,
WAITING FOR THE
EXPECTED NEWS OF
ABDICATION.

BELOW:
HOW THE *DAILY MAIL*
REPORTED THE ROYAL
CRISIS.

The Daily Mail, FRIDAY, DECEMBER 11, 1936. 13

DUKE OF YORK THE NEW KING

Edward VIII. To Leave England To-day

BROADCAST TO-NIGHT

Farewell Dinner With His Successor

SAME CORONATION DATE FOR NEW KING AND QUEEN

KING EDWARD VIII. has abdicated the throne and will leave the Country to-night. His destination late last night was a secret, but it will not be Cannes.

He announced his "final and irrevocable decision" in a message to Parliament yesterday. To-day he will sign the Act of Abdication, which will be taken to him at Fort Belvedere. It will be his last act as King.

LAST NIGHT AT FORT BELVEDERE

Lighted windows shining through last night's fog at Fort Belvedere, where King Edward stayed throughout the crisis.

PRINCESS ELIZABETH TOLD AT

Stricken Silence of the Commons

From PERCY CATER

WESTMINSTER, Thursday.

DWARD VIII:

This happy picture of the Duke and Duchess of York was taken during the Jubilee celebrations in May last year.

The Text Issued Last Night of

THE BILL OF ABDICATION

...ermined ...ance ...rone..."

...en Mr. Baldwin, the Prime

KING GEORGE VI APPEARS ON THE BALCONY AT BUCKINGHAM PALACE AFTER HIS CORONATION ON 12 MAY 1937.

THE CORONATION OF THEIR MAJESTIES
KING GEORGE VI AND QUEEN ELIZABETH.

SCOTCH SALMON   MAYONNAISE SAUCE
CUCUMBER
—
EGG MAYONNAISE
—
ROAST SURREY FOWL   GLAZED YORK HAM
DERBY ROUND BEEF
SADDLE SOUTHDOWN LAMB IN ASPIC
GLAZED OX TONGUE
CHAUDFROID OF CHICKEN ROSE MARIE
—
SALADS
POTATO   RUSSIAN
FRENCH
—
CORONATION TRIFLE
FRUIT SALAD & CREAM   FRUIT JELLIES & CREAM
CHARLOTTE RUSSE
ASSORTED BAVAROIS   CREAM CARAMEL
—
CHEESE   BUTTER   BISCUITS
—
DESSERT
—
COFFEE

Servants' Hall,
Buckingham Palace.

12th May, 1937.

MENU FOR THE CELEBRATORY MEAL SERVED IN THE SERVANTS' HALL, BUCKINGHAM PALACE

RIGHT: THE KING AND QUEEN, FOLLOWED BY QUEEN MARY AND PRINCESS ELIZABETH AT THEIR FIRST PALACE GARDEN PARTY, HELD ON 22 JUNE 1937.

her in moments of crisis, called her daughters' governess into her bedroom where she lay in bed propped up with pillows. 'I'm afraid there are going to be great changes in our lives, Crawfie,' she said. George V was dead, his successor Edward VIII preparing to abdicate. 'We must take what is coming and make the best of it,' the Duchess counselled.

DEVOTED TO DUTY. THE
KING AND QUEEN WITH
PRINCESS ELIZABETH
IN LONDON IN 1947.

BELOW:
DEVOTED TO
PLEASURE. THE DUKE
AND DUCHESS OF
WINDSOR IN NEW
YORK IN 1946.

At 11 o'clock on 12 December 1936 King George VI, as he now was, left One Four Five in his uniform of Admiral of the Fleet, to attend his Accession Council. Crawfie explained to the two Princesses, who had given their grave-looking father a farewell hug, that when he came home he would be King and they would have to curtsey to him.

THE DUKE OF WINDSOR AND MRS SIMPSON TOGETHER IN THE GARDENS OF THE CHATEAU DE LA CROË, 1937

'When the King returned, both little girls swept a beautiful curtsey,' Crawfie recalled. 'I think perhaps nothing that had occurred had brought the change in his condition to him as clearly as this did. He stood for a moment touched and taken aback.'

That afternoon the King, the two Princesses and Queen Elizabeth watched the proclamation ceremony from a room overlooking Friary Court at St James's Palace before returning to One Four Five for the last time. They then moved out into the impersonal vastness of Buckingham Palace.

Not a stone or vestige remains today of the original building in Piccadilly. It was bombed to rubble in the war and later demolished. The Intercontinental Hotel now stands on the site. The Queen Mother sometimes has difficulty remembering it at all. 'Poor Piccadilly got a direct hit in the war you know, did we really live there?' she asked.

She did, and very happy she was there, too, for it was at One Four Five that she had come to terms with her role within the Royal Family. Now she was a Queen in a palace, facing a challenging future.

CHAPTER 6

MOTHERHOOD

Like many women, Elizabeth performed better as a grandmother than as a mother. Prince Charles, her eldest and most favoured grandson, described her thus: 'She belongs to the priceless band of human beings whose greatest gift is to enhance life for others through her own effervescent enthusiasm for life.'

To her own daughters, however, she was a remote, rather magisterial figure. She was an affectionate enough presence when she was with them but as soon as the clarion call of 'duty' sounded she would be gone again, sometimes for months on end, and they spent their young lives having to get to know her – and then having to get to know her all over again when she returned from yet another long absence.

Even when she was present, a certain distance was maintained between mother and offspring. For instance, when the Yorks decamped from London to Glamis for the grouse-shooting, the three-month-old 'Baby' Elizabeth travelled north the day before with her nanny; her parents followed on the night sleeper with their dog, a golden retriever called Glen. And when, at the end of August, the Duke and Duchess left the castle for a round of visits with friends, their little daughter remained behind. It set a pattern that would continue to the outbreak of the Second World War.

By her own lights and the standards of her class, Elizabeth, Duchess of York, was a dutiful mother who devoted time and attention to her children. That view is not wholly without validity.

THE QUEEN, THE QUEEN MOTHER AND PRINCESS MARGARET AT ROYAL ASCOT, 1956

Certainly enough affection was generated in those early years to ensure that in adulthood Elizabeth formed the closest of friendships with her namesake whom she called Lilibet and her younger daughter, Margaret Rose. The three women grew to prefer each other's company to all others. They holidayed together, out of royal tradition but also out of choice, and gossiped together, often in French. They spoke to each other on the telephone every day and the switchboard operators at Buckingham Palace derived particular amusement from saying, as they put the Queen Mother through to the Queen, 'Your Majesty? Her Majesty, Your Majesty'.

They also delighted in letting their hair down (in old age Elizabeth's hair, when it was unfurled, reached almost to her waist, much to the annoyance of Princess Margaret who was forever telling her mother to get her hair cut and stop dropping her hairgrips all over the place). All three were partial to a stiff martini or three. That could sometimes lead to scenes more suited to a *Carry On* film than the studious decorum of their public images. One Christmas evening at Sandringham they got through nearly a whole bottle of gin and another of Dubonnet at pre-dinner drinks in the oak-lined salon. When they eventually took their precarious seats on the dining-room chairs that had been brought over from 145 Piccadilly, the Queen Mother, as she now was, could not get the vegetables out of the silver serving dish the stoical footman was holding. Spoonfuls

THE DUCHESS OF YORK
AND QUEEN MARY TAKE
BABY ELIZABETH FOR A
WALK AT BALMORAL.
HER GRANDMOTHER'S
STRICT APPROACH FOR
TEACHING ETIQUETTE
WAS SOFTENED BY HER
MOTHER'S LOVING
CONCERN.

of peas were sent cascading to the floor, accompanied by regal peals of high-pitched, inebriated laughter.

Such intimacy had to wait until they were grown-up. In infancy Lilibet and Margaret Rose were allowed no breaches of etiquette. Elizabeth poached her old nursery maid, Allah, from her sister Mary, Lady Elphinstone, and gave her the task of turning the girls into well-behaved upper-class English country ladies who knew how to hold their knives and forks and say please and thank you. A governess was later engaged to teach them to read and write but book-learning was never a pressing priority; according to Elizabeth, whose own formal education had ended at the outbreak of the First World War when she was just fourteen years old, childhood was there to provide 'lots of pleasant memories stored up against the days that might come and, later, happy marriage'.

THE DUKE AND DUCHESS OF YORK, AND THE EARL AND COUNTESS OF STRATHMORE AT THE CHRISTENING OF PRINCESS ELIZABETH, MAY 1926.

This was hardly the mental equipment needed for dealing with the modern world but Elizabeth, as the governess, Marion Crawford observed, 'had a definite idea of the sort of training she wished her daughters to receive, and pursued her course untroubled by other people's doubts'.

All she wanted for her daughters, she said in summary, was for them 'to spend as long as possible in the open air, to enjoy to the full the pleasures of the country, to be able to dance and draw and appreciate music, to acquire good manners and perfect deportment, and to cultivate all the distinctive feminine graces'.

Marion Crawford remarked: 'I often had the feeling that the Duke and Duchess, most happy in their own married life, were not over-concerned with the higher education of their daughters.' What was important was a sense of propriety, and there to ensure that it was instilled as early as possible were Elizabeth's formidable in-laws, Queen Mary and King George V.

Both were sticklers for doing everything by a very strict book, and their own children had been brought up in an atmosphere of stifling formality. James Stuart, Bertie's former equerry and Elizabeth's former suitor, said of the King: 'In his relations with his children there remained something of the manner of a stern and caustic naval commander.' The royal couple were, so Queen Mary's friend Mabell, Countess of Airlie insisted, 'more truly devoted to their children than the majority of parents of that era', but even she was forced to conclude: 'The tragedy was that neither had any understanding of a child's mind.'

This lack of parental understanding would have the direst effect on their four sons. The eldest, the future Duke of Windsor, grew into an irresponsible wastrel, Henry, Duke of Gloucester, a bad-tempered curmudgeon with an over-fondness for drink, George, Duke of Kent, a drug-abusing transvestite, while Elizabeth's husband, the shy and uncertain Bertie, Duke of York, developed the stutter which caused him such distress throughout his life.

By the time George and Mary's grandchildren arrived, age had leavened their approach, but not by very much. Elizabeth had

spent the first eighteen months of her life sleeping in a cradle at her mother's, the Countess of Strathmore's, bedside, but that was not the regal way. Hugs and kisses were never a feature of the Royal Family's parental agenda and their strictures were carried through into the next generation. This goes a long way towards explaining the emotional problems which have continued to beset the Royal Family. The irascible George V did not like little boys, as his daughter Mary's son, George, the future Earl of Harewood, quickly discovered. 'The possibility of getting something wrong

FAMILY GROUP, DATED JUNE 1931, WHEN PRINCESS ELIZABETH WAS FIVE YEARS OLD AND PRINCESS MARGARET ROSE TEN MONTHS.

was, where Grandfather was concerned, raised to the heights of extreme probability, and our visits to Windsor for Easter usually provided their quota of uneasy moments,' he recorded. Even indisposition would provoke the royal wrath. When George developed a sneeze, 'either from the pollinated grass or sheer nerves', the King shouted: 'Get that damn child away from me', which made a rather strong impression on an awakening imagination.

Queen Mary was equally intimidating. Princess Margaret would recall how a visit from that stiff, imposing woman brought a 'hollow, empty feeling to the pit of the stomach'.

Had the young Duchess been left to bring up her daughters in her own way, the two girls, and Lilibet in particular, might have enjoyed a more relaxed childhood than they did. But the flighty and warm-hearted Elizabeth was not in charge of her own destiny, nor indeed, of her own children.

Driving through Hyde Park one day, Lilibet asked her mother why people were waving their handkerchiefs and raising their hats as they passed. 'Because you are a little princess,' the Duchess replied.

'Were you a princess when you were small?' her daughter enquired. No, her mother explained, her royal status had come through marriage.

'Then if I grow up and marry a man will he be a prince because I am a princess,' the child persisted.

'No dear, not necessarily,' the Duchess answered. It was an early lesson in the arcane rules of royalty. Others were to follow. The King and Queen dictated how their granddaughters were raised and when Queen Mary said she was going to visit a museum or an exhibition and asked if her granddaughters might like to accompany her, the 'suggestion' was taken as a royal command. Under her watchful eye Lilibet was taught to smile for the

THE DUCHESS OF YORK WITH HER BROTHER, DAVID, HER MOTHER, THE COUNTESS OF STRATHMORE AND PRINCESS ELIZABETH AT GLAMIS.

THE QUEEN MOTHER
WITH TWO-YEAR-OLD
PRINCE CHARLES AT
PRINCESS ANNE'S
CHRISTENING.

BELOW:
THE QUEEN, THE
QUEEN MOTHER,
PRINCE CHARLES AND
PRINCESS ANNE. A
STARK CONTRAST WITH
THE FORMALITY OF
PRINCESS ELIZABETH'S
CHRISTENING.

photographers, wave to the crowd and control her bladder in return for the reward of a biscuit. 'Teach that child not to fidget,' Queen Mary ordered and, to ensure that she did not, the pockets of her dress were sewn up. And all this before she was three years old.

When they visited Glamis in the summer, the girls liked to stretch some chewing-gum across the railway track and watch what happened when the express train roared through. And both developed the habit of biting their nails, which no amount of ticking-off could cure. These were the rarest gestures of juvenile independence, however. Only once in her life was Lilibet allowed on to a beach to build sandcastles. That was in 1928 when she was two years old and staying with King George, who was convalescing in Bognor Regis after a severe illness which rendered him too unwell to object to this pastime.

Elizabeth might well have resented her interfering in-laws' dominating influence, but if she did she was careful to keep her thoughts to herself. Her behaviour must be viewed in context, however. What would seem bizarre and decidedly uncaring to later generations was accepted as perfectly normal at the time – and Elizabeth was always of her Edwardian time. She had married into a family which was governed by its own rules and, never one to court confrontation if it could possibly be avoided, she simply gave in. The daughter of an earl, she had been brought up by her own family to believe in rank and due deference. Unlike Diana Spencer, also the daughter of an earl but a woman of very different character, she was not prepared to challenge the system of which marriage had made her a part. She bowed to the ways of her Sovereign and his Consort, regardless of the heartache that might cause. It would have been regarded as disturbingly odd by the public as well as the Royal Family, if she had behaved otherwise. In 1927 when she left the ten-month-old Lilibet and set off with her husband on a six-month-long world tour, she was generally applauded for doing her wifely duty.

Even so, the parting was not an easy one and she was in such floods of tears when she left her baby daughter. There would be more tears when she came home again, though this time they were Lilibet's. Allah had taught the infant to say 'Mummy' – with the result that she called everyone and everything by that name. When the real Mama at last reappeared, Lilibet had clung pathetically to her nanny's skirts and had to be prized loose to join the Duchess on the balcony of Buckingham Palace for the obligatory homecoming welcome. It was hardly an auspicious return and in an effort to restore some sense of maternal normality to the situation, Elizabeth set about establishing a proper home for Lilibet and her sister Margaret Rose.

The Yorks moved out of Elizabeth's father's home in Bruton Street just off Berkeley Square, which had been their London base since their marriage, and into a large mansion at 145 Piccadilly overlooking Hyde Park Corner. The King gave them the Royal Lodge, in Windsor Great Park, for their weekend retreat. A well-ordered, upper-class routine was established, with Allah as its fulcrum.

At seven thirty a.m. the nanny would get the girls out of bed and give them breakfast in the top-floor nursery before taking them downstairs to spend all of fifteen minutes with their parents. The morning was spent at lessons with Marion Crawford, with a break at eleven for a biscuit and a glass of orangeade, before a light lunch at one fifteen. The afternoons were spent outside or, if it happened to be raining, in the drawing-room, learning to sew and knit and studying music. They were given afternoon tea at four forty-five. Their mother, if she happened to be in town, would join them in the nursery at five thirty for an hour's play and reading. Supper followed. Then, at seven fifteen on the dot, after spending a few more minutes with their mother in either the morning room or the drawing

MOTHER AND
DAUGHTERS.
ABOVE:
AT THE ROYAL
WINDSOR HORSE
SHOW WITH QUEEN
ELIZABETH, 1954.
LEFT:
WITH QUEEN
ELIZABETH AND
PRINCESS MARGARET,
1973.

room, Nanny would enter and firmly declare: 'I think it's bedtime now,' and they would be taken up by the specially installed lift to the nursery floor, across the cherry-coloured carpet and put into

bed. Encouraged by his wife, the Duke would sometimes break with the convention which all but barred fathers from the nursery floor, and join them on bath nights.

It was safe, methodical, disciplined – and very lonely.

Marion Crawford arrived at 145 Piccadilly when Princess Elizabeth was five years old. 'Until I came she had never been allowed to get dirty,' the governess later recalled. 'Life had consisted of drives in the park, or quiet ladylike games in Hamilton Garden, keep-

THE QUEEN MOTHER WITH HER FAVOURITE GRANDCHILD, PRINCE CHARLES. THEY HAVE ALWAYS BEEN TOTALLY AT EASE IN EACH OTHER'S COMPANY REGARDLESS OF THE OCCASION.

ing to the paths; or leisurely drives around London in an open carriage, waving graciously to people when Allah told her to.' Crawfie, as the Princesses called her, introduced her young charges to games of hide-and-seek and Red Indians. She took them for a ride on the top floor of a double-decker bus and, once, on the underground to Tottenham Court Road. She even allowed them to get dirty, just as their mother had done when she was little. And, as with her mother, companions of their own age were most notable by their absence. Their best friends were either their toys – Lilibet had a large collection of foot-high model horses which she stabled on the nursery landing – or those they made in their imagination.

'Other children always had an enormous fascination, like mystic beings from a different world, and the little girls used to smile shyly at those they liked the look of,' Crawfie remembered. 'They would have loved to speak to them and make friends, but this was never encouraged. They seldom had other children to tea.'

The governess thought that 'a pity'. It is doubtful if their mother thought about it at all. She had, after all, been brought up in a very similar manner, and what had gone before was always good enough for the Duchess.

The death of George V and the Abdication of Edward VIII meant that the family were forced to leave Piccadilly for the cavernous vastness of Buckingham Palace (and most disheartened by the move they were). The essence remained the same, however. Queen Mary continued to exert her influence from the shadows, the new King and Queen continued on their round of social and official engagements, and the Princesses' existence was as ordered as it ever had been.

Where life did differ from what had gone before, and differ substantially, was in the way that Elizabeth and her daughters were allowed to deal with the trauma of war.

It was on the evening of her fourteenth birthday that Lady Elizabeth's future father-in-law King George V declared war on Germany. Princess Elizabeth was only seven months younger when her father, George VI, committed Britain and her Empire and Dominions to war with Germany in 1939. But whereas Elizabeth had been permitted to nurse wounded soldiers, her elder daughter was prevented from playing any but the smallest part in the next World War.

Elizabeth was at the Coliseum when Britain's ultimatum expired in August 1914. The show had just ended when the theatre manager walked on stage to announce that hostilities had begun. 'It all seemed so terribly exciting,' Elizabeth recalled. 'People throwing their hats in the air, shouting and cheering. The atmosphere was electric and everyone couldn't wait to get at the enemy.'

THE QUEEN MOTHER WITH PRINCE CHARLES ON THE STEPS OF ST PAUL'S, 1977.

A few days later Elizabeth and her mother returned to Glamis, which was being converted into a hospital. In December the first of the wounded started arriving. They were put in the oak-panelled dining-room now converted into a ward. By January the number of patients was up to twenty. For the next four years Elizabeth would be charged with tending the smashed bodies and broken minds of soldiers invalided back from the Western Front. She ran errands for them, bought them cigarettes, wrote their letters for them, dressed their injuries and kept their spirits up with sing-songs, card games, practical jokes and the ebullience of her own good humour. Elizabeth had to come to terms with the death of one brother, Fergus, killed in action at the Battle of Loos in 1915, and the capture of another brother, Michael, who was initially posted missing, presumed dead, in 1917. She had to help her beloved mother in her subsequent nervous breakdown. And, in 1916, when Glamis Castle was in danger of burning to the ground, it was Elizabeth who took charge of the fire-fighting operation until the fire brigade arrived, and who personally led the rescue parties battling to remove as many valuables as they could from the flames.

They were four exciting, frightening, depressing, exhilarating years which tempered her character, gave her the opportunity of mixing with people from outside her own social circle, taught her the priceless value of a well-directed smile and a considerate word, and turned her from a girl into a woman.

Elizabeth's elder daughter was all but denied a similar rite of passage. While the country her father reigned fought for its existence, Princess Elizabeth lived in the comparative safety of Windsor Castle. The soldiers she met were not battle-ravaged evacuees from the front line, but guardsmen detailed to protect her should German paratroopers land in the vicinity, which they never did. Instead of the practical nurse's outfit her mother had worn, she was dressed either in the uniform of a Girl Guide or the same little girl's clothes her sister Margaret was wearing. She attended a madrigal society every Thursday. At Christmas she staged and starred in her own pantomime.

Her situation was, of course, very different from the one in which her mother found herself. Elizabeth was born a commoner; her daughter was Heir Presumptive to the throne. And, as Marion Crawford noted, the King 'was at first very reluctant to allow her to join up and face what could not help being a certain amount of danger'. It was a risk the young Princess Elizabeth was more than prepared to take. Since the age of sixteen, when she had registered with the local Labour Exchange at Windsor as the law required, she had badgered and pleaded with her father to be allowed to join one of the women's services. 'I ought to do as other girls of my own age do,' she said.

THE QUEEN MOTHER WITH THE QUEEN AT EPSOM ON DERBY DAY, 1988.

It was not until she was eighteen, however, that she was allowed to enrol in the Auxiliary Territorial Service as Second Subaltern Elizabeth Windsor and learn how to adjust a carburettor and drive a truck. By then the war was all but over, and the dangers George VI had been so anxious that his daughter should avoid were almost past. Consequently the aloof and introverted Elizabeth was never given the chance to mix with girls of her own age, to share in their privations, to broaden her outlook.

The King's attitude can be explained. Brought up in a self-contained family which made a point of not exposing itself to competition and scrutiny, and pessimistic by nature, he saw his public obligations as a burden rather than an opportunity or a challenge, and it was his urgent wish to shield his daughter from those same predestined responsibilities for as long as possible.

The more outgoing Elizabeth's reasons for acceding to her husband on a matter so vital to her daughter's development were more complex. The maternal desire to protect her offspring played its obvious part, as did her old-fashioned notion of a wife's duty which dictated that a husband have the final say. But more than that, her stance is indicative of how deeply she had been absorbed into the Royal Family.

Her status afforded her everything she wanted from life – respect, esteem and the opportunity to do something of value. It meant that she never really had to think about money. Queen Mary set the tone when she declared: 'Money is not a subject of practical concern to the Royal Family.' This was just as well, because throughout her life Elizabeth spent it lavishly.

Perhaps most important of all, being royal allowed her to create for herself a secure and comfortable setting in which change was only an occasional visitor, standards of a bygone age could be maintained, and the day-to-day problems of ordinary life kept firmly in their place. Seamless continuity was what counted: what the King wanted, and what her royal parents-in-law had demanded, was good enough for Elizabeth and, in turn, for her daughters. There was no place in her carefully ordered environment for waywardness – and certainly not for anything as disruptive as passionate infatuation. When Princess Margaret's relationship with Peter Townsend was no longer possible to ignore, the Queen Mother, as she then was, did what she always did when faced with something unpalatable, and refused to get involved. The Queen Mother was, in fact, just about the only person in the royal circle who seemed to have been unaware of what was developing between her younger daughter and the recently appointed Comptroller of her own Household. She had always been very close to her younger daughter, who shared her mischievous sense of humour and sometimes caustic wit. She still regarded her as a little girl and refused to acknowledge her burgeoning sexuality.

Group Captain Peter Townsend had been appointed equerry to George VI in 1944. The King liked his insouciant sense of humour and reciprocated in kind; when the equerry served him sherry one evening instead of his usual dry martini he joked, 'Do you know, that dreadful fellow Townsend tried to poison me.' Elizabeth admired his looks, responded to his deferential English charm and enjoyed dancing the hokey-cokey with him at Balmoral.

It was not long before the closeted Margaret also became attracted by the Hurricane pilot and much-decorated Battle of Britain hero sixteen years her senior. She developed a schoolgirl crush on him. He, in turn, noted her 'large, purple-blue eyes, generous sensitive lips and complexion as smooth as peach'.

They got to know each other better than her parents suspected during the tour of South Africa in 1947. Each night the White Train bearing the royal party and the accompanying journalists would stop in a siding. One morning in the Karoo, the semi-desert vastness north of Cape Town where the bushmen used to roam, horses were brought up. Townsend and the laughing, animated Princess Margaret saddled up and galloped off together. The gentleman from *The Times*, showing a discretion unusual in his calling, gallantly rode away in the opposite direction.

Queen Elizabeth had always been closer to Margaret than to her elder daughter. Both were excellent mimics, liked late nights and dancing and shared the same sense of humour. (Asked where she had learnt some modern slang words, Margaret replied: 'At my mother's knee, or some such low joint.') They delighted in the frivolity of life in a way the future Queen, constrained and reliable and very much her father's daughter, never could. They also enjoyed the company of handsome men and they regarded Townsend, understated and with an air of melancholy about him, as very good-looking. Others took a much sterner view.

Townsend was a married man. Two months before the King's death in February 1952, he was finally divorced from his wife, Rosemary, on the grounds of her adultery with John, the banker son of portrait-painter Philip de Laszlo . That made Townsend, in the eyes of the law at least, the innocent party. In the closed, moralistic Court of the early Fifties that was irrelevant. Townsend was a divorcee and that, by the rules of the day, made it impossible for him to marry the King's daughter.

There was another and darker shading to this tale of blighted love, however, which may explain the angry reaction of the new Queen's private secretary, Sir Alan Lascelles, who, when confronted by Townsend, declared: 'You must be either mad or bad.'

Rosemary Townsend's great friend was Eileen Parker whose husband, Mike, was equerry to Prince Philip. She recalled: 'Rosemary and I were both married to men frequently lured from us by the lustre of glittering prizes. But it was slightly easier for me then. At least, to the best of my knowledge, Mike was not having an affair and creating public humiliation. Rosemary as a wife and mother had to stand to one side while Princess Margaret, hardly out of ankle socks, entertained her husband. Understandably, she had every reason to sound bitter sometimes.' According to Mrs Parker, it was only 'in her frustration' that Rosemary became involved

LEFT:
PRINCE WILLIAM
GREETS THE QUEEN
MOTHER WITH A ROYAL
BOW AT THE GUARDS
POLO CLUB, WINDSOR.
BELOW:
WITH PRINCE
CHARLES AT THE
CELEBRATIONS FOR
THE QUEEN'S 50TH
WEDDING
ANNIVERSARY,
WESTMINSTER ABBEY,
20 NOVEMBER 1997.

with another man. 'Despite the fact that all in the Household were fully aware of what was going on, Townsend reacted to Rosemary's own affair with the stung indignation of a true cuckold.'

When Margaret brushed a fleck of fluff off Townsend's uniform at her sister's Coronation, the circumspection shown in South Africa by the journalist from *The Times* was not echoed by his colleagues on other newspapers, and the affair burst into public view.

The ensuing furore makes dismal reading today. The Church of England started braying about 'an affront to religion' and a violation of the 'law of Christ'. The Archbishop of Canterbury, Geoffrey Fisher, thundered on about 'God's will', labelled the unedifying situation 'the Townsend affair' and ended up dismissing the whole business as 'purely a stunt'. The Prime Minister, Sir Anthony Eden, himself divorced, advised the Queen that it was impossible for her sister to marry a divorced man. Margaret, faced with a choice between love and her royal status, chose the latter. Townsend was shuffled off into continental exile where he made a successful marriage with Margaret look-alike Marie-Luce Jamagne; Margaret went on to make an unsuccessful marriage to the photographer Anthony Armstrong-Jones, the Earl of Snowdon, and ended up a divorcee.

Only the Queen Mother emerged unscathed. With sublime nonchalance she coasted through the whole affair, offering neither advice nor condemnation. Townsend recalled how, when he and Margaret broke the news of their relationship to her, she 'listened with characteristic understanding. I imagine that [her] immediate – and natural – reaction was "this simply cannot be". But thoughtful as ever for the feelings of others, for her daughter's above all and for mine as well, she did not hurt us by saying so. Without a sign that she felt angered or outraged – or, on the other hand, that she acquiesced – the Queen Mother was never anything but considerate in her attitude to me. Indeed she never once hurt either of us throughout the whole difficult affair, behaving always with a regard for us both, for which I felt all the more grateful because of my own responsibility in the crisis.'

This hands-off attitude was typical of her style. With touching naïvety, the Queen her daughter once observed: 'She has been the most marvellous mother – always standing back and never interfering.' Whenever a crisis confronted her, she would turn away or retire to bed, in the belief that when she got up again, be it in a day or a fortnight, the situation would have eased and she would be able to carry on as before, almost as if nothing had happened. She had taken to her room at the height of the Abdication. She did so again during the Townsend affair. The problem, she declared, was for her elder daughter, as Queen, to resolve.

That led to inevitable friction between the two young women. The Queen felt bound by the advice of her ministers. Margaret peevishly informed her sister: 'You look after the Empire and I'll look after my life.' While they bickered, their mother remained serenely detached.

It was an approach better suited to a grandmother than to a mother. Love for her daughters there undoubtedly was, but the strong hand of maternal guidance was notable by its absence. Whether the Queen Mother's advice would have made any difference is open to question. Britain was a nation in the throes of transition. An Empire was being surrendered, and government ministers, churchmen, trade unionists and the Royal Family were struggling, for the most part unsuccessfully, to come to terms with the new political and social realities. Life for the younger royals was bound to be difficult, as the youthful notions of an increasingly self-devoted age blundered blindly into the rocks of the older traditions of duty and decorum. A woman as pledged to the status quo as Elizabeth was never likely to adapt well to the new order. She barely attempted to do so, with the result that her daughters were left to negotiate their own way through life and, in Margaret's case, through the emotional hazards that lay before her.

Once she was released from her day-to-day responsibilities, however, the Queen Mother was able to settle into the part to which she was far better suited. With the Queen preoccupied and often overwhelmed by her sovereign duties, and Prince Philip determinedly pursuing first his naval career and then his own life, their children had an emotional gap in their lives.

Prince Charles was born in 1948, his sister, Princess Anne, two years later. The Queen, observed Godfrey Talbot, the BBC's Court Correspondent at the time, 'had been trained since the cradle by her father that duty came before everything, including family. She reluctantly had to abandon her family and they virtually didn't see their parents for months on end. During the first years of the Queen's reign the Queen Mother was both mother and father.'

It was the same role that Queen Mary had fulfilled a generation earlier but, unlike her demanding mother-in-law, the Queen Mother was happy to allow the children to develop at their own pace, in their own way, without bringing any undue pressure to bear on her charges.

Rules and regulations had to be maintained, of course. When Charles was 'incarcerated', as he put it, at Gordonstoun, the spartan school in the north of Scotland he so disliked, he would seek weekend refuge with his grandmother at Birkhall, her home on the Balmoral estate. He adored it there. It was, he said, 'an unique haven of cosiness and character' where the tea table was laden with freshly-baked cakes and scones and the log fires kept everyone snug in winter. When he pleaded not to be sent back to Gordonstoun, however, the Queen Mother gently but firmly insisted he should go, with the inevitable reminder: 'All good things must come to an end.' But she did sometimes take him back late, explaining to Robert Whitby, Charles's testy house-master, 'You know what grannies are like.' In her words, 'Half the fun of being a grandmother is being able to spoil your grandchildren.'

There was a certain selectivity in her approach, it must be said. She doted on Prince Charles and on Princess Margaret's son, Viscount Linley, and his sister, Lady Sarah Armstrong-Jones. She was more circumspect in her dealings with Prince Andrew and Prince Edward, but only because the Queen, by then more comfortable in her role of Sovereign, had afforded them more time than she had their two elder siblings. Only Princess Anne was immune to her charm and then only for a while. Anne explained it thus: 'The Queen Mother is a wonderful family person and when I was a child and up to my teens I don't think I went along with the family bit, so my appreciation of my grandmother probably developed later than anybody else's.'

PRINCE WILLIAM HELPS HIS GREAT-GRANDMOTHER UP THE STEPS AFTER THE 1992 EASTER SERVICE AT WINDSOR.

Another explanation might be that, as usual, the males drew more out of the Queen Mother. But all the royal grandchildren, at one time or another, felt moved to comment on how much comfort and affection their grandmother had given them. It was a role she made her own. She provided them, Prince Charles said, with 'fun, laughter, warmth and infinite security'.

Indeed, looking at the bright, smiling, sympathetic figure who wafted across the nation's stage for the next five decades swathed in chiffon and floral scent, it is hard to imagine her as anything else but the grandmother she turned herself into, in fact as well as title.

CHAPTER 7

BY INVITATION ONLY

Of her four houses, Royal Lodge is the one that best reflects Elizabeth's style and personality. It is grand but comfortable, extravagant in concept and execution yet still very much a family home. It was here that she and her husband the King were at their happiest, where they brought up their daughters, where they worked together to create one of the finest gardens of the Thirties. It was their private sanctuary and it was where in widowhood Elizabeth continued to live a life of privilege, preserved in the aspic of Edwardian splendour.

And it was here as Duchess of York that she came face to face in private for the first time with Wallis Simpson, the woman who thought she could be Queen – and made Elizabeth one instead.

The Yorks were given the house by George V in 1931. It was in a dilapidated condition, both inside and out, and on their first visit they had to hack their way through the undergrowth and clamber in through an old greenhouse. The nation was in an equally parlous condition. The Great Depression had thrown two million out of work, the first Labour government had fallen, Britain had been forced off the Gold Standard and the pound had been devalued by 30 per cent; there were riots in London and 12,000 Royal Navy ratings stationed at Invergordon on the Cromarty Firth had staged a near mutiny.

The Royal Family were not immune to the troubles. George V gave up £50,000 of his Civil List and the Duke of York gave up hunting with the Pytchley and sold his six hunters for 965 guineas. 'It has come as a great shock to me that with the economy...my hunting should have been one of the things I must do without,' he wrote to the Master of the Pytchley, the immensely rich American Ronald Tree who had first employed the services of Sir Geoffrey Jellicoe, the most influential landscape gardener of the period. 'And I must sell my horses too. This is the worst part of all and the parting with them will be terrible.'

Despite the dire economic circumstances, however, the Duke and his Duchess were set on having a country home of their own: somewhere they could escape to from 145 Piccadilly. They did not like being beholden to others for their country weekends. They wanted a place where, as the Duke explained to his father, they could bring up their daughters, and teach them the ways of the countryside. Bertie's elder brother, the Prince of Wales, had already been given Fort Belvedere on the Windsor Estate and when George V made his offer of the nearby Royal Lodge the Yorks accepted with alacrity.

Situated in fifteen acres of Windsor Great Park, it was convenient for London even in those pre-motorway days and, as one observer noted, 'there was an air of grandeur about it which appealed to them.'

After that first intrepid inspection, the Duke wrote to his father: 'Having seen it I think it will suit us admirably.' The King replied: 'I am so pleased to hear that both you and Elizabeth liked the Royal Lodge and would like to live there. I hope you will always call it the Royal Lodge, by which name it has been known ever since George IV built it.'

The rose-washed neo-gothic house had suffered a chequered history since the Prince Regent had gone to work on the original Queen Anne building. He employed the architectural skills of John Nash who transformed it from a cottage in the woods into a romantic and elaborate (and notorious) 'cottage *orné*'. The entrance was given gables and a gothic door, the tiles were removed and replaced by thatch, sash windows were replaced by mullioned ones and coloured plaster covered the brick walls. A large conservatory, a trellised temple and tall elegant chimneys completed the transformation in 1814.

The cost came to an astronomical £52,000. And all for nothing, because when the Prince's highly unpopular reign as George IV ended in 1830, one of the first things his brother, William IV, did was pull most of it down, leaving only the Chapel and the last addition, the still unroofed salon designed by Wyatville.

Over the next century the remaining core had extra rooms tacked on and it was used as a grace and favour residence by various royal retainers including a Major Fetherstonhaugh, the manager of King George V's racing stables. To bring the house up to standard was clearly going to cost a great deal of money. It would certainly have been much cheaper to have continued to hunt instead of embarking on a renovation programme of such magnitude. But the Duke and Duchess were inspired by the challenge of creating a home and garden of their own design and, working on the principle that if they looked after the pennies by getting rid of a few horses, the tens of thousands of pounds needed to refurbish the Lodge would look after themselves, they set about their task.

They began with the great Wyatville salon, pulling down the partitions and restoring it to its original proportions. They had new wings built on either side and bathrooms installed. While the builders worked on the house, the royal couple concentrated on the gardens. For Elizabeth this was merely the continuation of an interest fostered in childhood by her mother, who had designed the two-acre Italian Garden at Glamis. For the Duke it was a completely new pursuit. His father had limited him, as a boy, to planting cabbages in military rows. Now he was able to let his imagination take bloom.

The Duke, wrote his official biographer, Sir John Wheeler-Bennett, had 'a genius for landscape gardening, a gift for design and display and the priceless possession of a "green finger"'. He also had the benefit of some very expert advice in addition to his wife's help. The Duke was able to draw on the services of Eric Savill, the Deputy Surveyor of Windsor Parks and Woods and creator of the Savill Garden, and Sir Geoffrey Jellicoe. Between them they laid out a romantic woodland garden which cut down on labour costs. At the same time their plan reflected 'a desire to create a more relaxed ambiance in tune with an emancipated era' in the words of the gardening historian and former director of the V&A museum Sir Roy Strong.

The Yorks took a hands-on approach to their gardening and everyone was expected to join in. Butlers, secretaries, equerries, policemen and princes were conscripted into the work-force, to spend afternoons hacking away at the thickets and digging and planting according to the Duke's drawings. One Saturday afternoon a tall guards officer became part of the gang. Wanting to wear in his new bearskin for a parade the following week, he kept it on while acting as wheelbarrow-boy for the Duke. As he became hotter and hotter and the Duke demanded he empty the wheelbarrow quicker and quicker, he stripped to the waist and ended up wearing only his khaki shorts and the bearskin. 'In full dress – but only down to his brow,' the Duchess remarked.

Jellicoe, who had also worked for Elizabeth's brother David at St Paul's Walden Bury, was developing what he called the psychology of gardening, which combined historical background and the physical character of the land with personal taste. George Plumptre wrote in *Royal Gardens*: 'It was the inspired fusion of these three motives which accounted for much of the royal couple's love of the place and which held the key to their success.'

Elizabeth loved her garden. So did the Duke, who, in an interesting psychological twist of his own, took to writing letters in what he called the language of flowers. Apologizing to the Countess of Stair for his wife's absence as a weekend guest at Lochinich Castle in the spring of 1935, he wrote: 'It was a great disappointment to me that my wife was unable to come too... I am glad to tell you that she is much better, though I found her looking Microleucrum (small and white). It was nice of you to say that I deputised well for her on Saturday but I feel that she could have done everything much better, as she has the Agastum (charming) way of Charidotes (giving joy).'

Elizabeth, one of whose great skills lay in steering her husband in the direction she wanted him to go and then standing back and allowing him to take the acclaim, gave all the credit to the Duke.

The Queen Mother's relaxed, loving relationship with her grandchildren is obvious from this portrait with six-year-old Charles and four-year-old Anne, taken at Royal Lodge in 1954.

'It had been a sort of jungle,' she said. 'The King made the garden all himself.'

By the end of his life Bertie had indeed become a proficient gardener, with a near professional knowledge of rhododendrons. Royal Lodge, though, was very much a joint effort and, as with all Elizabeth's horticultural ventures, the gardens were designed to give the effect of 'coming into the house', as the Prince of Wales's are today. To sustain that impression, Jellicoe added a new terrace which ran the length of the rear facade and a 'starkly modern' swimming-pool.

With the passage of years it is hard to recall that there was a time when Elizabeth was regarded as the epitome of modernity.

The romantic side of her nature, based on its stylized reflection of an idyllic past, would come to dominate her popular image. In the Thirties, however, she was seen as riding in the vanguard of contemporary taste. Throughout his life the Duke remained staunchly conservative in his artistic preferences. The Duchess, on the other hand, was much more adventurous. She took an interest in modern art and, under the tutelage of Sir Jasper Ridley and Kenneth Clark, who later presented the BBC Television's *Civilisation* series, she started collecting pictures by, amongst others, Augustus John, John Piper, and Edward Seago.

After the war she bought a seascape by Monet, which, according to Christopher Lloyd, the Surveyor of the Queen's Pictures is 'a spectacular picture'.

Lloyd declared that the Queen Mother had a very good eye for painting and knew what she was doing. 'Her collection in Clarence House, most of which was acquired in the 1940s constitutes a marvellous entity, but it is a private collection and no-one knows what will happen to it. If it should come into the Royal Collection, which it may well not by the terms of her will, then it would be a kind of stepping-stone. Besides the Monet she has a Latour, and some good Duncan Grants and a very good Sir John Everett Millais, the Pre-Raphaelite artist whom Queen Victoria totally ignored.'

Although the Queen Mother was the one with the prime interest in art, the King played his part in the design of both the interiors and exteriors of Royal Lodge. Jellicoe's terrace became part of the whole, and here the royal couple could drink their cocktails and lounge around in the sun on wicker-work planters' chairs which Elizabeth had painted white, the colour made intensely fashionable by interior decorator Syrie Maugham.

Syrie's husband, the author and playwright W. Somerset Maugham, who left her for his male secretary, cruelly remarked that she had stolen the idea from the wife of a Sandgate coal merchant. It mattered not a jot; white was the colour she had decreed, and white it was. Elizabeth did not go quite as far as Syrie, in whose own drawing-room, as the photographer Cecil Beaton noted, every piece of furniture had been stripped and bleached, the flowers were white and 'white sheepskin rugs were strewn on the eggshell surface floors, vast white sofas were flanked with crackled white walls, white ostrich and peacock feathers were put in white vases against white walls.' But Elizabeth's use of the colour in her décor showed that she was attuned to the latest trends. *Country Life* magazine, the guide to gracious country living, praised the 'streamlined' design of the 'clean-cut modern building' Royal Lodge had become.

As well as art and design, Elizabeth also introduced culture to the house, a commodity most notice-able by its absence in the court of George V and Queen Mary, who, according to Loelia Ponsonby, 'were considered so stuffy and frumpish that they were very much sneered at behind their backs'. Elizabeth started attending the Sunday-night poetry readings given by such luminaries as T.S.Eliot and the Poet Laureate John Masefield and organized by Edith and Osbert Sitwell. She introduced the idea to Royal Lodge, where in later years actors including Edward Fox and the Oscar-winning Jeremy Irons would be invited to dine and deliver.

Those intellectual forays notwith-standing, Elizabeth was not regarded as one of the great hostesses of the period. That dubious honour belonged to the likes of the Marchioness of London-derry, Emerald, wife of shipping mag-nate Sir Bache Cunard, and, most egregiously, Mrs Ronald Greville. Harold Nicolson called the latter 'a fat slug filled with venom'. Cecil Beaton described her as 'a galumphing, greedy, snobbish old toad who watered at the chops at the sight of royalty'. (The Duke and Duchess of York spent part of their honeymoon at Polesden Lacey, Mrs Greville's Regency house in Surrey.) The Duchess did not have the physical stamina, the political acumen or the social ambition to compete in that league. Nor did she share the determined disregard for convention which was the mark of so many of her contemporaries, some of her royal relations included.

PRINCE CHARLES AND PRINCESS ANNE WITH THEIR GRANDMOTHER IN THE GARDENS OF ROYAL LODGE.

Having a good time had always been a privilege of the upper classes, and in the Twenties and Thirties they set about it with a vengeance. It was the age of nightclubs and parties, endless parties – Circus parties, Cowboys and Indians parties, Russian parties, swimming parties. In 1927 the Duchess of Sutherland gave a Baby party. The Prince of Wales and the Duke of Kent went dressed as little boys, Lord Ednam dressed as a nanny pushing a pram in which sat his wife wearing a baby's mask. Lord Portarlington and his son came dressed as Victorian dowager and daughter, 'no hideous detail omitted'.

The Twenties and Thirties also saw many of the old taboos start to break down. Subjects like drug addiction and adultery, which were barely mentioned before, provided Noel Coward with the material for his hit plays *The Vortex* and *Private Lives*. And people who, for all their talent, might otherwise have remained beyond the pale were able to make their way in what was still called Society. Noel Coward, whose mother ran a boarding-house, became a friend of the Duchess. So did the art historian Kenneth Clark. The son of a thread-maker (and father of the future Tory MP Alan Clark) he was beaten unmercifully at school 'because I was not a gentleman', but rose to become Director of the National Gallery and Surveyor of the King's Pictures.

Despite the period's newly tolerant attitudes, the Duke and Duchess remained circumscribed in their behaviour. While Lady Eleanor Smith, the Earl of Birkenhead's daughter, and Loelia Ponsonby, who married the immensely rich 2nd Duke of Westminster in 1930, were tearing through London's East End or climbing Queen Victoria's memorial in front of Buckingham Palace on one of their all-night treasure hunts, the Duchess of York was at home having children and putting on weight.

Elizabeth was certainly not a prude. She was understanding of the Duke of Kent's problems when his lascivious letters to a young man in Paris produced a threat of blackmail, and when his fondness for drugs got out of hand and led to his removal to Fort Belvedere for a period of drying out.

She regarded Jamie Stuart's extra marital shenanigans with the same worldly insouciance. Not one to be restricted by the oaths of matrimony, Stuart was a serial adulterer. One lover was the Duchess of Buccleuch, whose nocturnal ramblings earned her the sobriquet of Midnight Moll. Another was Penelope Clive, wife of a brigadier in the Grenadier Guards and sister of Viscount Portman. Stuart was cited in Mrs Clive's divorce, a scandalous thing to happen in 1949. However, it did not disturb his friendship with Elizabeth which had resumed (at a safe distance, it must be said) when he returned from his Oklahoman exile and continued to his death in 1971.

Elizabeth's tolerance of other people's foibles and weaknesses extended to her younger daughter, and she appeared unperturbed when Princess Margaret became romantically entangled with Roddy Llewellyn, a man seventeen years her junior. He was invited to stay at Royal Lodge where, unable to fasten the studs of his dinner-shirt, he went looking for assistance in the ironing-room. There he encountered the Queen Mother, who did his studs up for him. Llewellyn had yet to put his trousers on and was standing in his underpants at the time.

The late ballet choreographer Sir Frederick Ashton was another who was caught with his trousers down. He recalled the occasion when he was weekending at Royal Lodge and the Queen Mother burst in on him with a party of friends she was showing round the house while he was sitting on the loo. 'And this,' the Queen Mother grandly announced, without so much as a blush, 'is Sir Frederick's bathroom.'

There was a decorum, a restraint to her own actions, however, which did not always endear her to others. She particularly irritated her sister-in-law, the impecunious but very royal Princess Marina of Kent, who referred to her as 'that common little Scottish girl' and complained that 'the Duchess of York's serene professionalism was so far ahead of everybody else that instead of helping by its example she set a standard that seemed almost impossible to reach.'

It was propriety woven in strands of steel, and the person who was destined to suffer the full force of Elizabeth's displeasure was, of course, Wallis Simpson.

Elizabeth had always got on well with her brother-in-law, the Prince of Wales, and he with her. Like almost everyone else, she had been captivated by his charm and he in turn had spoken poignantly to his brother of the 'one matchless blessing enjoyed by so many of you and not by me – a happy home with wife and children.' Elizabeth passed no judgement on the Prince's adulterous love affairs with Freda Dudley Ward and Thelma, Lady Furness, and the two households spent a great deal of time in each other's company.

One weekend when Lady Furness was in residence at Fort Belvedere, the four of them had a crazy time hurling the Prince's new plastic records across the terrace. 'Come on David, let's see if these are really unbreakable, as the label says', Bertie cried. The women ducked as the two brothers flung records around like Frisbees. They repaired to the drawing-room to continue the game, which only came to an abrupt halt when one of the Prince's more valuable lamps was broken by a direct hit.

On another occasion they went skating on the frozen lake of Virginia Water. Lady Furness and the Duchess hung on to a couple of old kitchen chairs as the men pulled them along. 'If I ever had to live in a bungalow in a small town,' Thelma said, 'this is the woman I would most like to have as a next door neighbour to gossip with whilst hanging out the washing in our back yards.'

It was very different with Mrs Simpson. There were no friendly exchanges between the Duchess and the Prince's new mistress. There never would be: Elizabeth took against her right from the start. She saw her at parties and receptions, but then she could hardly avoid her: the Prince saw to that. Casting discretion aside, he positively flaunted Wallis. He even managed to have her received at Court.

Mrs Simpson was not received by the Duchess of York, however. Like the King and Queen, her parents-in-law, she was alarmed by 'that woman's' influence over the Prince and deeply suspicious of her motives. She was too well-mannered to follow the example of others in Court circles who deliberately turned away when Wallis approached, but she went out of her way to avoid her.

Only once did the two women come face to face in private. This took place at Royal Lodge shortly after the death of George V; David had ascended the throne for his brief, uncrowned reign as Edward VIII. Determined to force the issue, the new King drove over from the Fort, ostensibly to show his brother his new American station wagon, in fact to introduce his lover to his brother and sister-in-law.

After the King had taken his brother for a spin in the new car, they walked around the garden and then went inside for afternoon tea. Wallis recalled: 'I had seen the Duchess of York before on several occasions at the Fort and York House. Her justly famous charm was highly evident. I was also aware of the beauty of her complexion and the almost startling blueness of her eyes. Our conversation was largely a discussion of the merits of the garden at the Fort and that at Royal Lodge. We returned to the house for tea, which was served in the drawing room. In a few moments the two little Princesses joined us. They were both so blonde so beautifully mannered, so brightly scrubbed, that they might have stepped straight from the pages of a picture book. Along with the tea things on a large table was a jug of orange juice for the little girls. David and his sister-in-law carried on the conversation with his brother throwing in only the occasional word.

'It was a pleasant hour; but I left with a distinct impression that while the Duke of York was sold on the American station wagon, the Duchess was not sold on David's other American interest.'

Indeed not. The little Princesses' governess Marion Crawford witnessed the scene. She remembered a 'smart, attractive woman, with the immediate friendliness American women have'. There was an embarrassing undercurrent, however, which Wallis's brittle gaiety could not disperse. Mrs Simpson, she noted, 'appeared to be entirely at her ease; if anything too much so'.

IT WAS AT ROYAL LODGE, AS DUCHESS OF YORK, THAT ELIZABETH CAME FACE TO FACE IN PRIVATE FOR THE FIRST TIME WITH WALLIS SIMPSON, THE WOMAN WHO THOUGHT SHE COULD BE QUEEN – AND MADE ELIZABETH ONE INSTEAD.

Crawfie said that she 'never admired the Duke and Duchess more than on that afternoon. With quiet and charming dignity they made the best of an awkward situation and gave no sign whatever of their feelings, but the atmosphere was not a comfortable one.

'No-one alluded to the visit when we met again later in the evening. As usual, nothing whatever was said, though I suppose most of us had the subject in our minds. Maybe the general hope was that if nothing was said, the whole business would blow over.' It was Elizabeth's custom throughout her life, when confronted with something she did not like, to pretend it either was not happening or was not there. That way she could block anything unpleasant out of her mind.

She could not block Wallis's influence out of her life, however, as a few short months later, in December 1936, Edward VIII abdicated his throne 'for the woman I love'. Bertie became King and sobbed piteously on his mother's shoulder at the prospect. Elizabeth retired to bed and David, now the Duke of Windsor, retired into exile. The new Queen made sure he remained there, for the rest of his life. On her prompting Wallis was denied the honorific of Her Royal Highness which should have been hers by right on her marriage to the ex-king. The Queen refused all her brother-in-law's entreaties to grant Wallis an audience, if only once and only for form's sake. Her hostility never abated and the Duke in his anger took to calling her 'that fat Scotch cook'. There would be no reconciliation. This was a feud that was destined to last a lifetime – as her grandson Prince Edward once remarked, referring to the vendetta: 'She takes no prisoners.'

That was partly to do with business. Elizabeth felt strongly that the Duke of Windsor had let down what her husband dubbed 'The Family Firm' by abdicating his responsibilities and thrusting the burden of kingship on her husband who, she believed, was driven to his early death by the stress.

Her real venom, however, was directed at Wallis.

Elizabeth was a dutiful aristocrat who regarded Wallis as an unscrupulous adventuress. She was unnerved by Wallis's glossy manner and envious of her chic. The fact that she was American did not help matters, either. David was charmed by Americans. Elizabeth, in common with many other Britons, was not. She found them too brash, too egalitarian, too democratic, too much of a challenge to the traditional British way of doing things; into her old age she took great delight in imitating the Duchess's Bostonian twang.

On a deeply personal level, she also found Wallis Simpson threatening. Elizabeth's priorities were hearth and home, husband and children. The thrice-married Wallis worked to a different agenda. The gossip was (and Elizabeth always had a well-tuned ear for gossip) that Mrs Simpson's hold over the former King was sexual; that during her time in Shanghai she had learnt some complicated and, to Elizabeth's way of thinking, highly undesirable bedroom tricks from a high-class Chinese concubine.

The idea, then, of 'that woman' being officially designated as a member of the Royal Family was something that Elizabeth simply would not countenance. She took the unyielding view that only by keeping the weakling Duke of Windsor and his unprincipled Duchess at arm's length could the integrity of the Royal Family be preserved. It was an uncompromising position but probably the right one, given the circumstances.

When Edward VII was on the throne he was more or less at liberty to enjoy himself as he saw fit, with barely a glance in the direction of popular opinion. The country had undergone a series of radical changes since then, however, not least in the area of public expectation. In 1886, the year Elizabeth's second oldest brother, John, was born, Robert, the Marquis of Salisbury, became Prime Minister for the second time. He formed a government which contained another marquis, two dukes, an earl, a viscount, three barons, two baronets and his own youthful nephew, Arthur Balfour, who would succeed him in 1902 (hence the expression 'Bob's your uncle').

When the Yorks acquired Royal Lodge the Labour Party was in power. Instead of dealing with Old Etonians and old friends, the Royal Family found itself having to do State business with a Cabinet made up of one-time engine-drivers, foundry labourers and mill-hands under the premiership of a former 'starvling clerk', Ramsay MacDonald. On the whole George V got on well with his Socialist ministers but there was no doubting who was in charge: when the King suggested that the Duke of York should become Governor-General of Canada, James Thomas, Secretary of State for the Dominions and former engine-driver, vetoed the idea on the dubious grounds that the Canadians didn't like royalty.

There was no place in this brave new world for the courtly excess of old, and no amount of charm could conceal the dire defects in David's character. Probity was the watchword and dull George V had personified this quality. So did his second son and his homely wife. Together with their daughters they presented a pastel-coloured picture of cosy domesticity which, to eyes

ROYAL LODGE – THE
EXTENSIVE GARDENS
CREATED BY THE DUKE
AND DUCHESS OF YORK
IN THE 1930S.

sharpened by the all too human failings of future generations of
royals, looks far too good to be true. In a sense it was. Elizabeth
never appeared downstairs before eleven o'clock in the morning –
she used the early hours of the day to catch up on her telephone

calls in bed – and Bertie's fragile temper ensured that the couple had their share of rows. Taken as a whole, however, they succeeded very well in living up to the unblemished, family-centric image the public and press had foisted on them.

Royal Lodge was a part of that image. There the Yorks created a little country world glowing with sentimentality and security. It even contained a world within a world in the form of a thatched cottage named 'The Little Cottage' ('Y Bwthyn Bach'), which the people of Wales presented to Princess Elizabeth for her sixth birthday. Set in its own garden complete with its own sundial and built on a scale for children, it had a tiny oil painting of the Duchess over the mantelpiece, tiny sets of china and linen and a kitchen with every conceivable utensil made in miniature. It is there to this day, just as it was, just as almost everything is at Royal Lodge.

The gardens are kept as exactly as Elizabeth and her husband created them. It is the same story inside the house where, health permitting, she has spent 6 February, the anniversary of George's death, every year since that sad day. Elizabeth still sleeps downstairs in her pale pastel bedroom with the dogs on their foldaway beds with their green slip-covers in the dressing-room next door, just as she did when he was alive. When the Wyatville drawing-room was refurbished in the early Eighties while she was away in Scotland she returned to find everything – the colours, the placement of the furniture, including the two desks where she and her late husband had worked side by side – back as it was when she first fell in love with the house half a century before.

The sport, too, continues to be conducted along the lines established when George VI was alive. By taking up gardening the King and his Consort were sharing the classless interest of millions of their subjects. In their other pastimes, however, their tastes were traditionally aristocratic. Elizabeth's childhood had been accompanied by the sound of gunfire. So had Bertie's.

His father, George V, was regarded as one of the four finest shots in the land. It was an accolade earned through hard practice; his annual cartridge count added up to an astonishing 30,000 and he was known to down a thousand pheasants in a single day. George VI shared his enthusiasm. He first ventured out with a gun on the evening of 23 December 1907, aged twelve, armed with the single-barrelled muzzle-loader which had also first served for his father and his grandfather, Edward VII. 'I shot three rabbits,' he recorded in the game book which he would dutifully keep for the next forty-five years, writing in the details, of weather and wind and the number and type of game killed, in his own hand at the end of each day.

Bertie's début was at Sandringham, the Royal Family's 20,000-acre Norfolk estate, which he loved and made the focal point of his sporting year. He was not quite as single-minded as his father had been in the quest to shoot birds; the appetite for huge bags had passed by the time he inherited. 'The wildlife of today is not ours to dispose of as we please,' he explained. 'We have it in trust. We must account for it to those who come after.'

His interest in shooting nonetheless amounted almost to an obsession and, given its importance in his life, it was only to be expected that he devoted time, energy and a considerable sum of money to maintaining the shoot at Windsor. It was never of a comparable quality to Sandringham's and those who have shot there are unimpressed by the pheasants which fly at neither a height nor a speed likely to test the skill of the better marksmen. There is more to a shoot than the shooting, however. It provides a social focus, where good company and good food is deemed to be almost as important as the number and the quality of the birds, and Elizabeth's hospitality is seen as ample compensation for any inadequacy in the pheasants.

Veronica Maclean, the adventurer and wife of author Sir Fitzroy Maclean, remembers weekends at Royal Lodge as being 'invariably happy. Queen Elizabeth is an inspired hostess, and as we are nearly always the same group of old friends, our company is very relaxed. There is walking and talking (occasionally shouting), swimming and sleeping, eating and feasting – and yes, singing.

'Our royal hostess is tireless: there are practically no visible signs that Queen Elizabeth's years have in any way diminished her, or have dimmed her enormous capacity for having and making what she calls "fun", but which is nearer to what philosophers might call enthusiasm, or pure happiness.'

A weekend house party at Royal Lodge is like stepping back in through the years. Guests are asked to be there on Friday evening in time to change for the first formal black-tie dinner of the weekend, and as soon as they arrive their cases are carried upstairs by a footman and everything is carefully unpacked. Each guest-bedroom has the name of its occupant typewritten on card and slipped into a brass slot on the door. The bedrooms are simple and have the air of faded, faintly distressed elegance much sought after at present by people wishing to create a certain type of fashionable interior. The larger ones have a dressing-room with a smaller bed for the husband to sleep in if he so chooses, as is the old-fashioned way. Each room has its own supply of Alka-Seltzer on the bedside table, alongside a jar of biscuits and a glass decanter of water.

In the morning a footman wakes the guests from their slumbers between cheerful yellow cotton sheets, not by knocking at the door, but by opening the curtains before slipping away to draw the bath. Few of the rooms have the luxury of an *en suite* bathroom. Instead guests must share a corridor bathroom. An assortment of cotton and linen and cotton towelling in a variety of sizes is laid out over a chrome heated towel-rail. The baths are large and old-fashioned with chrome taps and huge plugs. Dusting powder with a puff is provided, and by the lavatory is a small mahogany box holding about eighty sheets of old-fashioned stiff Bronco loo paper.

Happily soft paper is also available: it is a rule of economic thumb amongst the British aristocracy that as a great country house declines the writing-paper gets thinner and the loo paper gets thicker. That does not apply at Royal Lodge where the writ-

THE MAIN DRAWING ROOM AT ROYAL LODGE WHERE THE QUEEN MOTHER'S GUESTS ASSEMBLE FOR DRINKS BEFORE AND AFTER DINNER.
BELOW:
THE QUEEN MOTHER'S DESK OVERLOOKING THE TERRACE.

ing paper is very thick indeed and carries the name of the local railway station with a small picture of a train. There is a separate card with the train times printed on it. Another card, typewritten, gives the hours at which staff collect post from the silver salver left in the hall for that purpose.

Neither the Queen Mother nor Princess Margaret ever appear for breakfast and it is considered correct form for the female guests to have their breakfast in bed, having made the choice of what they want to eat the night before. It is brought to them by a footman carrying what is known in royal circles as a calling tray. For the men who are shooting, breakfast is downstairs in the dining-room at eight-thirty a.m., where they help themselves to a full English breakfast from a hotplate.

Shooting on the royal estates remains essentially a male preserve and, once the men have departed, the women are left to get up at their own leisurely pace in time to be collected by the chauffeur who takes them out to join the shoot for 'elevenses' – coffee, fruit cake and a nip of home-made sloe gin.

After the three or four morning drives, in which the beaters raise the birds and drive them towards the guns, the party repairs for lunch to one of the village halls in the centre of the park. Single-storeyed and built of wood, each has a stage at one end; down the centre of the room the long trestle-tables covered with linen cloths are properly laid up with 'number two' silver and plain white shooting china which dates back to the First World War. These plates will have been pre-heated at the house and wrapped in blankets to keep them warm while they are transported by footmen wearing the traditional navy blue livery with the Queen Mother's cipher in red on the collar.

The idea of a full, formal, hot shooting lunch was introduced by Prince Albert who, when surveying the cold food which had hitherto been served in England, complained to Queen Victoria: 'Heaven defend my stomach.' Building on his example, shooting lunches became increasingly ostentatious until, by the reign of George V, a guest counted ten liveried servants – half in dark blue with gold buttons, the others in red, waiting on a party of eight.

Such extravagance would be out of keeping in the comparatively suburban environs of Windsor, but there is still a decidedly courtly style to the shooting lunches held in the Great Park.

The Queen Mother, Princess Margaret and sometimes the Queen will have arrived ahead of the shooting party. The Queen Mother, distinctive in her delphinium blue coat and blue tweed suit, felt hat with a jaunty feather clasped by a silver buckle on the band and triple string of pearls around her neck, is the only lady apart from Princess Margaret not to be wearing the traditional green and brown shooting clothes.

Once inside the warmth of the hut, guests change from their shooting boots to casual shoes and the atmosphere is one of a small cocktail party. There is a choice of drinks on offer and footmen pass around hot sausages served on a plate with a pot of mustard. It is not a time to linger, however. Shooting is dictated by the availability of light, and promptly at one o'clock the guns and their accompanying ladies sit down to a luncheon of Irish stew, steak and kidney pudding or *poulet au riz*, kept in silver dishes which are enclosed in padded containers. There is also a choice of cold collations of meat, poultry and salad, followed by hot mince pies, treacle tart and large selection of cheeses to accompany liqueurs. There is no formal placement, although Princess Margaret usually manages to seat herself next to the best-looking man.

After lunch, the Queen Mother leads everyone outside the hut for a group photograph before they decamp into their various Land Rovers for the afternoon drives. On a fine autumn afternoon she might stand with one of the guns for a drive before returning to the house, leaving the Queen working with her gun dogs, using a whistle to instil total discipline as they retrieve the birds. One young house guest recalls turning slightly to get a bird and being taken aback to find the Queen standing directly behind him, ready to start picking up.

After two or three more drives, it is time to return for tea in Royal Lodge's Chinese Room. It is nowhere near as formal as the Sandringham shooting teas hosted by King George V, who adamantly maintained the strictest of sartorial standards. The King would change after shooting into a specially designed velvet or tartan suit and expect his guests to be equally elegantly attired. On one occasion his eldest son appeared in his outdoor clothes and was immediately reprimanded by his father, who refused to listen to his excuse of having to attend to a sick dog in the kennels.

The Queen Mother does insist on a certain Edwardian formality, however. Muddy boots are pulled off and left in the back porch and there is just time for a quick dash upstairs to change – a 'sensible skirt' for the girls and cords and sweaters for the men, who are expected still to be wearing their shooting shirt and tie.

Again there is no formal seating plan. 'Everyone sits wherever they can and it is all very relaxed with corgis running around under the table foraging for titbits and everyone talking at once,' says one regular guest.

Once tea is over the Queen Mother retires to her room and her drinks tray is taken to her while she changes for dinner. For the rest of the house party there is time for a game of snooker or a brief glance at the newspapers which are spread out in the traditional 'Sandringham fan' in the drawing-room, before heading upstairs for a bath and another change of clothes.

Dinner attire is always formal black tie or velvet smoking-jackets for the men and long dresses for the women. Nothing is ever spelt out but a silent dress code is adhered to and, although it would never be mentioned, black dresses are frowned upon as they are reserved for mourning.

By eight o'clock everyone is assembled in the main salon for pre-dinner drinks served by a footman from the silver 'grog tray'. This drawing-room, which occupies much of the ground floor, is painted pale green with the gothic mouldings picked out in white. It is not the large stone fireplace which is the centre of the room, but the large gothic windows which lead out on to Jellicoe's terrace and the garden beyond. The seamless union of house and garden is heightened by the profusion of potted plants and flowers arranged around the room. Family photographs proliferate as do books which are piled on chairs, tables and the floor. An old-fashioned gramophone plays favourites such as songs by Frank Sinatra, and all the weekend gifts are displayed on the grand piano or on a table nearby.

This ritual of the presents is carefully adhered to and, when the giver returns, the gift is placed in a conspicuous position. One guest who had presented Elizabeth with an etching of Glamis Castle was duly flattered, as it was intended she should be, to see it prominently on show on her second visit.

When their hostess finally enters the room, the ladies curtsey and the men bow their heads. A few minutes' chat ensues, with the Queen Mother exercising her talent of putting her guests at their ease by the simple expedient of asking them about themselves and listening to what they say. Then, after ten minutes or so, a footman comes in to announce, 'dinner is served.' The Queen Mother leads the way into the dining-room, escorted by whomever she happened to be chatting to at the time.

In an increasingly utilitarian world, dinner with the Queen Mother is a reminder of a more gracious age. The table is always lit by candles held by as many as four silver candelabra, depending on the number of diners. The only other light in the room comes from the concealed strips which illuminate the pictures hung on the cream walls and the polished dining-table laid with silver, crystal and porcelain.

This time there is a formal placement, changed each night and organized by Princess Margaret or sometimes her son, Viscount

Linley, so as to ensure that the Queen Mother has amusing company either side of her. Place cards with the name of each guest are slipped into a mahogany wooden board so that everyone can see where they are sitting. The Queen Mother sits at the head of the table in her special chair, a fine carver with arms. She has a footstool placed underneath and her own silver bucket, full of ice, is on the table beside her to cool her half-bottle of champagne. She is almost invariably the only person at the table drinking champagne, but the other guests do not go thirsty – the wines are excellent and dispensed liberally.

Manners dictate that she chats to the guest on her left for the first two courses and then turns to the person on her right. Others follow her example,

ABOVE: DRESS AND COAT OF SILK CHIFFON PRINTED IN A SWIRLING DESIGN, 1970. THE BODICE AND WAIST OF THE DRESS ARE SOFTLY DRAPED IN CROSS-OVER PANELS. WORN WITH A HAT OF POINTED CHIFFON PETALS BY SIMONE MIRMAN FOR HER BIRTHDAY IN 1970, AND SEEN HERE WITH HER GRANDCHILDREN, PRINCE EDWARD, LADY SARAH ARMSTRONG-JONES AND VISCOUNT LINLEY.

watching carefully to see when she makes the change. The conversation around the table is lively, although heated discussions are politely avoided and any embarrassing moments studiously ignored. One young guest remembers being startled as a footman dropped a spoon down the back of her dress while serving her the vegetables. As she was pondering on how to handle this tricky and uncomfortable situation, she felt the young footman's hand sliding down her back to retrieve the spoon. She glanced at her dinner companions, but no-one appeared to have noticed so she carried on with her conversation as if nothing had happened.

THE QUEEN MOTHER AT ASCOT IN 1968, WEARING A MATCHING DRESS AND COAT BY NORMAN HARTNELL AND A PINK NET HAT WITH WHITE DOTS BY FRENCH MILLINER SIMONE MIRMAN (DETAIL BELOW), WHO SET UP BUSINESS IN LONDON IN 1947.

As at all Elizabeth's homes, the food is excellent. The vegetables are always fresh from the garden or the Windsor greenhouses. Unlike the Queen, the Queen Mother sees her chef every day, who brings her the menu book. Having grown up at a time when it was only possible to eat food when it was in season, she enjoys choosing things that are expensive or out of season, saying, 'Oh just a little treat!'

Dinner invariably includes a small starter followed by a light fish mousse, and then meat or game which the Queen Mother does not like to be too 'high'. Salad on separate plates is always served with the main course, and used by the Queen Mother, as by all the Royal Family as a prop. Having a small appetite herself, she is conscious that not everyone eats at the same speed. If one of her guests is slow, she keeps a fork in her hand and toys with her salad until the moment is right to ring for the staff to come and clear.

For the third course there is either a sweet or a savoury soufflé, special favourites being a mild kipper soufflé or a *crème brûlee*. Cheese is never served with dinner.

Towards the end of the meal, when people are slightly flushed, the Queen Mother or Princess Margaret will raise their glass and make a series of toasts such as – before the last election – 'Up John Major – down Tony Blair' and everyone cheers or boos. Depending on the amount that has been drunk, these toasts become more and more extreme, with each guest taking it in turn to think one up.

Before matters get too out of hand, the ladies leave the room after dinner to 'powder their noses', as going to the lavatory is euphemistically called even in royal circles, taking it in turn to use Princess Margaret's loo, which is on the ground floor, and making sure the Queen Mother is not left alone in the drawing-room.

The men, meanwhile, remain in the dining-room, passing the decanter around to the left as custom demands, but never lingering too long over their port before joining the ladies for what the Queen Mother calls 'fun'. Any guest who can play the piano is always prized, and everyone gathers round to unite in such songs as 'Land of Hope and Glory' and 'She'll be Coming Round the Mountain When She Comes'. Sometimes a game of charades is played, and if anyone feels like dancing the gramophone is switched on.

The Queen Mother will often stay up quite late, although in her later years it was Princess Margaret who led the revels into the early hours. (It is considered rude for younger guests to sneak off to bed before the Princess, and anyone who does so is unlikely to be asked again.)

On Sundays everyone has to be ready for church at 11 a.m., so there is little time for a lie-in. After breakfast in bed, guests drive or walk the few minutes to the church. Clothes are Sunday best – frocks for the ladies, flannels for the men – and the guests often join the Queen Mother in her special 'box' high in the sanctuary of the Victorian chapel, which was built by Queen Victoria as a memorial to her children.

After church the guests return to Royal Lodge, where they are joined by the vicar and his wife and a few notable neighbours – often including the Queen – for a glass of pre-luncheon sherry. All the ladies wear hats in church. The Queen Mother continues to wear hers at lunch, where a traditional roast is always served.

Unlike the Queen, whose house parties come to an end after lunch, the Queen Mother likes her guests to stay on. Weather permitting, this is the moment to inspect her garden. One of her pleasures is to see young people enjoying themselves, and she once cheered along an entire house party as they danced around the little Welsh cottage in front of her.

It is then time to sign the large, leather-bound visitors' book in the drawing-room. It is considered *infra dig* to write anything in this book other than your name and the dates of your stay, though the Queen Mother is charmed if her guests can place a small photograph of themselves by their signature.

Behind the scenes the staff have been hard at work. While the guests were at church the maids will have packed their clothes and checked to make sure that nothing has been left behind. Everything will have been laundered and packed in tissue paper – one guest recalls her embarrassment when she discovered her favourite old teddy bear, who always accompanied her, lying on top of her clothes in royal grandeur in a sea of tissue paper. The men's guns will have been cleaned for them and a brace of birds, boxed for travelling, will have been added to the luggage. As a final touch the car will have been cleaned and the suitcases packed neatly in the back.

The Queen Mother always comes to see her guests off, politely saying, 'Do you have to leave so soon?' and, 'So looking forward to seeing you again'. The guests respond in kind with a formal but hopefully entertaining 'bread-and-butter' thank-you letter. Those who have amused her will usually be invited again to step back through the looking glass into the private world of our last Queen- Empress.

CHAPTER 8

ℐNFLUENCE ABROAD

On 10 December 1936, Edward VIII had abdicated and handed the throne and its burdens to his brother, Bertie, who was duly crowned on 12 May the following year. The Coronation had been a masterly exercise in pomp and ceremony, specifically designed to paper over the fissures in public confidence in the Royal Family which Edward VIII's flight had caused.

On the prompting of the Archbishop of Canterbury, Dr Cosmo Lang, the thousand-year-old ceremony was subtly revised so as to emphasise the link between the Crown and the Church of England, thereby re-establishing the position of the Sovereign, as the constitution expert Walter Bagehot put, as 'head of our morality'. The Bishop of Winchester and future Archbishop of York observed: 'Throughout the service the Archbishop (of Canterbury) blessing and exhorting the King is also hallowing the State.'

To ensure the public's involvement, the BBC was permitted to broadcast the ceremony live on radio and twelve tons of equipment and 472 miles of cable were installed in Westminster Abbey. Millions listened in while hundreds of thousands more chose to line the route to see the two-mile-long procession which took forty minutes to pass any given point.

For the leading players in this great Imperial pageant and for the King in particular who admitted to 'a sinking feeling inside', it was an occasion for reflection and on the night of 11 May Dr Lang visited the royal couple at Buckingham Palace to lend his spiritual support, They three knelt together and prayed for 'their realm and Empire'. 'I was much moved and so were they,' Dr Lang noted. 'Indeed there were tears in their eyes when we rose from our knees.'

For all its solemnity, the ceremony itself was not without its lighter moments. The Lord Great Chamberlain hands so shook with nerves that the King had to fasten his own belt and sword. Due to a muddle between the Dean of the Abbey and Dr Lang, who kept 'jiggling' with it, the 7 lb crown was put on the King's head the wrong way round. And one of the bishops stood on the King's robes as he tried to make his way down from the Coronation chair. 'I had to tell him to get off pretty sharply as I nearly fell down,' the King recorded.

The Princess Elizabeth and Margaret-Rose were excited but well-behaved, except for the moment when Margaret started playing with her prayer book and had to be nudged to behave by her older sister.

Elizabeth, weighed down by a velvet train several yards long supported by six trainbearers, sailed through it all with aplomb. Chips Channon recorded in his diary: 'She appeared, dignified but smiling and much more bosomy ... my thoughts travelled back to the old days when I called her "Elizabeth" and was a little in love with her.'

The whole occasion was generally deemed a great success which had more than fulfilled its purpose of drawing the country together after the shock of the Abdication. Events beyond Britain's shores were not so easily stage managed, however, and there was no disguising the new King's distress as he saw the direction Europe was drifting.

He and his wife, fervently believing in peace, gave their full support to their Prime Minister Neville Chamberlain's self-deluding efforts to preserve it. He was confused and frightened and would sit late into every night anxiously studying the contents of his dispatch-boxes, taxing his limited stamina by worrying about what to do, what action if any to take.

The new Queen, in her own phlegmatic way, was also deeply concerned. She had lost a brother in the Great War. Two others had been wounded. She had seen, while nursing the servicemen who had come to Glamis to convalesce, how modern warfare can wreck men's bodies and souls.

But it was too late now for appeasement. Idealism and goodwill were being knocked aside as Europe, a truck without brakes, rolled down the political incline towards the abyss of war. All across the continent the steel foundries and machine factories were starting to churn out, not the ploughshares of the peace promised by the 1914-18 war to end all wars, but the murderous weaponry needed for a further conflict.

And as the armaments emerged from the factories and foundries, so the new Queen began to equip herself for what lay ahead. The transformation of the motherly homemaker into a Queen-Empress would cost a great deal of money and at a time of hunger marches and mass unemployment on an unprecedented scale, it smacks now of ill-considered extravagance. But no-one complained, at least not very loudly; each age has its own sense of priorities and proprieties. And besides, Elizabeth chose her weapons well, brilliantly in fact. Always aware of the power of appearances, she set about dressing for the part, and her clothes proved themselves even more effective than she could ever have anticipated when she first picked them out from the designs offered to her.

She had always protested that she was terrified of becoming Queen and she was probably telling the truth. Her husband did not want the job and her daughters had not wanted to leave the domestic comfort of 145 Piccadilly for the draughty coldness of Buckingham Palace. Elizabeth had soon settled into her role, though, as the Duchess of Windsor was quick to notice.

Shortly after the Coronation Wallis, who could not yet bring herself to refer to her sister-in-law as Queen, wrote to her husband: 'Really David, the pleased expression on the Duchess of York's face is funny to see. How she is loving it all.'

Up until then Elizabeth had played a part of her own making. She was a Duchess in her own chiffon-swathed, tweed-lined fairyland, looking after her daughters, supporting her husband, dispensing smiles and platitudes and basking in the pleasant glow of the deferential and, for the most part, unquestioning adoration that was still royalty's prerogative.

Through the irresponsibility of her brother-in-law in exile across the water, however, a greater role was now being thrust upon her. Britain, under-armed and isolated, was in desperate need of allies and it was beholden to the King and, more especially, his Queen, to venture out into the international arena and revive the mildewed friendships and alliances the politicians had for so long neglected. And, to fulfil such obligations, Elizabeth had to be equipped and properly kitted out.

Charm she already had. It had always been a component of her arsenal, and it was to prove vital as she set about her task of wooing the support of people who had no natural affection either for her country or for the institution of which she was now the leading representative. She had already had the opportunity of employing her charm on the French, with telling effect.

In 1931 the Yorks were in Paris to open a British Week. At a trade exhibition the Duchess was seated next to the old colonial administrator, Marshal Lyautey, who was in less than jovial humour. The Duchess suddenly asked, 'Monsieur le Maréchal, you are so powerful. You have created the beautiful country of Morocco and you have made this fine exhibition. Would you do something for me?'

'What can I do for Your Royal Highness?' the marshal enquired.

'Why, this,' the Duchess replied. 'The sun is in my eyes. Will you make it disappear?'

Bang on cue, the sun vanished behind a cloud. The Duchess feigned wide-eyed surprise. It was a trick, of course – the Duchess later confided that she had seen the cloud approaching – but it worked: the Marshal was suitably charmed. As her friend Lady Cynthia Asquith noted, she never looked bewildered, but frequently managed to look surprised, which, when one takes into account the tedious, stupefying, repetitive similarity of most of her duties, was a priceless knack.

It was going to be harder to impress the French this time round, however, and it was in Paris that the increasingly jittery

Chamberlain government had decreed the Queen was to open her campaign. This was a full-blown State visit and, in a city which conducted most of its daily business in the public theatre of its markets and pavements, theatres, cafés and restaurants, first impressions were going to count for a great deal. That meant clothes. And clothes had never been Elizabeth's strongest point.

She had not compared well with the elegance of That Woman, the detested Wallis Simpson who was now her sister-in-law by marriage, and, with the exception of those cloche hats which had become the vogue after her visit to Australia, she had never succeeded in setting a fashion. Just keeping up with it had proved hard enough; she was a country lady and, as Kenneth (later Lord) Clark noted, she dressed the part – i.e. poorly. That had proved no handicap at the Court she had married into, where anything and anyone too à la mode was regarded with suspicion.

Clothes have always been an integral part of royal display. They stand at the very heart of royalty itself. Queen Victoria had recognized this when she wrote to her son, the future Edward VII, when he was only ten years old: 'Dress is a trifling matter which might not be raised to too much importance in our own eyes. But it gives also the one outward sign from which people in general can and often do judge upon the <u>inward</u> state of mind and feeling of a person; for this they all see, while the other they cannot see. On that account it is of some importance particularly in persons of high rank.'

It was a maxim Victoria's grandson George V placed great store by (as of course did his own son, the Duke of Windsor – often to the point of sartorial absurdity). The trouble was that to George's blinkered eyes the only clothes that were acceptable were the ones he had known as a young man.

That was problem enough for his sons. Men's clothes have changed little in their fundamentals since the end of the First World War, and the changes that have taken place were more a matter of the reinterpretation of a basic theme than any radical redesign. To George V, however, any variation was considered an inexcusable vanity. The Duke of Windsor recalled: 'With my father, it was not so much a discussion as to who he considered to be well or badly dressed; it was more usually a diatribe against anyone who dressed differently from himself. Those who did he called "cads". Unfortunately the "cads" were the majority of my generation, by the time I grew up, and I was, of course, one of them.'

For the royal womenfolk it was a fashion nightmare. They were hobbled by the King's attitude: in the case of his wife, Queen Mary, quite literally. George V believed that women should dress as they did when they were first married; and that any change was tantamount to infidelity. His poor wife was therefore condemned to spend her life corseted, physically and mentally, in floor-length Edwardian dress. Her friend Mabell, Countess of Airlie, recalled: 'She never even wore a colour he did not like. Her style of dressing was dictated by his conservative prejudices.'

According to Lady Airlie, who was one of the very few to have seen them, the Queen had 'perfect' legs and once, in the 1920s when skirt lengths had risen to the knee, she tentatively suggested shortening her own by a modest two or three inches. Lady Airlie volunteered to be the guinea-pig but such was the ferocity of the King's reaction that the project had to be abandoned.

Nail varnish was predictably frowned upon. When Princess Marina, who was to save George, Duke of Kent, from himself by marrying him, first arrived at Buckingham Palace in 1934 Queen Mary took one look at her blood-red talons and coldly observed: 'I'm afraid the King does not like painted nails. Can you do something about it?'

Marina, more royal in her own right than any Teck and imbued with the confidence that her status bestowed, replied: 'Your George may not. But mine does.'

It was not the kind of remark Elizabeth, always the team player and dutiful daughter-in-law, would ever have made. She disapproved of Marina and her flighty ways. For her trip to the French capital in 1938, however, the Queen had no sensible alternative but to take a leaf out of Marina's style book and dress herself up accordingly.

Had the task fallen to the ever-chic sister-in-law, she would doubtless have turned to Paris itself to provide her with her wardrobe. The city, then as now, was the world centre for women's fashion, while London was a mere provincial outpost (the great Spanish couturier Balenciaga had considered setting up in London after leaving his homeland, only to think better of it and establish himself in Paris where the British connection was confined to his address: Number 10, Avenue George V).

Elizabeth, the mistress of keeping up appearances, preferred to follow the example set by Queen Victoria, who had made an ostentatious point of only buying goods made in Britain or its Empire. There was, however, an element of deception in that when it came to her clothes. Victoria did indeed order these from a London dress-maker. The actual making, though, was the responsibility of John Frederick Worth, the top Parisian couturier of the day. The Queen's measurements and details were sent to him in Paris where he had clothes made up. The finished garments were then dispatched to London where the court dress-maker would cut out Worth's labels before delivering them to the Queen.

The Lincolnshire-born Worth was happy enough to go along with the deceit. Victoria rarely wore a dress more than once, which meant that his workshops were kept in steady and highly profitable employment. The fact that most of Victoria's dresses were copies of ones she had already had only increased the financial attraction.

Such a deception would have been impossible by the 1930s. The photographs and sketches that appeared in the newspapers and the proliferation of magazines devoted to the subject had brought fashion, and the intricacies of the different French fashion houses in particular, to a mass audience. If the new Queen was to make a favourable impression, she would have to do so with imagination and flair. It was a daunting assignment, but one the brash young designer she chose had no hesitation about confronting. Quite the contrary: Norman Hartnell regarded royal patronage as a necessary career move and had actively sought it.

Born in London into a solidly middle-class family in 1901, the original plan was that he should become an architect. But he had always been fond of drawing dresses. 'I was a sickly child, forced to remain in bed for long periods,' he explained. To allay the boredom, he was given crayons, then a box of watercolour paints. When he went up to Cambridge he joined the Footlights Revue and put his skills with the paint-box to use designing the costumes for a production of *The Bedder's Opera* (Bedder is the Cambridge name for a college servant). A one-off production of the show in

London earned him a mention in the *Evening Standard*. So encouraged, he decided on a career in dress design and dropped out of university.

There followed a picaresque series of setbacks and rejections. Hartnell had one set of designs stolen by Lady Duff Gordon (who traded under the name of Lucille), sued and was awarded £50. He was fired from one job and failed to get the commission to design the uniforms for the lift girls at Selfridges.

Finally, in 1923, unable to find employment with any of the established fashion houses, he sank the £300 he had inherited from his mother and, equipped with a paint-box and 'the enthusiasm of ignorance', he opened his own *maison de couture* in Bruton Street off Mayfair, declaring 'I despise simplicity, it is the negation of all that is beautiful.' His father paid the first year's rent.

Hartnell lived where he worked. When he complained that he wanted rooms of his own 'in, say, St James's,' his father replied, 'My boy, it is better to live over your business than over your income.'

In 1924 he held his first show which was well received. 'I think there is not a good word to be said for the shortskirt fashion,' he haughtily declared. 'Ankle-length dresses are delightfully graceful but they certainly should not be shorter.'

Slowly but surely he built up his client list and Daphne Vivian chose a Hartnell dress decorated with silver and gold lilies for her wedding to the future Marquess of Bath. Business, however, refused to thrive at the rate he wanted. The French ruled the fashion roost and, as Hartnell drily observed: 'I suffered from the unforgivable disadvantage of being English in England.'

But Hartnell was nothing if not a pushy young man with a brazenness to match his talent. In 1927 he brashly went to Paris to show his collection. When that failed to generate the business he was looking for he tried again and, despite the sneers of his French counterparts, walked away with the season's plaudits.

There would be the occasional *faux pas*, as on the occasion when he dressed the actresses Evelyn Laye and Bebe Daniels in the same lemon yellow ball-gown for the same ball and was greeted the following morning by two telegrams, one from Laye which read, 'I hate you and I hate Bebe Daniels. Close my account at once'; the other from Daniels which said, 'I hate you and I hate Evelyn Laye. Close my account at once.' By 1934, however, Hartnell was the dominant force in London fashion. His business, which would eventually employ 385 staff, had started making what he called 'considerable financial profit' and he was able to move out of his cramped premises and into a grand Georgian house a few important doors further along Bruton Street. His client list included many of the society beauties of the day and, despite the hiccup over those lemon yellow ball-gowns, many of the leading actresses.

It was now time for Hartnell to raise his game and take the next step up the social ladder of his success. As he noted, 'everything revolved around the Courts' and it was on the Court that he set the sights of his prodigious ambition. And, as always, he was not shy about pushing himself forward.

In the autumn of 1935 George V's third surviving son, the Duke of Gloucester, became engaged to the Duke of Buccleuch's daughter, Lady Alice Montagu-Douglas-Scott. Hartnell, encouraged he said, by the 'romantic flavour of the betrothal' wrote to Lady Alice 'asking if I might be permitted to submit some ideas for her wedding dress'.

Once again his audacity was rewarded. He was commissioned to design the dress. It was to be, Lady Alice commanded, 'of a strict simplicity', which must have hurt. He nonetheless followed her instructions. Nor did he have any compunction, when it came to designing the outfits for the bridesmaids, in adhering to the instruction of King George V that 'the little ones should wear girlish dresses'. So their frocks were made short.

Hartnell's willingness to tailor his designs to suit his royal clients met with their approval. The bridesmaids included the Duke and Duchess of York's two daughters, the Princesses Elizabeth and Margaret Rose.

King George V died on Monday 20 January 1936, put to eternal sleep a few minutes before midnight by a lethal injection of cocaine and morphine into his jugular administered by his doctor Lord Dawson. The timing was such that the formal announcement could be made, in the proper manner, in the following morning's *Times*.

The Duchess of York was most upset by his death and wrote, 'Unlike his own children, I was never afraid of him, and in all the twelve years of having me as a daughter-in-law he never spoke one unkind or abrupt word to me.'

It was sadness leavened with relief, in one respect at least. Freed from the icy grip of his displeasure, the ladies of the Court were able, for the first time in a quarter of a century, to dress as fashion and good taste decreed. Even Queen Mary emerged, if only gingerly, from out of the louring shadow he had cast. Her sister-in-law, Princess Alice, remarked how 'she blossomed out once more', to the extent of daringly ordering three dresses from Hartnell – and paying for them, too.

DRESSES DESIGNED BY HARTNELL FOR PRINCESS ELIZABETH AND PRINCESS MARGARET ROSE, WORN AT THE MARRIAGE OF THEIR UNCLE, H.R.H. THE DUKE OF GLOUCESTER TO LADY ALICE MONTAGU-DOUGLAS-SCOTT.

Queen Mary was so notorious for taking things and not paying for them that Bond Street store-owners shut up shop when they heard she was in the vicinity. Hartnell was more fortunate. He had wanted to charge 35 guineas per dress, but then decided to drop the price to 25 guineas. While he was wavering he received a telephone call from a lady-in-waiting who informed him; 'Her Majesty approves of all the three sketches you sent – but I am commanded to inform you that your estimate of 25 guineas for the blue embroidered dress does not meet with the Queen's approval.'

It was a familiar cry which usually ended in the tradesman's tears. But, as Hartnell started to protest, the lady-in-waiting interrupted to say: 'Her Majesty desires me to say that the price of 25 guineas for the dress is much too little. Her Majesty desires to pay 45 guineas for the dress, and the same amount for the other dresses.'

149

Hartnell rightly took such rare generosity as a singular sign of royal approval. It was not with the old Queen that his future lay, however, but with the new one.

As Duchess of York, Elizabeth had had her clothes made by the safe and conservative Madame Handley Seymour and it was she who was entrusted with designing the Coronation dress. But this was a new reign and George VI was determined to put his own mark on his own Court. And, as always, he looked to his wife to set the pace.

He was never as flamboyant as his elder brother but like all the Windsor men, George VI took a detailed interest in clothes and would spend long hours being fitted for his suits. These were beautifully tailored for him by Benson and Clegg in the Savile Row area of London's West End.

He was just as interested in women's fashion. As a boy he had been fascinated by the clothes his mother wore for receptions and balls, and would sit entranced as he watched her make the final adjustments to her toilette. He had taken it upon himself to advise on the dresses worn by the train-bearers at the Coronation. Now he was most anxious that his wife should dress in a manner befitting the role he foresaw for her.

That presented one substantial problem. Elizabeth had never been notably slim, and a healthy appetite and two children had not been kind to her figure. Indeed, her weight had burgeoned to the point where rumours had started to circulate that she was again pregnant.

No concerted action had been taken to halt the advance of inches. 'At the time the average woman never thought of dieting,' Hartnell would recall. 'Gladys Cooper was the first woman of whom I heard it said that she had subjected herself to a diet in order to stay slim.'

Cooper relied on a diet of milk and potatoes two days a week to keep herself in check. The Queen preferred the more appetizing alternative of Hartnell's dressmaking skills. By way of a taster, she had invited him to make her a number of black dresses for the period of Court mourning for George V. She had then asked him to design the dresses for the Queen's Coronation maids of honour. The following year he designed Elizabeth's dresses for visits to Britain of the kings of Belgium and Rumania.

At last, in 1938, it was time for the main course – and what a banquet it proved to be. Hartnell was summoned to Buckingham Palace. 'The Queen told me of the coming State visit to France, the first big event of the new reign, and I was asked to make Her Majesty's dresses.' He had reached the pinnacle of his profession and he knew it. 'I came away from the Palace that morning in a mood of exultation,' he glowed.

The tour would only last four days but the Queen would be on display from 'morning to midnight'. Thirty dresses were therefore required and Hartnell was determined that she should stand out in the capital of couture – and to hell with the cost. Money was not a subject for discussion between the designer (known as Normie to his friends, but always as Mr Hartnell and later, Sir Norman, to the Queen) and his clients.

The King did not, as far as we know, ever query his accounts – or question his wife's extravagance. He did pay close attention to the finished result, though. He had definite ideas about how he wanted his wife to look and had made quite certain that Hartnell knew exactly what he had in mind. He invited the designer to Buckingham Palace, and led him to one of the picture galleries and then on into the State Apartments. There he showed him the paintings by Franz Xavier Winterhalter of Empress Eugénie of France and the beautiful but unstable Empress Elisabeth of Austria.

'His Majesty made it clear in his quiet way that I should attempt to capture this picturesque grace in the dresses I was to design for the Queen,' Hartnell recalled.

Even as the clothes were being readied for their final fitting, however, all the colour was washed out of them by the death of the Queen's mother, Lady Strathmore, at the age of seventy-five.

Elizabeth was distraught. She wrote to Neville Chamberlain: 'I have been dreading this moment ever since I was a little child and now that it has come, one can hardly believe it. She was a true Rock of Defence for us, her children, & Thank God her influence and wonderful example will remain with us all our lives... We all used to laugh together and have such fun.'

In ordinary circumstances the tour would have been cancelled. But the circumstances were anything but ordinary, and instead the visit was merely postponed for a month. It was barely long enough for the Queen to come to terms with her grief. It did,

THEIR MAJESTIES
KING GEORGE VI AND
QUEEN ELIZABETH AT
BAGATELLE DURING
THEIR STATE VISIT TO
PARIS, JULY 1938.

though, give Hartnell just enough time to remake many outfits
needed for the tour.

By tradition black is the colour of mourning. Hartnell, however, did not believe black suitable. 'Could she possibly visit the
gay city of Paris in mid summer and for such a festive occasion,
dressed in deep mourning,' he pondered. 'As a nation the French
might have a taste for heavy and excessive black, but would they
appreciate it on an occasion designed as happy evidence of an
entente in an already troubled Europe?'

The answer to that rhetorical question was a resounding *Non*.
Instead he decided to remake everything in bridal white which
had been an alternative colour of mourning since 1862, when
Queen Victoria's daughter, Princess Alice, had married Prince
Louis of Hesse seven months after the death of her father the
Prince Consort.

'From a dressmaker's point of view white is much easier to handle, as there is no matching material required and no special dyeing to cause delay,' Hartnell observed. With only a fortnight to get the work done it was still an enormous job, but complete it he did and when the King and Queen crossed the Channel aboard the First Lord of Admiralty's yacht, *Enchantress*, the Queen's thirty dresses went with them.

But if Hartnell were filled with anticipation, the King was in an altogether more circumspect mood.

HARTNELL'S SKETCH AND (INSET) THE DRESS WORN FOR THE GARDEN PARTY AT BAGATELLE ON THE STATE VISIT TO FRANCE, JULY 1938. DESCRIBED BY HARTNELL AS 'OF THE FINEST COBWEB LACE AND TULLE'.

He was, according to one contemporary, 'rather preoccupied', a polite way of saying worried. He had cause for concern. The mission was one of great importance. Thirty-four years earlier his grandfather, Edward VII, had personally sealed the Entente Cordiale which allied Britain and France. Now it was his job to reconfirm it and, as always happened when he was forced to shoulder royal responsibilities, he fell to questioning his abilities.

He was not alone in this. The new French premier, Edouard Daladier, had visited Windsor Castle in April and had formed the none too private opinion that the King was 'a moron'. Nor had he succumbed to the Queen's charm. A more sceptical man than old Marshal Lyautey, Daladier described her as 'an excessively ambitious woman who would be ready to sacrifice every other country in the world in order that she might remain Queen of England'.

Compounding these problems was the very real security risk. The last royal visit to Paris, of King Alexander of Yugoslavia in 1934, had ended in that unfortunate monarch's assassination. Now two groups of Spanish anarchists, one bearing the melodramatic name of the Dwarfs, were threatening to kill the King of England. There were also rumours of a plot by the Gestapo. In consequence Paris was a city under virtual siege when the King and Queen arrived on 19 July. The entire Parisian police force had been mobilized and supplemented by 9,000 reservists; 20,000 troops lined the royal route; the public was banned from the rooftops along the way. Even nature was guarded against; Lady Diana Cooper recorded that hefty men were delegated to lean against the trees 'lest they should fall on the procession'.

The Queen could see what was happening around her – she would have been blind not to have done – but she chose to ignore it. Instead she carried on, a regal actress on a sublime high,

SKETCH OF A DESIGN FOR A DRESS FOR ELIZABETH, WHILST STILL H.R.H. THE DUCHESS OF YORK.

1937

Specially designed for
HER MAJESTY THE QUEEN

Specially designed for
H. M. THE QUEEN.

SKETCHES OF DESIGNS
FIT FOR A QUEEN.
EVENING GOWNS FOR
FORMAL AND STATE
OCCASIONS ARE A
TRIUMPH OF REGAL
SPLENDOUR.
HARTNELL'S MASTERY
IN CREATING HEAVILY
EMBROIDERED AND
BEJEWELLED DESIGNS
MATCHED THE
PRICELESS JEWELS
WORN WITH THEM.

dipping her head very slightly, waving and smiling all the time at the crowds pressed ten deep against the barricade of gendarmes. Her audience was waiting, wanting, demanding to be captivated, and she played her role to perfection. The French newspapers screamed their approval. 'Today France is a Monarchy again,' one headline declared. 'We have taken the Queen to our hearts. She rules over two nations.'

Even those publications which could not bring themselves to abandon completely their hostility to England felt compelled to find a way of joining in the chorus of praise. The Queen, as *L'Illustration* reminded its readers, was descended from the royal house of Scotland which had given France the '*charmante* Mary Stuart'.

There was a magnificent luncheon at the Galerie des Glaces at Versailles where thirteen different wines, all bottled on the birthdays of kings or presidents, were served. Winston Churchill, no favourite of the King and Queen at this stage in his career, was on hand to witness the royal couple's arrival at the Opera 'and was like a schoolboy, he was so delighted', Lady Diana noted. A crowd of over 10,000 gathered to cheer them when they appeared on the balcony of the Foreign Ministry.

And everywhere the Queen went, people gasped at the splendour of her clothes. They were nothing short of spectacular. At Versailles she wore a spreading floor-length dress of white organdie. The one she wore for the evening reception at the Elysée Palace had a bodice and billowing skirt made out of 'hundreds of yards of narrow Valençiennes lace, sprinkled with silver'. For the Gala at the Opera, Hartnell recorded, she wore 'a spreading gown of thick white satin, the skirt draped with festoons of satin, held by clusters of white camellias. At the garden party at the Bagatelle she wore a dress of the finest white cobweb lace and tulle, that trailed on the green grass of the lawn.'

No Queen this century has ever made such an impression, and Elizabeth was thrilled. So, of course, was Hartnell. In his autobiography he quotes Christian Dior as saying: 'Whenever I try to think of something particularly beautiful I think always of those lovely dresses that Mr Hartnell made for your beautiful Queen when she visited Paris.'

For a while it even looked as if the visit might have achieved its political objectives. The King, in his speech at the Elysée Palace, had been at pains to emphasize that the 'friendship' between Britain and France was 'not directed at any other power'. No-one was fooled. The spectre of a resurgent Germany was looming ever larger and the Allies were at last being forced to respond with their own shows of brawn. In March Chamberlain had informed the House of Commons of the 'almost terrifying power' being created by Britain's rearmament programme, while the march past by 50,000 French troops the King had just witnessed had illustrated the might of the French arm of the Entente. It was an alliance of formidable military strength (on paper, at least) that was now arrayed against Hitler and his bellicose Axis partner Mussolini. For the next few months Europe settled into an uneasy peace, which Chamberlain in September declared to be permanent. Czechoslovakia was dismembered on the altar of appeasement and the Prime Minister returned from his meeting with Hitler in Munich to announce: 'I believe it is peace for our time.'

A CRINOLINE OF DRAPED WHITE SATIN, SILVER LACE AND CAMELLIAS DESIGNED BY HARTNELL AND WORN BY HER MAJESTY QUEEN ELIZABETH AT THE PARIS OPERA HOUSE.

The Royal Family certainly thought so. In a gesture of unprecedented (and probably unconstitutional) support for their Prime Minister, Chamberlain was invited to Buckingham Palace to become the first politician ever to appear on the balcony.

'The time of anxiety is past,' the King declared. 'After the magnificent efforts of the Prime Minister in the cause of peace it is my fervent hope that a new era of friendship and prosperity may be dawning among the people of the world.'

As for the pawns in this power game, the King believed that 'some day the Czechs will see that what we did was to save them for a happier fate.' The policy of appeasement had been given the seal of royal approval.

It was neither the most edifying nor the most politically adept pronouncement of his reign, and by the following spring even the King and his Queen were forced to face up to the hard fact that by feeding Hitler scraps all that Britain had succeeded in doing was whetting his appetite.

In 1935 George V had told Lloyd George, his Prime Minister during the latter part of the Great War: 'I will not have another war. *I will not.* The last one was none of my doing and if there is another one and we are threatened with being brought into it, I will go to Trafalgar Square and wave the red flag myself sooner than allow this country to be brought in.' His son would never have dreamt of waving the red flag; his wife would not have allowed it. Instead they set about doing what they – or, more accurately, she – did best, which was to fly the flag of British interests.

On 5 May 1939 the King and Queen set sail aboard the *Empress of Australia*, bound for North America. It was to prove the most important tour of their lives. Queen Mary and their daughters were at the quayside to see them off, and as the 21,850-ton liner cast off Princess Elizabeth produced her handkerchief and sternly told her younger sister, 'To wave, not to cry'.

The King had not wanted to go, believing that he could be of more use sitting at his desk in Buckingham Palace than touring Canada and the United States. It was pointed out to him, diplomatically but firmly, that this was not the case; that he would better serve his country by visiting Canada to confirm the Imperial ties and then crossing over to tour the United States and meeting President Franklin D. Roosevelt. He reluctantly agreed. Even so, it was clear that it would again be beholden to his Queen to make the tour a success.

Once more the odds appeared to be against them, particularly in the United States. Many Americans regarded George VI as a weak and colourless man made, according to *Scribner's* magazine, of 'poorer royal timber than has occupied England's throne in many decades'; a usurper who had stolen the Crown from his popular brother.

FACING PAGE:
ON THEIR WAY TO
AMERICA, THE KING
AND QUEEN SURVEY
THE SPOT WHERE THE
TITANIC WAS LOST.

'As for Queen Elizabeth,' the magazine opined, 'by Park Avenue standards she appears to be far too plump of figure, too dowdy in dress, to meet American specifications of a reigning Queen. The living contrasts of Queen Mary (as regal as a woman

can be) and the Duchess of Windsor (chic and charmingly American) certainly do not help Elizabeth.'

The elements were equally unfriendly. Three days out the liner and its escort of two cruisers were hit by a storm which ripped three royal standards to shreds. The following day they sailed into a field of icebergs and for three and a half days the *Empress of Australia* was fogbound in the freezing waters of the North Atlantic. The Queen wrote to her mother-in-law: 'The fog was so thick that it was like a white cloud around the ship, and the foghorn blew incessantly. Its melancholy blasts were echoed back by the icebergs like the twang of a piece of wire.' As she went on to remind Queen Mary, they were on the same latitude on almost the same date as the *Titanic* was in 1912 when it hit an iceberg and sank.

The Queen was not a woman who took much notice of portents, though, no matter how ominous. The *Sunday Graphic* recorded: 'Throughout all the liner's adventures those on board have been impressed by the Queen's unfailing cheerfulness. Neither gale, rain, fog, nor ice has discouraged her in the slightest.'

She had served her apprenticeship and learned her trade. She knew what worked and she stuck to the tried and tested. In seven gruelling weeks the royal party rumbled across the Americas, from Quebec to Vancouver, down to Washington, up to New York, and then back again into Canada. They covered 10,000 miles and an estimated fifteen million people turned out to greet and cheer them.

It was an Imperial progress. They travelled in their own specially appointed, twelve-carriage, royal-blue-painted train. The Queen's suite, in Car Number One, was described as being 'as charming as a country cottage'. Her bedroom and dressing-room were painted blue-grey, 'with dust-pink damask coverings, curtains to match, and a white eiderdown. Even the linen-bag and the clothes hangers were in material to match the hangings. The bathroom was of mauve tiles, with a full-sized bath and shower and gleaming white fixtures.'

There was a dining-room and sitting-rooms, telephones and air-conditioning and the King's office was oak-panelled.

The King had brought his own bottles of whisky and gin with him, and in the United States special water was provided for the

Queen's tea. President Roosevelt's housekeeper, Henrietta Nesbitt recalled: 'Since Washington drinking water is chlorinated and does not make good tea, we asked London to send over samples of the drinking water. Our Government chemists "tore it down" and then built up American water "to a Queen's taste."'

Breakfast was always at 9.15 (tea, fruit, eggs and bacon and toast for the King; tea, toast and fruit for the Queen). Wherever they dined, strict instructions were given that the King-Emperor was to be served exactly thirty seconds before his Queen.

The June temperature in Washington was in the nineties but the royal staff insisted that the Queen be provided with woollen blankets, hot-water bottles and hot milk.

'My lady likes to sleep warm,' one of the Queen's maids explained.

The royal staff did not endear themselves to their hosts. Very status-conscious, they were more royal than the royals (and often are to this day). They were, so both the Americans and the Canadians said, snobbish in the extreme. Even the gentleman from *The Times*, official organ of the British Establishment, agreed.

The Queen, on the other hand, was far from stand-offish. In Canada, just as she had in New Zealand and Australia, a decade before, she made a point of singling out former servicemen and plunging, unaccompanied, into the crowds that thronged around.

She charmed the French Canadians and converted Montreal's pro-Fascist mayor, Houde, just as she had won over the old communist she met in New Zealand, who announced that he became a confirmed royalist after she had smiled at him.

She captivated Fiorello La Guardia, the mayor of New York, echoing her success with the old French marshal, Lyautey, by saying, 'There is nothing nicer than friendship. Friendship is about the nicest thing in the world, isn't it?'

Eleanor Roosevelt, the strong-minded wife of the President, was equally entranced by the way she had of 'actually looking at people in the crowd so I am sure many of them felt that her bow was really for them personally...My admiration for her grew every minute she spent with us.' (The Queen, she later learned, sat on a a cushion with special springs which eased the long hours spent sitting and waving.)

The eight-year-old daughter of the President's aide, Harry Hopkins, said she sparkled like a 'fairy queen'.

It was a white crinoline gown sprinkled with diamonds that had excited the little girl's imagination. As in Paris, clothes had been used to stunning effect. The Queen called them 'my props'. And, once again, it was Hartnell who designed and made them. It was a mammoth job, with six or seven different changes of outfit required for each day.

The grander dresses could only be worn once. Hartnell explained: 'Should Her Majesty wear a magnificent dress of white satin and turquoise in Ottawa, she would not appear, even for an exactly similar occasion, in that same outfit in Montreal. The people of Montreal would expect to see a new and different dress and might consider it a slight if the Queen wore the Ottawa dress which they would have seen in their morning papers.'

Only those clothes needed immediately were kept on the train. The rest were sent ahead to await the Queen's arrival. It was a glittering, bejewelled procession which drew the King along in its diamond-encrusted wake.

Some of his wife's fairy dust settled on him. Chivvied on by her, he overcame his in-built reserve and followed her into the crowds. 'The capacity of Their Majesties for getting in touch with the people amounts to genius,' Canada's Governor-General Lord Tweedsmuir noted approvingly. 'It is the small unscheduled things that count most, and for these they have an infallible instinct.'

He was really referring to the Queen who, he said, 'has a perfect genius for the right kind of publicity, the unrehearsed episodes here were marvellous.'

In his other role as John Buchan, author of *The Thirty-nine Steps*, Tweedsmuir had a well-exercized facility for writing fiction. On this occasion, however, he was dealing in hard fact; the tour was an outstanding success.

The King had achieved a rapport with the President. Roosevelt, older, wiser and more assured in his personal authority, had treated the ruler of a quarter of the world with avuncular condescension, patting him on the knee one night and telling him: 'Time for bed, young man.' The two men nonetheless got on well.

Joseph Kennedy, the American ambassador in London and father of the future president, was certainly no friend of Britain. Indeed, his attitude was such that he was quickly recalled once war started. Kennedy was still astute enough, however, to recognize the importance of the camaraderie the King and the President had established, and described their handshake as 'perhaps the most important handclasp in modern times'. It was a friendship that would serve Britain well in the dark days to come.

The Queen basked in his success and was fully aware of its significance, not only on a political but also on a personal level. 'That tour made us,' she told Mackenzie King. The Canadian Prime Minister took that to mean that it had helped reinforce Canada's loyalty to the Empire. The Queen did not mean that at all. Pointing to herself, she said, 'I mean us, the King and myself.'

When the royal couple left Washington one newspaper headline declared, 'Au Revoir – to the Queen of Hearts.' Six decades later another royal wife of Windsor would lay claim to that title. For the next five decades, however, it belonged to Elizabeth alone.

CHAPTER 9

$\int$ TANDING FIRM

At 11.15 on the morning of 3 September 1939 Prime Minister Neville Chamberlain announced that he had received no reply to Britain's ultimatum to Adolf Hitler to stop his attack on Poland and that 'consequently this country is at war with Germany.'

The Second World War confirmed Queen Elizabeth in the country's affections. It was a battle hard-won, resulting in establishing her as the national mother figure – a role she would adeptly fulfil for the rest of her life – in the mind of a public anxious for a symbol of security. To achieve this status took guts, determination and an intuitive feel for the mood of the time.

The circumstances that led to the huge upswing in the Queen's popularity are written into folklore. What was not broadcast – it was officially suppressed at the time, and is only vaguely remembered today – is the crisis of popularity the Royal Family faced in those early days of the conflict. Luck born out of potentially fatal disaster was required to change that. This came about on the ill-omened Friday 13 September 1940, when six bombs hit Buckingham Palace.

Two landed in the courtyard, two in the forecourt, another in the garden. The sixth destroyed the chapel where the old family Bible in which the Royal Family's births, marriages and deaths were recorded was the only thing that survived intact.

The royal couple were in their small office overlooking the courtyard when the bombs landed. The Palace rocked with the explosions and shards of glass flew through the morning air.

The King later recounted how he and the Queen had watched the German plane approach the Palace from the direction of St James's Palace; how they had seen it release its bombs; how, when the King suddenly realized that the missiles were heading straight for them, he had grabbed hold of his wife, the Queen-Empress, and unceremoniously dragged her down on to the red carpet.

'We all wondered why we weren't dead,' the King wrote afterwards in awe and relief. Unnerved, he continued: 'It was a ghastly experience & I don't want it to be repeated.'

The reaction of his Queen was very different. Without thought for her own safety or the good fortune of her escape, she said: 'I'm glad we've been bombed. It makes me feel I can look the East End in the face.'

Once more she had defied the portents. Again her unerring instinct for saying just the right thing at the right time had

come to the fore. It was the defining quote, certainly of her war, possibly of her life, and the reaction was immediate and, as it happened, very welcome.

Later the forty-year-old Queen described, in a letter to Queen Mary, the horror of the devastation she had witnessed in the East End the same afternoon. 'The damage there was ghastly,' she wrote. 'I really felt as if we were walking in a dead city when we walked down the little empty street. All the houses were evacuated and yet through the broken windows one saw all the poor

THE KING AND QUEEN VISITING MINERS AND THEIR FAMILIES DURING THE WAR. SHE ALWAYS MADE AN EFFORT TO LOOK HER BEST ON THESE OCCASIONS COMPLETE WITH JEWELLERY AND LONG GLOVES.

little possessions, photographs, beds, just as they were left...It does affect me seeing this terrible and senseless destruction. I think I mind it much more than being bombed myself.'

When the war the royal couple had worked so hard to prevent broke out in 1939, they had immediately put themselves forward as the inspirational focus for their embattled nation.

The King practised pistol-shooting every morning in the grounds of Buckingham Palace and announced that if the Germans landed he intended to 'die there fighting.'

QUEEN ELIZABETH VISITS THE EAST END OF LONDON DURING WORLD WAR II.

The Queen, her inner eye fixed on the target of public opinion, followed his kingly example and took instruction in how to shoot a revolver. 'I shall not go down like the others,' she declared.

When it was suggested that the young Princesses, Elizabeth and Margaret Rose, should be evacuated to Canada, the Queen replied: 'The children will not go without me. I won't leave the King. And the King will never leave.'

It was good, stirring stuff. But it had not been enough.

By the autumn of 1940 the war was in full, terrifying flow and going very badly indeed. The King was in despair. 'There is not a bright spot anywhere,' he wrote on 29 October 1940. France had fallen and Britain was fighting for its very existence. The skies above southern England had become a battlefield as the RAF threw men and machines in the desperate fight to stem the dark tide of German warplanes pouring in from over the Channel.

The East End of London was taking a terrible pounding. Night after flaming night the bombs rained down on the working-class heartland of the Empire's capital.

The King and Queen made frequent trips to inspect the devastation and offer the comfort of their presence. They were not always well received. The spirit of the Blitz, as it came to be called, would become a rallying cry. At the height of the actual bombing, however, morale sometimes dipped alarmingly. Soldiers from the Guards regiments originally raised to protect the Sovereign were deployed in the East End to keep order. In two weeks in September 1940 more than 8,000 Londoners were killed or maimed by bombs and, in a country where class divisions were never far beneath the surface, there was a quickening swell of resentment in the East End at the way the Royal Family, living in the apparent safety of the West End, were spared the worst of the carnage.

The Information Minister Harold Nicolson MP recorded in his diary that during one excursion to the bomb-wrecked streets the King and Queen were booed. 'Everyone is much concerned about the feeling in the East End where there is much bitterness,' he noted.

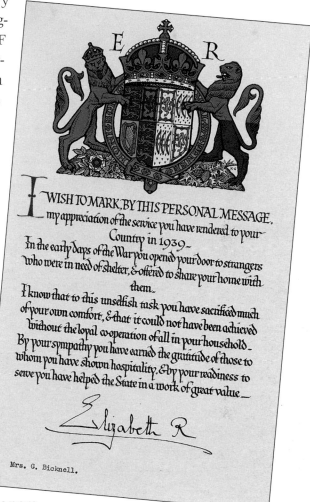

I WISH TO MARK BY THIS PERSONAL MESSAGE my appreciation of the service you have rendered to your Country in 1939.

In the early days of the War you opened your door to strangers who were in need of shelter, & offered to share your home with them.

I know that to this unselfish task you have sacrificed much of your own comfort, & that it could not have been achieved without the loyal co-operation of all in your household. By your sympathy you have earned the gratitude of those to whom you have shown hospitality. & by your readiness to serve you have helped the State in a work of great value.

Elizabeth R

Mrs. G. Bicknell.

A SIGNED CERTIFICATE GIVEN TO FAMILIES WITHIN THE UNITED KINGDOM WHO TOOK IN EVACUEES DURING THE WAR.

After one visit by the King and Queen, a cockney housewife was quoted as saying, 'It's all very well for them traipsing around saying how their hearts bleed for us and they share our suffering, and then going home to a roaring fire in one of their six houses.'

THE KING AND QUEEN AT STONEY CASTLE RANGES, ALDERSHOT IN 1939, TO SEE A SECTION OF VICKERS MACHINE-GUNS IN ACTION SHOOTING AT TARGETS.

That attitude changed after Buckingham Palace was bombed and the Queen had delivered her famous remark. Now, when she ventured forth into the East End, great crowds turned out to cheer her.

The Queen's heart continued to bleed. 'I feel quite exhausted after seeing and hearing so much sadness, sorrow, heroism and magnificent spirit,' she wrote to Queen Mary the following month. There were no sneering class-driven complaints this time, however. 'Oh, ain't she luverley! Ain't she bloody luverley!' said the next cockney housewife to be quoted.

The Queen dressed to fit the description. Despite the wartime deprivations, she wore clothes befitting her station. 'If the poor people had come to see me, *they* would have put on their best clothes,' she explained.

The King wore uniform throughout the war, only donning his well-cut Savile Row suits and jackets in the privacy of Royal Lodge where they escaped, when they could, for rare moments of relaxation.

The Queen *never* wore uniform. She was, in name if not in fact, the head of all the three women's services and the Colonel of several regiments. 'There are too many of them,' she explained. 'One would have been changing all day long.'

The real reason was that she did not feel that such outfits suited her. Uniforms, she decided, were simply not her style and instead she stuck to the tried and tested 'props' Norman Hartnell continued to make for her. Even her gas mask was converted into a fashion accessory. At the outbreak of war she carried it in the regulation-issue khaki case that hung from her shoulder on a white strap. Before very long, however, she had hidden it away in a satchel which she had covered in velvet to match the colour of whichever coat she was wearing.

It was a clever touch and a subtle one; Hartnell, as aware of the importance of her image as she was herself, was always careful to ensure that the Queen was outfitted in a manner appropriate to the circumstances. The war, he noted, had brought a new dress problem for his most illustrious client.

'What could she wear when visiting bombed sites and the devastated areas all over the country?' he asked. 'How could she appear before the distressed women and children whose own kingdoms, their small homes, had been shattered and lay crumbled at her feet?'

Black was ruled out. Black, he sagely deduced, 'does not appear in the rainbow of hope.' Instead he dressed her in gentle dusty shades of pink and blue and lilac 'to convey the most comforting, encouraging and sympathetic note possible'. The Queen observed: '*Dusty* is an apt colour. It doesn't show all the dust on bomb sites.'

Throughout the war great play was made of how the Royal Family stuck rigorously to the rationing rules. A line, it was announced, had been painted five inches from the bottom of all the royal baths so that they would be certain only the permitted amount of water was used. Heat was provided, not by the blazing fires that East End woman had imagined, but by tiny electric fires. Only one light was allowed in each bedroom. The Big House at Sandringham was shut up and dust-sheets drawn over the furniture. The Windsor deer were culled from 1,000 down to a breeding herd of a hundred.

Food, too, was said to be carefully measured and Eleanor Roosevelt, who visited Buckingham Palace in 1942, noted that the portions served to her at dinner were as meagre as the rationing laws allowed (although the food was still served on solid gold plates). 'At Buckingham Palace we are very careful to observe the rationing regulations,' the Queen declared and everyone at the Palace, from the King and Queen downwards and including

Norway's King Haakon and Queen Wilhelmina of the Netherlands who had fled to Britain after the Germans invaded their homelands, had their own ration books. They were kept in a safe in the office of Frederick Corbitt, the Palace's Deputy Controller of Supply, who recalled that the stock of Tabasco sauce ('an essential item of the cocktail mixture') soon ran out, as did the Negri toothpicks which the King used after every meal.

Despite such deprivations, the Royal Family fared considerably better than most of the rest of the population. At a particularly splendid civic reception in Lancashire, the Queen had taken one look at the groaning table and then stiffly informed the Mayor, 'We don't have any more food on the table at Buckingham Palace than is allowed to the ordinary householder according to the rations of the week.' That was technically correct. But there was never any rationing of fish, game or vegetables and, with their own large estates to supply them, the King and Queen were always able to eat well.

Each week eighty rabbits were delivered to Windsor alone. For tea there were potted shrimps which arrived from Morecambe Bay in Lancashire in small aluminium containers. During the season which began in May two or three fine salmon, each weighing from eight and a half to sixteen pounds, were sent down from Balmoral every week; and grilled salmon steak was a regular feature on the royal menu.

The King, as it happened, did not like salmon steaks (he much preferred trimmed lean lamb cutlets) and had to make do instead with fried fillet of sole, poached turbot or halibut. There was no shortage, however, of eggs and while most of the rest of the country was making do with the powdered variety, the King and Queen were able to breakfast off fresh ones. They also enjoyed freshly-made cream cheeses and strawberries and raspberries and freshly-picked vegetables – Corbitt recalled that 'young broad beans, new peas, and carrots, small lettuce and new potatoes just out of the ground' were particular favourites – which, like the eggs, came from the royal farms at Windsor. And while everyone else at the Palace had to make do with margarine, it was Windsor butter that was served at the royal table.

When the royal estates could not satisfy the royal appetites, a call to one of the big London hotels or, failing that, to the Windsor

Castle public house in Victoria, usually could. 'I had many friends among the West End tradesmen and caterers,' Corbitt later observed laconically.

When Queen Mary remarked that it had been a long time since she had tasted foie gras the King instructed Corbitt to rectify that gastronomic shortfall and a quarter-pound terrine was quickly obtained – at a cost of £5. And when the Queen ordered dressed crab for one of the luncheon parties she continued to host throughout the war, the chef at the Dorchester Hotel was persuaded to part with half a dozen 'on loan'.

In the same way, a supply of Tabasco – 'enough to last for years, as long as only a few drops of it were used in making the lobster cocktail' as Corbitt informed the Queen – along with ten thousand toothpicks – enough, as it turned out, to last the King for the rest of his life – were soon acquired.

If the Royal Family ever wondered how, during the hungry days of the war, their staff were able to conjure up such luxuries, they were decorous enough not to enquire.

As with food, so with clothes. From June 1941 onwards, there were precise regulations governing clothing. Hartnell would later insist: 'To these limitations in dress, which stipulated how much material, how many seams a dress could comprise, how much adornment and how wide the collar or belt of a dress might be, the Queen adhered strictly.'

What Hartnell tactfully failed to mention was that the Queen received many times more than her allotted number of clothing coupons. The Queen told a member of her family that many of her old dresses were being altered for Princess Elizabeth. 'Margaret gets Lilibet's clothes then, so with the three of us we manage in relays.' The need for such economies was not quite as pressing as it might have been, however. The coupon allowance for ordinary people was gradually reduced from sixty-six to forty-eight a year: the Queen and members of the Royal Family received an average of 1,277 a year.

There were sound arguments to justify the deception. For propaganda purposes, the King and his family had to be seen to be sharing his subjects' hardships. At the same time, and again for reasons of propaganda, the Government did not want to see the Queen looking shabby in old and increasingly threadbare clothes.

Clothes convey their own message and a well-dressed Queen was regarded as vital to national morale.

It was a subterfuge the Queen was more than happy to support. She enjoyed clothes and recognized their importance. Plump and short in stature, they gave her a majesty denied her by nature.

For all the attention paid to cut and colour and the 'ornaments of diamonds and rubies' Hartnell insisted on adding to her ensembles, the Queen's progresses were more than just a fashion parade. To the people she saw and spoke to she had indeed become a symbol of hope, of continuity, of belief in the possibility that somewhere ahead burnt the light of victory.

The Queen, for her part, drew moral encouragement from her visits to the bomb sites. 'Often we would come back from seeing the most terrible devastation feeling quite cheerful,' she later said. 'There was something so uplifting about people's behaviour. So many times people would say to me, "Ah well, no use complaining." They were always ready to tackle whatever had to be done. Everybody worked wonderfully well together. Really, we would come home feeling quite cheered up.'

She was considerably less happy with some of the other work she was called upon to perform. Nazism threatened nothing less than the total destruction of Britain and all the civilized values it cherished, and there was no room in this conflict for social niceties of the kind the Queen, brought up in a more chivalrous age, still held dear. A religious woman, she had a simple but deep belief in what constituted right and wrong, and she was very uncomfortable with the duplicities and falsehoods of many of the Government's stratagems.

Having learnt that plans were afoot to invade neutral Norway ahead of the Germans, she refused to send a message to the Young Women's Christian Association in the United States. She explained why in a letter to the Foreign Secretary, Lord Halifax.

EASTENDERS CHEERED THE KING AND QUEEN ON THIS VISIT TO A BOMB SITE IN APRIL 1941. LIKE THEM, THE ROYAL FAMILY HAD SUFFERED IN THE BLITZ BUT HAD PUT A BRAVE FACE ON IT.

Duke of Marlborough, has been described as 'one of the most disreputable men ever to have debased the highest rank in the British peerage'. The future Edward VII called him, 'the greatest blackguard alive'. He was banished from Court, as was his son, the ninth Duke, whose licentious behaviour continued this social ostracism into the reign of George V.

In 1885 the 15th Earl of Derby had dismissed Churchill's syphilitic father, Lord Randolph, as 'thoroughly untrustworthy, scarcely a gentleman and probably more or less mad'. Three decades later Derby's nephew, the 17th Earl, described Lord Randolph's son as 'absolutely untrustworthy, as was his father before him'.

A moralist of conventional hue, the Queen was concerned that the war was loosening the traditional restraints on the minds and mores of the general populace. Over dinner at the Palace one night in March 1940, she told the BBC's first director-general, Lord Reith, that 'the Christian ethic should be the basis of post-war policy.' In the Queen's view, Churchill, whose boundless energy did not embrace a noticeable respect for either religious beliefs or spiritual values, was not the man willing or capable of implementing such a strategy.

It was not just his bad name, however, that stood between the new Prime Minister and his Sovereign and his influential wife. There was also personal animosity, certainly on the Queen's side. Churchill had been the Duke of Windsor's greatest supporter during the Abdication crisis and for that the Queen had most certainly not excused him.

What might even now be construed as mere pettiness was based on solid concern. The Duke's Abdication had destroyed his reputation with Britain's political Establishment but he still continued to enjoy wide public support. Mass Observation, the government organization which monitored audience responses to newsreel footage, reported that the Duke of Windsor drew considerably more applause than either his brother or sister-in-law.

At first overawed by what she called the 'intolerable honour' that had been thrust upon them, Elizabeth had soon discovered that she felt very comfortable in the mantle of sovereignty. To the new Queen the threat from the former king in exile across the water was very real indeed.

Churchill, buoyed by his unassailable self-confidence and understandably preoccupied by matters of greater consequence, seemed sublimely indifferent to such Palace sensibilities. He was curt, almost to the point of discourtesy, in his weekly meetings with the King, sometimes arriving late and usually leaving early. Halifax noted that the King and Queen were 'a little ruffled by the

offhand way in which he treats them. Winston says he will come at 6.00, puts it off by telephone till 6.30 and is inclined to turn up for ten hectic minutes at 7.00.'

He was equally offhand with the Queen. Unwilling to allow her animosity towards the Prime Minister to ruffle her good manners, she would ask Churchill to join her in charades or one of the word games she was so fond of, only to have her invitation rejected.

The exigencies of war can make for strange bedfellows, however, and, despite their obvious differences, a mutual admiration started to develop between the royal couple and their Prime Minister. The King and Queen, as Mrs Ronnie Greville noted, had initially felt that 'Winston puts them in the shade – he is forever sending messages for the nation that the King ought to send.' They were soon to appreciate the bulldog grit, the energy and the oratory power of Britain's real wartime leader, and astutely came to

THE LADIES OF THE WOMEN'S KNITTING GUILD JOIN THE QUEEN IN THE BLUE DRAWING ROOM OF BUCKINGHAM PALACE DURING WORLD WAR II.

terms with their roles as Churchill's supporting players. For his part Churchill, ever the committed monarchist, managed to curtail his sometimes boorish exuberance and found the time to pay the King the attention his constitutional position demanded.

Instead of those hurried briefings, Churchill took to lunching with the King on Tuesdays. Bertie, who did not care for cold meals, arranged for a self-service buffet of grilled fish or legs of chicken to be laid out on the sideboard in the small sitting-room next to the Caernarvon Room. Next to the food would be two small decanters, one containing whisky for the King, the other brandy for the Prime Minister. Frederick Corbitt recalled that there were 'always two or three of the finest cigars from the Palace stock for Mr Churchill'. Not surprisingly, the lunches rarely lasted less than two hours. The Queen, by then something of a fan of Churchill's, would occasionally join them for coffee.

What really cemented their relationship, though, was not so much the flow of cigars which the Queen so thoughtfully arranged – as the war progressed the Prime Minister found decent Havanas ever harder to come by – but the transformation in Churchill's attitude to the Duke of Windsor.

The Prime Minister's growing disenchantment with the charismatic but fatally flawed ex-king he had once championed flamboyantly came to its head shortly after the fall of France in the summer of 1940.

The Duke was in Paris in the uniform of a major-general, serving with the Military Mission as a liaison officer between the British and French armies, when the German forces broke through the Allied lines and bore down on Dunkirk. Putting his duty to 'the woman I love' before that to his country, he left his post and fled to Biarritz to join Wallis. From there the couple retreated to La Croe, their villa on the Riviera outside Cannes.

THE QUEEN IS GIVEN A
LESSON IN LORRY
MAINTENANCE BY A
UNIFORMED PRINCESS
ELIZABETH IN MARCH
1945.

Italy's entry into the war on 10 June again drove them to panicky flight and they set off for the Spanish border in a three-vehicle convoy which included a lorry laden with their clothes. They made it to Madrid, capital of pro-German Spain, where they spent several days before decamping to Lisbon in neutral Portugal.

By then they were at the centre of a sinister intrigue from which the Duke's reputation would never fully recover. With the prize of the disgruntled, right-wing and possibly pro-Nazi ex-king almost within his grasp, the German Foreign minister Von Ribbentrop, an old friend of Wallis's from his days as Ambassador to London, set in motion a scheme to 'persuade or compel' the Duke and his Duchess to remain in Europe.

German intentions were transparently clear. Ribbentrop said: 'Germany is determined to force England to peace by every means of power and, upon this happening, would be prepared to accommodate any desire expressed by the Duke, especially with a view to the assumption of the English Throne by the Duke and Duchess.'

German Intelligence officers descended on Lisbon with orders to lure the Windsors back across the border into Fascist Spain. British Secret Service agents took up their positions around the villa in Estoril fifteen miles outside Lisbon, where the Windsors were staying, to ensure that this did not happen.

Ribbentrop put Walter Schellenberg, head of the SD (German Secret Intelligence) in charge of the operation and informed him: 'The Führer feels that if the atmosphere seemed propitious you might perhaps make the Duke some material offer. We should be prepared to deposit in Switzerland a sum of 50 million Swiss Francs – if he were ready to make some official gesture disassociating himself from the manoeuvres of the British Royal Family.

'The Fuhrer would of course prefer him to live in Switzerland, though any neutral country would do so long as it is not outside the economic influence of the German Reich.'

In today's money, Hitler's bribe amounted to £45 million.

Quite how far the Duke went along with what would have amounted to treason still remains a matter for conjecture. In 1996 Elizabeth's grandson, Prince Edward, produced and presented a television documentary which exonerated his great-uncle from this most heinous of charges.

Prince Edward's grandfather, George VI, was far less certain, particularly where his sister-in-law Wallis was concerned. In a handwritten note to Churchill, marked Private and Confidential, he would later state: 'I must tell you quite honestly that I do not trust the Duchess's loyalty.'

The King could not bring himself to commit to paper his doubts about his own brother's loyalty. Churchill admitted no such restraint. As Prime Minister he had unique access to the most secret reports provided by Britain's Intelligence Services and they led him to draw the direst of conclusions. He was outraged at what he regarded as the Duke's petty and, in the circumstances, highly suspicious procrastinations.

On 27 June, when the Duke had shown reluctance to leave Madrid, Churchill had taken the extraordinary step of writing to inform him of the consequences of further delay. His enciphered cable read: 'Your Royal Highness has taken active military rank and refusal to obey direct orders of competent military authority would create a serious situation. I hope it will not be necessary for such orders to be sent. Already there is a great deal of doubt as to the circumstances in which Your Royal Highness left Paris. I strongly urge immediate compliance with wishes of the Government.' The missive was tantamount to a threat of court martial.

Still the Duke delayed. The British government wanted him off the Continent and safely back on British soil as quickly as possible. The Duke, however, insisted that he would not return to England unless he had a job befitting his status to come back to – or until his wife was raised to the rank of Her Royal Highness and was duly received by the King and Queen.

Churchill was unmoved. He coldly informed him that, while the Duchess would be welcome back in Britain, no royal title would be bestowed upon her. As for a job, all the Prime Minister was prepared to offer the Duke who had been trained from birth to become King-Emperor was the trifling governorship of the out-of-the-way, strategically insignificant Bahamas. With the threat of court martial hanging over him and a swarm of British agents shadowing his movements, however, the Duke had no choice but to accept, and on 1 August the Windsors at last set sail for the West Indies aboard the *Excalibur*.

Churchill had written to the leaders of the Dominions of Australia, Canada, New Zealand and South Africa at the beginning of July, informing them of the Duke's appointment to the Bahamas. It read: 'The position of the Duke of Windsor on the Continent in recent months has been causing HM and HMG embarrassment as though his loyalties are unimpeachable there is always a backwash of Nazi intrigue which seeks to make trouble about him. The Continent is now in enemy hands. There are personal and family difficulties about his return to this country. In all the circumstances it has been felt that an appointment abroad might appeal to him and his wife and I have with HM's approval offered him the Governorship of the Bahamas. I think he may render useful service and find a suitable occupation there.'

The draft of that letter, written in his own hand, is a more accurate insight into Churchill's estimation of the Duke. The document, dated 4 July 1941, bears the instruction, 'Most Secret & personal. Decipher Yourself.'

It reads: 'The activities of the Duke of Windsor on the Continent in recent months have caused HM and myself grave uneasiness as his inclinations are well known to be pro-Nazi and he may become the centre of intrigue. We regard it as a real danger that he should move freely on the Continent. Even if he were willing to return to this country his presence here would be most embarrassing to HM and to the Government. In all the circumstances it has been felt necessary to try and tie him down to some appointment which might appeal to him and his wife, and I have decided with HM's approval to offer him the Governorship of the Bahamas. Despite the obvious objections, we felt that it was the least of possible evils.'

It was in the interests of morale and political expediency that Churchill decided to tone down his letter to the Dominion Prime Ministers. Given this dire background, however, there was no question of the Duke being granted any appointment of consequence – or of his wife being received by the King and Queen.

The Queen vehemently opposed her brother-in-law's appointment to the Bahamas, just as she had resisted all his previous attempts to find a new role for himself following the Abdication. In 1938, when Chamberlain suggested that the Duke should henceforth be treated as a younger brother who would take on some of the more minor royal duties, George VI did not object. His Queen, however, did and declared as recorded by Walter Monckton, the former Attorney General 'that it was undesirable to give the Duke any effective sphere of work. I felt then, as always, that she naturally thought she must be on her guard because the Duke of Windsor...was an attractive, vital creature who might be the rallying point for any who might be critical of the new King.'

THE QUEEN WITH PRINCESS ELIZABETH AND PRINCESS MARGARET ROSE IN HYDE PARK, 1944.

Her attitude had not softened. On 6 July 1940 she wrote to the Colonial Secretary, Lord Lloyd: 'The people in our own lands are used to *looking up* to their King's representative – the Duchess of Windsor is looked upon as the lowest of the low – it will be first lowering the standard hitherto set, and may lead to unimaginable troubles, if a Governor's wife such as she is to lead and set an example in the Bahamas. These objections are on moral grounds, but in this world of broken promises and lowered standards who is to keep a high standard of honour, but the British Empire?'

In the event, the Queen could do nothing to block the Duke's appointment. Churchill, who had observed that 'the Duke of Windsor's views on the war are such as to render his banishment a wise move,' wanted him out of the way. So did the King, who, according to Lord Lloyd, wanted to 'keep him at all costs out of England' and may indeed have been the one who first suggested that he be exiled to the Caribbean. For appearances' sake, the former King had to be seen to be doing something and the Bahamas was the least the Government could offer, which is precisely why they offered it to him.

On the matter of the Duchess's title, however, the Queen had a more decisive say.

On his Abdication the Duke had pleaded with his brother not to cause them the 'embarrassment' of denying what Wallis chose to call 'the extra chic' of being styled Her Royal Highness. As the son of a King, the Duke's H.R.H. was his by 'unalienable right'. That should have entitled his wife to the same appellation. It had been stated in *The Times* of 28 April 1923, 'in accordance with the general settled rule, that a wife takes the status of her husband, Lady Elizabeth Bowes Lyon on her marriage has become Her Royal Highness the Duchess of York.' What held true for the Lady Elizabeth, the Duke argued, also applied to Wallis.

The Abdication, however, and the unprecedented issues it raised had further confused the always arcane business of titles, and the former Lady Elizabeth had no qualms about using that to her advantage in the row that ensued. Wallis, she declared, had been found unfit to be a Queen: *ergo*, she was unfit to be a member of the Royal Family.

The King agreed. George VI argued that, by abdicating in order to marry Wallis, his brother had renounced his royal rank and, at the same time, accepted implicitly the constitutional judgement that his wife should not hold royal status. Out of courtesy and familial affection, Bertie 'restored' his brother's royal rank. He was quite adamant, however, that the thrice-married Wallis should remain a commoner.

Legal opinion was against him but the King, backed wholeheartedly by his Queen, refused to budge. As the 'Fountain of all Honours', royal titles were his box of toys and Wallis was not going to be allowed to play. As he explained to his Prime Minister in a typed letter dated 8 December 1942: 'I cannot alter a decision which I made with considerable reluctance at the time of his marriage.

'The reason for his abdication was that he wished to marry a lady who, having already two husbands living, was not considered by the country to be a suitable Queen of England.

'When he abdicated, he renounced all rights and privileges of succession for himself and his children – including the title of Royal Highness in respect of himself and his wife. There is therefore no question of the title being 'restored' to the Duchess – because she never had it.

'I am sure that there are still large numbers of people in this country, and in the Empire, to whom it would be most distasteful to have to do honour to the Duchess as a member of our family. I know you will understand how disagreeable this is to me personally but the good of my country and my family come first.'

He concluded: 'I have consulted my family, who share my views.'

The member of his family consulted most closely by the King was, of course, his wife. And Elizabeth was implacable in her hostility towards the Duke and, more specifically, the Duchess whom she held responsible for the change in the man she had held in such high esteem (and may indeed once have carried a torch for). When the Windsors finally arrived in Nassau they discovered, to their further humiliation, that the Queen's reach had got there before them: officials at Government House had received a telegram sent some weeks earlier instructing them that they were not to bow or curtsey to the Duchess or address her as 'Your Royal Highness'.

Despite his all too obvious failings, Churchill would always retain a sentimental attachment to the Duke. When it came down to matters of policy, though, he sided with the King and that only increased the Queen's growing regard for the pugnacious old warhorse.

The Queen's attitude towards the Windsors bordered on a vendetta. It was yet another example of the essential toughness which underlay the crinoline. It prompted Peter Townsend, who joined the Palace staff as an equerry to the King in 1944, to remark that 'beneath her graciousness, her gaiety and her unfailing thoughtfulness for others, she possessed a steely will.'

This was not the side that was put on general display. The Queen was an estimable actress with an inborn ability to give – by look, by gesture, by always saying the right thing at the right time – the public what they wanted.

She shared their tragedies. In 1942 her brother-in-law, the Duke of Kent, an Air Commodore in the RAF, was killed when his Sunderland flying boat *en route* to Iceland, crashed into a Scottish mountain. The year before one of her nephews, John Patrick, the Master of Glamis, was killed in action; another, Andrew Elphinstone, was taken prisoner.

She suffered their fears. While on a flight to visit the British armies in North Africa, the King's York aircraft suddenly went out of radio contact. 'I had an anxious few hours,' she recalled. 'Of course I imagined every sort of horror and walked up and down my room staring at the telephone.'

These private concerns and tragedies were not allowed to interfere with what she saw as her vital war work. She searched through the storerooms at Windsor and unearthed sixty suites of furniture which were given to families who had lost all their possessions in the bombing.

At the suggestion of the Minister of Food, the future Earl of Woolton, she helped distribute provisions to the victims of the German Blitz. 'I think food and kindliness indicate the things that Your Majesty means to the people of this country – practical sympathy,' Woolton said. To which she replied: 'Do you really think that the people think of me like that, because it is so much what I want them to think – and it's true. It's what I try to be.'

With the King at her side, she journeyed tens of thousands of miles around the country, visiting bombed cities and naval dockyards, factories and RAF bases. (The royal couple usually travelled in the royal train with its ten carriages dating from the reign of Queen Victoria, which had been equipped with a mobile telephone link to Buckingham Palace that enabled the Queen to stay in daily touch with her daughters.) Old complaints were forgotten in the flood of patriotic emotion she generated as she picked her way through the rubble. 'She had a kind word for everyone,' recalled Pearly King Chris Friend. 'She acted as if she had known us all her life.'

Lord Harlech, who accompanied the Queen on a January visit to Sheffield, recounted to Harold Nicolson how she worked a crowd. 'He says that when the car stops, the Queen nips out into the snow and goes straight into the middle of the crowd and starts talking to them,' Nicolson wrote in his diary. 'For a moment or two they just gaze and gape in astonishment. But then they all start talking at once. "Hi! Your Majesty! Look here!" She has that quality of making everybody feel that they and they alone are being spoken to. It is, I think, because she has very large eyes which she opens very wide and turns straight upon one.'

And everywhere she went she took her smile with her. 'I find it's hard to know when *not* to smile,' she told the Society photographer Cecil Beaton.

Shortly after 3 p.m. on 8 May 1945, that smile was witnessed by the multitude who gathered in the Mall to celebrate the victory over Nazi Germany. Hand in hand, the Queen, the King and their two princesses emerged on to the balcony of Buckingham Palace, which had been specially reinforced for the occasion, to be greeted by a tumultuous welcome. It was the first of eight appearances the Royal Family would make that memorable day. And standing beside them was Winston Churchill.

No-one questioned the constitutional right of this Prime Minister to be there. The war had confirmed him as one of the greatest Englishmen in history. It had also secured for the Queen an unrivalled place in the hearts of her husband's subjects.

$\mathcal{I}$MPERIAL CURTAIN CALL

When the war ended in 1945 the aftermath of victory was nation-wide euphoria. The arms of righteousness had prevailed, an evil foe had been vanquished and the country celebrated. It was a giddy time, a time for a new beginning. The terrors of the past six years had been laid to rest and the Queen, in her middle forties but in her own mind still a young woman, was in high step with the national mood.

The King, bowed by his sense of duty, committed by instinct and upbringing to the old ways, was much more circumspect. He observed the changes sweeping the country and he did not like what he saw. His Queen, as always, took a more flighty view. Blessed since childhood with unselfconscious grace and an ability to see only what she wanted to see, she did what she could to keep her husband's flagging spirits above the Plimsoll line of depression, while at the same time beginning to enjoy herself.

When Mrs Roosevelt came to stay, it was Elizabeth the Queen-Empress who cajoled everyone into her own version of charades called The Game, still enjoyed by the Royal Family today. Chips

Channon reported that the house party 'became quite childish with the Queen wearing a beard, etc'. (Mrs Roosevelt was exhausted; Churchill, as curmudgeonly as ever when it came to party games, refused to join in.)

On another occasion a nursery game of Murder ended with her hiding under the piano where she was joined by her artistic advisor, Ben Nicholson, who recalled poking his finger into what he thought was a cushion only to discover it to be the Queen's bosom.

It was at the Queen's instigation that the Princesses Lilibet and Margaret were allowed to mix with young men of their own age. Mabell, Countess of Airlie, who had been so instrumental in bringing Bertie and Elizabeth together, remarked on the way 'both sisters teased, and were teased by the young Guardsmen.'

It was the pre-television age, when cinema attendance soared to unrepeatable heights. Like millions of others, the Royal Family went to 'the pictures', as they called it, once a week. They were spared the queues: they took their entertainment in the private cinema owned by Sir Alexander Korda, producer of such lavish historical melodramas as *The Four Feathers*. Sometimes Korda himself would join the royal party, accompanied by his beautiful wife Merle Oberon.

The audience usually comprised the King and Queen and their two daughters; Marina, Duchess of Kent, and her daughter, Princess Alexandra; and members of the Household who happened to be around – including the Queen's equerry Peter Townsend. The Royal Family took particular delight in seeing themselves in the newsreels and provided their own running commentary. There were cries of, 'Look at the face she's pulling!' and 'How could you wear that hat?' Princess Margaret, still a teenager and behaving like one, would prop her feet on the seat in front of her (the King did not approve and was forever telling her to put them down).

Afterwards everyone would motor back to the Palace in the royal Daimlers for a supper of fish and chips – of the royal variety. Not for them battered cod eaten out of the traditional wrapping of newspaper. Instead, they tucked into breadcrumbed sole prepared in the Palace kitchens and served on fine china plates by liveried footmen.

Compared to the rigid etiquette of the previous reign, however, when everybody was required to change into evening clothes and medals and decorations were always worn, these were markedly informal occasions. The men dressed in tweeds or flannels, the women in day dresses (no hats).

'It was much more like ordinary family life than it had been in the old days,' Lady Airlie commented.

Elizabeth was by now too much the Queen to be in favour of all of these changes. When Princess Elizabeth's first lady-in-waiting appeared without a hat she declared, 'She can't come here like that!' The Princess replied: 'Don't be old-fashioned, Mummy. These days, many girls don't have a hat.'

Zest usually got the better of the Queen's reservations, however. When the dancing began at eleven thirty she was the most eager of participants, sometimes ordering the bandleader Maurice Winnock to carry on playing until five the following morning. At one dance, ostensibly for the staff, the comedians Frankie Howerd and Jimmy Edwards provided the cabaret and the Queen, dressed in a lime green silk dress and wearing a tiara, took great delight in skipping around the ballroom floor in the arms of Freddie Mayes, the footman who wound the Palace clocks.

She made friends with the flamboyant Sir Philip Sassoon, whose mother was a Rothschild and whose father's family were Parsees from Bombay. He entertained her at his home in Kent, where scented lilies adorned the lake and the dining-room was lapis lazuli blue and decorated with a decadent Glyn Philpot frieze of white cows being herded by Negroes.

The painter John Piper, who was one of the Queen's favourite house guests, remembered her as being 'frightfully jolly – a generous warm country house-girl'. Other observers were of the more caustic opinion that she was in the throes of second youth. Chips Channon said she was becoming 'slack'. But all she was doing was what her husband found so difficult – letting off steam after the hardship and pressure of the war. Nor was she was alone in wishing to release the tension of the recent past with jollity and dance.

Queen Mary, nearing eighty and still as stiff and formal as ever in public, was seen to throw aside decorum and shake an elegant leg when a country-dance record was playing on the gramophone. One night, at the Queen's prompting, she got up and danced the hokey-cokey. Even the King was swept up by the gaiety once in a while and on one noteworthy occasion, urged on by his wife, he joined in a conga line as it snaked its way through the halls and corridors of Buckingham Palace.

For Bertie, however, these were but brief interludes of relaxation in the constant round of duties. There were the government dispatch-boxes to be dealt with, endless letters to write and reply to and his estates to manage. He took each and every one of his responsibilities with equal seriousness and no detail, however trivial, escaped his attention. Sir John Wheeler-Bennett wrote: 'No addition could be made to a cottage at either Sandringham or Balmoral, no new tenant taken on, no employee discharged, no tree cut down, without the King's approval, the decision being submitted to him personally, even if he was in London.'

He was just as concerned with the moral welfare of his employees. Both the King and Queen were regular church attenders, and he expected others to follow their royal example. At both Sandringham and Balmoral 'he liked to see all the heads of departments on his estate present in church, together with their wives, and if he noticed an absentee (and he always noticed), he made immediate and emphatic enquiries after his health.'

Had Bertie been simply a country squire, the workload he insisted on setting himself would have been burdensome. As a King-Emperor, with all the demands that that entailed, it became health-threatening, especially for someone of such fragile constitution. Britain was in Imperial retreat but, a quarter of the world's map was still painted red. Over four hundred million people owed allegiance to this small, troubled man, and it was a part of his duty to be seen by as many of them as possible.

The Queen had always revelled in foreign tours and it was with her customary enthusiasm that she set about preparing in 1947 for the royal visit to South Africa, the one Dominion she had yet to visit. As always, a great number of new frocks were ordered, both for herself and for the two princesses who were to accompany them.

Carte blanche was no longer one of the royal prerogatives, however. Before the war the Queen had been able to order whatever she liked. Now she was subject (in theory at least) to the same restrictions as everyone else. The Labour government, faced with mounting economic problems and with its in-built ideological distaste for 'upper-class' display, had already baulked at what they regarded as the Queen's extravagance. Board of Trade officials had complained at the way the royal coupon requirement had 'increased considerably since the end of the war...and our efforts to check this tendency seem so far to have been unsuccessful.'

In the end the Queen and the two Princesses got their extra coupon allowance, on the grounds that the Royal Family had to dress according to their status. For the soundest of public relations reasons, however, the public was not informed that 4,329 extra coupons – enough to keep a hundred people in clothes for a year – were issued for the South African tour. But the press photographs and the newsreels told their own story, and an opinion poll taken at the time found that 32 per cent disapproved of the tour because they felt it 'inappropriate' for the Royal Family to indulge in 'expensive junketing'.

To add a further dampener, the most savage winter weather swept across Britain just as the royal entourage of thirty-seven set sail for sunnier climes aboard the nation's latest and last battleship HMS *Vanguard* (which had been launched by Princess Elizabeth three years before). Railways froze, coal ran out and hundreds of people literally froze to death under fourteen foot snowdrifts and 16 degrees of frost. At one point the situation became so critical that mass starvation seemed a possibility.

The King, consumed with guilt, wanted to call off the trip and return to Britain. There were many aboard ship who agreed with him. All the senior officers' cabins had been taken over by the royal party and an extra eighteen midshipmen from the Dominions had been drafted in to help entertain the two Princesses. This led to intense congestion on the lower decks, where sailors were forced to vacate their bunks and make do with hammocks.

THEIR MAJESTIES KING GEORGE VI AND QUEEN ELIZABETH
WITH THEIR DAUGHTERS
H.R.H. PRINCESS ELIZABETH AND H.R.H. PRINCESS MARGARET ROSE.

PICTURE POSTCARD OF THE ROYAL FAMILY ISSUED BY VALENTINE'S IN 1947.

The Queen organized her by now familiar conga lines and the Princesses enjoyed themselves. But the voyage was ill-omened. *Vanguard* ran into severe storms which tore away the Royal Standard and on the day before they arrived at Cape Town the weather was so bad that only the ladies-in-waiting, Lady Harlech and Lady Delia Peel, managed to get through the morning service in the ship's chapel. That added to the festering disquiet amongst the crew, many of whom were 'hostilities only' men who saw little reason why they should be ferrying the Royal Family to Africa instead being at home. Poor food – reconstituted potatoes and cabbage featured regularly – only exacerbated the situation.

Matters came to their unpleasant head while the Royal Family were in Bechuanaland (now Botswana) and the battleship was cruising off Durban. The Admiral in command cabled the King's private secretary, Sir Alan Lascelles, with the disturbing news that there had been 'slight mutiny'.

The rebellion was quickly quelled and the incident was hushed up, to the extent that many of the ratings serving in different parts of the ship never knew that it had taken place. But the King knew and when the royal party arrived back in Portsmouth he refused, on the advice of the Cabinet, to hold the traditional end-of-voyage investiture on the quarterdeck.

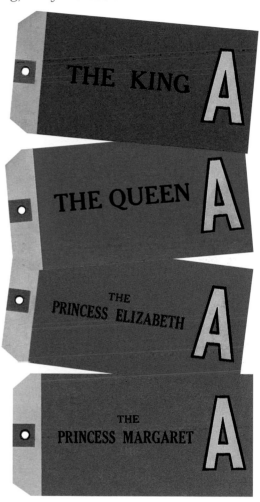

THE COLOUR-CODED LUGGAGE LABELS USED DURING THE ROYAL TOUR OF SOUTH AFRICA IN 1947

Despite the problems, however, there was never a chance of the mission being cancelled. The beleaguered Prime Minister, Clement Attlee, refused to allow it. 'Apart from other effects,' he wrote, 'the curtailment of the tour would magnify unduly the extent of the difficulties we are facing and surmounting at home, especially in the eyes of foreign observers.'

The Queen wrote to her mother-in-law: 'This tour is being very strenuous as I feared it would be & doubly hard for Bertie who feels he should be at home.' Then, with typical common sense, she

193

added: 'But there is very little he could do now, and even if he interrupted the tour & flew home, it would be very exhausting & possibly make it difficult to return here.'

In other words, the royal show had to go on. And so it did – in glorious style. The Queen watched her daughters being chased around the foredeck by the young officers, went down on her hands and knees for rifle practice and was the first of the royal party to start waving as the great battleship drew into Cape Town harbour.

THE WHITE TRAIN.

For the next two months her home was the specially furbished White Train which was fourteen carriages and a third of a mile long. Eight of the carriages had been specially shipped out from Britain, six had been borrowed from the famed Johannesburg to Cape Town express and together they made the longest train ever seen in South Africa. The King, the Queen and the Princesses each had their own bedroom with *en suite* bathroom. Dressed in ivory and gold, the White Train was preceded by the Pilot Train carrying officials and reporters and followed by the Ghost Train laden with spares and equipment. A fleet of cars followed by road, poised to ferry the royal party to places of interest. In addition, four Viking aircraft of the King's Flight were on standby for the longer hops.

Wherever they went they were greeted by cheering, flag-waving crowds. In the other Dominions of Canada, New Zealand and Australia, Elizabeth had made a point of following her own spontaneous schedule and plunging into the multitude to shake hands and exchange words of greeting. She continued to do so.

At Camper she was asked to read a message to a young boy. When she learnt that he was confined to an invalid chair she led her daughters over to him for a chat. In Basutoland (now Lesotho), where she reviewed a parade of Girl Guides, she insisted on going across to say a special hello to a coachload of Guides. They were inmates of the local leper colony.

In the Afrikaner citadel of Bloemfontein, the Queen even succeeded in winning the goodwill of the Boers. It was less than fifty years since the end of the Boer War and anti-English feelings still ran deep. The legacy of that brutal conflict was mistrust and suspicion and it was with barely contained hostility that one citizen informed her that the Afrikaners had never forgiven the English. With unstudied aplomb the Queen replied: 'I understand perfectly. We feel very much the same in Scotland, too.' The atmosphere improved immediately.

THE KING AND QUEEN, FOLLOWED BY THE PRINCESSES ELIZABETH AND MARGARET, LEAVING THE GOVERNOR GENERAL'S HOUSE IN BLOEMFONTEIN.

It was her charm which saved the situation at an ostrich farm in Oudtshoorn where the King, invited to snip the tail feather off one of the giant birds which had its head stuck in a sack, only succeeded in cutting a quarter of an inch out of its backside. The Queen immediately took over the scissors and finished the job properly. 'We do a lot of gardening at home,' she explained.' The King is good at digging and weeding. It is I who concentrate on the secateurs.'

In what was then still Rhodesia the Royal Family made a pilgrimage to the granite slab called World's View in the Matopo Hills, which is the last resting-place of the empire-builder and dia-

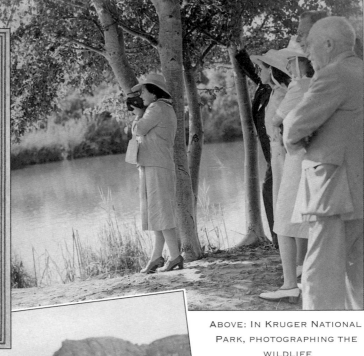

ABOVE: IN KRUGER NATIONAL
PARK, PHOTOGRAPHING THE
WILDLIFE

ABOVE:
IN NATAL NATIONAL
PARK WITH PRIME
MINISTER JAN SMUTS.

RIGHT:
DRESSED FORMALLY FOR A
BANQUET GIVEN IN THEIR
HONOUR

ABOVE: THE ROYAL PARTY DISEMBARK
FROM ONE OF THE FOUR VIKING AIRCRAFT
OF THE KING'S FLIGHT, WHICH WERE
USED FOR THE LONGER HOPS. PETER
TOWNSEND CAN BE SEEN (IN SHORTS) IN
CONVERSATION WITH PRINCESS
MARGARET.

BELOW:
THE KING AND QUEEN
AND THE PRINCESSES
ELIZABETH AND
MARGARET STAND IN
LINE FOR THE FORMAL
INTRODUCTIONS AT
ONE OF THE
NUMEROUS GARDEN
PARTIES THEY
ATTENDED DURING
THEIR TOUR.

THE ROYAL FAMILY
AND THEIR STAFF POSE
FOR A FORMAL GROUP
PHOTOGRAPH AT THE
END OF THE TOUR.
GROUP CAPTAIN PETER
TOWNSEND IS BACK
ROW FAR LEFT.

mond czar Cecil Rhodes. As they paid homage to the only Englishman to give his name to a country (and in the process playing a provocative part in the events that led to the Boer War), Princess Elizabeth wandered off on her own to gaze at the African vastness. The King turned to the Queen and remarked: 'Poor Elizabeth. Already she is realizing that she will be alone and lonely all her life; that no matter who she has by her side, only she can make the final decision.'

At that precise moment Princess Elizabeth was probably thinking more of her sore feet than her lonely future. The Queen had started the climb wearing her trademark peek-a-boo high-heeled sandals which slipped on the stony path. Princess Elizabeth, more sensibly, was wearing flat shoes. She took them off, gave them to her mother and continued up the hill in her bare feet, accompanied by an occasional cry of pain.

There were other incidents and exigencies which no amount of forward planning could have foreseen. In Durban a fight following accusations of race-fixing erupted at the racecourse a few minutes after they had left. In Cape Town the Queen was almost swept off her feet when the red carpet she was standing on got caught in the royal train whilst it was reversing.

The most disturbing moment came in Benoni when a Zulu man suddenly burst out of the crowd and lunged at the royal car. The Queen, with what at first looked like great presence of mind, set about him with her parasol which she broke over his head. She then turned and continued waving to the crowds as if nothing had happened. The South African police took over where she left off and beat the unfortunate man unconscious.

It later transpired that all he had been trying to do was hand Princess Elizabeth a ten-shilling note as a twenty-first birthday present. The Queen described it as 'the worst mistake of my life'.

From a political standpoint, however, the tour was adjudged a great success. The sun was going down on the Empire and the

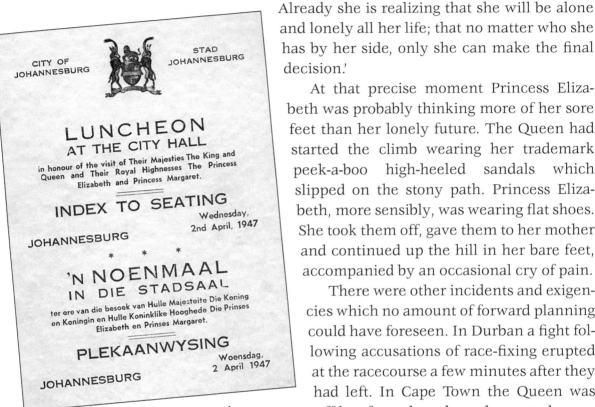

THE SEATING PLAN FOR A LUNCHEON IN JOHANNESBURG. POLITICS REQUIRED THAT IT WAS PRINTED IN AFRIKAANS AS WELL AS ENGLISH.

King's belief that his duty lay at home was indicative of the way Britain was retracting into itself. The process of Imperial withdrawal had begun.

The Queen had believed that 'if the dividing lines in South Africa go deep, the reconciling appeal of royalty goes deeper still.' Before the Queen spoke those words, however, Nelson Mandela had formed the African National Congress Party to battle for majority rule by any means possible. And within a year South Africa's all-white electorate had voted in the Boer-dominated Nationalist party, whose policy of Apartheid would lead the country out of the Commonwealth.

That same year, 1947, Ireland finally severed its political links with mainland Britain – links which stretched back over 800 years. By then, of course, the jewel in the crown of Empire had already been removed. On 15 August 1947 Britain marched out of India. An epoch was at an end.

The handover of power had been completed by the last Viceroy, Earl Mountbatten of Burma. He was the King's cousin and probably his closest friend and Bertie was proud that this onerous, climactic task of winding up two centuries of British rule had been entrusted to a member of his own family. Indeed, the King had pressed for Mountbatten's appointment. It was with inevitable sadness and no small amount of concern that George VI saw himself shorn of the grandest of his titles. Overnight he ceased to be Emperor.

When Disraeli had arranged for the Imperial title to be bestowed on Bertie's great-great-grandmother, Victoria, not quite seventy years before, Gladstone had dismissed it as 'theatrical bombast and folly'. The Royal Family, on the other hand, for whom titles were and are of immense importance, had rejoiced in this grand

THE LAST DAYS OF THE ROYAL TOUR OF SOUTH AFRICA. GENERAL SMUTS RECEIVED A FEATHER FROM THE QUEEN'S HAT. HER MAJESTY'S HAT BLEW OFF ON TABLE MOUNTAIN AND THE PRIME MINISTER RESCUED IT, BUT NOT BEFORE ONE OF THE FEATHERS HAD BEEN BROKEN OFF. THIS WAS DULY PRESENTED TO GENERAL SMUTS AND ARRANGED IN HIS HAT BY THE KING.

appellation. Now it was gone. No longer was George entitled to sign himself 'G.R.I.' The *Imperator* had been removed. Henceforth he was merely a King. Three days later he wrote to Queen Mary, who commented, 'the first time Bertie wrote me with the I for Emperor of India left out. Very sad.'

The King, indeed, during the final months leading up to the handover had fretted about how in future he would sign himself in letters addressed to leaders of Commonwealth countries which no longer recognized his sovereignty.

Like most of her husband's subjects, the Queen took an altogether more relaxed view of the matter. The Imperial legacy in India includes the graves of one and a half million Britons. The great majority of people, however, were untouched and, to a greater or lesser extent, unmoved by what, with hindsight, was the most dramatic and far-reaching change in Britain's world role since the loss of the American colonies a century and a half earlier. Before the advent of the jet plane, the Indian sub-continent was a far and distant place of little practical interest outside history and geography classrooms.

Dreams of Imperial glory, like the empire which had fostered them, were fading into irrelevance as the baton of international might passed from Great Britain to the United States. It was to America that Britain was forced to look – for military protection and for the funds with which to rebuild its shattered industrial base. Britain would receive $1.5 billion in Marshall Plan aid, a third more than Germany.

In symbolic recognition of that dependency, George VI asked Harry Truman for his autograph when he met the new American President in 1945. The very notion of his father George V, never mind his great-grandmother Queen Victoria, asking the leader of any foreign country for his signature as a keepsake was inconceivable. It was a measure of where Britain now stood in the league table of world power. This change in status, however, went all but unremarked. By then Britain was consumed with problems on its own doorstep.

In 1945 the British electorate had made it emphatically, irrefutably clear that they would not tolerate a return to the old pre-war order. There had been troubles then. The Depression. A General Strike. The growth of trade union power which had so worried George V. But then the social fabric, if wearing thin, had held fast. Now it was being rent by the pressing, widespread desire for radical change.

Churchill, the Prime Minister who had led the country to victory over Germany and who only a few weeks before had stood triumphant with the Royal Family on the balcony at Buckingham Palace, was ruthlessly voted out of office. Labour was swept to power in a landslide on the promise of far-reaching reforms which amounted to what the King himself called a 'Social Revolution'.

The King was upset by this seismic shift. He deeply regretted the departure of Churchill, the bravura politician he and his Queen had been so suspicious of but had come to rely on so heavily. He recorded: 'It was a great shock to me to have to lose Churchill as my chief adviser, and I am sure the People did not want to lose him as their leader, after all the stupendous work he did on our behalf in the War.' To Churchill he wrote: 'I regret what has happened more than perhaps anyone else. I shall miss your counsel to me more than I can say.'

He was ill at ease with the new Labour ministers with whom he was now obliged to treat. His weekly meetings with the new Prime Minister, Clement Attlee, were stilted affairs, marked by long and embarrassing silences. 'My new Government is not too easy & the people are rather difficult to talk to,' he admitted to his brother, Henry, Duke of Gloucester.

George was profoundly worried by the drastic innovations which he correctly suspected would destroy the aristocratic way of life upon which the Royal Family's position rested. He advised Attlee to moderate the pace of reform. 'I thought he was going too fast in the new nationalizing legislation,' he wrote.

It was a cry in the wind. Earl Mountbatten wrote to him that 'you are now the old and experienced campaigner on whom a new and partly inexperienced Government will lean for advice and guidance' but that was just flattery, Mountbatten style. The hard truth was that the Labour government had no intention of listening to any Conservative voice, the King's included. At breakneck speed it set about creating the Welfare State. The coalmines, the railways, gas and electricity, road transport were nationalized. The iron and steel industry would follow.

Taxation soared to punitive levels. Attlee declared: 'Controls were desirable not for their own sake but because they were necessary in order to gain freedom from the economic power of the owners of capital. A juster distribution of wealth was not a policy to soak the rich or to take revenge, but because a society with gross inequalities of wealth and opportunity is fundamentally unhealthy.'

The rich did not see it that way. They railed against the petrol rationing, the controls on investments, luxury consumer goods and on meals taken in restaurants, and the stringent currency allowance for foreign travel, all of which were the preserves of the well-to-do. They believed that they were being put to the sword of Socialism and an American newspaper agreed. In 1946 it was noted: 'Where, before the war, Britain could count some seven thousand people who kept incomes of £6000 or over after taxes, the Britain of today counts only sixty people who still retain £6000.' As far as the rich were concerned it was not a soaking they were getting – they were being bled dry.

The King and his Queen were not directly affected by Labour's punitive tax policies. Sometime between 1936 and 1939, by a judicious exercise of his prerogative and the application of royal pressure in the right quarters, the King had persuaded the Treasury to allow him to reclaim the tax deducted from his investments. In other words, he had made the monarchy tax-free.

The Queen's family, however, was no so fortunate. The Bowes Lyons' wealth was founded on now-nationalized coal and iron works. Faced with debts and demands he could not meet, Elizabeth's nephew, Timothy, who in 1944 had succeeded to the earldom of Strathmore, started selling thousands of acres of land. To add social insult to ancestral injury, Glamis Castle was opened to the public (admission charge: 2/-). For 10p the general public was allowed to traipse through the Queen's childhood holiday home. Royalty had taken yet another irreversible step down the road to becoming a money-spinning part of the tourist industry – and Elizabeth's own kin had joined the bandwagon.

By 1947 the King was depressed enough to write to his mother: 'Never in the whole history of mankind have things looked gloomier than they do now.' His despondency was understandable. The optimism which had greeted Labour's historic victory ran aground on the banks of austerity, as military victory started to look depressingly like economic defeat.

Britain, which within memory had been the richest country on earth, was rushing towards bankruptcy. The pound, the very symbol of national strength, was devalued and gold reserves shrank to crisis level. Rationing was more severe than ever. In 1946 bread was added to the list of rationed goods for the first time. Socialism, it seemed, was being bought at a great cost which even huge American loans could not meet. Conditions were harsher than they had been at the height of the war and in February of that year the King wrote to Attlee to complain. He noted in his diary: 'I said we must all have new clothes & my family are down to the lowest ebb.'

On the question of clothes the King was as punctilious as ever. He always made a point of dressing correctly: when King Peter of Yugoslavia called upon him wearing the uniform of the Royal Yugoslav Air Force, the King noticed a gold watch-chain strung between the upper pockets of the jacket. 'Is that part of the uniform?' he asked. King Peter replied: 'No'. 'Then take it off. It looks damned silly and damned sloppy,' Bertie commanded.

The Labour ministers were not monarchs, to be told how to dress, and what irritated the King as much as anything was the refusal of his government to observe the niceties he valued so highly. He was shocked by the steadfast refusal of Aneurin Bevan, the Health Minister who provocatively described the hierarchy of Churchill's Conservative party as 'lower than vermin', to wear evening dress on the grounds that it was an 'upper-class uniform.'

Nettled, the King's response was to seek the security of family and friends. In 1948 Mrs Eleanor Roosevelt, the widow of America's wartime president, visited Britain and weekended at Windsor. The ousted Prime Minister Winston Churchill and his wife Clementine were there. Churchill, for whom conflicts of policy were never allowed to stand in the way of good fellowship, commented that there were no Labour politicians amongst the guests. The King coldly replied: 'This is a private family party.'

Part of George VI's problem was that, fine gardener though he was, he found it hard to differentiate between wood and tree. Meticulous to the point of obsession, he was forever getting himself entangled in the undergrowth of minutiae. As his official biographer Sir John Wheeler-Bennett noted: 'Indeed he wore himself out with his care for detail.'

The war had left him exhausted, both physically and psychologically. 'I feel burned out', he was forever saying.

He had no hobbies other than shooting and gardening, no interests outside his family other than the well-being of the amorphous masses. He saw himself, so Wheeler-Bennett said, as 'The People's King'. The trouble was that the proletariat in question no longer saw themselves as the King's People in quite the unquestioning way they had before the war. They had their own hopes and ambitions.

Even his own staff were imbued by this vision of a future where welfare was available by right, not charity. They formed a trade union and demanded higher wages. The King was 'hurt'. One commentator remarked, 'It was as though he had been tossed by a wave and left stranded on a new beach, unfamiliar and empty of his beliefs and ideals.'

In its most far-reaching reform the Government took the health services into public ownership and created the National Health Service. The King did not grasp the point nor appreciate how important and inspirational the ideal of free medical treatment was to people for whom ill-health had all too often led to financial ruin. Hugh Gaitskell, future leader of the Labour party, recorded the King saying to him: '"I really don't see why people should have false teeth free any more than they should have shoes free", waving his foot at me as he said it,' Gaitskell commented. 'He is of course a fairly reactionary person.'

Elizabeth, never one to face a problem head-on if it could be avoided, had made her regal way through the post-war years with an almost sublime indifference to the tremors rumbling through the nation's foundations. For her, life continued much as it always had. She had her good works and her gardens, her children, her houses and her creature comforts. She had seen her elder daughter married in spectacular state and the following year had celebrated her Silver Jubilee, the climax of which was a drive of twenty-two miles through the streets of London where the crowds lined the pavements twenty deep.

She continued to entertain on a scale even the grandest of her husband's subjects were either unable or loth to emulate.

Elizabeth's year still followed the calendar of outdoor activities which a minority were starting to refer to as blood sports. From her perspective everything was very much as it always had been. That was how she wished it to stay. Life, as she was fond of saying, was what you make of it and she was quite happy, thank you, with the way it was made. One of her favourite maxims was 'Traditions exist to be kept.'

Tradition, however, was not standing up well to the chronic economic problems that had taken such an iron grip on the country. The Queen expressed her sympathy. In her eve of Silver Wedding broadcast she said: 'At this time my heart goes out to all those who are living in uncongenial surroundings and who are longing for a time when they will have a home of their own. I am sure that patience, tolerance and love will help them to keep their faith undimmed and their courage undaunted when things seem difficult.'

It was to try and bring cheer to a public beset by economic woes that the wedding in 1947 of Princess Elizabeth to Prince Philip of Greece was conducted on such an extravagant scale. Ceremonial pomp was no longer the bromide it had been, however, and the plan was not quite the success the Palace hierarchy had hoped it would be or many royal biographers would insist it was. There was strident criticism from the Labour benches in Parliament and an opinion poll revealed that one in three considered the wedding arrangements 'too elaborate'.

Again there were rows over the number of clothing coupons – and this time the Government won the argument. The Palace had asked for 800 coupons for the Princess. When it was pointed out that the Palace's request was likely to become public knowledge, the request was scaled down to 100. Even so, there was still a great deal of rancour at what many regarded as the Royal Family's prodigality. According to University College of Wales lecturer Ina Zweiniger-Bargielowska: 'The Royal Family did not set an example to the nation during the post-war shortages. Rather, they were able to benefit from their privileged status and it is a symptom of intense frustration with austerity that these privileges aroused appreciable resentment.'

The King, too, harboured misgivings, though for very different reasons. His life revolved around his family – 'Our family, us four' as he touchingly called it – and he was most unhappy at his elder daughter's departure from what his wife referred to as 'the family circle' ('It sounds so close and safe and happy,' the Queen said). When, at the age of eighteen, Princess Elizabeth's interest in her handsome but impecunious cousin became obvious to everyone, her parents refused to countenance an early engagement. 'We both think she is too young for that now...P. had better not think any more about it for the present.'

It was to delay the inevitable that they had embarked on their tour of South Africa – and taken their daughters with them, hoping that the old adage 'out of sight, out of mind' would indeed prove to be right.

When the opposite turned out to be the case, the King was concerned in case any ill will had been generated. It was therefore with relief that he told his daughter and heir: 'I am so glad you wrote and told Mummy that you think the long wait before your engagement and the long time before the wedding was for the best. I was rather afraid that you had thought I was being hard hearted about it.'

His sense of loss, however, was almost palpable. After the wedding he wrote to her: 'when I handed your hand to the Archbishop I felt that I had lost something very precious.'

Again it was left to the Queen to give the situation the perspective of common sense. With simple nursery logic she stated: 'They grow up and leave us, and we must make the best of it.'

Trying to steer her husband round to her sensible way of thinking was proving ever more difficult, however. It had never been easy – his self-doubt was too deeply embedded – but with a supportive word or gentle hand of encouragement, the Queen had usually been able to lift the King's spirits. Now she found herself in competition with his health. It was an unequal contest.

The Queen would come to hold the Duchess of Windsor responsible for her husband's death. Had it not been for her, she argued, Edward VIII would never have abdicated and her beloved Bertie would never have been called upon to shoulder the burdens of office which, as he had plaintively exclaimed, 'I'm quite unprepared for'.

In the event he had acquitted himself with far more ability than he ever acknowledged. Now he was killing himself with worry, cigarettes and alcohol. As his health gave way so did his temper; his tantrums, always fierce, became ever more unpredictable. (His great-grandmother, Queen Victoria, was prone to unaccountable screaming fits; she was the granddaughter of Mad King George III.)

By the autumn of 1948 the King was in almost constant pain. He was diagnosed as having arteriosclerosis. It was feared that his right leg would have to be amputated. He was operated on but the decline was irreversible. Now the diagnosis was cancer. The Queen was told. He wasn't. The death-watch had begun.

To disguise his sickly pallor, he took to wearing thick brown make-up, as his father had done in the last days of his life. He was cheered when Churchill was returned to power in 1951 but by the winter he was too ill to travel. He pulled out of his planned tour of Australia and New Zealand and sent Princess Elizabeth and his newly-ennobled son-in-law the Duke of Edinburgh in his stead (as a farewell celebration the whole family went to see *South Pacific* at Drury Lane).

The last sighting the public would have of him was standing on the tarmac at Heathrow airport, hair blown thin, a gaunt, forlorn figure staring into the sky long after his daughter's plane had disappeared from view. The Queen on whom he so depended – and who, through a long and happy marriage, had come to depend on him – stood behind him, as she always had.

That evening the Queen, giving her nothing-is-wrong-if-you-carry-on-as-normal performance, visited the City of London Squadron of the Royal Auxiliary Air Force of which she was honorary Air Commodore. The following day the ailing King and his wife retired to Sandringham, taking Princess Margaret and their grandchildren, Prince Charles and Princess Anne, with them.

On Tuesday 5 February 1952 the King went out on the 'keeper's day' shoot to clear what remained of the season's game. He shot nine hares and a pigeon. 'A good day's sport,' he declared as he bade farewell to the nineteen other guns. 'I will expect you here at nine o'clock on Thursday.'

While the king was enjoying his recreation the Queen was lunching with Edward Seago, one of her favourite artists, who lived in nearby Ludham. Afterwards Seago took her by the hired motor cruiser *Sandra* for tea with friends at Barton Hall. It was late when she arrived back at the 'big house'. She went straight to the King's bedroom and showed him the Seago pictures of Sandringham that she had commissioned.

Dinner that night was, so the Queen wrote to inform Seago, 'a truly gay' occasion. The King listened to the BBC news on his Roberts wireless and learnt that all was well with his daughter in Kenya. He then went out to the kennels to check on his golden retriever, Roddy, who had cut his paw on a thorn. 'Poor Roddy, he and I are both too keen on shooting for our own good,' he told a groom.

Back inside, he listened to Princess Margaret play the piano for half an hour before deciding on an early night. He took a country magazine with him, telling his wife as he went: 'I'll see you in the morning.' A valet brought him a cup of hot chocolate and shortly after midnight a watchman patrolling the lawns below saw him fasten a latch on his bedroom window.

At 7.30 on the morning of 6 February 1952 his valet, James Macdonald, brought a cup of tea to the King's bedroom and drew back the curtains. The King did not stir. He would never stir again. The life and reign of George VI was at its end.

Elizabeth was already awake when her maid Gwen Suckling brought her her morning tea. A moment later the equerry on duty, Commander Sir Harold Campbell, hurried in and told her that her husband, her King, her support, was no more. She immediately went to his study and ordered that a vigil must be kept outside his open bedroom door. 'The King must not be left,' she said. Campbell remarked: 'I never knew a woman could be so brave.'

When she went downstairs to see her grandchildren, however, her composure, for once, understandably, deserted her and tears flowed down her face. Prince Charles cuddled up to her and said: 'Don't cry, Grannie.'

Charles was too young to appreciate it, but by the death of his grandfather he had moved up a notch on the ladder of the royal hierarchy to the rank of heir apparent. For Grannie the situation was the reverse. She had been demoted. The reins of sovereignty had passed to George's daughter – the new Queen Elizabeth.

There was sorrow at the King's passing (80,000 filed by in the cold to see his body lying in state) but at the same time there was a general and genuine feeling of optimism in the air. A new Queen

THE NEW QUEEN, DRESSED ALL IN BLACK, IS SALUTED AS SHE ARRIVES BACK IN LONDON. AFTER SHE HEARD THE NEWS OF HER FATHER'S DEATH, SHE TRAVELLED THROUGH THE NIGHT FROM KENYA TO COMFORT HER MOTHER.

promised a new beginning and people started calling themselves the 'new Elizabethans'. Suddenly the world seemed fresh with opportunity.

Where did that leave the woman who, until that morning, had been Queen? Upon the death of her husband, she sent a message to the British people. It amounted to a plea. She said: 'My only wish now is that I may be allowed to continue the work we sought to do together.'

Elizabeth's concern for her future was as pressing as it was poignant. For twenty-nine years, sixteen of them as Queen, Elizabeth had stood at the centre of royal life. She had served as an example and a focus through the constitutional traumas of the Abdication and the tumult of the war. She had given strength and backbone to her husband and made a king out of him, in fact as well as name. And in so doing she had stamped her indelible seal on the monarchy. It was her style which had been the keynote of George VI's reign. She had given it the colour and cheerful fortitude which had helped to lighten the tone of the Royal Family.

Now, at the age of fifty-one, she found herself without a defined role in a realm where royalty's station was no longer cer-

tain or inviolate. She was still popular. But now George VI was dead and for the moment her outlook was as bleak as the flat Norfolk landscape that morning of 6 February 1952, when his reign and life had come to its premature end. She was marooned in the winter-grey uncertainty of widowhood, no longer Queen, but the mother of the Queen. It was an uncomfortable position for Elizabeth, made doubly so by the way her daughter took up the mantle of her responsibilities – and relegated her mother to the sidelines.

On 2 June 1953 she was back in Westminster Abbey for another Coronation. Seventeen years earlier she had occupied the centre stage. Now she was relegated by protocol to a seat in the front row of the Royal Gallery, her grandson Prince Charles beside her.

The Prince, still only 4 years old, was too young to be imbued with the solemnity of the occasion and kept bobbing up and down on his seat. He wiped his hands through his newly brilliantined hair and smelt the unfamiliar fragrance. He covered his eyes and peeked at the ceremony unfolding before him through the spread of his fingers. He fired a stream of questions at his grandmother and aunt who was sitting on his other side which continued unchecked for almost an hour. At one point he disappeared from view altogether, to emerge a few moments later triumphant holding his grandmother's handbag. Then the gold plate on display caught his eye, and his grandmother had to haul him back as he started to lean too far over the Gallery to get a better look at it.

Elizabeth, glittering in diamonds, handled the little Heir to the Throne, as she did the whole occasion, with her stately composure, dispensing courtly bows to the assembled peers and dignitaries, never hesitating, always with a smile ready for the crowds and the television cameras which for the first time had been allowed to film this most sacred of royal events.

The press, their minds on more temporal matters, saw Princess Margaret pick a speck of fluff off the uniform of her mother's recently divorced equerry Peter Townsend, so providing the first visible proof of a romance which had long been the subject of Court gossip. The old Queen feigned not to notice and proceeded sedately on her regal way.

Even this most self-contained of ladies cannot have failed but to have sensed the significance of the day, however. A new Queen was on the throne and the old order was passing. Cecil Beaton wrote: 'In the Queen Widow's expression we read sadness combined with pride.'

The British constitution makes no allowance for and affords no official place to the widow of a king and even a queen as formidable as Mary had found herself exiled to the shadows. Chips Channon, the diarist MP quoted the Duke of Devonshire's observation that the new Queen 'makes it very plain to (her mother) that whereas she...is a commoner, she, Princess Elizabeth, is of royal blood.'

Officially Elizabeth was now the Dowager Queen, a title she detested and which carried no specified responsibilities. She didn't even have a home – Sandringham and Balmoral became the property of her daughter, the Queen, and within six weeks she would be out of Buckingham Palace – 'to get out of the way of the new Queen', as Lord Home said, but also because she had to. At Bertie's State funeral she was photographed alongside her mother-in-law and daughter: three Queens united in mourning. It was noted that, for the first time anyone could remember, Elizabeth was photographed without a smile.

In grief, she retreated to Scotland to stay with her friend Lady Doris Vyner at her home situated on a peak in Caithness. There were those who feared that she might go the way of Queen

Victoria, who, upon the death of Prince Albert, swathed herself in black and withdrew from public life for several years.

But her capacity to shrug aside life's misfortunes by putting them behind her was not going to allow her to remain cloistered in bereavement indefinitely. Winston Churchill's promptings helped (in typically grandiloquent style, he informed her: 'Your country needs you, Ma'am'). So did Edith Evans, whose poetry readings she had attended during the war. The actress sent her an anthology of verse. The Queen Mother wrote back: 'It is giving me the greatest pleasure. I took it out with me and started to read it sitting by the river. It was a day when one felt engulfed by great black clouds of unhappiness and misery. I found a sort of peace stealing round my heart. I found hope in George Herbert's poem, "who could have thought my shrivel'd heart could have recovered greenness…' And I thought how small and selfish is sorrow. But it bangs one about until one is senseless, and I can never thank you enough for giving me such a delicious book wherein I found so much beauty and hope, quite suddenly one day by the river.'

An even greater help was the comfort she drew from spiritualism – just as Princess Diana did.

The Bowes Lyons have long believed themselves gifted with second sight, and a passing acquaintanceship with what her family called 'the other side ' made its impression on Elizabeth as she grew up at Glamis. When her elder brother Michael was reported killed in action during the First World War, her beloved David refused to accept it, claiming that he was only injured. Elizabeth, convinced of her 'darling bruvver's' powers of 'seeing', supported him, and their faith was rewarded when Michael was discovered in a field hospital on the Western Front.

Her sister Rose, who married Lord Granville, would also recall how, as children, they frequently encountered apparitions in the castle, including the spectre of a grey lady who would appear in the the chapel. 'She was praying,' Lady Granville recalled. 'I distinctly saw the detail of her dress and the outline of her figure – but the sun, shining through the windows, shone through her and made a pattern on the floor.'

The Royal Family, too, as George VI once admitted, 'are no strangers to spiritualism.' This was not something to be broadcast. As Defender of the Faith and the Supreme Governor of the

Established Church of England, it was not deemed wise or sensible to publicly attach his name to something which many of his subjects regarded as dangerous and irreligious mumbo-jumbo. It was to 'the other side', however, that Elizabeth turned for solace in her grief.

Early in 1953 a medium called Lilian Bailey was called from her home in Wembley and taken to an address in Kensington where she was blindfolded and then taken on to another house. When the blindfold was removed she found herself in the company of the Queen Mother, whose husband had just died, the Queen, Prince Philip, the Duchess of Kent whose husband had been killed in the war, and the Duchess's daughter, Princess Alexandra. Mrs Bailey then put herself into a trance and started talking to the dead. Or so she claimed.

Intriguingly, though, Mrs Bailey's account was never officially denied. And, to lend it substance, there is the fact that she was a friend of long and good standing of Lionel Logue. He was the Australian speech therapist who did so much to assist George VI, and was himself a committed believer in spiritualism.

According to Mrs Bailey, the Queen Mother attended several more sessions with her. Whether Mrs Bailey ever managed to make contact with the late King, only the Queen Mother knows. Mrs Bailey said that because she was in a trance she has no recollection. And the Queen Mother, one eye always on her dignity and reputation, has made no comment.

Diana was equally circumspect about her dealings with mystics, astrologers, faith-healers and psychics. 'I'd never discuss it with anyone,' the Princess said. 'If I did they would think I was a nut.'

By her own choice, however, Diana's life was much more open than the Queen Mother's, and her visits to a succession of astrologers, including Penny Thornton and Felix Lyle, the go-between she used in her dealings with her biographer Andrew Morton, were soon widely reported. And, less than three weeks before her death, she took her fated lover Dodi Fayed with her when she flew to Derbyshire by helicopter to see her psychic, Rita Rogers.

This was not a subject the two women ever discussed. Diana was always wary of and, in truth, rather disconcerted by the

Queen Mother, who regarded her impetuous and, to her way of thinking, irresponsible granddaughter-in-law with ever-mounting suspicion. The simple fact is that they never saw eye to eye – even when it came to an interest which they both shared.

For Diana this reliance on the paranormal was a search for fulfilment and direction which never produced quite the result she was looking for, and she remained forever troubled and unsure of herself and where her destiny lay.

For the Queen Mother, more self-contained and a great deal more certain of her position, it was simply a means to an end and it helped rekindle her sense of hope. This in turn produced a determination to get back to work. In another of her nannyisms Elizabeth declared: 'The work you do is the rent you pay for the room you occupy on earth.' She chose for herself on the death of her husband the title of Queen Elizabeth The Queen Mother, anxious to avoid the term 'Dowager' and, so armed, put her shoulder to the royal wheel and applied herself with an energy that would carry her through into her nineties.

Quite what that work was would remain ill-defined. It involved opening factories and launching ships, patronizing this institution, serving as a figurehead for that association, but that was really only the means to an end. And the end, as far as she was concerned, was to spread her royal radiance as far and as wide as she possibly could, for her own sake as well as for others.

Her friend and lady-in-waiting Ruth, Lady Fermoy observed: 'Loneliness is the hardest thing to bear, not having by you the one person to whom you can say anything and everything. This was probably worse for her because, as Queen, she had many friends but not many intimates – the reserve she had learned as Queen made her lonelier than others would otherwise have been. To resume work was the right and natural decision for her.'

And the sooner she got back to it the better, as she herself acknowledged. On the day after George VI's death the Queen who was now the Queen's mother came downstairs to play with her grandchildren. She explained: 'I have to start sometime, and it is better now than later.'

She had set her course to become the most popular grandmother in the world.

CHAPTER 11

IN HER OWN FASHION

'I have nothing to wear!' This has always been the Queen Mother's refrain, constantly repeated to her husband, to her dressmaker, to her daughters.

Her lament is an elaborate exaggeration. She has rows of clothes, racks of them, lining her dressing room and spilling into the corridor. Ball gowns, day dresses, tea gowns, pastel gardening frocks, summer clothes, winter clothes, suits, coats, belted dresses, buttoned dresses, bejewelled dresses, coat dresses, fur-trimmed dresses, clothes for every occasion and many more besides.

'I'll never know why she wants all those clothes, as they are all the same,' the Queen once complained. With a shrug of resignation she added,: 'But you won't change her.'

True enough. Still her mother's clothes kept coming, in their tens, in their hundreds, until the whole of Clarence House was awash in tulle and taffeta, silks and the finest wools, with hats, shoes and handbags to match. There might be a dozen pale blue coats hanging in her wardrobe, but as far as Elizabeth was concerned, that was never a reason for not ordering yet another.

'What have you bought me now, you temptress?' she would joke when Evelyn Elliott, her vendeuse for half a century, arrived with her latest sample of beautiful fabric.

Cost was never a consideration. The late Ian Thomas, the Queen's couturier, recalled how, at the time of Princess Margaret's wedding, the Queen Mother's milliner, Madame Claude St Cyr, arrived from Paris with a hat to complement a gold lamé dress Norman Hartnell had designed for her. It was made of aigrettes in cream shading to a pale toast

THE QUEEN AS AN ELEGANT, MATURE WOMAN WEARING A MAGNIFICENT BLACK VELVET CRINOLINE. IT WAS CECIL BEATON'S IDEA TO PHOTOGRAPH THE QUEEN IN UNACCUSTOMED BLACK AND HARTNELL MADE THE COSTUME SPECIALLY FOR THIS PHOTOGRAPHIC SESSION IN 1948.

colour. As a golden rule prices were never discussed with the Queen Mother, but on this occasion Madame St Cyr insisted that her royal client be told just how much the little spray of feathers was going to cost.

When the Queen Mother was seated at her dressing-table with the creation on her head, Hartnell whispered that the feathers alone came to over £100 – almost three months' wages for the average working man in 1960.

The Queen Mother continued to move her head from side to side, admiring her reflection in the mirror. Then, after what Thomas, who was working for Hartnell at the time, called 'a fairly long silence', she looked up and said: 'Yes – and I think I'll have one in white too.'

That was the end of the matter. The bill, when it was presented, was left discreetly on her dressing-room table, eventually to be settled with a personal cheque. The price was never mentioned again. To a gentlewoman of the Queen Mother's generation money was a vulgarity to which one never alluded.

Elizabeth's taste in clothes, like her attitude towards their expense, had been fashioned by her mother. As a child she had amused herself for hours with the great dressing-up box at Glamis Castle, which was stuffed with clothes and hats and wigs accumulated and then discarded by generations of Lyons. This was supplemented by costumes devised for her by Lady Strathmore, who was both imaginative and deft with a needle. While Nanny made and altered Elizabeth's day-to-day clothes, often inherited from her elder sisters, Lady Strathmore turned her hand to producing her youngest daughter's fancy-dress and party outfits. Elizabeth had one particular favourite, a long dress of rose pink and silver, which her mother copied from a Velázquez picture described by Lady Cynthia Asquith as 'a long dress of rose coloured brocade, full pleated and gathered at the waist, stiffened with a hoop and coming right down to her feet'.

On another occasion Lady Strathmore copied a painting of a Van Dyck child and created a dress with a high square bodice and stiff satin skirts, which made little Elizabeth 'look exactly like one of the children of Charles I.'

The habit of drawing inspiration from the works of painters continued into Elizabeth's womanhood. Sir George Hayter's picture of Queen Victoria's Coronation gave her the idea of using wheat-ear motifs for the dresses of the maids of honour for her own Coronation, and Court dressmaker Madame Handley Seymour incorporated the square *décolleté*, after Van Dyck's portraits in the Royal Collection, into the Coronation gown itself.

Most notably, this same source of inspiration also furnished Elizabeth with the basis for what became her defining style. This time the creative spur was provided by Franz Xavier Winterhalter, whose paintings George VI had shown to Norman Hartnell.

'Thus it is to the King and Winterhalter that are owed...the regal renaissance of the romantic crinoline,' Hartnell recorded. A style had been realized and the Queen was to stay with it for the rest of her life.

Elizabeth was thirty-six when Bertie ascended the throne – late to start the quest for a look of her own, even in an era when, as Evelyn Elliot said, 'the teenage market did not exist and "fashion" was only for women aged from twenty-eight upwards.' But then dressing for the cutting edge of society, with all its capricious ostentation, had not played any noteworthy part in the life of this mother and dutiful wife. Fashion was led by her brother-in-law the Prince of Wales, whose carefully nurtured look of unstudied elegance provided the sartorial template for a generation.

David was pictured whenever he sallied forth and a selection of photographs of what he was wearing, together with patterns of materials and samples of collars, ties, socks and waistcoats were immediately dispatched to America where they created a series of overnight fashions. When the dye came out of his red bathing-costume while on holiday in Le Touquet in Northern France, giving him what was described as 'the temporary appearance of a Red Indian', it was the talk of towns on both sides of the Atlantic.

This was certainly not an example either Elizabeth or her husband were inclined to follow. Their clothes were safe, staid, respectable – and dowdy. When Lord David Cecil described Elizabeth as 'picturesquely unfashionable' he was being kind. Help was close at hand, had she cared to look out of her parents' window: Hartnell had set up shop across the road from the Strathmores' home in Bruton Street in 1924, and soon established himself as the most talked-about designer in London. But Elizabeth, mirroring her husband's sartorial conservatism, had continued to patronize

STATE EVENING DRESS OF DUCHESSE SATIN WITH BEADED DECORATION. THE FULL CIRCULAR SKIRT WAS WORN WITH A HOOPED PETTICOAT. WORN FOR A GALA PERFORMANCE OF THE SADLER'S WELLS BALLET AT COVENT GARDEN, 1950.

the altogether more conventional Handley Seymour who had been her mother's dressmaker, and had her salon just around the corner in New Bond Street.

The mantle of sovereignty is a flamboyant one, however, and, as her queenly confidence grew, so did her desire to set her own royal fashion. And it was Norman Hartnell she entrusted with the assignment.

By then the designer had moved out of his rooms above the shop and below the actress Gladys Cooper, who was running a business called Gladys Cooper Beauty Preparations, and into

220

Number 26 Bruton Street, a few doors away. For the next forty years this imposing Georgian house, complete with ballroom which had once been the London home of Viscount Hereford, served as his headquarters.

There were six workrooms, which would today be called illegal sweatshops, each employing over fifty girls. Altogether Hartnell had some 400 people labouring to produce 2,000 commissions each year. The embroidery rooms were on the top floor. There a workforce of fifty-six women sat either side of long wooden frames slowly attaching beads, using special long beading needles and a double thread for strength. The material was kept tight on the frames and each piece of the dress was marked so that it could be put together like a patchwork quilt. Hartnell's trademark sequins and rhinestones were sewn on individually.

The attention to detail was painstaking, with perfection the goal. A traineeship of eighteen months was not uncommon before an apprentice even so much as stitched a sleeve. 'No-one became a "hand" – allowed to put a complete dress together – without at least five years 'and sometimes eight years' experience,' said Evelyn Elliot. As a consequence there were very few fitters or cutters under the age of forty.

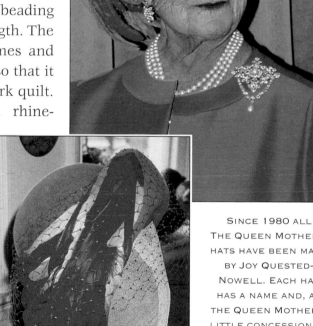

SINCE 1980 ALL THE QUEEN MOTHER'S HATS HAVE BEEN MADE BY JOY QUESTED-NOWELL. EACH HAT HAS A NAME AND, AS THE QUEEN MOTHER'S LITTLE CONCESSION TO ECONOMY, IS RETURNED TO JOY'S CHELSEA WORKROOM TO BE REDYED AND RETRIMMED WHENEVER NECESSARY.

As with the staff, so with the materials. In the three tailors' rooms the bolts of materials were lined with a wet cloth and wrapped in bales before being cut and when the dress or suit was tried on, the tailor would hang a tape down the length of material to ensure it was not going off the grain. If it was, it was discarded.

Mrs Louise Bowen joined Hartnell in 1923 as a fifteen-year-old straight out of a convent, 'to pick up the pins.' She rose to become his head stockkeeper and adviser on the cost and quality of fabrics. She recalled his attention to detail. Everything, he told her, had to look as glamorous from the inside as it did on the outside, and in the workrooms all the silk underslips were scalloped and tucked by hand, using thin organza or chiffon as a borderline. Almost everything in that age before synthetics, including fabrics such as *eau de toile* and tulle, came from France, brought over by 'travellers' who were agents for the great material houses. They called at Bruton Street every day to see if there were any orders and one, a stately lace agent named Mr Elms, always arrived in a horse and carriage.

There was an entire floor for furs run by Mr Bell the furrier. For those who could afford it, silver fox was the most adaptable. It was fashionably worn as a small cape over an afternoon dress or draped from the shoulder as a stole. It was used as a trimming for hats and collars and cuffs, for cloth coats and suits, and could be dyed to match any outfit. Silver-fox fur is seen by some as the epitome of feminine glamour and the Queen Mother has worn it for many years.

She was wearing it the day she first visited Hartnell's emporium, 'silver grey georgette clouded with the palest grey fox' as Louise Bowen remembered. It was October 1935 and Elizabeth was there to oversee the fittings for the bridesmaids' dresses her daughters were to wear at the wedding of their uncle the Duke of Gloucester to Lady Alice Montagu-Douglas-Scott. The girls arrived in identical blue jackets and small grey hats.

Hartnell, a perennial snob, had given his staff precise instruction on how to curtsey to the Duchess of York, as she still was.

'Not so quick and jerky,' he ordered. 'Not like a pecking sparrow, more like a swooning swan.'

Once she had been bowed in, the Duchess was ushered through the crowded showroom to a small private room at the rear of the building where, to Hartnell's considerable delight, she asked to see his collection. The Princesses, having tried on their bridesmaids' dresses, were more interested in watching the cars come and go in the mews at the back. The Duchess obviously liked what she had seen, for three years later when, as Queen, she set off to France, it was Hartnell and not Handley Seymour who was commissioned to design her wardrobe. Soon he was providing her with everything, from underwear to overcoats, gloves, furs and parasols with handles of diamonds and sapphires. It was the start of an association which would last until Hartnell's death in 1979. When he died, the Queen and Princess Margaret turned to each other and said in unison, 'What are we going to do about Mummy and her clothes now?'

Mummy knew, even if they didn't. Hartnell had set her style and the imprint was indelible. Hartnell was succeeded by a former employee of the House of Hartnell, John Anderson, who ran his own couture business with the essential workroom from London's Chiltern Street. Gentle and unassuming, he continued to make the Queen Mother's clothes until his death in 1996. Then the job was taken over by Evelyn Elliot who always knows exactly what the Queen Mother wants to wear. 'She's not going to change now' says Evelyn, who habitually did the sketches even in the days of Hartnell.

'She knows exactly what suits her and once we have chosen the materials the garments are made up from my sketches by Mr Roy Allen in Hampstead.' The grand days of Hartnell's empire were over but his influence continued. At the beginning, though, it had been touch and go. The gown in silver with a deep collar of silver lace Hartnell produced for the State visit of the King of the Belgiums in 1937 had won the approval of the new King and Queen. However, the Queen never wore the one in grey satin embroidered with pearls and amethysts he had made for the visit of King Carol of Rumania.

'On the morning of the day of the banquet, there appeared in a newspaper a detailed description, though with no mention of the designer's name, of this important dress,' Hartnell lamented. 'His Majesty was most displeased and the dress was abandoned.'

The King's anger was as predictable as it was extreme. The notion that a couturier, even one he had personally conducted through Buckingham Palace, should appear to be using his newly-forged royal connections for publicity violated George's sense of propriety. Only Elizabeth's intercession prevented Hartnell being dismissed from the royal service. She loved the clothes he made for her and she was not going to let him go. She diplomatically accepted his explanation that 'some over-zealous member of my staff must have let slip, or given away, the news of the dress before it was delivered to the Palace' and persuaded her husband to accept it too. Madame Handley Seymour was duly relegated to the past and in later years the Queen Mother feigned hardly to remember the lady who had made her Coronation dress. Handley Seymour was, she said, already an 'oldish woman' when she first went to her in the Twenties – and, as Queen, Elizabeth was determined to champion a new order, including the delight of shopping for clothes.

DRESS AND COAT IN STRIKING LIME GREEN COLOUR, LACE LINED AND EDGED IN SILK CHIFFON WITH MATCHING HAT OF OSPREY BY SIMONE MIRMAN, WORN FOR THE INVESTITURE OF THE PRINCE OF WALES, CAERNARVON, 1 JULY 1969.

'One went to one of the small houses in Bond Street when one wanted something special,' the Queen Mother remembered. At the time such forays were still considered something of a novelty and women such as Lady Airlie, who, as Lady of the Bedchamber to Queen Mary, needed a great many changes of outfits, much preferred to have their clothes made up from patterns bought in a shop. Accompanied by a maid, Lady Airlie would choose the designs and order the paper patterns before buying the material from one of the big stores in Oxford Street, such as Selfridges.

A sewing-woman would then be engaged. 'The work went on all day from 9 a.m. to 6 p.m., but eventually quite a credible collection was produced,' Lady Airlie recalled.

Credible it may have been, but chic it wasn't – that was a French monopoly. As the Queen Mother remembered: 'If they wanted couture, they went to Paris as there was virtually no-one in London in those days.'

This Gallic domination was not always popular in Britain. There had been fierce criticism in 1909 when the Prime Minister's wife, the notable Margot Asquith, invited the fashionable French couturier Paul Poiret to 10 Downing Street to show his collection of brilliant red, violet, gold-green and blue corset-free draped dresses. Glancing in on the party, the Prime Minister was reported to be 'looking grave', as well he might. The British textile and dress industries were in crisis, and increased taxes had been levied on the rich to pay for social reform. This was not a time for frippery, and the popular press thundered at the stupidity of what it called Mrs Asquith's 'Gowning Street Parade'.

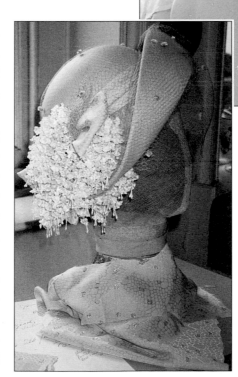

THIS CREATION BY JOY QUESTED-NOWELL WAS MADE FOR THE QUEEN MOTHER'S 90TH BIRTHDAY IN 1990. SHE LIKED IT SO MUCH SHE WORE IT ON MANY OCCASIONS THAT YEAR.

Such rantings did nothing to loosen the French stranglehold, of course. Those who could afford it continued to look to Paris for their inspiration, Elizabeth amongst them (she had some of her clothes made by a French house called Vionet). The British couturiers who started opening up in the Thirties tried to add a French gloss to their work by adding Monsieur or Madame as a prefix to their names. Mrs Hughes, who employed the young Hartnell for a brief three months after the First World War called herself Madame Desirée, while Lady Duff Gordon, briefly London's grandest couturier, changed her name to Lucille. Hartnell continued the tradition, and the new Queen was attended by a host of hard-working English girls bearing French names. There was Madame Emilienne who fitted her day clothes and the Mademoiselles David who looked after those for the evening. Louise Bowen somehow survived as an English Miss – but only after her Christian name had been Gallicized to Louie. Presiding over them all was Hartnell's Directrice, Madame Jeanne, who rinsed her white hair in a particularly fetching shade of purple and was known in consequence as Madame Mauve.

Then there was Madame Claude St Cyr who did the hats and the advantage of actually being French. Elegantly swathed in mink over a grey or beige suit or dress, she was perpetually involved in what one staff member described as 'well-mannered fights' with Hartnell over 'Norman's big 'ats' as she called them. Like two cranes they would circle each other, pecking away with choice and well-turned phrases, intent on ruffling each other's feathers.

Another milliner who enjoyed Elizabeth's patronage was Aage Thaarp. On his first visit to Buckingham Palace, the Danish-born Thaarp recalled being 'shot' at from behind a sofa by Princess Margaret Rose, who was engaged in a private game of cowboys and Indians. Always flamboyant, Thaarp once tried to persuade the new Queen-Empress to have her hat trimmed with plastic vegetables, thereby provoking the King, who happened to be in the room, to declare: 'You're mad.' It was a rare disagreement with his wife, for as Evelyn Elliot said: 'You couldn't disagree with her. Somehow you wouldn't get round to that – if there was something she didn't want you to talk about she would change the subject.'

The trick, the *vendeuse* recalled, was to lead Elizabeth gently towards a cut or fabric, while being careful never to put her in a position where she had to take a firm stand. It was all done by hint and nuance, as were most things in her long life.

'If she says "I don't think so, do you?" you can tell her, "I don't think so either,"' Ms Elliot said. 'But if she said, "What do you think of that?" and I would say "it's very nice", she would say. "Then let's just say we like that. So put that on one side."'

It required practice, tact and intuition to read these regal rules, but once they had been deciphered there was never really doubt as to what Elizabeth liked – and what she didn't. Brown and navy blue 'were a no-no', nor could she ever be persuaded to wear a coat and dress in different colours. And no matter how many heavy hints Hartnell and his staff let drop, she still insisted on wearing her signature white shoes, made for her by Edward Rayne, rather than the coloured ones they were suggesting. 'She was no pushover,' Ms Elliot said.

Conversely, if Elizabeth liked something, no amount of pleading from her dresser could dissuade her from wearing it again and again. During her ninetieth birthday celebrations she developed a fondness for a hat with little bells of feather on the side which tinkled in the breeze. She wore it to a ceremony in her honour on Horse Guards Parade and then again a couple of days later, ignoring gentle hints that she looked identical in every photograph. She has her look – and she sticks to it.

When milliner Zdenko Rudolf von Ehrenfeld arrived from Prague in 1948, he was unknown in the fashion world and spoke very little English. His designs soon won him acclaim, however, and two years later he held his first London show. Former Worth model Joy Quested-Nowell was one of the girls chosen to show Rudolf's collection, and it was the start of a partnership which was to last until his death in 1980.

When Evelyn Elliot introduced the Queen Mother to Rudolf in 1969, the Queen and the Prague-born milliner formed an instant rapport and spent the afternoon discussing hats. Joy Quested-Nowell was present at their first meeting and recalls taking a selection of half a dozen hats for the Queen Mother to try on. Rudolf placed his hands around the head of his royal client that so he could feel the shape. He found the Queen Mother's cranium to be large and squarish, which, with her broad face, is ideal for hats. He discovered that the Queen Mother was very definite about what she liked. Her distinctive style in millinery, which was to last her the rest of her life, had begun to be outlined.

Each creation Rudolf made was, in a way, two hats. Underneath is a cloche-like bandeau, which fits closely over her bun of hair at the back. The actual hat is then mounted on the bandeau.

'Rudolf found a look that suited her,' Joy recalled, 'and she stayed with it. She finds it very soft and feminine and it doesn't obscure her face.'

When Rudolf died Joy lost interest in the business, but when the Queen Mother's Royal Warrant was transferred to her she decided to carry on designing – but only for the Queen Mother.

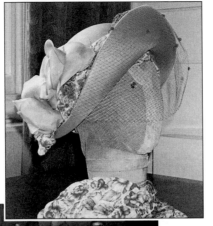

THE QUEEN MOTHER AT THE SANDRINGHAM FLOWER SHOW, JULY 1993.

The two women still spend many an afternoon in the dressing-room at Clarence House, discussing various trims for the dozens of new hats the Queen Mother orders each year. Often the afternoon edition of *The Archers* can be heard playing in the background. And while the dogs snuffle around the floor and dresser Betty Leek flicks through the hanging rails to find the correct outfit, Joy and the Queen Mother work together on the complete look before they go 'on parade'. Each hat is designed in conjunction with a specific outfit, and each has a name. The Queen Mother sometimes suggests themes like 'Bersagliere', prompted by the memories of her childhood visits to Florence, where she recalled seeing foot-soldiers wearing hats trimmed with feathers.

To the average eye all the hats appear identical, but there are, so Joy explained, six or seven different upturned brims which are the royal favourites. If necessary Joy goes to Paris to buy materials and trimmings, but she also relies on her 'three boys', fellow milliners Philip Sommerville, Freddie Fox and Graham Smith, who supply her with the small amount of fine straw she needs. She keeps meticulous notes on how each hat was made, together with a sample of the material and details of any alterations. She then takes a snapshot before she delivers the finished version, which helps when it comes to repairs.

The Queen Mother's little concession to economy is to allow her hats to be redyed and retrimmed whenever they look 'tired'. Joy makes and repairs the hats in her Chelsea kitchen, which, having natural light, doubles as a workroom. After the only fitting, the finished version is placed in one of the mahogany cupboards which line the Queen Mother's Clarence House dressing-room while those needed for the current season swing jauntily from a wire hat tree on a sofa table in the centre of the room.

Some of Joy's most charming creations are never seen by the public. These are the Queen Mother's gardening hats which, like her 'country' hats, are worn when she's off duty. The country hats are fashioned so that she can pull them low over her face and tie a scarf around them, but the gardening hats are made of straw and the Queen Mother wears them for tending to her gardens with all the style and panache she displays on official engagements.

Elizabeth has an important collection of jewellery but prefers to stick to her three strands of pearls, a couple of favoured pairs of earrings, the pearl ring set in a diamond cluster which she wears instead of her sapphire engagement ring, and two

THE QUEEN MOTHER HAS BEEN KNOWN TO WEAR THE SAME HAT ON MORE THAN ONE OCCASION.
ABOVE: ON AN OFFICIAL VISIT TO THE ELIZABETH HOSPITAL, HACKNEY, JULY 1992.
LEFT: AT THE V.E. DAY 50TH ANNIVERSARY CELEBRATIONS IN MAY 1995 AT BUCKINGHAM PALACE.

or three brooches. By well-practised sleight of hand, she can transfer whichever brooch she is wearing from her coat to her dress without anyone noticing, thereby saving herself the trouble of having to wear two.

When the Queen Mother was Queen, society was considerably more formal than now, and on any average day she was expected to wear different outfits in the morning, for lunch, in the afternoon and in the evening. Care had to be taken to ensure the clothes were suitable for each occasion.

'If there was a big ball at the Australian embassy, for instance, there would be mimosa on the dress, embroidered on or let into it somewhere as a tribute to the Australians,' Ms Elliot said. If Elizabeth were attending a dinner where insignia were to be worn, a clash of colour between dress and emblem had to be avoided at all cost.

Foreign tours – and as Queen Mother she was constantly on the move – added to the problem. Clothes not only had to complement the occasion but also the country, and outfits had to be carefully juggled to avoid undue repetition. That was the responsibility of her dresser – Miss Suckling who was succeeded by her sister Miss Beale, and finally Miss Betty Leek. Each in their turn would make careful note of when a dress had been worn, and where. It was also the dresser's job to check the garment after each wearing for rips, stains, tears or creases, and then press it ready for its next outing.

The Queen Mother took great enjoyment in selecting her clothes. Sometimes her dresser would summon Hartnell by telephone and he would go to Buckingham Palace with an armful of coloured sketches drawn for her by Ian Thomas, who was working for the couturier at the time. On other occasions Elizabeth would venture forth to Bruton Street, usually with Princess Margaret in tow. She would be ushered into the showroom where a few other select clients would have been assembled 'so that the room didn't look empty,' as Ms Elliot explained.

At one point Hartnell employed nearly a hundred models and they paraded his offerings. Elizabeth would never discuss the clothes while they were being displayed before her. 'She would just look,' Ms Elliot said. The final decision was left until later, after she had talked over her forthcoming engagements and her needs with Hartnell and the *vendeuse*. Once the choice had been made, Hartnell's staff, which in his heyday totalled nearly 400, would be put to priority work.

Two fittings were usually needed. Winterhalter had dealt with paint on canvas; Hartnell had the more exacting task of fitting fabric to flesh. It was a talent which required all the skills of his workrooms, for the royal client's figure was not without its little irregularities.

Low in the bosom, Elizabeth eschewed round necks, preferring the V-neck which, everyone agreed, was more flattering to her particular shape. The heavy brooches she wore did not help the hang of the dresses but, set in her ways, she refused to pin them to her bra, preferring to leave the problem to the skill of her designer.

Length was another consideration. In her declining years Elizabeth has suffered from an ulcerated leg. This is not something she ever mentions. A product of the old school that taught that one's problems should be kept to oneself, she would simply say that she had a 'little scratch'. She did however have a small scar on her leg which she said dated from the day when, as a little girl, she fell out of an apple tree while playing with her brother David. This served as a reminder to the fitters of the correct length she liked her dresses, and they adjusted them according to the scar.

The choice of colour was also important, especially for her evening clothes. Because of the number of decorations she was called upon to wear, her gowns were usually in neutral white, apart from one she had made in lilac taffeta. When Ms Elliot told her how attractive it looked, the Queen Mother replied: 'Yes, Princess Margaret says it's her favourite dress.'

The Queen Mother, needless to say, was very fond of it too. Evelyn Elliot said: 'She knows what suits her and what she is comfortable in and she keeps that line. She feels she dresses for herself, but at the same time she dresses as she thinks people like to see her. She knows they all like her in blue, so she wears lots of blue, she has done so for more than half a century.'

Fashions have changed and the great couture houses have down-sized. Hartnell is dead, many of the fabric manufacturers have gone out of business and the quality of workmanship is nothing like it used to be. According to Evelyn Elliot, British couture started to crumble with the advent of rock 'n' roll, when

manufacturers turned away from their old customers to exploit the disposable incomes of young people who no longer wanted to look like their mothers. Most of the old aristocratic clients were disappearing anyway, driven from the arena by taxation, rising costs and social change.

Yet the Queen Mother sails calmly on as if everything is as it was, swathed in tulle and crinoline, ordering new clothes for each new season, unconcerned by the cost, adding, always adding to her collection.

The clothes are stored in polythene bags and hung in free-standing mahogany wardrobes which line a corridor in Clarence House. Occasionally a dress or a ball gown is lent to a museum. Sometimes the Queen Mother, whose figure has survived the passing of the years, will take out an old favourite and wear it, pleased it still fits her, thrilled by its old-fashioned quality. But in the main the clothes just hang there on their racks, the reminders of a bygone age when the Empress's new clothes were as grand as the Empire itself.

People are inclined to dress in a way which reflects the happiest times of their lives, and the Queen Mother was at her happiest when she was Queen and her husband reigned over a quarter of the world. That is when she established her own style. It is the style she has clung to ever since. The world has changed beyond recognition since those days. The Queen Mother never has seen the need to follow suit.

THE OUTFIT (AND DETAIL OF HAT, RIGHT) WORN BY THE QUEEN MOTHER TO THE BRAEMAR GAMES, BRAEMAR, SCOTLAND IN SEPTEMBER 1996.

CHAPTER 12

ℋIGHLAND RETREAT

Elizabeth has never been one to be overawed by grandeur. Brought up with a great fortress as one of her homes, she settled easily into the splendour of the royal environment of palaces and villas, mansions and castles. She moves between them at a leisurely pace, in majestic style. The demands of royalty, she quickly realized, had their material compensations and she continues to enjoy them, to the end of her life.

While the Queen has been forced to cut back and make stringent economies, Elizabeth has always carried on is if nothing has changed and the sun is still high in an Imperial sky. While her daughter is forever looking for ways to cut down on the number of royal staff, the Queen Mother has never ventured north to Scotland without a full complement of retainers in tow. They include a dresser, a personal housemaid, a brace of footmen, a page, a chef, as well as an equerry and the attendant ladies-in-waiting. Her entourage would sometimes comprise a staff of twenty who followed her in their own coach as she made her regal progression around the Highlands in a chauffeur-driven Daimler, moving backwards and forwards between the Castle of Mey and Birkhall. (The latter is situated on the south-east corner of the 50,000-acre Balmoral estate.)

The Castle of Mey is one of the great royal extravagances of the century. It is only used for six weeks. Its annual upkeep is half a million pounds.

It was to this Highland remoteness that she retreated after the death of her husband the King in 1952. She built a luxurious redoubt for herself on a lonely outcrop of rock looking out across the Pentland Firth towards the Arctic Circle, where in old age she watched the passage of time and season, untroubled by exigencies of change or expense.

Even the Queen, who was usually prepared to overlook her mother's extravagances, came to question the wisdom of maintaining, in full running order, a castle that stands empty for nearly eleven months a year. Trying to make a Queen, who in all her royal life has never had to account for anything, see economic sense proved a task beyond the nerve of any of her advisers, however. The Queen Mother would protest that she has made economies – that the tablecloth has been patched, that the damp has peeled away the wallpaper, rush matting was so worn in places that a house guest once tripped over it and fell.

There is nothing threadbare about the entertainment, though. Even the dogs – never fewer than two – live well. At night they sleep in her dressing-room in their own metal-framed foldaway beds with slip-covers for easy washing. And before the guests are served their afternoon tea a footman brings out a silver tray of dog bowls so that the Queen Mother can have the enjoyment of feeding them herself.

This attention to food, of both the canine and the human variety, is an essential part of the routine at both Birkhall and Mey where the days revolve around eating, with the emphasis on fresh, home-grown produce. At Mey that represents a triumph of will and money over nature. Even the vegetables find the going tough there. The Queen Mother chose this desolate outpost of mainland Britain to put down roots, but the cabbages are not always so successful. Sandy and Jane Webster, the resident couple, have seen them torn from the ground and hurled over the highest wall by the force of winds that regularly top ninety miles an hour. To provide the kitchen with the fresh garden produce the Queen Mother loves, and fill the garden with the flowers which are timed to bloom with her arrival, is a constant battle against formidable odds involving net, wire, glass, and stone lashed together with faith and optimism.

'The uncertainties of our intractable climate,' as the Queen Mother calls them, have never deterred her, however, from venturing out. She usually visits the gardens at Mey twice a day to supervise her *sous-chef* in his checked trousers and white apron collecting the surviving redcurrants and fruits. The footman picks the simple cottage flowers such as marigolds, roses and daisies which she arranges in vases inside. The seashore also beckons and until her health failed she was regularly to be seen tramping the beach, collecting seashells and looking out for seals. Dressed in an old blue mackintosh, sturdy walking shoes and a felt hat secured by a scarf, she was oblivious to the ocean raging a few feet away.

The Swedish-born Mrs McKee, who cooked for both Queen Elizabeths, wrote: 'At Balmoral, all the royal family would lead an outdoor life, but of all the ladies it was the Queen Mother who was the most energetic.'

Neither cold mists nor driving rain have ever prevented Elizabeth from drawing her house-guests outside for yet another of the picnics so dear to her heart. The wind, she says dismissively, 'will blow the cobwebs away' and if there is even a glimmer of hope, picnic chairs and tables will be erected and everyone will sit down for lunch wrapped in rugs and surrounded by wind-breaks. On one occasion when her house party was picnicking in the lee of a farmhouse and it was discovered that they did not have enough chairs, one of the guests knocked on the farmhouse door to ask if they had any to spare. A sullen Scots voice enquired from within: 'Who's there?' The Queen Mother, who was sitting a few yards away, shouted back: 'Don't worry, it's only the Queen!' When the door opened, only good manners restrained her party from bolting inside for shelter.

This love affair with the outdoors was echoed at Birkhall, where every day had to include at least one long stroll, and on untold occasions she climbed the 3,786 feet to the top of what Lord Byron called the 'frowning glories' of Lochnagar which dominates the estate. Even when creaking limbs put such walks beyond her range, she still refused to forsake the heather-clad 'hills', as the verbally parsimonious Highlanders call their towering mountains. Field sports are the main preoccupations at Balmoral. It was not the stalking nor the grouse-shooting so beloved by her husband which excited Elizabeth's interest, but the fishing. She had been taught to cast a line as a little girl at Glamis, and the pursuit of salmon became her lifelong passion

'She loves her fishing,' said her friend, the Marchioness of Salisbury. 'All her life she has been a keen and highly skilful fisherman'. Elizabeth's son-in-law Prince Philip shares her enthusiasm, and on one memorable day took fifteen salmon out of the Muick's peaty water which Lady Salisbury called 'as brown as brown ale'. Fishing

has an almost mystical allure for her favourite grandson, Prince Charles, and he once said: 'I can pray when I'm fishing but I can't fish in church'. It was always the Queen Mother who set the standard in what for the Royal Family is a highly competitive sport, however. It was not until she was well into her eighties that her family, fearful for her safety, finally persuaded her to give up the pleasure of wading waist deep in the fast-flowing Dee or its tributary the Muick, pronounced Mick ('Means pigs, *not* a pretty name,' Queen Victoria observed).

Her devotion to rod and line was not allowed to interfere with the lunches which were an essential part of every shooting day, and well into old age the Queen Mother continued to insist on joining the guns at their repast, regardless of the weather, allowing herself to be driven up the rough deer tracks to the appropriate picnic spot.

While she was still able to shoot, she used a large canvas tent which had belonged to her late husband, the King, and which she continued to cherish. The staff who had to erect it did not share her enthusiasm. If it was windy, which it often was, her steward and her chauffeur would be outside desperately trying to hold the tent down while the royal shooting party was inside, lunching off a table laid with fine glass, silver and china. Sometimes the only way to keep the tent on the ground was to park the Land Rovers on the corner flaps.

The lunches, like the help-yourself-breakfasts which the Queen Mother provides at Birkhall, are comparatively casual affairs. The women arrive half an hour early at the designated point to spread

LUNCH *AL FRESCO* SCOTTISH STYLE OUTSIDE THE QUEEN MOTHER'S LOG CABIN BESIDE THE RIVER DEE. AMONGST THE GUESTS ARE PRINCESS ALEXANDRA AND SIR ANGUS OGILVY, HER LADIES-IN-WAITING, LADY JEAN RANKIN AND LADY ANGELA OSWALD AND HER HUSBAND, SIR MICHAEL OSWALD, MANAGER OF THE ROYAL STUDS.

the tartan rugs over the heather and lay out the food, which is towed up by Land Rover in a dark green trailer specially designed for the purpose by Prince Philip. The sides open to reveal compartments stuffed with cold cuts, mutton pieces (rolls), cheese, sandwiches and fruit cake. The back undoes to reveal a well-stocked bar containing, amongst the claret, champagne, beer and whisky, the gin and Dubonnet the Queen Mother gallops through.

When there is no shooting, the Royal Family still prefer to eat their midday meal out of doors, or, if the weather makes that too uncomfortable even for this hardy clan, in one of the many huts and cabins Queen Victoria had erected all over the estate, or, when the mood takes them, in a luxurious chalet beside the Dee which was their eightieth birthday present to the Queen Mother. It is, as one former member of the Household explained, 'a chance for them to be on their own.' There are no staff in attendance, 'which allows the Queen the opportunity to pretend to be an ordinary housewife.'

This Rousseau-like return to nature continues into the night on at least a couple of days each week, when the Family again decamp from the comfort of their houses and head into the hills for one of the barbecues they so enjoy (and which Diana so disliked). Wind and hail are no deterrent and while the men do the cooking, with Prince Philip very much in command, the Queen mixes her special salad dressing of olive oil, cream, balsamic vinegar and mustard (and woe betide anyone who tries to usurp her task; if they do so they are sternly informed that they have got the measures wrong). It is another opportunity to put to practical use Victoria's lodges and huts, some of which are equipped with their own china and one or two of which have bedrooms.

From time to time the organization has been known to go awry. On one occasion the Queen got to the appointed hut only to discover that she had left the key behind. Arriving back at Birkhall she was greeted by the Queen Mother who drolly remarked: 'How very odd, darling, I thought if it was you all you had to say was "Open-sesame!"'

Rather than getting annoyed by such mishaps, the Royal Family tend to treat them as a joke. No-one else is allowed to share their humour, however. One year an absence of grouse caused the Queen Mother to cancel her house parties, in the mistaken belief that with no birds to shoot, no-one would want to come. If the Royal Family worried about the hurt feelings of friends, they did not show it, and took delight in spending their days in kilts, climbing the hills, eating sandwiches out of old Huntley & Palmer biscuit tins, and brewing their afternoon tea in spirit kettles.

There was a limit to how much informality the Queen Mother was prepared to entertain, however. In Scotland, so her late husband declared, he could 'put off being King' and they both enjoyed the sturdy independence of the Highland character exemplified by the stalker who turned to Edward VII's brother, the Duke of Connaught, and declared, after he had missed two easy shots: 'Ye blithering idiot, you've ruined the whole thing.' But Balmoral, as some critics have noted, is run along almost feudal lines, with everyone knowing their place – and knowing how to keep it. When the present Queen first went stalking (she shot her first stag at the age of sixteen), the accompanying ghillies would eat their lunchtime sandwich or roll sitting on one side of a large rock while she ate hers on the other. That deferential separation of servant and master is still maintained. Prince Charles's late valet, Stephen Barry, observed: 'At lunch the royals sit on their section of the moorland, while the staff sit a respectable distance away on their bit of territory.'

That decorum was kept up throughout the day. On picnics, while the other royal women vied with each other for the right to lay the table and do the clearing-up afterwards, the Queen Mother would sit regally to one side, surveying the activity and offering encouragement, ever the grand matriarch, aware, perhaps, of the element of make-believe in this royal idyll. As one of her staff remarked, 'She never got the gist of that kind of living.'

Her afternoon tea, served at the royal hour of 5 p.m., is a lavish event wrapped in ritual. Everyone is expected to change – the men, bathed after their sporting exertions, into shirt and tie, corduroys and tweed jackets, the women into day dresses – before gathering in the hostess's sitting-room to be treated to a a veritable meal of potted shrimps, cucumber sandwiches, a choice of ginger, chocolate and digestive biscuits and her favourite chocolate and coffee cake which she insists on having freshly baked every day even if the previous day's offering has remained untouched. When Elizabeth first arrived at Birkhall she would exercise what

Lady Cynthia Asquith called 'her Scotch skill in making of scones and cakes'. She soon came to leave the baking to the kitchen staff.

After tea the guests retire to their rooms to rest and to freshen up (one bathroom has a trio of original bowls marked in Gothic script, 'Teeth', 'Hands' and 'Face'; in the late King's bathroom there is a sign that says: 'Cleanliness is next to Godliness') and to change yet again.

BIRKHALL, SITUATED ON THE SOUTH-EAST CORNER OF THE 50,000 ACRE BALMORAL ESTATE.

When they are on their own the Queen and Prince Philip prefer to dine in their tweeds. The Queen Mother, on the other hand, like a Victorian caricature of the district officer in some far-flung outpost of Empire always dresses for dinner, even on the very rare instances when she is alone. And where she leads, others follow, the Queen included. When the Queen Mother stayed at Balmoral it was long dresses every evening.

The timings, too, are adjusted to accommodate the habits of Britain's last Queen-Empress. Everyone assembles at seven o'clock in the drawing-room for a couple of cocktails mixed by the equerry to a strength liable to knock the unsuspecting sideways, including, on occasion, the Queen Mother herself. The Queen and Prince Philip like to go through to the dining-room at eight fifteen sharp but the Queen Mother will not even contemplate eating until eight thirty at the earliest, and sometimes much later. There are eleven long-case clocks in the dining-room at Birkhall, gathered there by the Queen Mother 'because it seemed rather amusing at the time', but they served no practical purpose. Elizabeth has always been a notoriously bad timekeeper and it was quite usual for the clocks to be chiming nine when the company made their way through, much to the annoyance of Prince Philip for whom patience was never a virtue.

Her own dinner parties at Birkhall and the Castle of Mey are sumptuous affairs. Elizabeth has always kept an excellent table in Scotland. The wines are French, featuring the first-growth clarets selected by the Queen Mother's page, Billy Tallon, who enjoys the responsibility – and devotes a great deal of time to it. The food is equally tempting. In the inter-war years dinner would often comprise seven courses. That slimmed down to five and then to three or four, as appetites changed and labour became scarcer (in the early years of her reign a staff of up to 200 would accompany the Queen to Balmoral). The quality, however, remains of the highest. A typical menu might include cold cherry soup followed by red mullet poached in dry white wine and flavoured with lemon and a pinch of cinnamon (the Queen Mother likes eating fish, as well as killing them). Duckling or perhaps chicken sauté Provençale (prepared without so much as a hint of garlic which the Royal Family are so wary of) could form the main course. The Queen Mother is particularly partial to eggs and chicken, and her guests have noted that many of the first courses are based on eggs, and a great many of the main courses feature chicken. Cream is often an ingredient,

THE DRAWING ROOM AT BIRKHALL SHOWING THE QUEEN MOTHER'S COLLECTION OF MISS MARPLE VIDEOS AND BOX OF CHOCOLATES WHICH SHE LOVES TO DIP INTO.

providing what one diner called 'pints and pints of cholesterol'. There would be cheese and, to follow, a pudding such as crêpes Suzette or pears in a maraschino sauce, which the Queen Mother likes to wash down with a glass of vintage champagne.

Tables would be decorated with freshly-cut flowers, and the vegetables freshly picked from the kitchen gardens. Befitting the locale and its larder of natural plenty, venison features prominently on the menu, as does the salmon so often caught by the Queen Mother herself. (When a fishbone got stuck in her throat, she called it, 'The salmon's revenge'.) Grouse is in such plentiful supply, those sporadic lean years which afflict every sporting estate excepted, that the royal chefs, driven to ever more bizarre extremes in their efforts to add variety to their cooking, on occasion have resorted to stuffing them with raspberries. 'It is,' says one frequent house guest, 'very old-fashioned country-house cooking, but quite delicious.' A Michelin-starred restaurant could hardly do it better.

According to the Royal Family's own standards, Scotland is a haven of informality where they can relax and safely let their hair down. In their Highland fastness they can walk and picnic and shoot and relax out of public sight. Only in Scotland do they feel that they have the liberty to be themselves. Victoria's Albert called this 'somewhat primitive, yet romantic life...a tonic to the nerves' and to this day the Family looks forward with agitated anticipation to moving there. They arrive in August for the grouse and the stalking and leave reluctantly when the unbending routine of their lives decrees it time for them to move south at the end of October. The Queen Mother is always the first to travel north and always the last to leave.

Outsiders, however, are not unfailingly enamoured of this way of life. Royalty has its own foibles and they can be unsettling.

At Mey when the night is clear it was not unusual for everyone to file out of the dining-room between courses to try and catch a glimpse of the northern lights over the Firth, and on particularly merry evenings guests have been known to do the conga around the table before sitting down again, each in a different place, to start on the next course.

Although dancing the conga might be permissible, heaven forbid that anyone should be so ill-bred as to tip their soup-plates

in order to spoon up the last dregs: the Queen Mother has decidedly old-fashioned views on table manners, which can sometimes
be disconcerting. The moment the footman puts their plate down,
for instance, guests start eating straight away without waiting for
anyone or anything else, including the vegetables. It is the same
at the end of each course, when the footman clears away each
person's plates as he or she finishes.

What happens after the meal can also have its unexpected
moments. It helps to be able to sing or play the piano, and a sense
of easy-going humour also comes in handy. The Queen Mother is
partial to after-dinner sing-songs and likes to give her own inter-
pretation to old Scottish ballads and such ditties as Sir Walter
Scott's 'Ca' the yowes to the knowe'.

Diana loathed the whole Scottish experience. The Queen, who
spent much of her childhood holidays at Birkhall, declared when
she was twelve years old, that it was 'the nicest place in the whole
world.' The Duchess of Kent said the house 'was made for a honeymoon'. She spent part of hers there, as did the Queen, Princess
Margaret and Princess Alexandra. And it was at Birkhall that the
Prince of Wales did much of his courting of Lady Diana Spencer –
and where he retreated when his marriage was razed to ruin.

Initially Diana too had professed to 'adore' the place but her
affection for it did not long survive her marriage. She spent part of
her honeymoon at Balmoral but that only proved to be an
unhappy harbinger of the troubles to come. Prince Charles summoned a psychiatrist from London to try, unsuccessfully as it
turned out, to bring some easing of mind to a young woman for
whom royal life, especially in its Scottish incarnation, was to
prove so difficult.

The Queen Mother was unsympathetic to Diana's unhappiness. Scotland was her territory and she was not going to allow her
holidays to be spoilt by what she dismissed as the Princess's juvenile petulance. If Diana wanted to mope around feeling sorry for
herself, that was her business. The Queen Mother, meanwhile,
remained as committed in old age as she had been in her youth to
enjoying herself, particularly at the two ghillies' balls which mark
the high points of the Royal Family's Scottish sojourn.

The first is held at the beginning of September just before
'Changeover Day', when the Queen's pared-down staff of fifty

THE DINING ROOM AT
THE CASTLE OF MEY.
THE CHAIRS ARE
STAMPED WITH THE
QUEEN MOTHER'S
CIPHER, WHICH AGAIN
IS DISPLAYED IN THE
FIRE SCREEN MADE
FOR HER BY SIR
MARTIN CHARTERIS,
FORMER PRIVATE
SECRETARY TO THE
QUEEN.

return to Buckingham Palace and are replaced by another fifty: the second takes place at the beginning of October, a few days before the Court packs up and returns to London. Held in the ballroom at Balmoral and hosted jointly by the Queen and the Queen Mother, they are joyous, exuberant nights notable for the energy that goes into the dancing of Scottish reels and the prodigious amounts of alcohol that are consumed. All the staff are invited, along with wives and husbands, and the barriers between masters and servants crumble in the giddy atmosphere as royals reel around the dance floor with stalkers and footmen, ladies' maids and dressers.

No-one stands on ceremony and the Queen Mother has always selected her own partners. One embarrassed young soldier was compelled to turn her down, explaining that he had already been booked by the Queen. When the Queen Mother danced by him a few moments later, she tapped the soldier on his shoulder and said: 'Snob!'

'The servants dance with the Royal Family without any sense of familiarity but with the utmost good friendship,' noted Princess Marina of Kent. Elizabeth, despite their obvious and sometimes abrasive differences, took the time to teach Marina to reel. This was not the cultivated Princess's usual social fare but with typical worldliness she revelled in the unsophisticated gaiety. Of her trips to Scotland she remarked: 'I was enchanted by one thing more than all else – the ghillies' ball.'

BIRKHALL – ENTRANCE HALL WITH THE MAIN STAIRCASE IN THE BACKGROUND, COVERED WITH CARICATURES DRAWN FOR *VANITY FAIR* BY SPY, THE PSEUDONYM OF SIR LESLIE WARD.

INSET:
THE ENTRANCE HALL WHERE A SMALL ARMY OF CORGIS GATHERS AT MEALTIMES.

The music is provided by the Jack Sinclair Band from Glasgow and when the Queen Mother retires from the fray, which, age having caught up with her, is now shortly after midnight, she invariably goes up to the band-

leader and says: 'Thank you so much, Mr Sinclair, you won't mind playing on to the end will you?' Without fail he replies: 'Oh no, Ma'am.'

By the time the end arrives, there are very few merrymakers still steady on their feet. It was always thus. As Queen Victoria's assistant private secretary Sir Frederick ('Fritz') Ponsonby observed: 'The amount of whisky consumed by the servants was truly stupendous.' Like her successors, Queen Victoria, too, joined in the dancing. 'But after she left it became an orgy of drink,' Ponsonby said.

In more recent times the sore heads that greeted the morning were not confined to the servants' quarters. There is a bar at the top of the *Gone With the Wind*-style double staircase at Balmoral and, as the Queen watched the Queen Mother negotiate her way up there late one night in search of yet another refill of her champagne glass, she turned to her page and said, 'For goodness' sake, don't let Mummy have another drink.' There was little chance of that instruction being followed. Such free-flowing nights are part of the Highland tradition, and traditions, as the Queen Mother is fond of repeating, 'exist to be kept.'

Even Diana, for whom Balmoral became an ever more unpleasant ordeal, entered into the spirit of the ball, and danced so energetically that she once tore the hem of her dress.

Once back at Birkhall, however, the gaiety quickly evaporated and Diana would start looking for excuses to leave. Another who remained unimpressed was Edward VII. The house was bought for him by his parents in 1849 when he was eight but he only ever stayed there once. Edward preferred the more lavish amenities of nearby Abergeldie Castle to the comparative simplicity of Birkhall where, when the Queen Mother is in residence, log fires blaze in every room even in summer, and the kitchens smell of baking.

Prince Charles, who is the only person allowed to sleep in George VI's bedroom, is particularly drawn to the house, which he expects to inherit. Like his grandmother, he much prefers it to Balmoral and stays there from choice whenever he can, as has Elizabeth since it was given to her and her husband by King George V shortly after their marriage in 1923. The Duke was determined to create a family life for himself as different as possible from the cramped and over-disciplined childhood he had endured at York House on the Sandringham estate, and Scotland provided an ideal setting.

To call Birkhall 'cosy' as Charles does, is stretching the meaning of the word, though. By any conventional description the house is imposing, its grounds impressive. The porch, which Queen Victoria had built so that she could descend from of her carriage without getting wet, is of wood and supported by four trunks of oak, stripped of their bark, but with the stumps of their branches still protruding. Once the visitor has passed that contrived piece of rustic-work, the décor is a meeting of Belgravia mansion with Highland lodge. There are stags' heads over doorways and paintings by Landseer, the

THE CASTLE OF MEY. PURCHASED BY THE QUEEN MOTHER AS A RUIN AND SUBSEQUENTLY RESTORED.

Victorian master of sporting scenes, hang in the corridors on dark green wallpaper embellished with Queen Victoria's gold cipher. A French tapestry is displayed in the drawing-room and a superb Persian rug lies under the fourteen-seat Georgian mahogany dining-table. The main staircase is lined with the caricatures drawn for *Vanity Fair* by Spy, the pseudonym of Sir Leslie Ward. Many have personal letters from the subjects attached to the backs, which the Queen would read as a young girl, when the weather kept her indoors.

When Wallis Simpson, the future Duchess of Windsor, made her first foray to Balmoral she declared: 'This tartan has to go.' Her rival and lifelong adversary had very different ideas about interior decoration. The walls of the entrance hall are covered in a Hunting Stuart fabric and tartan carpets proliferate, giving Birkhall the look which so inspired the New York designer Ralph Lauren. It is, says the Queen Mother, 'a small big house or a big small house.'

It is certainly bigger than it was, for the first thing the Queen Mother did when she moved back in in 1952 was to build on a wing, thereby adding four more bedrooms, bathrooms, a modern kitchen and a large new drawing-room to what was already a substantial property.

As Birkhall grew, so did the division between upstairs and downstairs. When Elizabeth first moved in there was only one staircase, which was used by both the royals and their maids whose bedrooms were above the royal apartments. John Gibson, a former footman, recalled: 'When we came back in the early hours there was only one way up to the attic. We'd let ourselves into the house by the kitchen door and once inside take off our shoes. Then clutching their shoes the girls would creep up the staircase, tiptoe past the royal bedroom door and up the attic stairs.' The new wing had its own staircase, which reduced the possibility of the royal slumbers being disturbed.

At Mey the desire to build and improve was given full rein. The castle was deserted and decayed when Elizabeth saw it. 'I've bought a villa in the most remote part of the world,' the new Queen Mother told Cecil Beaton in 1952. 'I've taken this villa to get away from everything, but I don't suppose I shall ever be able to get there.'

But get there she did, and for the next quarter of a century the climbing roses planted around the castle walls struggled against the winds off the Firth in their efforts to bloom around the only home she has ever personally owned. It required time and money to make it habitable but, in those early years of her widowhood, they were the two things she had in abundance.

When the King died Elizabeth's usual ebullience deserted her. For thirty years she had devoted her energies to supporting her husband, an almost full-time job. Now she was without him and her life, so carefully ordered, so secure, suddenly lacked purpose.

She had been deeply affected by the death of her father-in-law George in 1936. 'I miss him dreadfully,' she said. 'Outwardly one's life goes on the same, yet everything is different, especially mentally and spiritually.' When her father died in 1944 at the age of eighty-nine she had wept openly at his graveside at Glamis.

The loss of her husband proved to be infinitely worse. Her reliance on Bertie had grown almost to equal his dependence on her. To compound matters, she was now effectively unemployed. 'One cannot yet believe that it has all happened,' she wrote. 'One feels rather dazed.'

Kemp, her page, commented: 'Poor woman. She never had time to cry.'

She went to Scotland to stay with the Lady Doris Vyner, sister of the Duke of Richmond and Gordon, and her husband at their romantically named House of the Northern Gate in Caithness. One afternoon they persuaded Elizabeth out of her private mourning and took her to look at some of the crumbling stone houses and castles that are a part of the barren Caithness landscapes. They spotted a ruined stronghold with most of its roof 'gone missing'.

Its bleak isolation reflected the mood of the Queen Mother. 'I was driving along' she recalled, 'and from the high road saw this old castle; when I heard it was going to be pulled down, I thought it must be saved.' So resolved, she returned for several subsequent inspections before throwing financial caution to the harsh winds that blow off the Pentland Firth. She bought the castle and its surrounding acres for £26,000 in the hope that the 'peace and tranquillity of the open countryside with the rugged glory of a magnificent coastline,' would help ease her despair.

The Queen Mother paid close attention to each phase of the restoration work, consulting with the builder over every small detail. (Her neighbour Lord Thurso, who had been using the same builder, was amused to note that, when the Queen Mother's plane landed at Wick airport twenty miles away, the contractor would mysteriously disappear from his employ.) And, as the building rose, so the loneliness of widowhood began to subside.

'It filled a gap in her life when she was not at all sure what her public duties might be,' Lord Thurso said.

The finished result was a castle and garden that reminded Elizabeth of Glamis and mirrored her love of romance and history. An avenue of sycamore trees forms the approach, their branches bent by the wind to provide a natural canopy. The sixteenth century keep, hidden from the road by storm-sculpted woods, appears to grow out of the landscape. The 'whirly wind' as they call it in Caithness, whistles round the tower where the Primrose Lady, the ghost of a nobleman's daughter who fell

RIGHT:
THE SYMMETRICAL
STONE DOUBLE
STAIRCASE AT THE
CASTLE OF MEY.

ABOVE:
THE QUEEN MOTHER'S
CLOAKROOM AT THE
CASTLE OF MEY.

RIGHT:
A COSY CORNER IN THE
DRAWING ROOM OF THE
CASTLE OF MEY — THE
WINDOWS OF WHICH
LOOK OUT OVER THE
PENTLAND FIRTH.

THE ANNUAL VISIT OF
BRITANNIA TO THE
CASTLE OF MEY.
LEFT: HER MAJESTY
THE QUEEN AND THE
QUEEN MOTHER ON
THE JETTY AT
SCRABSTER.
BELOW: PRINCE
CHARLES IN
CONVERSATION WITH
THE QUEEN MOTHER.
SERENA LINLEY AND
SARAH CHATTO ARE
WELCOMED BY THE
QUEEN MOTHER.

unsuitably in love and jumped to her death on the stones below, is said to linger. The sandstone walls are six feet thick and have gun-holes at ground-floor and first-floor levels. Further protection is afforded by a castellated low stone wall surmounted by cannons, moved from a nearby ruined coastal battery. According to the Queen Mother, 'they were originally intended for use against Napoleon and in the last war there was a fighter squadron stationed up here to fight Hitler.'

The garden, like the one at Birkhall, is filled with flowers which are timed to bloom with her arrival. The bell-shaped garden at Birkhall is a traditional Scottish pleasance in which flowers, vegetables and fruit are mixed together, as they were at Glamis when she was a child. Everything is organically fertilized with well-rotted horse manure. The Queen Mother does not hold with chemical fertilizers. 'Nobody likes them,' she claims.

Once a year the royal yacht *Britannia* called by, and then all pretence at economy was promptly abandoned. Out would come the best linen and china and silver while

Mrs Webster, aided by the staff brought up from London, would be set to work in the kitchens to produce a meal fit, not for one, but for two Queens.

The visit by *Britannia* was always the most important day of the castle's year. For forty-two years the royal yacht called at Mey *en route* for Aberdeen and Balmoral on the Queen and her family's annual cruise around the Western Isles. 'Dressed overall' in the flags she flew whenever members of the Royal Family were embarked, the ship would anchor in the bay below, her single yellow funnel etched against the huge Caithness sky. The royal barge would motor slowly into the small fishing port of Scrabster with its cargo of royal passengers, all of whom, children included, would be be wearing kilts (the royal rule is that the kilt must never be worn south of Perth except at official Caledonian balls). The Queen Mother, also wearing a kilt or tartan suit with the inevitable blue wool coat and one of her country felt hats, and accompanied by the Lord Lieutenant of Caithness, would meet them at the jetty. A fleet of Land Rovers would then ferry the royal party up to the castle for lunch, eaten, weather permitting (and sometimes even when it wasn't) on the lawn. (Staff and crew from *Britannia* would also be given lunch, but, being less hardy than their employers, they would eat theirs indoors.) After a tour of the walled garden or a walk along the beach to look for seals, it would be back to the castle for a sumptuous tea of freshly-baked scones, home-made jam and some of Mrs Webster's chocolate cake.

In the light of the northern evening, the Queen Mother would then escort the royal party to Scrabster harbour to board the royal barge and return to the royal yacht. She would always be back at the castle in time to see *Britannia* as she steamed by at exactly 7.30 p.m., sailing as close in as possible to the shore. As *Britannia* passed, she sent up flares and the display was reciprocated with fireworks from the castle. From the windows of Mey and the deck of *Britannia* large white towels were waved in a farewell salute.

August 1997 was the royal yacht's swansong, but as she steamed past the Castle of Mey for the last time she was still queen of the waters. It was her last dance, but, like the last Queen-Empress who stood waving her goodbye, this lady of the ocean knew all the steps. It was with grace and style that she swept away over the horizon and into memory.

The castle and its owner is heading in the same direction. In 1996 the Queen Mother handed Mey over to a charitable trust, thereby ensuring that it will not be sold, as would otherwise have happened, but at the same time giving clear indication that its time as a royal residence is running out. When the Queen Mother's standard is finally lowered, its royal connection will be severed and the Castle will become the most northerly museum in Britain, open to the public, a monument to the woman who created it: an elegant, romantic, enchanting indulgence where she succeeded in maintaining the air and atmosphere of her gilded childhood.

Change was all around, but for Queen Elizabeth The Queen Mother the rhythms remained very much as they were when she was growing up at Glamis nearly a century ago.

CHAPTER 13

$\mathcal{A}$ LADY AT HOME

At 7.30 every morning, regardless of the season or the time she got to bed the night before, or wherever she happens to be, the Queen Mother is woken by her dresser who drops a deep curtsey and says, 'Good morning, ma'am.'

Waking her up and getting her up are two different things, however. All her life people have remarked, sometimes with amusement, more often with exasperation, on her inability to get herself out of bed and into the day in anything under three hours. From her first-floor bedroom in Clarence House she can hear the traffic of the modern world roaring down the Mall, but it is only the sound, never the driven purpose which intrudes. The Queen Mother moves to the leisurely rhythm of an older era. While others have jobs, she has her routine.

It begins with a cup of appropriately named Royal Blend tea especially mixed for her by Twinings, served in a pink china cup with a gold rim, bearing the crest of her late husband and delivered by her dresser Betty Leek. The tea served, Mrs Leek's next task is to shoo the royal corgis which sleep in the next-door dressing-room on their miniature camp beds out into the long corridor and into the care of a waiting footman dressed in full livery, who takes them out for a quick trot in the garden.

Their mistress never joins them at what she considers an unearthly hour when, she has been brought up to believe, any lady of quality and breeding was expected to be in her boudoir. And there she remains, her long hair cascading over the pillows she is propped up on, glancing through the newspapers, listening to the morning news on the radio she always calls the wireless, reading her letters, studying the *Sporting Life*, the trade paper of the horse-racing industry which became her consuming interest. She is joined by her dogs as soon as they are back from their walk and have had their paws dried by the liveried footman.

By the time her large, old-fashioned breakfast tray which extends right across the bed is brought in at nine o'clock, she may well have had the first of her several daily chats with her elder daughter, who would be up, and with

THE QUEEN MOTHER'S CORGIS 'ESCORTED' FROM THE PLANE BY HER PAGE AND STEWARD, WILLIAM TALLON. HE WEARS THE UNIFORM DESIGNED BY KING GEORGE VI DURING WORLD WAR II TO CUT DOWN ON LAUNDRY EXPENSES.

Princess Margaret, who never is. The Queen Mother, as ever, eats sparingly – fresh fruit, perhaps a slice of toast and marmalade, washed down with another cup of tea drunk out of the same china but served this time in a teapot warmed by a spirit lamp.

But if the meal is frugal, the service and the setting is not. The Queen Mother's London home, built at the beginning of the nineteenth century, was improved upon by John Nash and has been added to and refined a number of times since. In 1949 Princess Elizabeth and her husband moved in after a much-needed refurbishment (Parliament had voted £50,000 for the works; the final cost is said to have topped £250,000). Upon the death of the King, the Queen and her young family very reluctantly moved up the Mall and into Buckingham Palace, while the Queen Mother went the other way. On May 18 1953, ten days before her daughter's Coronation, the Queen Mother's standard flew over Clarence House for the first time. It has been her London residence ever since.

It is an elegant house filled with fine pictures and exceptional furniture, a little threadbare in places but only because, as Elizabeth grew older, she grew to dislike change more and more, preferring the comfort of the familiar and the recollections that are carried with it. The pale blue damask sitting-room, across a corridor but on the same Mall side of the house, is a museum of memorabilia. It is filled with clocks, *objets d'art*, favourite books, photographs of her family and of Prince Charles in particular, sketches of dogs and children, her lifetime collection of Chelsea china vegetables and plates and, busts and portraits of her husband.

The bedroom, too, is filled with reminders of the past which remained such a tangible part of her present. Above the fireplace hangs an oval painting of 'Madonna and Child' by Raffaelino del Garbo inherited from Mrs Scott, the grandmother with whom Elizabeth enjoyed her childhood holidays in Florence. And on the posts each side of the bedhead, which was painted for her in the Renaissance style by Riccardo Meacci in 1923, are the two angels she bought in the market in Bordighera when she was eight years old. The past, as she was fond of saying, is to be savoured.

But then so is the here and now. The cloth on her breakfast tray is always of the finest, with her cipher in the corner. The teapot is Georgian silver. The bell with which the Queen Mother summons her staff was made by Fabergé, court jeweller to the czars of Russia. Her clothes are laid out for her in her dressing-room. The footmen and pages who wait on her twenty-four hours a day, who get up at five o'clock in the morning to go to Covent Garden to buy the flowers she adores and do not go to bed until she does often past midnight, all wear the uniforms specially designed for them by the late King during the war. Elizabeth's existence is as luxurious as her embroidered linen sheets and she revels in it, taking her time to sample its enjoyments.

Not until eleven o'clock is she settled at the antique writing desk in her sitting-room, answering her correspondence, working on her itinerary, discussing her schedule with the ladies-in-waiting. She devotes time and effort to her letter-writing, and despite her great age still writes in a firm hand with a fountain-pen, using a pithy turn of phrase. Those tasks completed, it is time to get down to the business of the day – fortified by a stiff 'sharpener'.

The Queen Mother is never alone. Even on those infrequent evenings when she stays in and watches television – she likes the soaps, *Dad's Army* and old films – the dinner she eats off a card-table laid with the finest linen is served by one of the hovering footmen. There are always people in attendance – friends, family, representatives of the charities she is involved in. And people, she maintains, are best put at their ease with a decent drink inside them.

The Queen Mother takes her first Dubonnet and gin at around twelve thirty in the afternoon. Her staff call it Communion.

'Just a splash,' she always says. 'What she means by that is pour in half the bottle,' commented one staff member whose job it was to serve her. This is an exaggeration. If the mixture is too weak for her taste, though, she walks across to the drinks tray where the ice is kept in an old chrome bucket with Bakelite handles, and instructs whoever is in charge: 'Just a splash more'.

In an era obsessed with health and concerned about the damaging effects of alcohol, the Queen Mother's drinking habits smack of dangerous excess. They do not appear to have done her any noticeable harm, however. On the contrary, she has kept her wits, outlived the doctors who had the impertinence to advocate temperance to her and sailed through to the cusp of the new century. And her fondness for liquor never once appeared to harm her public performance in any way. With an energy and enthusiasm that defied her years, she has spent her widowhood tirelessly fulfilling the role she created for herself, a smile on her face – and a drink never far from her hand.

It was a punishing schedule she set herself. Shortly after the death of her husband, George VI, she came down the staircase and announced to her steward, William Tallon: 'I am going to travel around the world. Would you like to come with me?'

With Tallon and a host of other staff, the Queen Mother spent the next forty years on the move, to Canada and Australia and Africa and the United States and all the way around Britain. As she travelled, the sun sank ever lower on the Empire her husband had ruled over, but his widow seemed unaffected by the change in either Britain's status, or her own.

Once, on a visit to an old people's home in Norwich, she stopped and cheerfully asked the first lady she encountered, 'Do

THE SOUTH SIDE OF
CLARENCE HOUSE
FROM THE GARDEN,
SHOWING THE BALCONY
WHERE THE QUEEN
MOTHER STANDS ON
HER BIRTHDAY.

you know who I am?' The old lady replied: 'If you don't know who you are, dear, go to the desk at the end of the corridor and they'll help you!' It is a story the Queen Mother tells against herself. But then she always knew who she was, even if others did not. The exterior world was changing, but she had created one of her own and she was happy in it.

Her staff are happy, too. They call her Auntie behind her back and over the years have acquired many of the habits and manner-isms of their royal employer. For a long time her two dressers, named Field and Suckling – in the old-fashioned way, the Queen Mother always referred to them by their surnames – looked after a dachshund called Pippin that once belonged to Princess Margaret and broke the ranks of pedigree, starting the line of corgi-dachshunds crossbreeds called dorgis. Like the former nursery-maid Bobo MacDonald who became the present Queen's friend and mirror image, Gwen Suckling came closely to resemble the Queen Mother – but was even grander in manner. Ivy Field was remembered for once coming down the steps of the aircraft in which the royal party was travelling carrying a hatbox which flew open – to reveal a bottle of gin. It was Ivy Field who created the Queen Mother's extraordinary handbags which matched what-ever dress she was wearing. This was achieved with material left over when the outfit was made.

Reg Wilcox, a forthright York-shireman and her page of forty years, came to Elizabeth via the Duke of Windsor, whose style he had observed closely. As did William Tallon, who learnt to imi-tate him with uncanny perfection. Recalling a meeting with the exiled ex-King, he recalled Edward asking him, in his fake cockney American accent; 'How are yer and whadda yer do?' When Tallon replied: 'I work for your sister-in-law, the Queen, Your Royal Highness,' the Duke commented: 'Verry nice too.' Reg Wilcox was retained to help the actor Edward Fox perfect his impersonation of the Duke in the TV series *Edward and Mrs Simpson*.

A SOUTHWARD VIEW OF THE HALL FROM THE STAIRCASE, WITH A PORTRAIT OF AUGUSTA, PRINCESS OF WALES. A COMPANION PORTRAIT OF KING GEORGE III WHEN PRINCE OF WALES CAN BE SEEN BEYOND.

This slight irreverence has always been a noticeable feature of the parallel but mutually supportive universes which make up the Queen Mother's Household. While she was upstairs dealing with or, more usually, ignoring the crises which have beset her family – abdication, broken love affairs, failed marriages, divorce, the swingeing changes in public opinion – downstairs the staff were wrestling with their own problems of broken love affairs, gay trysts and wounded feelings. There is tolerance on both sides of the social divide.

One of Elizabeth's footmen once caused a rumpus when he tried to inveigle Princess Margaret's nanny to join him for a drink.

She retreated into the nursery and barricaded herself in. Princess Margaret's only remark was: 'I wouldn't mind but he knows that Nanny only likes sherry. Can you believe he was trying to force a whisky on her?'

Some time later the same footman was discovered by the Queen Mother passed out, dead drunk, in the hall. But he kept his job.

Her chef, Michael Sealey, came to her in a fit of pique after he had worked for the Queen for seventeen years and she failed to recognize him – a mistake the Queen Mother has been careful to avoid. She values Sealey's culinary expertise highly and takes great pleasure in choosing the menus, which are always written in French. Where she partakes of Sealey's cooking depends on her mood and, to some extent, the weather.

Following the early Victorian custom, the Queen Mother likes eating in different rooms. Some days she will eat in the morning-room, where paintings by Monet, Augustus John, Sickert and Fantin-Latour adorn the walls. Paintings by other artists are propped in contrived casualness here and there. In a corner is a bust of herself by David Cregeen, on a stand made by David Linley. On other days her luncheon, as she calls it, will be served in the library where the backs of the bookshelves are painted maroon and the porcelain figures are by Sèvres.

The Queen Mother's special delight, however, is to eat under a canopy of plane trees in her walled garden which she calls 'my *salles vertes*', green rooms. This is no picnic, however; it could almost be a scene from the court at Versailles. The mahogany table is set with crystal glasses decorated with her late husband's cipher. The dishes and cutlery are silver. The table decorations are solid gold. The atmosphere is always what she calls 'cosy'.

The Queen Mother refrains from giving direct orders. If she does not like what someone says or disagrees with them, she will either change the subject or convey her displeasure by euphemism, droll witticism or pointed politeness. She loathes cooking smells and, should she detect the faintest whiff of bacon and eggs, she will say to her page, 'Do you think someone could do something about that?' Someone always does.

In a spirit of give and take, she displays an amused curiosity about her staff's comings and goings, about their habits and their tastes. William Tallon lives in a doll's house of a cottage at the foot of the Clarence House garden, overlooking the Mall. When the Queen Mother came to inspect it she glanced into the bathroom and declared: 'What fun. Isn't it marvellous to be able to bathe in the Mall. Do you know, I've always wanted to.'

The humour is reciprocated. On New Year's Eve at Sandringham the Royal Family abide by the traditions of the Scottish Hogmanay the Queen Mother enjoyed as a child. A dark-haired man is delegated to go outside, knock on the door and come in carrying a piece of coal for good luck. The man is always one of their own footmen, but the Royal Family never fail to feign surprise and pleasure. There was a moment of flustered anticipation, however, the year the task fell to Tallon. Fergie and Diana had recently departed, the Family had been reduced to turmoil and when Tallon proposed the toast to absent friends, an embarrassed silence fell. Tallon raised his glass as Prince Philip, determined to ride out the moment in his own brash way, started speaking German. 'To...the Sultan of Brunei.' The world's richest man has been exceedingly generous to the Windsors. The Royal Family thought the toast intensely amusing and laughed about it for weeks afterwards.

This is the kind of light-hearted, in-house interchange which the Queen Mother's parents, and her father especially, enjoyed with their retainers. As a result of this tolerant atmosphere her staff stay with her for years, old people growing older together, content in each other's company. Many years ago her very old under-butler James Frost was asked how long he had been in royal service. He replied: 'I have boiled water for five Queens,' which meant that he must have first worked for Victoria. As exceptional as such longevity may have been, it is indicative of the bonds of attachment the Queen Mother forges. Her households do not experience the staff turnover which has become the mark of other royal homes in recent times.

Sweetness and light does not always prevail, however. The Queen Mother can be quite cutting. Once surveying the crowd gathered for luncheon in Clarence House's formal and rather gloomy ground-floor dining-room, she dismissively remarked: 'They're only here for the gilt.'

Should the mood so take her, she can also behave with the petulance of an indulged child. At a State banquet at Buckingham

Palace for the visiting Sultan of Oman, the Queen Mother discovered that the footstool which is always placed under her seat was missing. Irritated, she waved to the Queen who was deep in conversation with her guest of honour. The two women started mouthing to each other across the table. 'What?' the Queen asked. 'My footstool,' her mother silently replied. 'What?' 'My *footstool!*'

The soundless conversation continued behind the Sultan's back when he stood up to make his speech. Convinced that the two women were talking about him, he became irritated. So did Prince Philip, who joined in and silently ordered them to stop it. Eventually the Queen realized what the problem was, and dispatched her page in search of the offending footrest. He could not find it and produced a small box instead. The Queen Mother refused to accept it and waved him away. As soon as dinner was over she left in a sulk. The stool was not found for another two months. It was eventually discovered hidden behind a curtain. 'It didn't get there by itself,' the Queen Mother remarked accusingly.

TABLE SETTING IN THE DINING ROOM AT CLARENCE HOUSE. INSET: DETAIL OF TABLE SETTING.

THE SITTING ROOM.
THE WRITING TABLE IS
SURROUNDED BY
PICTURES OF FRIENDS
AND FAMILY, WITH
PARTICULAR
PROMINENCE BEING
GIVEN TO PRINCE
CHARLES.

This was a singular tumble from the pedestal of good manners
which the Queen Mother usually occupies, and it is a measure of
the pain she has endured in her later years. The spirit never
wilted: it was the body that slowly but inexorably started to give
way. From the mid 1950s onwards she became increasingly acci-
dent-prone. Ankles were twisted, bones in her feet were cracked,
fishbones became stuck in her throat. In 1966 she had a colostomy.
In 1996 she had a cataract operation, followed by a hip replacement which, according to the Queen, 'gave my mother a new lease
of life'. In 1998 she broke her hip and had to have it replaced. Yet on
she soldiers, refusing to surrender to any discomfort. Before her

cataract operation she pretended to see when she couldn't, some-times holding her menu upside down, too vain to wear her specta-cles anywhere except in private. When in 1995 the Queen insisted on installing a electric invalid-chair lift to ferry her up the stairs in Sandringham, the Queen Mother at first refused to use it.

Her mind, however, remains as sharp as ever. Her lively inter-est in current affairs, would surprise and embarrass by its breadth the younger members of her family. She reads a lot, an unusual habit amongst the Windsors. She retains her sense of humour – when she was finally persuaded into the chair lift she did so with a regal smile and wave, looking for all the world, or at least that priv-ileged part of it gathered in the hall to see her on her way, as if she were in a coach setting off to a State function. And when she was being escorted around the Royal Agricultural Show by the hon-orary director, Sir Dudley Forwood, he put his hand on her head to stop her hat blowing away. 'Oh, Sir Dudley,' she said, 'In a more gracious age I would have made you my Comptroller of Hats.'

If being seen is one of royalty's functions, then the Queen Mother is more than happy to keep up appearances. That has included paying close attention to the endless portraits that were painted of her. The artists who had been commissioned by her various charities and regiments were invited to the garden room, where the furniture had been covered in dust-sheets in readiness for the sitting. She would dress for the occasion, prattle cheerfully if she thought that would help to put the painter at ease, sit silently if he needed to concentrate. Brian Stonehouse, who painted her portrait for the Special Forces Club in London's West End, had worked with the Resistance during the war and still lived in France. She spoke to him in French.

'During the three months of sittings I became so absorbed with what she was saying, I used to pretend to paint and, once the Queen Mother had left the room, worked from memory,' said Stonehouse. During this time he never showed the portrait to the Queen Mother, but she confessed to him, 'I came down and had a peek.'

She takes an equally lively interest in horses and there has never been any waning of her enthusiasm for the Turf. Elizabeth first became involved in racing in 1949 when, after a dinner at Windsor with the former champion amateur jump jockey Lord

Mildmay, she took a half share in a horse called Monaveen with her elder daughter. The horse did well, winning at Fontwell, Sandown and Hurst Park. 'And of course I got hooked,' the Queen Mother recalled.

The future Queen's attention quickly moved on to flat-racing. In unusual deference to her daughter, her mother has confined herself to steeplechasing and over the years has had the pleasure of seeing over 400 of what she called 'my darlings' ride to victory wearing the buff and blue she describes as the 'not quite royal blue' Strathmore colours she inherited. Racing runs in the Queen Mother's blood. The 5th and 9th Earls of Strathmore bred horses and John Bowes, the natural son of the 10th Earl, won the Derby four times. Their successes and her own are honoured in what she calls the 'horse corridor' on the ground floor at Clarence House. This is lined with pictures and sketches of horses and jockeys, including a painting of her three horses which won on the same day at Cheltenham in 1961. 'I've loved horses ever since I was a little girl,' said the woman whose favourite book in childhood was *Black Beauty*. 'Probably one gets too fond of them.'

She has certainly afforded these animals a great deal of care. Elizabeth has always placed a great deal of faith in homeopathy, just as her husband did. From 1936 until his death in 1952, the King's Physician in Ordinary (his GP, in more prosaic language) was Dr John Weir, a firm believer in the medicinal powers of herbs. In 1946 the King wrote to his brother Henry, the Duke of Gloucester: 'I've been suffering from an awful reaction from the strain of war...medicine, not even Weir's, is of any use as I really want a rest...'

Despite that setback and the fact that at the time homeopathy was regarded as quackery, Weir continued to influence the Royal Family. He would boast how, on the day of the King's funeral, he wrote out prescriptions for three kings and four queens, and he was present at the births of Prince Charles and Princess Anne. He so impressed George VI that the King named one of his racehorses after a homeopathic remedy, hypericum, used to treat abrasions, broken skin, bites and crash injuries.

Elizabeth takes the view that what was good enough for a king and his family was probably good enough for her horses, and on her instructions they receive a variety of herbal mixes often dis-

pensed by herself, together with a carrot but never a sugar lump. Sugar, she insists, is bad for them – though not, it seems, for her. She always indulges her own sweet tooth, most especially with chocolates. 'But only the soft ones': the ones with the hard centres are removed from the box and put on the mantelpiece to be handed out later to the corgis (much to the confusion of the housemaids, who are never quite sure how long the chocolates have been sitting there and whether to throw them out or not).

As well as taking a professional interest in her horses' health, the Queen Mother also concerns herself with their psychological well-being. In 1989 she invited Monty Roberts, the American who listens and talks to horses, to give a demonstration at Windsor Castle. After fifteen minutes of whispering Roberts was able to throw a saddle over one of her highly-strung, unbroken thorough-bred fillies. The Queen Mother, with rare tears of emotion in her eyes, declared it to be 'one of the most wonderful things I've ever seen in my life'.

But then, as Michael Oswald observed, horses and horse-racing are 'her real passion in life'.

Oswald is the manager of the royal stud in Norfolk where the Queen Mother keeps her mares and their foals, and where she sustained the fall in January 1998 which necessitated the hip replacement. And all the time she was in hospital and despite the pain, she was constantly on the telephone, checking to see how her mares were doing.

The interest is not merely academic. Like many of her daughter's subjects, she enjoys what she calls 'a little flutter' and in 1965 had a blower – the racecourse commentary service relayed to betting shops – rigged up at Clarence House. That system has now been superseded by modern electronics: the bookmakers' satellite racing television channel, piped into her hospital room to keep her amused while she lay recuperating from her hip operation. When the *Sporting Life* went on strike, the publishers continued to print a special copy for her and one for

IN THE SUMMER, THE QUEEN MOTHER MAKES GOOD USE OF WHAT SHE CALLS HER 'SALLES VERTES'. GUESTS ARE ENTERTAINED TO LUNCH UNDER THE GRACEFUL HANGING BRANCHES.

the Queen. She organizes her engagements around the racing calendar and thought nothing of standing in the winter chill at a race meeting, exchanging gossip, evaluating the horseflesh, enjoying a drink with the trainers, relishing the companionship.

One bitterly cold Cheltenham the Queen saw her on television wearing an inadequate three-quarter-length-sleeved coat and a silk scarf. She telephoned her mother that evening to admonish her for not taking proper care of herself. The Queen Mother replied: 'Don't worry – I've got my pearls to keep me warm.'

It is a passion which comes with a price. Steeplechasing is a dangerous sport for both riders and ridden, and a number of the Queen Mother's horses have been killed – starting with Monaveen which had to be put down after falling at the water at Hurst Park in 1951.

She has always reacted to these mishaps with an upper lip stiffly in place. 'It's terribly sad, isn't it,' was all she said to the crowds who rushed to console her after Monaveen's demise. She was equally phlegmatic when Devon Loch, in the lead with Dick Francis, her jockey (and later a successful thriller writer) in the saddle, collapsed fifty yards from the winning-post during the 1956 Grand National. The crowd, imagining the horse had won, turned towards the royal box yelling their approval. Then they realized there had been an accident. 'The ovation stopped suddenly as if a light had been switched off and there was a complete hush,' Harold Nicolson recalled. 'The Queen Mother never turned a hair. Instead she left the box with the words, "I must go down and comfort those poor people."'

'That's racing,' she said as she dried her jockey's tears. 'There will be another time.'

The Duke of Westminster, who was a spectator, called her reaction 'the most perfect display of dignity I have ever witnessed.' To modern eyes it might have looked more like callousness. But then the Queen Mother is never one to wear her heart on her sleeve. The only emotion she ever allows herself to display is that of radiant happiness. Only at the funeral of her husband did the public catch a glimpse – and then through a black veil – of feelings more acute or painful. She had no time and less sympathy for the emotional openness of Diana. It ran contrary to everything she had been taught – and everything she had taught herself – in the years she had been a member of the family which she came to dominate.

In 1992 the Queen felt moved to declare the year *annus horribilis* and bemoan the marital disasters that had in turn beset her two elder sons and her daughter. The Queen Mother went to stay with her at Sandringham shortly afterwards. She sternly informed her daughter: 'It's another generation – let them get on with it'. That said, she calmly went back to her hand of Patience.

She has not always been so complacent or understanding. As long ago as 1960, years before her grandson the Prince of Wales took up the theme and made it his own, she was emphasizing the need for a firm spiritual foundation at a time when technology was seen as a cure for all human ills. 'The ages in which the world has made some of its greatest advances,' she told London University, 'are those in which men of piety and vision have caught sight of levels higher than those in which the world is moving.' Age, however, is a great mellower and having made her point, she then retired from the fray and went back to doing what she has always done best, which is playing to the image she has created for herself.

Direct action has never been the Queen Mother's forte. She prefers to exert her influence behind the scenes. And her control has never been anything less than considerable. She made a king out of her husband's unpromising material. Deep into her declining years she continued to hold sway over her daughter the Queen. She played a great part in the moulding of Prince Charles, who shares many of her values and ideas. The British crown may not be what it was, but the Biblical 'crown of glory' of her old age continues to sit on a shrewd and powerful head.

Although the Queen Mother's conversation is seasoned with dated expressions, she always gets her point across and even Prince Philip, a man of strong opinions who believes in expressing them forcefully, finds her hard to persuade. He is usually able to bring others round to his way of thinking, but, if the Queen Mother is against an idea, it is her viewpoint that almost always prevails. In the 1950s, for instance, when the Prince argued that the Royal Family should invite the Duke and Duchess of Windsor back to Britain, it was the Queen Mother who put her foot down. Implacable in her opposition, she feared that if her brother-in-law and the wife she so despised returned, they would inveigle themselves back into Court life. This would have a damaging effect on the Royal Family she had helped create – and therefore on herself.

Prince Philip was also of the belief that Princess Margaret should have been allowed to marry Peter Townsend. The Queen Mother, however, was against the match and again it was she who held sway.

The one common ground she shared with Philip was the question of Diana. If anything, the Prince was even more hostile to the Princess and her problems – and a great deal more vocal about it. For the most part, though, the Prince prefers to keep a wary distance from his indefatigable mother-in-law. After the 1992 fire had reduced Windsor Castle to charred rubble, the Queen Mother offered the Queen the use of Royal Lodge. The Prince is said to have 'paled under his tan' at the suggestion. The prospect of weekends at Royal Lodge with the Queen, the Queen Mother and Princess Margaret chatting together in French and excluding him was not one which appealed, and it was on his insistence that the invitation was declined.

The Queen Mother's nephew, the Earl of Harewood, is another who has felt the cold draught of her disapproval. After his divorce from the concert pianist Marion Stein, who later married the disgraced former leader of the Liberal party, Jeremy Thorpe, he found himself excluded from the Court circle. Harewood blamed the Queen Mother for his banishment.

It is not her determination and underlying toughness, however, that has secured the Queen Mother in the affections of the country she has served for the better part of a century. The nation's devotion was earned by indomitable good humour, grace, her willingness to do her duty and a smile that embraced and enchanted almost everyone who came into contact with her. She belongs to a vanished age whose emotional values have been discarded and whose distinctions, of class, race and background, have been discredited. Her younger daughter's marriage ended in divorce, as did the unions of her grandchildren, Charles, Anne and Andrew. The great houses of her youth have all but gone, and even the House of Windsor has started to rock on its foundations.

Yet the Queen Mother has managed to ride out the changes, to emerge unscathed, the tangible link to a fading past best viewed through the sepia tint of wistful nostalgia.

Her world remains as she wanted it to be – secure, pampered, inviolate – and that is how her daughter's subjects wish it to remain for her. She has lived her life in glorious style and no-one ever seriously suggested that it should be otherwise.

When she retires for the night at Clarence House a watchman takes up his position outside her door, just as he does all her life at all her homes. When she rings her bell her staff whisper to each other: 'Auntie has her hand on the Fabergé.'

The signal means that the Queen Mother has gone to bed. Lights are dimmed and the house settles down into peaceful, timeless silence, safe and sound with its memories.

ℬIBLIOGRAPHY

Alice, HRH The Duchess of Gloucester, *Memoirs*, (London 1983)

Aronson, Theo, *Princess Alice, Countess of Athlone*, (London 1981)

Aronson, Theo, *Royal Family: Years of Transition*, (London 1983)

Aronson, Theo, *The Royal Family at War*, (London 1993)

Asquith, Lady Cynthia, *The Duchess of York*, (London 1937)

Barrow, Andrew, *Gossip 1920-1970*, (London 1978)

Barry, Stephen, *Royal Secrets*, (New York 1985)

Barry, Stephen, *Royal Service*, (New York 1983)

Barstow, Phyllida, *The English Country Houseparty*, (London 1989)

Beaton, Cecil, *Self Portrait with Friends*, (London 1979)

Bloch, Michael, *The Duke of Windsor's War* (London 1982)

Boothroyd, Basil, *Philip*, (London 1971)

Bradford, Sarah, *George VI*, (London 1989)

Buxton, Aubrey, *The King in his Country*, (London 1955)

Carol, Valerie, *From Belfast's Sandy Row to Buckingham Palace*, (Cork 1994)

Churchill Papers, Churchill College, Cambridge

Colville, Lady Cynthia, *Crowded Life*, (London 1963)

Corbitt, F J, *My Twenty Years in Buckingham Palace*, (New York 1956)

Cornforth, John, *Queen Elizabeth The Queen Mother*, (London 1996)

Coward, Noël, *Diaries*, (London 1982)

Crawford, Marion, *The Little Princesses*, (London 1950)

Dale, John, *The Prince and the Paranormal*, (London 1986)

De Courcy, Anne, *The Last Season*, (London 1989)

De-la-Noy, Michael, *The Queen Behind The Throne*, (London 1994)

Dempster, Nigel, *Princess Margaret*, (London 1981)

Dempster, Nigel, *Diaries of Sir Henry Channon*, (London 1967)

Donaldson, Frances, *King Edward VIII*, (London 1974)

Dorling Kindersley, *Chronicle of the Queen Mother*, (London 1995)

Duchess of Windsor, The, *The Heart Has Its Reasons*, (London 1956)

Duff, David, *Elizabeth of Glamis*, (London 1973)

Duff, David, *Geoge and Elizabeth* (London 1983)

HRH The Duke of Windsor, *A King's Story*, (London 1951)

Edwards, Ann, *Matriarch*, (London 1984)

Forbes, Grania, *My Darling Buffy*, (London 1998)

Gathorne-Hardy, Jonathan, *The Rise and Fall of the British Nanny*, (London 1972)

Heald, Tim, *The Duke: A Portrait of Prince Philip*, (London 1991)

Hoey, Brian, *Mountbatten*, (London 1988)

Howell, Georgina, *In Vogue*, (London 1991)

Julian, Philippe, *Edward and the Edwardians* (London 1967)

Lacey, Robert, *Majesty*, (London 1977)

Lane, Peter, *The Queen Mother*, (London 1979)

Longford, Elizabeth, *Queen Elizabeth The Queen Mother*, (London 1981)

Lurie, Alison, *The Language of Clothes*, (London 1998)

Mabell, Countess of Airlie, *Thatched with Gold*, (London 1962)

Maclean, Veronica, *Crowned Heads*, (London 1993)

Massie, Robert K, *Dreadnought*, (USA 1992)

McDowell, Colin, *One Hundred Years of Royal Style*, (London, 1985)

McKee, Mrs *The Royal Cookery Book*, (London 1983)

Menkes, Suzy, *The Royal Jewels*, (London 1985)

Menkes, Suzy, *Queen and Country*, (London 1992)

Morrah, Dermot, *The Royal Family in Africa*, (London 1947)

Morrow, Ann, *The Queen Mother*, (London 1984)

Mortimer, Penelope, *Queen Elizabeth The Queen Mother*, (London 1995)

Nicolson, Harold, *King George V*, (London 1952)

Noblesse Oblige, *Our Old Nobility*, (London 1879)

Oliver, Charles, *Dinner at Buckingham Palace* (New York 1972)

Payne, Graham, *My Life with Noel Coward*, (London 1994)

Pope-Hennessey, James, *Queen Mary*, (London 1959)

Rhodes-James, Robert, *Chips: The Diaries of Sir Henry Channon*, (London 1993)

Roberts, Andrew, *Eminent Churchillians*, (London 1994)

Rose, Kenneth, *King George V*, (London 1983)

Ross, Josephine, *Royalty in Vogue*, (London 1989)

Salisbury, Marchioness of, *The Gardens of Queen Elizabeth The Queen Mother*, (London 1988)

Sinclair, David, *Queen and Country*, (London 1979)

Sitwell, Osbert, *Queen Mary and Others*, (London 1974)

Sitwell, Osbert, *Rat Week*, (London 1986)

Strong, Roy, *Royal Gardens*, (London 1995)

Talbot, Godfrey, *Queen Elizabeth the Queen Mother*, (London 1989)

Townsend, Peter, *Time and Chance* (London 1978)

Tweedsmuir, Susan, *The Edwardian Lady*, (London 1966)

Wakeford, Geoffrey, *Thirty Years a Queen*, (London 1968)

Warwick, Christopher, *King George VI and Queen Elizabeth* (London 1985)

Wentworth Day, James, *The Queen Mother's Family Story* (London 1967)

Wheeler-Bennett, Sir John, *King George VI*, (London 1958)

Zec, Donald, *The Queen Mother*, (London 1990)

INDEX

PHOTOGRAPHIC ACKNOWLEDGEMENTS

Jo Little: 1, 233, 251

Alpha: 5, 9, 10, 11, 16, 19, 26, 39, 42, 49, 55, 58, 63, 71, 72, 73, 75, 77, 82, 83, 95, 96, 98, 103, 104, 106, 107, 110, 111, 115, 121, 136, 137, 166, 168, 177, 183, 212, 216, 221, 224, 225, 228, 229, 232, 251, 254, 255

The Royal Collection by gracious permission of Her Majesty The Queen: 21, 259, 263, 266

The E O Hoppé Trust Curatorial Assistance: iii, 29

Press Association: 35, 36, 40, 53

Jim Kershaw: 41, 45, 136, 137, 153, 217, 220, 224

Ian Shapiro: 68, 92, 167, 192, 194, 195, 196, 197, 199

Topham Picturepoint: 87, 119, 140, 152, 159

Rita Burns: 97

Camera Press: 99, 104, 217, 220

Popperfoto: 101, 159

UK Press/Julian Parker: 114

Derry Moore: 128/9, 132, 258

Author's archive: 147, 149, 153, 154, 155, 157, 164

Hulton-Getty: 173

The Interior Archive/C Simon Sykes: 236/7, 240, 241, 245, 247

Geoffrey Shakerley: 244, 250, 252, 262

Other photographs courtesy of the *Daily Mail* library or private collections.